IVAN TURGENEV was the first of the great Russian novelists to be read widely in Europe. Born of a landowning family in the province of Orel in 1818, he grew up with sympathy for the plight of the serfs, a feeling reflected in his early short stories. A collection of these stories under the title *A Sportsman's Sketches* caused his arrest in 1852, but also helped to bring about the emancipation of the serfs nine years later. Best known for his masterpiece *Fathers and Sons* (1862), he is also the author of *A House of Gentlefolk* (1858), *On the Eve* (1860), *Smoke* (1867), *Spring Torrents* (1871), *Virgin Soil* (1877), several plays, and many short stories

DAVID MAGARSHACK was born in Riga, Latvia, and received his secondary-school education in Russia. Settling in London, he received his B.A. from London University, and is now a British subject. Among the books Mr. Magarshack has written are *Stanislavsky on the Art of the Stage*, *Stanislavsky, a Life*, *Chekhov the Dramatist*, *Chekhov, a Life*, *Turgenev*, and *Gogol*. His major translations include works of Chekhov, Dostoevsky, Tolstoy, Leskov, and Ostrovsky. His translations of six of Gogol's short stories are published in the Norton Library under the title *"The Overcoat" and Other Tales of Good and Evil* (N304).

RUSSIAN LITERATURE
IN NORTON PAPERBOUND EDITIONS

THE NORTON LIBRARY

Anton Chekhov *Seven Short Novels* (translated by Barbara Makanowitzky)

George Gibian, Tr. and Ed. *Russia's Lost Literature of the Absurd:
Selected Works of Daniil Kharms and
Alexander Vvedensky*

Nicolai V. Gogol *Dead Souls* (translated by George Reavey)
"The Overcoat" and Other Tales of Good and Evil
(translated by David Magarshack)

Alexandr Sergeyevitch Pushkin *The Complete Prose Tales*
(translated by Gillon R. Aitken)

F. D. Reeve, Tr. and Ed. *Nineteenth-Century Russian Plays
Twentieth-Century Russian Plays*

Aleksandr Solzhenitsyn *"We Never Make Mistakes"*
(translated by Paul W. Blackstock)

Ivan Turgenev *"First Love" and Other Tales*
(translated by David Magarshack)

NORTON CRITICAL EDITIONS

Feodor Dostoevsky *Crime and Punishment* (the Coulson translation;
George Gibian, ed.)

Leo Tolstoy *Anna Karenina* (the Maude translation; George Gibian, ed.)
War and Peace (the Maude translation; George Gibian, ed.)

Ivan Turgenev *Fathers and Sons* (a substantially new translation;
Ralph E. Matlaw, ed.)

Ivan Turgenev

First Love

and Other Tales

Translated with an Introduction

by David Magarshack

The Norton Library

W · W · NORTON & COMPANY · INC ·

NEW YORK

W. W. Norton & Company, Inc. also publishes *The Norton Anthology of English Literature*, edited by M. H. Abrams et al; *The Norton Anthology of Poetry*, edited by Arthur M. Eastman et al; *World Masterpieces*, edited by Maynard Mack et al; *The Norton Reader*, edited by Arthur M. Eastman et al; *The Norton Facsimile of the First Folio of Shakespeare*, prepared by Charlton Hinman; *The Norton Anthology of Modern Poetry*, edited by Richard Ellmann and Robert O'Clair; and the *Norton Critical Editions*.

ISBN 0 393 00444 9

Printed in the United States of America
6 7 8 9 0

CONTENTS

INTRODUCTION

AN eminent English critic recently summed up his idea of Turgenev's style in the following sentence: "We are transported by his [i.e., Turgenev's] sensuous, elegiac prose to a Russia dulcet with the lark and the nightingale, scented with tobacco plant and lilac, rustling with aspens, glimmering with girls in white frocks, pensive among the pale, moonlit birch trees."

Quite apart from the fact that the whole idea of Turgenev's Russia in the above passage is a grotesque travesty of the truth, no one who can read Turgenev in the original could possibly describe his style as exclusively or even predominantly "sensuous," "elegiac," or "luminous," as it is also sometimes described. Broadly speaking, Turgenev's writings can be divided into five distinct periods, each of which has a decided style of its own. As a young man Turgenev fell under the influence of the German idealist philosophers, especially of Hegel. In that period he wrote a large number of highly romantic poems, of which only several poems and one three-act poetic drama are extant. In his second period Turgenev got over his romantic obsessions but was still determined to remain a poet. He wrote a number of lyric and narrative poems in which he attempted to express himself in a style of the utmost simplicity. The only trace of his romantic period in these poems can be detected in their descriptive passages, which are also characteristic of his first stories. These purely poetic passages are, unfortunately, considered by certain critics to be one of the essential constituents of Turgenev's prose style. His third and rather brief period was as a dramatist (Turgenev gave up writing plays because his comedies, as he expressed it, "do not show the slightest dramatic talent"), and after it Turgenev turned to prose. The most notable achievement of his fourth period was his already mentioned series of stories, most of them written in France between 1848 and 1850, in *A Sportsman's Sketches*. According to Turgenev's own admission in his *Literary Reminiscences*, his realisation that he would never become a great poet nearly made him give up literature altogether. It was by mere chance that he turned to fiction.

"It was only because of the repeated requests of Ivan Panayev [editor of *The Contemporary Review*, a monthly in which Turgenev took a great interest], who had nothing with which to fill the miscellaneous section of *The Contemporary*," Turgenev wrote, "that I left him a sketch entitled *Khor and Kalinych* (the words *From a Sportsman's Sketches* were invented and added by the same Panayev, with the intention of winning the reader's favour). The success of this sketch made me write others; and I returned to literature."

The interesting stylistic feature of *A Sportsman's Sketches*, as well as of Turgenev's other stories belonging to the same period, is the presence of the long descriptive passages which have very little relation to the subject matter of the story. Indeed, Turgenev was for a time so obsessed with his ability to paint landscapes in words that even his letters of the period abound in descriptive passages of the same kind. The first break with this practice and the transition to his last period —or, as Turgenev described it, his attempt to write "in a new manner"—begins with his story "The Inn" in 1852. In Turgenev's opinion the chief merit of this story lay in its "greater simplicity," by which he meant the complete absence of descriptive passages. "In my new stories," Turgenev wrote in a letter to a friend on December 27, 1852 (*O.S.*), "I have struck out on quite a new path. My sketches seem to me now to have been written by a complete stranger."

Turgenev's fifth and last period is, therefore, first of all characterised by the absence of descriptive passages which have nothing to do either with the mood or the particular circumstances of the story. In this period Turgenev has gradually succeeded in achieving a compactness of style which makes any of his earlier "poetic" efforts seem extravagant. At the same time it would be quite absurd to claim, as is so often done, that during the remaining twenty years of his authorship Turgenev's style stayed the same throughout. Indeed, Turgenev's greatness as a writer consists mainly in the variety of styles in which his different stories and novels were written, a variety that to a large extent depends on their subject matter and the particular mood evoked by certain scenes. It is obvious, however, that, in spite of this variety, certain stylistic features predominate in all his writings, features that make them unmistakably his own (this is not true of his articles and reviews). Some of these features, such as the occasional scansion of his sentences and the few onomatopoeic passages in his stories, which still show the influence of his early purely poetic period, are much less remarkable than certain critics believe them to be. They are certainly not enough to characterise his style as a whole.

Turgenev wrote "The Singers" and "Bezhin Meadow,"

two of the finest stories from *A Sportsman's Sketches*, in 1850 and 1851, after his return to Russia from France. Of the first story, Turgenev wrote from Petersburg on November 7, 1850, to Pauline Viardot, the celebrated operatic singer whose devoted slave he was all his life: "I have depicted in a somewhat highly coloured manner the contest between two folk singers at which I was present two months ago. The childhoods of all peoples are alike, and my singers reminded me of Homer. Then I stopped thinking about it, for otherwise the pen would have dropped out of my hand. The contest took place in a country tavern in the presence of many original characters whom I tried to depict *à la* Teniers. . . ."

"Bezhin Meadow," published in February, 1851, contains some autobiographical material, such as the story of the ghost seen walking on the dam over the large pond. The ghost was that of Turgenev's great-uncle Lutovinov, the original owner of Turgenev's estate at Spasskoye and a notorious miser. The peasants of the estate claimed to have seen his ghost walking on the dam of one of the larger ponds, bending down and looking at something on the ground, as he had often been seen doing in his lifetime. Turgenev must have heard this story many times as a child, as well as many of the other superstitious folk tales which the children tell in "Bezhin Meadow." Turgenev objected to the description of this story as "fantastic." "I had no intention," he wrote to a friend on March 16, 1851, "to give this story a fantastic character—these are not German but Russian boys. The truest criticism I have had," he concluded, "is that the boys in my story talk like grown-up people."

The stories in *A Sportsman's Sketches* were instrumental in enlightening Russian public opinion about the intolerable position of the serfs and in this way helped to bring about their emancipation ten years later. Turgenev's story "Mumu" can be said to have delivered the *coup de grâce* to a system in which the majority of the population were treated worse than cattle.

Turgenev wrote "Mumu" while under arrest in Petersburg from April 16 to May 16, 1852, for publishing an obituary on Gogol in which he was incautious enough to describe him as "a great man." "Mumu" is based on an actual incident that had taken place in the house of Turgenev's mother. Gerasim, the hero of the story, was his mother's deaf-and-dumb caretaker Andrey, who had also been compelled to drown his dog in circumstances very similar to those related in this story; but, unlike Gerasim, Andrey did not run away.

"Mumu" was published in *The Contemporary Review* in 1854, and the censor who had passed it was severely reprimanded for failing to realise the dangerous implications in showing up "the improper use of the landowners' powers over their serfs" and in this way arousing the readers' sympathy for the peasants.

"Assya" shows Turgenev at the height of his powers. He began writing it in Sinzig, the German watering place near Coblenz (the S. of the story), in May, 1857, and finished it in Rome in December of the same year. It was published in January, 1858, in *The Contemporary Review*.

Turgenev wrote "Assya," as he wrote to Leo Tolstoy from Vienna on April 8, 1858, "at white heat and with tears." In fact, he had been going through one of the greatest emotional crises of his life, having discovered that Pauline Viardot had been unfaithful to him. Pauline Viardot figures in the story under the guise of the designing widow, "the cruel charmer," who preferred a "red-cheeked Bavarian lieutenant" to the anonymous hero of the story. There is even a stronger, if indirect, connection between Pauline Viardot and Assya, the heroine of the story, for it was to Pauline Viardot that

Turgenev had sent this detailed description of Assya's prototype, the natural daughter of Turgenev's uncle.

"Do you remember," Turgenev wrote to Pauline Viardot on September 9, 1850, "the little five-year-old girl I wrote to you about in one of my letters? I saw her again and I still find this child a rather strange little creature. Imagine a very pretty little face with features of extraordinary delicacy, a charming smile, and eyes such as I have never seen before, the eyes of a grown-up woman, sometimes gentle and caressing and sometimes sharp and observant, a face that changes its expression every minute, and every expression of which is amazingly true and original. She possesses a great fund of common sense and a remarkable precision of sensations and feelings; she thinks a lot and is never dishonest; it is remarkable with what an instinctive directness her little brain moves towards truth, passes a correct judgement upon everything round her, beginning with my mother. And yet she is a child, a *real* child, for all that. There are moments when her eyes assume a dreamy and mournful expression which makes you feel sorry for her. But, as a rule, she is very cheerful and entirely self-composed. She loves me very much and at times looks at me with such gentle and tender eyes that I can't help being deeply moved.

"Her name is Anna; she is the natural daughter of an uncle of mine and a peasant woman. My mother took her into the house and treats her like a doll. . . . When you tell her something that strikes her as unusual she moves her head and eyebrows in a way that I find irresistible; she seems to subject everything she hears to a careful examination in her childish mind and then proceeds to give you the most remarkable answers. She is light-haired and with a fair complexion. Her eyes are bluish-grey flecked with black; her little teeth are like real pearls. She is a very loving and very sensitive little creature. . . . I assure you she is an extremely strange little human being and I am studying her with interest. She is not five yet."

The impression Assya or Anna left on Turgenev was so strong that seven years later he made her into one of his most fascinating heroines. (Assya herself eventually married, prosaically enough, Turgenev's cook.)

Turgenev claimed "First Love," one of his most famous stories, to be the most autobiographical of all his stories. He began it in Petersburg in January, 1860, and finished it on March 22, 1860—"at three o'clock in the morning," as he noted down on the manuscript. He dedicated it to the critic and memoirist Pavel Annenkov, one of his closest friends and literary executor. It was at the age of thirteen (and not sixteen, as in the story) that Turgenev had experienced his first "crush" on a young woman who turned out to be his father's mistress. He described it all in "First Love," a story which, he told a correspondent, was not invented, but given him entirely by life. Even the incident of the knife with which the young boy in the story had got ready to stab his rival before he discovered that it was his father, he assured another correspondent, had actually taken place. Turgenev's relations with his father and his father's relations with his mother are also faithfully reproduced in the story.

"Knock . . . Knock . . . Knock . . ." was published in 1871. Turgenev regarded it as one of the most serious things he had written. "It is a study of suicide," he wrote to a woman correspondent on January 16, 1877, from Paris, "a vain, stupid, superstitious, absurd suicide, which is as interesting and important a subject as any other grave and important social problem . . . for it adds a document to the analysis of man's personality, and, in effect, all creative writing . . . has no other object than that."

Turgenev began "Living Relics," one of the most

moving stories in *A Sportsman's Sketches,* in 1850, but only finished it in 1874. "Originally," he wrote to the poet Yakov Polonsky on January 13, 1874, from Paris, "I had prepared about thirty sketches, but only twenty-two of them were published. Some of them remained unfinished because I was afraid the censors would not pass them, others because they seemed to me to be insufficiently interesting, or because I thought them unsuitable. 'Living Relics' belonged to the last category." He sent it as his contribution to a symposium in aid of the famine-stricken peasants of the Samara Province. It was this story that elicited the often-quoted enthusiastic tribute from George Sand. *"Maître,"* she wrote to Turgenev, *"nous devons aller tous à votre école!"*

"Clara Milich," which Turgenev first entitled "After Death," is one of the finest stories in the Turgenev canon. If it has never been appreciated as it should be for its remarkable insight into the human mind, it is mainly because of the absurd literary convention which associates Turgenev with a "style" of writing to which this particular story does not conform. The story is based—like many of his other writings—on an actual incident related to Turgenev by the poet Polonsky, concerning a friend of his, V. D. Alinitsyn, a young zoologist, who fell in love with a young actress and operatic singer *after* she had committed suicide. The actress, E. P. Kadmina, took poison on November 4, 1881, while acting in one of Ostrovsky's plays in Kharkov. Turgenev had met Alinitsyn at Polonsky's house, and he had also seen Kadmina acting in an opera. "The psychological fact you wrote to me about," Turgenev wrote to Polonsky, "is truly remarkable. One could write a semi-fantastic story about it in the style of Edgar Allan Poe. I remember seeing Kadmina once on the stage. She had a very expressive face. . . . Just think of it: wherever you look, there is the drama in life, and there are still writers who complain that all subjects have been exhausted."

"Clara Milich" is the last story Turgenev wrote. At the time (in 1882) he had already been stricken down by his fatal illness.

D. M.

THE SINGERS

THE small village of Kolotovka, which once belonged to a lady nicknamed in the neighbourhood "Mistress Trouncer," because of her vicious and uncontrollable temper (her real name is not recorded), and now owned by some Petersburg German, lies on the slope of a bare hill cleft from top to bottom by a terrible ravine. Yawning like a chasm, this ravine winds its torn and eroded way across the very middle of the village street, dividing the poor little village in two, worse than any river (for a river could at least be bridged). A few spindly willows cling precariously to its sandy sides; at the bottom, dry and reddish like copper, lie huge flagstones of shale. A cheerless sight—no doubt about it—and yet the road to Kolotovka is well known to the people in the neighbourhood: they go there readily and often.

At the very top of the ravine, a few yards from the spot where it begins as a narrow crack in the ground, a small square peasant's cottage stands solitary, apart from the others. It is thatched and has a chimney; a single window, like a watchful eye, looks towards the

1

ravine and, lighted up from within on winter evenings, can be seen from afar through the dim frosty haze, shining like a guiding star to many a peasant who happens to be driving that way. Over the door of the cottage is nailed a little blue board; the cottage is a country pub, known as the Cosy Corner. In this pub, drinks are in all probability sold no cheaper than the fixed price, but it is much better attended than all similar establishments in the neighbourhood, and the reason for that is the publican Nikolai Ivanych.

Nikolai Ivanych was once a slender, curly-headed and rosy-cheeked lad, but now he has grown into an inordinately fat and grey-haired man with a bloated face, a pair of sly, genial little eyes, and a fleshy forehead with deep furrows running right across it. He has lived in Kolotovka for over twenty years. Nikolai Ivanych is a wide-awake, resourceful fellow, as indeed most publicans are. Without being particularly amiable or talkative, he has the knack of attracting and keeping customers, who somehow feel at ease sitting in front of his counter, under the calm and affable, though rather watchful, eye of their phlegmatic host. He has a great deal of common sense, and he is well acquainted with the mode of life of the landowner, the peasant, and the tradesman; in difficult circumstances he could give good advice, were it not for the fact that as a cautious man and an egoist he prefers to keep his own counsel and guide his customers (and only those he particularly favours) out of trouble's way by rather obscure and indirect hints, dropped, as it were, in passing. He is an excellent judge of what a true Russian considers to be either interesting or important: of horses and cattle, timber, bricks, crockery, textiles, leather, singing, and dancing. When there are no customers he can usually be seen sitting like a sack on the ground in front of his cottage, his thin legs tucked up under him, exchanging pleasantries with every passer-by. He has seen much in

his life, outlived more than a dozen of the small landowners who used to drop in for a glass of vodka; he
knows everything that happens for a hundred miles
round but never breathes a word about it and does not
ever let on that he knows what even the most astute
district police officer does not so much as suspect. All
he does is keep mum, chuckle to himself quietly, and
busy himself with the glasses.

His neighbours respect him: one of them, a certain
Shcherepenko, a civil servant of the rank of a general
and one of the most influential landowners in the neighbourhood, always bows to him courteously when driving
past his little cottage. Nikolai Ivanych is a man of influence too: he forced a well-known horse thief to return a horse stolen from one of his acquaintances; he
made the peasants of a neighbouring village listen to
reason when they refused to accept a new agent; and
so on. However, it would be a mistake to think that he
did it all out of love of justice, or out of zeal for the
welfare of his neighbours. No! He was simply trying to
nip in the bud anything that might disturb his peace
of mind.

Nikolai Ivanych is married and has children. His wife,
a brisk, sharp-nosed, and quick-eyed tradeswoman, has
also put on a good deal of weight lately, just like her
husband. He defers to her judgement in everything, and
she keeps a tight hand on the purse-strings. Rowdy
drunkards are afraid of her; she dislikes them, for there
is little profit and a lot of noise from them; she would
much rather deal with the silent and gloomy ones. Nikolai Ivanych's children are still small; the first all died,
and those who survived resemble their parents: it makes
one feel good to look at the clever little faces of these
healthy children.

It was an unbearably hot July day when, scarcely able
to drag one foot after the other, I walked slowly, accompanied by my dog, up the Kolotovka ravine in the

direction of the Cosy Corner. The sun was blazing away in the sky with a kind of fury; it was scorchingly, piteously hot; the air was saturated with choking dust. The rooks and crows, their feathers gleaming in the sunlight, gazed dolefully at the passers-by, their beaks gaping, as though begging them for sympathy; the sparrows alone did not seem to mind and, fluffing up their feathers, went on chirping more furiously than ever as they kept fighting each other along the fences, flying up from the dusty road in flocks and hovering in grey clouds over the green hemp fields. I was tortured by thirst. There was no water anywhere near: in Kolotovka, as in many another steppe village, there are no springs or wells, and the peasants drink a sort of liquid filth from the pond—but who would give the name of *water* to that horrible hogwash? I was thinking of asking Nikolai Ivanych for a glass of beer, or kvas.

It must be admitted that at no season of the year does Kolotovka present a cheerful sight; but it arouses a particularly mournful feeling when the blazing July sun glares down with its pitiless rays upon the half-crumbling brown roofs, the deep ravine, the scorched, dust-laden common on which some lean, long-legged chickens are wandering about despondently, the grey aspen-timbered shell of a former mansion, grown over with nettles, weeds, and wormwood, and the pond, black and almost incandescent, covered with goose feathers, with its fringe of half-dried mud and its lopsided dam; near the dam, on the fine, trampled, cinder-like earth, sheep, hardly able to draw their breath and sneezing from the heat, crowd sorrowfully together and with dismal patience hang their heads low, as though waiting for the moment when this unbearable sultriness will pass at last.

Barely dragging my feet, I drew near at last to Nikolai Ivanych's cottage, as usual making the children stare in intense amazement at me and arousing in the dogs a feeling of indignation expressed by vicious and hoarse barking which seemed to tear their insides and make them choke and cough. Suddenly a tall, bare-headed man in a frieze overcoat with a blue belt round the waist appeared in the doorway of the country pub. He looked like a house-serf; his thick grey hair rose untidily over his thin wrinkled face. He was calling somebody with rapid movements of his arms, which were quite obviously swinging out much farther than he intended. It was clear that he had already had a drop too many.

"Come on, come on," he babbled, "come on, Blinker, come on! Good heavens, you're just crawling along! It isn't nice at all, old fellow. Not nice at all. They're waiting for you here and you're crawling along. Come on, come on now!"

"All right, I'm coming, I'm coming," a quavering voice cried, and a short, stout, lame fellow appeared from behind a peasant's cottage on the right. He wore a fairly clean farm labourer's cotton coat, with only one sleeve; a high, pointed hat, pulled straight over his forehead, gave his round, podgy face a cunning, sardonic look. His little yellow eyes darted about; a restrained, forced smile never left his thin lips; and his nose, long and pointed, was thrust forwards impudently, like a rudder. "I'm coming, my dear fellow," he went on, limping in the direction of the pub. "Why are you calling me? Anyone waiting for me?"

"Why am I calling you?" the man in the frieze overcoat cried reproachfully. "What a funny fellow you are, to be sure, Blinker! You're called to a pub and you ask why? There are all sorts of excellent fellows waiting for you: Yashka the Turk, the Wild Gentleman, and the contractor from Zhizdra. Yashka and the contractor have made a bet: they've wagered a quart of beer to see who wins—I mean who sings best—see?"

"Yashka's going to sing?" the man nicknamed Blinker cried excitedly. "You're not telling a lie, Booby?"

"No, I am not!" Booby replied with dignity. "It's you

who're talking a lot of nonsense. Of course he's going to sing if he's made a bet, you stupid insect, you twister, you!"

"Oh, come along, you ninny," said Blinker.

"Come, give me a kiss at least, my dear fellow," Booby babbled, flinging his arms out wide.

"Get away with you, you great milksop!" Blinker replied contemptuously, elbowing him aside, and they both, stooping, went in through the low doorway.

The conversation I had overheard greatly aroused my curiosity. More than once rumours had reached me of Yashka the Turk as the best singer in the neighbourhood, and all of a sudden I was given the chance to hear him in competition with another master. I redoubled my steps and entered the pub.

I don't expect many of my readers have had occasion to look into a country pub, but we sportsmen go everywhere. The arrangement of these country pubs is very simple. They usually consist of a dark passage and a large room divided in two by a partition, behind which no customer is allowed to go. A big oblong opening is cut in this partition above a broad oak table. On this table or counter vodka is sold. Sealed bottles of different sizes stand side by side on shelves immediately opposite the opening. In the front part of the room are benches, two or three empty barrels, and a corner table put at the disposal of the customers. Village pubs are mostly rather dark, and on their timbered walls you hardly ever see any brightly coloured popular prints, without which very few peasant cottages are complete.

When I went into the Cosy Corner a fairly large company was already assembled there.

Behind the counter, as was only to be expected, and filling almost the whole width of the opening, stood Nikolai Ivanych, in a gay cotton shirt, and with a lazy smile on his chubby cheeks, pouring out two glasses of vodka with his podgy white hand for the two friends,

Blinker and Booby, who had just come in. His sharp-eyed
wife could be seen behind him in the corner near the
window. In the middle of the room stood Yashka the
Turk, a lean, slender man of twenty-three, wearing a
long-skirted blue nankeen coat. He looked like a dashing
factory hand and, so far as I could judge, his health was
nothing to boast about. His sunken cheeks, large, restless grey eyes, straight nose with thin, mobile nostrils,
his white receding forehead with light brown curls
thrust back from it, his large but handsome and expressive lips—his whole face revealed an impressionable, passionate nature. He was in a state of great excitement: he
blinked, breathed irregularly; his hands trembled as
though he were feverish—and, as a matter of fact, he
had a fever, that sudden, shaking fever which is so familiar to all who speak or sing in public.

Beside him stood a man of about forty, broad-
shouldered, with broad cheekbones, a low forehead, narrow Tartar eyes, a short, flat nose, a square chin, and
black, shiny hair, hard as bristles. The expression of his
face, swarthy with a leaden hue, and especially of his
pale lips, might almost have been called ferocious, if it
had not been so calmly reflective. He hardly stirred and
just kept looking round slowly like an ox from under the
yoke. He wore a sort of threadbare frock coat with shiny
copper buttons; an old black silk handkerchief was
wrapped round his massive neck. He was nicknamed the
Wild Gentleman.

Yashka's competitor, the contractor from Zhizdra, sat
right in front of him on the bench under the icons. He
was a short, thickset man of about thirty, pock-marked
and curly-headed, with a blunt, tipped-up nose, lively
brown eyes, and a scanty beard. He was looking round
boldly, with his hands tucked under him, carelessly
swinging and tapping his feet, on which he wore smart
boots with trimmings. He had on a thin new peasant's
overcoat of grey cloth with a velveteen collar, against

7

which a strip of scarlet shirt, buttoned up tightly round his throat, stood out sharply.

In the opposite corner a peasant in a threadbare greyish coat with an enormous hole on the shoulder sat at a table to the right of the door. The sunlight came through the dusty panes of the two small windows in a fine yellowish shaft of light and seemed unable to dispel the habitual darkness of the room; all the objects in it were dimly illuminated, their outlines blurred. On the other hand, it was almost cool in the room, and the moment I crossed the threshold the sensation of closeness and sultriness fell from my shoulders like a heavy load.

My arrival—I could see it—at first disconcerted Nikolai Ivanych's guests a little; but, observing that he bowed to me as to an old acquaintance, they set their minds at rest and paid no more attention to me. I ordered some beer and sat down in the corner beside the little peasant in the torn coat.

"Well," Booby cried suddenly, after having drained a glass of vodka at one gulp, accompanying his exclamation with those strange gesticulations without which he evidently could not utter a single word, "well, what are we waiting for? Let's begin, eh, Yashka?"

"Yes, yes, let's begin," Nikolai Ivanych echoed approvingly.

"Let's begin, by all means," the contractor said coolly and with a self-confident smirk. "I'm ready."

"Me—too," Yashka declared with a catch in his voice.

"Well then, begin, my lads, begin," Blinker squeaked.

But notwithstanding this unanimously expressed wish, neither of them began; the contractor did not even stir from his bench; they all seemed to be waiting for something to happen.

"Begin!" the Wild Gentleman said sharply and sullenly.

Yashka gave a start. The contractor got up, pushed down his belt, and cleared his throat. "Who's to begin?"

he asked in a slightly changed voice, addressing himself to the Wild Gentleman, who was still standing motionless in the middle of the room, his thick legs planted wide apart and his powerful arms thrust almost to the elbows into the pockets of his billowing wide trousers.

"You, Contractor, you," Booby babbled. "You, my lad."

The Wild Gentleman glanced at him frowningly. Booby uttered a faint squeak, faltered, threw a hasty glance at the ceiling, wriggled his shoulders, and fell silent.

"Draw for it," said the Wild Gentleman with deliberation, "and put the quart of beer on the counter."

Nikolai Ivanych bent down, picked up, grunting, the quart from the floor and put it on the table.

The Wild Gentleman glanced at Yashka and said, "Well?"

Yashka fumbled in his pockets, found a half-copeck piece, and marked it with his teeth. The contractor took out a new leather purse from the skirt of his coat, slowly undid the strings, and, pouring out a lot of small change into his hand, chose a new half-copeck piece. Booby held out his battered old cap with its loose and broken peak; Yashka threw his half-copeck into it, and so did the contractor.

"You choose," said the Wild Gentleman, addressing Blinker.

Blinker smirked with a self-satisfied air, took the cap in both hands and began shaking it.

A dead hush fell for a moment upon the room; the coins chinked faintly against each other. I looked round attentively: every face expressed strained anticipation; even the Wild Gentleman half closed his eyes; my neighbour, the little peasant in the torn coat, also craned his neck inquisitively. Blinker thrust his hand into the cap and drew out the contractor's half-copeck; there was a general sigh. Yashka flushed, and the contractor passed his hand through his hair.

"I said it was you, didn't I?" cried Booby. "I said so!"

"All right, all right, stop your cackle!" the Wild Gentleman observed contemptuously. "Begin!" he went on, nodding to the contractor.

"What shall I sing?" asked the contractor, with mounting excitement.

"Anything you like," replied Blinker. "Just think of something and sing it."

"Yes, of course, anything you like," added Nikolai Ivanych, slowly folding his arms across his chest. "We have no right to tell you what you should sing. Sing any song you like. Only, mind, sing it well, and we shall afterwards decide without fear or favour."

"Aye," Booby put in, licking the rim of his empty glass, "so we shall—without fear or favour."

"Let me first clear my throat a little, friends," said the contractor, passing his fingers along the inside of the collar of his coat.

"Come now, don't waste time—begin!" the Wild Gentleman said forcefully and dropped his eyes.

The contractor thought for a moment, shook his head, and stepped forward. Yashka stared fixedly at him.

But before proceeding with the description of the contest itself, it may be as well to say a few words about each of the characters of my story. The circumstances of life of some of them I already knew when I met them in the Cosy Corner; I found out all about the rest subsequently.

Let us begin with Booby. His real name was Eugraph Ivanov, but no one in the neighbourhood ever called him anything but Booby, and he referred to himself by the same nickname, so well did it fit him. And, to be sure, it seemed to go perfectly with his insignificant, perpetually worried features. He was a dissolute, unmarried house-serf, whom his masters had long since given up as beyond redemption and who, having no job of any kind and receiving no wages whatever, nevertheless found means of making merry at someone else's expense. He had a great many acquaintances who treated him to drinks and to tea without themselves knowing why, for, far from being amusing in company, he made everybody sick and tired of his senseless chatter, his unbearable importunity, his feverish fidgetings, and his ceaseless, unnatural laughter. He could neither sing nor dance, and he had never been known to utter an intelligent, let alone sensible, word: he just babbled and talked a lot of nonsense—a regular booby! And yet there was not a single drinking party for forty miles round at which his spindle-shanked figure did not turn up among the guests; people had become so used to him that they tolerated his presence as a necessary evil. It is true, they treated him with contempt; but the Wild Gentleman alone could check his absurd outbursts.

Blinker was not at all like Booby. His nickname, too, fitted him well, though he did not blink more than anyone else; it is a well-known fact that the Russians are past-masters at giving nicknames. In spite of my efforts to unearth as many details of his past as possible, there remained for me—as well as for many others, I suppose— many dark spots in his life, places which, to use a literary cliché, were shrouded in mystery. All I could discover was that at one time he had been coachman to an old, childless lady, had run away with the team of three horses entrusted to his care, disappeared for a whole year, and, no doubt convinced by experience of the disadvantages and hardships of a vagrant's life, returned, now a lame cripple, thrown himself at his mistress's feet, and, having made amends for his crime by many years of exemplary conduct, won his way back into her favour and at last earned her full confidence; he had been appointed bailiff and, on his mistress's death, had somehow or other gained his freedom, registered as a member of the tradesmen's class, leased melon fields from the neighbours, grown rich, and now lived in clover. He was a man of great experience, knew which side his bread was buttered on, was neither good nor bad, but very calculating; a man who had been through the mill and who understood people and knew how to make use of them. He was cautious and at the same time resourceful, like a fox; talkative as an old woman, but never let out a secret, while making everybody else speak his mind freely; still, he never posed as a simpleton, as many cunning fellows of his kind do, and in fact he would have found it difficult to pretend: I have never seen shrewder and more intelligent eyes than his tiny, cunning "peepers."* They never just looked; they were always reconnoitring and spying. Blinker would sometimes spend whole weeks in thinking over some apparently simple enterprise, and at other times suddenly make up his mind to undertake some desperately daring business deal, and you'd think he'd be ruined; but no! his deal had come off and all was plain sailing again. He was lucky, and he believed in his luck, believed in omens. He was, in general, highly superstitious. He was not liked, because he did not care what happened to others, but he was respected. His entire family consisted of one small son who was the apple of his eye and who, brought up by such a father, would probably go far. "Little Blinky is the very spit of his father," the old men were already saying of him in an undertone as they sat gossiping on the mounds of earth outside their cottages on summer evenings; and everyone understood what that meant, and there was no need to say more.

Of Yashka the Turk and the contractor there is not much to be said. Yashka, nicknamed the Turk because he really was descended from a captured Turkish

---

* The people of Oryol Province call eyes "peepers," in the same way that they call a mouth a "gobbler." AUTHOR.

woman, was at heart an artist in every sense of the word, but was employed as a dipper in a paper-mill; as for the contractor, about whom, I'm afraid, I found out nothing, he appeared to me to be a highly resourceful and smart tradesman. But of the Wild Gentleman it is worth speaking at somewhat greater length.

The first impression the appearance of this man made was one of barbaric, ponderous, but irresistible strength. He was clumsily built—"rough-hewn," as we say—but he exuded rude health, and, strangely enough, his bearlike figure was not without a certain peculiar kind of grace, which was perhaps the result of his absolute, calm confidence in his own strength. It was difficult to decide at first glance to what social class this Hercules belonged; he did not look like a house-serf or a tradesman or a retired and impoverished scrivener or a pugnacious, huntin' small country squire: he did indeed seem to be an exceptional case. Nobody knew from where he had descended on our district; it was said that he belonged to the class of free smallholders and had previously been in government service somewhere, but nothing definite was known about it; and indeed there was no one to find it out from, certainly not from the man himself: there was no more surly and taciturn man in the world. Neither could anyone say positively what he lived on: he was engaged in no trade; he visited no one; he scarcely knew anyone; and yet he had money—not much money, it is true, but he certainly had some money. He conducted himself not so much modestly—there was nothing modest about him—as quietly; he lived as though he never noticed anyone round him and he most certainly wanted nothing from anyone.

The Wild Gentleman (this was his nickname; his real name was Perevlesov) enjoyed enormous influence in all the district; he was obeyed instantly and eagerly, although he had no right whatever to give anyone orders —but then, he never made the slightest claim on the obedience of people with whom he happened to come in contact. He spoke and was obeyed: power always claims its due. He hardly ever drank, had no dealings with women, and was passionately fond of singing. There was much that was mysterious about this man; it was as if tremendous forces were sullenly hidden within him, as though he knew that, once aroused, once let loose, they must destroy themselves and everything they touched; and I am sadly mistaken if some such explosion had not already happened in that man's life and that, taught by experience and having just escaped destruction, he was now holding himself inexorably under iron control. What struck me particularly about him was the mixture of a sort of innate natural ferocity with a similarly innate nobility—a mixture such as I have never come across in any other person.

And so the contractor stepped forward, half closed his eyes, and began to sing in a very high falsetto. His voice was quite sweet and agreeable, though a little husky; he played with it, twirled it about like a top, dwelt lovingly and with abandon on the high notes, with constant downwards trills and modulations and constant returns to the top notes, which he held and drew out with a special effort, stopped, then suddenly took up his previous tune with a sort of rollicking, arrogant boldness. His transitions were sometimes rather daring, sometimes rather amusing; they would have given the connoisseur great pleasure; they would have greatly shocked the German. It was a Russian *tenore di grazia, tenor léger*. He sang a gay dance tune whose words, so far as I could make them out among the endless embellishments, extra consonants, and exclamations, were as follows:

> A little plot of land, my love,
> I'll sow,
> A little scarlet flower, my love,
> I'll grow.

He sang, and everyone listened to him with rapt attention. He evidently felt that he was dealing with experts and that was why he simply put his best leg forward, as the saying goes. And, indeed, in our part of the country people are good judges of singing, and it is not for nothing that the large village of Sergeyevskoye, on the Oryol Highway, is renowned throughout all Russia for its especially agreeable and harmonious singing.

The contractor sang for a long time without arousing any particular enthusiasm in his hearers; he missed the support of a choir; at last, after one particularly successful transition, which made even the Wild Gentleman smile, Booby could not restrain himself and uttered a cry of delight. We all gave a start. Booby and Blinker began to take up the tune in an undertone, humming, calling out, "Well done! Hold it, you dirty rascal! Hold it—higher, higher, you villain! Up, up! Make it hotter, hotter, you dirty dog, you cur, the devil take you!" and so on. Behind the counter Nikolai Ivanych shook his head to right and left approvingly. At length Booby began stamping, dancing about, and twitching his shoulder, and Yashka's eyes blazed like coals, and he shook all over like a leaf and smiled confusedly. The Wild Gentleman alone did not change countenance and remained motionless as before; but his gaze, fixed on the contractor, softened a little, though his lips kept their contemptuous expression.

Encouraged by these signs of general satisfaction, the contractor let himself go in good earnest and went off into such flourishes, such tongue-clickings and drummings, such frantic throat play, that when, at last exhausted, pale, and bathed in hot perspiration, he threw himself back and let out a last dying note, a loud burst of general exclamation was the instantaneous response of his audience. Booby threw himself on his neck and fell to smothering him in his long bony arms; Nikolai Ivanych's fat face flushed, and he seemed to have grown younger. Yashka shouted like a madman, "Well done, well done!"—and even my neighbour, the peasant in the torn coat, could bear it no longer and, striking his fist on the table, exclaimed, "A-*ha!* Good, damn good!" and, turning his head, spat with conviction.

"Well, my lad, you've given us a treat!" Booby cried, not without letting the exhausted contractor out of his embrace. "A real treat, and that's the truth! You've won, my dear fellow, you've won! Congratulations—the quart is yours! That fellow Yashka can't touch you. I'm telling you—he can't touch you. You must believe me!" And he again pressed the contractor to his bosom.

"Let him go, for heaven's sake," Blinker said with annoyance. "Let him go, you leech! Let him sit down on the bench here. Can't you see how tired he is? Oh, what a silly fool you are, my lad, what a silly fool! Why are you still sticking to him like a leaf from the whisk in a bath-house?"

"Why, of course, let him sit down and I'll drink to his health," replied Booby, going up to the counter. "It's on you, old fellow," he added, turning to the contractor.

The contractor nodded, sat down on the bench, pulled a towel out of his cap, and started wiping his face. Booby emptied his glass with eager haste and, as is the custom with confirmed drunkards, grunted and looked sad and preoccupied.

"You sing well, my boy, you sing well," Nikolai Ivanych observed graciously. "Now it's your turn, Yashka, dear fellow. Don't be nervous, mind. We shall see who's best, we shall. But the contractor sings well. Aye, so he does."

"He does that," observed Nikolai Ivanych's wife, glancing at Yashka with a smile.

"Aye, he does that!" my neighbour repeated in an undertone.

"Eh, you savage woodlander!"† Booby suddenly

† The inhabitants of the Southern wooded districts, a long woodland belt beginning on the borders of the Bolkhovsk

shouted and, walking up to the peasant with the hole in
the shoulder of his coat, pointed a finger at him, began
jumping up and down, and went off into a jarring
laugh. "Woodlander, woodlander! Ha, gee-up, wood
savage! What brings you here, wood savage?" he
shouted through his laughter.

The poor peasant looked embarrassed and was about
to get up and depart hurriedly, when all of a sudden
the brasslike voice of the Wild Gentleman resounded
through the room. "What kind of disgusting animal is
that?" he said, grinding his teeth.

"I—I didn't mean anything," Booby muttered. "I—I
didn't—er—I just——"

"All right then, shut up!" said the Wild Gentleman.
"Yashka, begin!"

Yashka touched his throat with his hand. "I'm afraid
I—I don't quite—er—I mean, I don't rightly know—er—I
don't quite——"

"For goodness' sake, man, don't be afraid. You ought
to be ashamed of yourself! You're not trying to wriggle
out of it, are you? Sing as God tells you." And the Wild
Gentleman looked down and waited.

Yashka said nothing, glanced round, and covered his
face with his hand. They all fixed their eyes on him,
especially the contractor, whose face, through its usual
expression of self-confidence and the triumph of his success, betrayed a faint unconscious anxiety. He leaned
against the wall and again tucked his hands under him,
but he no longer swung his legs. At last Yashka uncov-
ered his face. It was as pale as a dead man's; his eyes
glowed faintly through their lowered lashes. He took
a deep breath and began to sing.

His first note was faint and uneven and seemed to

---

and the Zhizdrinsk districts, are known as woodlanders. They
are distinguished by many peculiarities in their way of life,
their customs and language. They are called savages because
of their suspicious and harsh natures. AUTHOR.

come not from his chest but from somewhere far away,
just as though it had come floating into the room by
accident. This trembling, ringing note had a strange
effect on us all; we glanced at one another, and Nikolai's
wife suddenly drew herself up to her full height. This
first note was followed by another, firmer and more
drawn out, but still perceptibly trembling like a string,
when, ringing out loudly after being suddenly plucked
by a strong finger, it wavers with a last fast-fading trill;
after the second came a third note, and, gradually
warming up and broadening, the mournful song flowed
on uninterruptedly.

"Across the fields many a path is winding," he sang,
and we all felt entranced and thrilled. I must confess I
have seldom heard such a voice: it was a little broken
and had a sort of cracked ring; at first, indeed, there
seemed to be an unhealthy note in it; but there was
in it also genuine deep passion, and youthfulness and
strength and sweetness, and a sort of charmingly careless, mournful grief. A warmhearted, truthful Russian
soul rang and breathed in it and fairly clutched you by
the heart, clutched straight at your Russian heartstrings.
The song expanded and went flowing on. Yashka was
evidently overcome by ecstasy: he was no longer diffident; he gave himself up entirely to his feeling of happiness; his voice no longer trembled—it quivered, but with
the barely perceptible inner quivering of passion which
pierces like an arrow into the hearer's soul, and it grew
continually in strength, firmness, and breadth. I remember once seeing in the evening, at low tide, a great white
seagull on the flat sandy shore of the sea which was
roaring away dully and menacingly in the distance: it
was sitting motionless, its silky breast turned towards
the scarlet radiance of sunset, only now and then spreading out its long wings towards the familiar sea, towards
the low, blood-red sun; I remembered that bird as I
listened to Yashka. He sang, completely oblivious of his

rival and of all of us, but visibly borne up, like a strong swimmer by the waves, by our silent, passionate attention. He sang, and every note recalled something that was very near and dear to us all, something that was immensely vast, just as though the familiar steppe opened up before you, stretching away into boundless distance.

I could feel tears welling up in my heart and rising to my eyes; suddenly I became aware of dull, muffled sobs. I looked round—the publican's wife was weeping, her bosom pressed against the window. Yashka threw a quick glance at her and his song rose even higher and flowed on more sweetly than before. Nikolai Ivanych looked down; Blinker turned away; Booby, overcome by emotion, stood with his mouth stupidly gaping; the coarse, ignorant little peasant was quietly whimpering in a corner, shaking his head as he muttered bitterly to himself; down the iron countenance of the Wild Gentleman, from beneath his beetling brows, slowly rolled a heavy tear; the contractor had raised a clenched fist to his forehead and never stirred.

I do not know how the general suspense would have been broken if Yashka had not suddenly ended on a high, extremely thin note—just as if his voice had broken. No one uttered a sound; no one even stirred; everyone seemed to be waiting to see if he would sing again; but he opened his eyes as if surprised at our silence, cast a questioning glance round at us all, and saw that victory was his.

"Yashka," said the Wild Gentleman, putting a hand on his shoulder and—fell silent.

We all stood there as though benumbed. The contractor got up quietly and went up to Yashka. "You— it's yours—you've won," he said at last with difficulty and rushed out of the room.

His quick, decided movement seemed to break the spell; everyone suddenly began talking loudly, joyfully.

Booby leapt up into the air, spluttered, and waved his arms like the sails of a windmill; Blinker went up limping to Yashka and began kissing him; Nikolai Ivanych stood up and announced solemnly that he would add another quart of beer on his own account; the Wild Gentleman kept laughing a sort of good-natured laugh which I had never expected to hear from him; the poor little peasant, wiping his eyes, cheeks, nose, and beard on both his sleeves, kept on repeating in his corner, "It's good, aye, it's good all right! Aye, I'm a son of a bitch if it ain't!" And Nikolai's wife, flushed all over, got up quickly and went out of the room.

Yashka enjoyed his victory like a child; his whole face was transfigured; his eyes, in particular, simply shone with happiness. He was dragged across to the counter; he called to the poor little peasant who had been crying to come over too, sent the publican's little son to fetch the contractor, and the revels began. "You'll sing to us again," Booby kept saying, raising his arms aloft, "you'll go on singing to us till the evening."

I cast another glance at Yashka and went out. I did not want to stay—I was afraid to spoil my impression. But the heat was still as unbearable as before. It seemed to hang over the earth in a thick, heavy layer; through the fine, almost black dust, little bright points of light seemed to whirl round and round in the dark blue sky. Everything was hushed; there was something hopeless, something oppressive about this deep silence of enervated nature. I made my way to a hayloft and lay down on the newly mown but already almost dried grass. For a long time I could not doze off; for a long time Yashka's overpowering voice rang in my ears; but at last heat and fatigue claimed their due and I sank into a deep sleep. When I awoke, it was dark; the grass I had heaped all round me exuded a strong scent and felt a little damp to the touch; through the thin rafters of the half-open roof, pale stars twinkled faintly. I went out. The sunset glow had died away long ago and its last trace could be just distinguished as a pale shaft of light low on the horizon; but through the coolness of the night one could still feel the warmth in the air which had been so glowing-hot only a short while before, and the breast still yearned for a cool breeze. There was no wind, no cloud; the sky all round was clear and translucently dark, quietly shimmering with countless, hardly visible stars. Lights gleamed in the village; from the brightly lit pub nearby came a discordant and confused uproar through which I seemed to recognise Yashka's voice. At times there were wild bursts of laughter.

I went across to the window and pressed my face against the pane. I saw a rather sad, though lively and animated, scene: everyone was dead drunk—everyone, beginning with Yashka. He was sitting bare-chested on a bench and, humming in a hoarse voice some popular dance tune, lazily plucked and fingered the strings of a guitar. Strands of moist hair hung over his terribly pale face. In the middle of the pub, Booby, completely unstrung and coatless, was leaping about on his haunches as he danced in front of the little peasant in the greyish coat; the little peasant, in his turn, was laboriously stamping and scraping with his exhausted feet, and, smiling stupidly through his tousled beard, kept waving a hand as if to say, "I don't care!" Nothing could have been funnier than his face; however much he tried to lift his eyebrows, his heavy lids would not stay up, drooping over his scarcely visible, bleary eyes which, nonetheless, kept their sweet, sugary expression. He was in the delectable condition of complete intoxication when every passer-by, looking at his face, would be quite sure to say, "You're in a fine pickle, old fellow, in a fine pickle!" Blinker, red as a lobster, his nostrils dilated as far as they would go, was laughing sardonically from a corner; Nikolai Ivanych alone, as befits a good publican, remained as imperturbable as ever. Many new faces had collected in the room, but there was no sign of the Wild Gentleman.

I turned round and walked away quickly down the hill on which Kolotovka stands. At the foot of this hill lay a broad valley; covered as it was with vaporous waves of evening mist, it seemed vaster than ever and appeared to merge with the darkened sky. I was walking with great strides down the road along the ravine when suddenly, from a long distance away in the valley, there came the ringing voice of a boy calling, "Antropka-a! Antropka-a!" in obstinate, tearful desperation, drawing out the last syllable a long time.

He was silent for a few moments and then began to call again. His voice carried clearly in the motionless, lightly dozing air. He must have called Antropka's name thirty times at least, when suddenly from the opposite side of the meadow, as though from a different world, there came a hardly audible reply. "Wha-a-at?"

The boy's voice called at once with joyful desperation, "Come here, you little devil!"

"What fo-o-or?" answered the other after a long pause.

"'Cause Dad wants to give you a good hiding!" the first voice called promptly.

The second voice made no further reply, and the little boy started calling for Antropka again. His cries, growing more infrequent and fainter, still reached my ears when it had grown completely dark and I was rounding the corner of the wood that surrounds my village, about four miles away from Kolotovka.

"Antropka-a-a!" I still seemed to hear in the air full of the shadows of the night.

1850

BEZHIN MEADOW

It was a beautiful July day, one of those days which come only after a long spell of settled weather. From the very early morning the sky is clear. The sunrise does not blaze fiercely but spreads in a gentle flush. The sun is neither fiery nor incandescent, as in a time of sultry drought; it is not dark crimson as before a storm, but bright and gently radiant—rising peacefully from behind a long, narrow cloud, shining freshly, and once more sinking into its lilac mist. The thin upper rim of the extended cloud sparkles sinuously; its brilliance is like the brilliance of beaten silver. But a moment later the dancing beams come shooting out again and the mighty luminary rises gaily and majestically, as though borne aloft on wings. About midday there usually appears a multitude of high, round clouds, golden-grey, with delicate white edges. Like islands, scattered over a boundless river in flood, flowing round them with deep, transparent arms of an even blueness, they scarcely seem to stir; farther off, towards the horizon, they come more closely together, they almost touch and merge, and one no longer sees any patches of blue between them, but they remain almost as azure as the sky; they are filled through and through with light and warmth. The colour of the horizon, light and of a pale lilac, does not change all day and is the same all round; there is no sign of a gathering, darkening storm, except that here and there bluish shafts can perhaps be seen coming down from above, but that is merely the scattering of an almost imperceptible shower. Towards evening these clouds vanish; the last of them, darkish and smudged like smoke, lie in pink puffs against the setting sun; over the place where it has set as calmly as it rose into the sky, a scarlet radiance lingers for a short time over the darkened earth and, flickering softly, like a candle that is carried with great care, the evening star twinkles faintly in the sky.

On such days all colours are softened; they are clear but not bright; the seal of some touching tenderness is set upon everything. On such days the heat is sometimes very great and sometimes it is even steaming on the slopes of the fields; but the wind disperses and breaks up the accumulated sultriness, and whirling eddies—an infallible sign of settled weather—move in tall white pillars along the roads and across the ploughland. There is a smell of wormwood, harvested rye, and buckwheat in the air; even an hour before nightfall you feel no dampness. It is for such weather that the husbandman prays to gather in his corn.

On such a day I once set off on a black-cock shoot in the Chern District of Tula Province. I had found and shot a fair number of game; a bulging game bag cut into my shoulders mercilessly; but when at last I made up my mind to return home, the sunset was fading, and in the air, still light, although no longer illumined by the rays of the setting sun, cold shadows were beginning to thicken and spread. At a brisk pace I walked across the long acreage of bushes, climbed a hill, and, instead of the familiar plain with the small oak wood on the right and the little white church in the distance, I saw a totally different and unfamiliar landscape. At my feet was a narrow valley, and, immediately opposite, a dense aspen wood rose like a high wall. I stopped dead in perplexity and looked round.

"Good heavens," I thought, "I've lost my way! I've kept too much to the right!" And, surprised at my own mistake, I quickly descended the hill. I was at once enveloped in a pocket of disagreeable, stagnant, damp air, just as though I had descended into a cellar; the thick, tall grass at the bottom of the valley, dripping wet, stretched far ahead in a white unbroken line; walking on it somehow gave me an eerie feeling. I clambered out on the other side as quickly as I could and, bearing to the left, walked along beside the aspen wood. Bats were already flitting above its slumbering treetops, wheeling mysteriously and quivering against the dimly radiant sky; a young, belated hawk flew sharply past in a straight line high up in the sky, hurrying back to its nest. "Let me just go round the corner," I thought to myself, "and I shall get to the road at once. I must have gone a good mile out of my way!"

I reached the corner of the wood at last, but there was no sign of a road there: some low, unclipped bushes stretched a long way before me, and behind them, far, far away, I could see a bare field. I stopped again. "What on earth? . . . Where am I?" I began going over in my mind the places I had been to and the direction I had come from during the whole of that day. "Good Lord, this must be the Parakhin bushes!" I exclaimed at last. "Why, of course, then that must be the Sindeyev copse. How in heaven's name did I get here? So far! How curious! Now I must bear to the right again."

I went to the right, through the bushes. Meanwhile night was falling and growing like a storm cloud; it

25

looked as though, together with the evening mists, the
darkness was rising from every quarter, and even streaming down from above. I lighted upon some untrodden,
overgrown path and walked along it, looking intently
ahead of me. Everything round me was quickly growing
dark and silent—only the quail could be heard calling
to one another from time to time. A small night bird,
flying noiselessly and low on its soft wings, almost
knocked against me and shied away in alarm. I came
out of the bushes and walked along the boundary of a
field. Already I found it difficult to distinguish distant
objects: all round me the field looked like a white blur;
beyond it an enormous mass rose up in the gloomy
darkness, moving nearer and nearer with every minute that passed. My footfalls sounded muffled in the
thickening air. The sky, which had gone pale, began to
grow blue once more, but that was already the blue of
the night. Little stars glimmered and twinkled in it.

What I had taken for a wood turned out to be a dark
round hillock. "But where on earth am I?" I again repeated aloud, stopping for the third time and looking
inquiringly at my skewbald English gun dog, Dianka,
without a doubt the cleverest of all four-legged creatures. But the cleverest of four-legged creatures merely
wagged her tail, blinked her weary eyes dejectedly, and
gave me no practical advice whatever.

I felt ashamed before her, and I hurried off ahead
desperately, as though realising suddenly which way I
ought to go. I rounded the hill and found myself in a
low-lying hollow, which was ploughed all round. I was
at once overcome by a strange feeling. This hollow was
shaped almost like a symmetrical cauldron with sloping
sides; at the bottom of it were some large white upright
stones—it looked as though they had crept down there
for some secret conference—and it was so lonely and
still there, the sky hung so flatly and gloomily above
that hollow, that my heart sank. Some little animal

squeaked faintly and piteously among the stones. I
hastened to get out onto the hillock again. Till that
moment I had still not given up hope of finding my way
home; but here I came finally to the conclusion that I
was completely lost, and without even trying to see if
I could recognise any of the surrounding landmarks,
which were almost completely blotted out in darkness,
anyway, I walked straight ahead, setting a course by
the stars and trusting to chance to find the right way.
I walked like that for half an hour, hardly able to drag
my feet. I had a feeling that I had never before been in
such a deserted, lonely place: there was not a glimmer
of light to be seen anywhere, not a sound to be heard.
One gently sloping hill followed another; field stretched
endlessly upon field; bushes seemed to rise suddenly
from under the ground under my very nose. I kept walking, and was already thinking of lying down somewhere
till morning, when suddenly I found myself at the edge
of a terrible precipice.

I drew back my raised foot quickly and through the
almost transparent dark of the night saw a vast plain
far below me. A broad river wound round it in a semi-
circle that turned away from me; the steely reflection
of the water, gleaming faintly here and there, marked
its course. The hill on which I was standing descended
in an almost sheer drop; its vast outlines stood out
black against the bluish void of the air; and directly
below me, in the corner formed by this precipice and
the plain, beside the river—which at this point was
motionless and dark—right beneath the steep slope of
the hill, two fires were throwing up smoke and red
flames close to each other. People were moving round
them; shadows were swaying; and from time to time the
front half of a small curly head was brightly lit up.

At last I recognised where I had got to. This meadow
was widely known in our neighbourhood under the
name of Bezhin Meadow. But there could be no ques-

tion of returning home, especially at night; my legs were
giving way under me from exhaustion. I decided to walk
up to the campfires and wait for the dawn in the
company of the people whom I took for drovers. I got
safely down, but before I had time to let go of the last
branch I had grasped, two big, shaggy white dogs suddenly threw themselves upon me, barking furiously. The
ringing voices of children sounded round the campfires.
Two or three boys got up quickly from the ground. I
called back to their questioning cries. They ran up to me
and at once called off the dogs, who were particularly
struck by the appearance of my Dianka, and I went up
to them.

I was wrong in taking the people who were sitting
round the campfires for drovers. They were simply
peasant boys from a nearby village who were minding
a drove of horses. In the hot summer weather, horses
in our part of the country are usually driven out at
night into the fields to graze: in daytime, flies and gnats
would give them no peace. To drive out the horses before
nightfall and to drive them back in the early morning is
a great adventure for the peasant boys. Sitting bare-
headed and in old sheepskins on the liveliest nags, they
gallop off with merry shouts and whoops of joy, swinging their arms and legs and jumping up high in the air
and laughing at the top of their voices. A fine dust rises
and is blown along the road in a yellow pillar; for a
long way off you can hear the rapid clatter of hoofs;
the horses are racing along, pricking up their ears; ahead
of them all, its tail in the air and continuously altering
its stride, gallops a shaggy sorrel with burrs in its shaggy
mane.

I told the boys that I had lost my way, and sat down
beside them. They asked me where I came from; then
they fell silent and made room for me. We talked a
little. I lay down under a bush with nibbled-off leaves
and began to look round. The picture was a wonderful

one: near the campfires a round, reddish glow of light trembled and then seemed to freeze as it leaned against the darkness; from time to time the flame blazed up and threw rapid reflections of light beyond the boundary of that circle; a thin tongue of light licked the bare willow twigs and immediately disappeared; long, thin shadows, bursting in for a moment in their turn, ran up to the very edge of the campfires; darkness was struggling with light. Sometimes, when the flame burned weaker and the circle of light narrowed, a horse's head would suddenly emerge from the encroaching darkness, a bay head with a white sinuous streak running from the forehead to the upper lip, or all white, stare intently and dully at us, quickly munching the long grass; and, dropping back again, instantly vanish. All we could hear was that it was still munching away and snorting. From the lighted place it was difficult to make out what was going on in the darkness, and that was why near at hand everything seemed to be hidden by an almost black curtain; but, farther away, towards the horizon, hills and woods could be dimly discerned as long smudges. The dark, clear sky stood solemn and immensely high above us in all its mysterious grandeur. My breast was filled with an aching sweetness when I breathed that peculiar, languorous, fresh fragrance, the fragrance of a Russian summer night. All round us hardly a sound could be heard. Only occasionally, in the nearby river, there came the sudden loud splash of a big fish and the faint rustling of the reeds on the banks stirring lightly as the ripples reached them. The fires crackled faintly.

The boys sat round them; there too sat the two dogs who had been so eager to devour me. They could not reconcile themselves to my presence for a long time, and, blinking and squinting sleepily at the fire, growled from time to time with quite an extraordinary sense of their own dignity, growling at first and then whining a little, as though regretting the impossibility of carrying out their desires. There were five boys there altogether: Fedya, Pavlusha, Ilyusha, Kostya, and Vanya. (I learnt the names from their talk, and I propose to introduce them to the reader at once.)

Fedya, the first and the eldest of them, you would say was about fourteen. He was slender, with handsome, fine, rather small features, fair, curly hair, bright eyes, and a perpetual half-gay, half-dreamy smile. He belonged by all appearances to a well-to-do family and had gone out to spend the night in the fields, not because he had to, but just for the fun of it. He wore a gay cotton shirt with a yellow border; a small, new peasant overcoat was thrown precariously over his slender shoulders; a little comb hung from his blue belt; his boots with low tops were most certainly his own and not his father's. The second boy, Pavlusha, had tousled black hair, grey eyes, broad cheekbones, a pale, pock-marked face, a large but regular mouth, a huge head "as large as a beer cauldron," as the saying is, and a squat, awkward body. He was an uncouth lad, there is no denying it, and yet I liked him for all that: he had an intelligent, frank look, and in his voice too there was a note of authority. His clothes were nothing to boast of: they consisted of an ordinary hemp shirt and a pair of patched trousers. The face of the third boy, Ilyusha, was rather insignificant: long, hawk-nosed, with shortsighted eyes, it expressed a sort of dull, sickly anxiety; his compressed lips never moved; his contracted eyebrows were never smooth—he seemed to be always screwing up his eyes at the fire. His tow-coloured, almost white hair stuck out in sharp tufts from under his low felt cap, which he kept pulling down over his ears with both hands. He wore new bast shoes, and his legs were bound round with rags; a thick rope, twisted three times round his waist, carefully tightened his clean black Ukrainian coat. Neither he nor Pavlusha looked more than twelve. The fourth, Kostya, a boy of ten, aroused my curiosity by his pensive and wistful look. His face was small, thin, freckled, with a pointed chin like a squirrel's; his lips one could barely make out; but his large black eyes, which glittered with a liquid brilliance, produced a strange impression; they seemed to wish to say something for which no tongue—his tongue, at least—had any words. He was short, of a puny build, and rather poorly dressed. The last boy, Vanya, I had not even noticed at first; he was lying on the ground, quietly curled up under an oblong piece of bast matting, and only occasionally thrust his curly head out from under it. This boy was only seven years of age.

And so I lay under a small bush, a little apart from the rest, and kept looking at the boys. A small pot hung over one of the campfires; in it "taters" were cooking. Pavlusha was keeping an eye on them and, kneeling, kept prodding with a small piece of wood in the boiling water. Fedya lay propped up on his elbow, with the skirts of his coat spread out. Ilyusha sat beside Kostya and all the time kept his eyes tensely screwed up. Kostya, his head drooping a little, gazed far away into the distance. Vanya did not stir under his matting. I pretended to be asleep. Little by little the boys began to talk again.

At first they chatted about all sorts of things—about the next day's work, about their horses—but suddenly Fedya turned to Ilyusha and, as though resuming an interrupted conversation, asked him, "Well, so you really saw a house goblin, did you?"

"No, I didn't see him, and besides, you can never really see him," replied Ilyusha in a weak, hoarse voice, the sound of which was entirely in keeping with the expression of his face, "but I heard him all right. And it wasn't me alone, either."

"And where does he live in your place?" asked Pavlusha.

"In the old pulping room of the paper-mill."

"Why, do you work at the paper-mill?"

"Course we do—my brother and Adruyshka and me all work in the pulping room."

"Fancy that! So you're factory hands, are you?"

"Well, how did you hear him?" asked Fedya.

"You see, it was like this. Me and my brother, and Fyodor from Mikheyevo and cross-eyed Ivashka, and the other Ivashka from the Red Hills and a third Ivashka with the withered arm, and some other boys—about ten of us all told; the whole shift, you see—had to spend the night in the pulping room. I mean, we didn't just happen to spend the night there, but Nazorov, our foreman, would not let us go home. 'What do you boys want to go home for?' he says. 'There's lots of work for you to-morrow, so you'd better not go home,' he says. So we stayed, and we all lay down together, and Adruyshka, he starts saying, 'What,' he says, 'if the house goblin was to come tonight, boys?' And before he—Adruyshka, that is—finished speaking, someone suddenly started walking over our heads. You see, we was lying downstairs, and he starts walking upstairs by the wheel. So we hears him walking about, the boards bending under him—creaking, they was—and now he passes over our heads; and suddenly the water starts making an awful noise over the wheel, and the wheel starts knocking and turning round and round, although, you see, the slides in the troughs was let down. So we was wondering who could have lifted them up to let the water go through. Anyway, the wheel turned and turned and then stopped. Then he goes to the door upstairs again and starts coming down the stairs. Aye, coming down slowly, he was, just as if he was in no hurry at all, so that the steps under him fairly groaned. Well, so he walks up to our door, he does, and there he stands waiting and waiting, and—then—all of a sudden the door just flies open! It scared the life out of us, I can tell you. We looked, but there was nothing there, nothing at all. . . . Suddenly

32

the net of one of the vats starts moving, then it starts rising, then dipping and floating about in the air, just as if someone was rinsing it, and then back it goes to its old place again. After that the hook of another vat comes off its nail, and then back on its nail it goes again. And then someone seems to walk up to the door, and there, suddenly, it starts coughing, clearing its throat just like it was a sheep, only very loud it was. Well, we just all falls down in a heap, and each of us tries to crawl under the other. Aye, we was scared all right that night!"

"Fancy that!" said Pavlusha. "What did he start coughing for?"

"Dunno. Must have been the damp."

They all fell silent for a while.

"What about the taters?" asked Fedya. "Are they done?"

Pavlusha felt them. "No, they're not done yet. . . . Hear that splash?" he added, turning his face in the direction of the river. "Must have been a pike. And there's a shooting star."

"I've got something to tell you too, boys," Kostya said in his thin little voice. "Just listen to what my dad told us the other day."

"Oh, all right," Fedya said with a patronising air, "we're listening."

"You know Gavrilo, the village carpenter, don't you?"

"Yes, we do."

"But do you know why he's always so glum and never speaks a word? You don't, do you? Well, I'll tell you why. One day, my dad says, he went into the woods to gather nuts. Well, so he went gathering nuts in the woods and lost his way. Didn't know where he was, he didn't. So he walked and walked and just couldn't find the way. And, you see, it was already getting dark, so he sits down under a tree. 'I'd better wait till the morning,' he says to himself. So he sits down and dozes off. But no sooner did he doze off than he heard someone calling him. He looks up. There's no one there. So he falls asleep again, and again someone is calling him. So again he looks and looks, and there, on a branch in front of him, he sees a water nymph. There she sits, swinging on the branch and calling him to come to her, and she herself is laughing—dying of laughter, she was. And the moon was shining bright, so bright and clear it shone that he could see everything—everything. And so she kept on calling him and she herself was so bright and so light, just like a dace or a gudgeon, or a carp which is sometimes whitish and silvery. . . . Well, boys, so Gavrilo the carpenter, he nearly dies of fright, but she just goes on laughing and beckoning to him with her hands. So poor old Gavrilo, he gets up, and he's about to do as the water nymph tells him, but at that moment, boys, God Himself, I suppose, must have told him what to do, for just in the nick of time he crossed himself. It wasn't any too soon, either, for you can't imagine how difficult it was for him to cross himself. 'My hand,' he says, 'seems to have been turned to stone: I could hardly move it. The devil's own work it was all right!' So no sooner did he cross himself than the little water nymph stopped laughing and suddenly she starts crying. And she cries and she cries, wiping her eyes with her hair, and her hair is as green as hemp. So Gavrilo looks and looks at her and then he starts asking her, 'What are you crying for, you little witch of the woods, you?' And the water nymph, she says to him, she says, 'What did you want to cross yourself for, you silly man?' she says. 'You could have lived happily with me to the end of your days,' she says, 'and now I'm crying and grieving,' she says, 'because you crossed yourself. And,' she says, 'I won't be the only one to grieve, either. You too,' she says, 'will grieve to the end of your days.' And right at that very moment she disappeared, and old Gavrilo, you see, immediately realised which way he had to go to get out of the wood, only ever since that night he has been going about looking unhappy."

"Well, I never!" Fedya said after a short pause. "But how can such an evil spirit of the woods harm a Christian soul—he didn't do what she wanted, did he?"

"Well, there you are," said Kostya. "And Gavrilo, you know, said she had such a thin, pitiful little voice, just like a toad's."

"Did you hear your dad tell that himself?" Fedya went on.

"Yes, himself. I was lying on the plank-bed under the ceiling and heard it all."

"Funny thing! Why should he be unhappy? I expect she must have liked him, if she called him."

"Aye, she liked him all right," Ilyusha put in. "Course she liked him. She wanted to tickle him to death, that's what she wanted to do. That's what they always does, them water nymphs."

"I suppose there ought to be water nymphs here too," observed Fedya.

"No," replied Kostya, "not in a clean, open place like this. One thing, though—the river is near."

They all fell silent. Suddenly, somewhere in the far distance, there came a drawn-out, ringing, almost wailing sound, one of those mysterious night sounds which sometimes come out of the dead silence, rise, hang in the air, and then slowly die away. You listen intently, and there seems to be nothing there, and yet it still keeps on reverberating. It was as if someone had uttered a long cry right under the very horizon, and as if someone else had answered him from the woods in a thin, sharp laugh; and a faint, low whistle went hissing along the surface of the river. The boys looked at each other and shuddered.

"Lord help us!" Ilyusha whispered.

"Oh, you gaping fools!" cried Pavlusha. "What are you scared of? Look, the taters are done!" They all moved nearer to the pot and began eating the steaming potatoes. Only Vanya did not stir.

"Why don't you come?" said Pavlusha. But Vanya did not crawl out from under his matting.

The pot was soon empty.

"And have you heard, boys," began Ilyusha, "what happened at Varnavitsy the other day?"

"At the dam, you mean?" asked Fedya.

"Yes, at the dam, at the burst dam. There's a haunted place for you, if you like. Haunted and lonely. Ravines and ditches all round, and lots of snakes in the ditches."

"Well, what happened? Come on, tell us."

"This is what happened. I don't suppose you, Fedya, know that there's a drowned man buried there. He drowned himself a long time ago when the pond was deep, but you can still see his grave, but only just. A little mound, that's all you can see of it. . . . Well, so the agent sent for the kennel-man Yermil the other day and told him to go to the post office in town. Yermil always drives to the post office. You see, he lets all his dogs die. He can't keep them alive, for some reason, and so they never lives long—and yet he's a good kennel-man, old Yermil is; everyone likes him. So Yermil went off for the post, but he stayed too long in town, and when he drove back he was a little tipsy. It was night. A bright night too. The moon was shining. So Yermil rides over the dam—that was the way he took. So the kennel-man Yermil, he rides across the dam, and what do you think he sees? On the drowned man's grave there's a little lamb, a white, curly, pretty little lamb, and it keeps walking about. So Yermil, he thinks to himself, 'Why not take the little lamb? If I leave him here he's sure to die.' Well, the little lamb doesn't mind a bit. So Yermil walks up to his horse, and the horse stares at him and starts snorting and shaking its head. But he cries, 'Whoa there!' and the horse quietened. He then mounts with the lamb and rides off, holding the lamb in front of him.

36

He looks at the lamb, and the lamb looks him straight in the face. Well, old Yermil, he got frightened, for, you see, he couldn't ever remember seeing a lamb looking a man straight in the face like that. Still, there didn't seem to be anything wrong, so he starts stroking the little lamb's fleece and says to it, 'Baa-baa!' And the little lamb suddenly bares its teeth and says to him too, 'Baa-baa!' "

Ilyusha had hardly uttered this last word when suddenly both dogs leapt up at once and, barking furiously, rushed away from the campfires and disappeared into the darkness. All the boys looked frightened. Vanya sprang out from under his matting, and Pavlusha ran shouting after the dogs. The barking quickly died away in the distance. One could hear the restless scamper of the frightened horses. Pavlusha shouted loudly, "Grey! Beetle!" After a few moments the barking stopped; Pavlusha's voice sounded a long way off. A little time passed. The boys exchanged bewildered glances, as though waiting for something to happen. Suddenly there came the thud of a galloping horse; it stopped abruptly at the very edge of the campfire, and Pavlusha, grasping the mane, jumped off it nimbly. The two dogs also rushed into the circle of light and at once sat down, with their red tongues hanging out.

"What was the matter there? What was it?" the boys asked.

"Nothing," replied Pavlusha, waving his hand at the horse. "The dogs must have scented something. I thought it was a wolf," he added in an indifferent voice, breathing quickly with his whole chest.

I could not help admiring Pavlusha. He looked very splendid at that moment. His unattractive face, animated by the rapid ride, blazed with fearless audacity and firm determination. Without a switch in his hand, at night, he had galloped off alone after a wolf without a moment's hesitation. "What a fine boy!" I thought, looking at him.

"You didn't see any wolves by any chance, did you?" Kostya, the coward, asked.

"There are always lots of 'em here," Pavlusha replied, "but they're only troublesome in winter." He settled down again in front of the fire. As he sat down on the ground, he dropped his hand on the shaggy neck of one of the dogs, and the delighted dog did not move its head for a long time, looking sideways at Pavlusha with grateful pride.

Vanya again crawled back under his matting.

"What a scarifying story you told us, Ilyusha," said Fedya, who as the son of a well-to-do peasant always called the tune (he spoke very little himself, as though afraid to lose his dignity). "And I suppose it was some evil spirit who made the dogs bark. No wonder! I was told that that place was haunted."

"Varnavitsy? I should think so! It's haunted, all right. I'm told they saw the old master there once—the one who's dead. They say he walks in a coat with long skirts and all the time he keeps groaning and looking for something on the ground. Grandpa Trofimich met him once and asked him, 'What are you looking for on the ground, sir?'"

"He asked him that?" Fedya interrupted in astonishment.

"Yes, he did."

"Oh, Trofimich must be a stout fellow to have done that! Well, and what did *he* say?"

"'I'm looking for a magic herb,' he said, and he said it in such a hollow, dull voice: 'Magic herb!' 'But, sir,' says Trofimich, 'what do you want a magic herb for?' 'The grave,' he says, 'presses heavily on me, Trofimich. I want to get out, to get out!'"

"Oh, so that's what he wanted!" Fedya observed. "I expect he hadn't lived enough."

"That's strange," said Kostya, "I thought you could only see the dead on All Saints' Day."

"You can see the dead at any hour of the day and night," Ilyusha put in with conviction; for, so far as I could see, he knew, or he seemed to know, all the country superstitions better than the other boys. "But on All Saints' Day you can see a living man too. I mean one whose turn it is to die in that year. All you have to do is sit at night on the porch of a church and keep on looking at the road. The people who go past you on the road are those who are going to die in the same year. In our village Ulyana went to sit like that on the porch of the church."

"Well, did she see anyone?" Kostya asked with interest.

"Of course she did. First of all, she sat there a long, long time and never saw or heard no one. She thought she could hear a dog barking, barking far away. Suddenly she saw a boy coming along the road, wearing nothing but a shirt. She looked closer—it was Ivashka Fedoseyev coming——"

"You mean the one who died in the spring?" Fedya interrupted.

"Yes, that's the one. There he was, coming along without lifting his head, but Ulyana recognised him. And then she looked and there was a woman coming along. She looked closer and closer, and, good Lord, there she was herself, walking along the road!"

"Really herself?" asked Fedya.

"Oh yes, yes—herself."

"Well, she hasn't died yet, has she?"

"But the year isn't finished yet, you see. Just look at her: she's on her last legs."

They all fell silent again. Pavlusha threw a handful of dried twigs on the fire; they showed up black against the sudden blaze of flame, crackled, smoked, and began to curl up with the heat. The reflection of the fire, trembling violently, struck out in all directions, especially upwards. Suddenly a white pigeon seemed to fly out of nowhere straight into its reflection, hovered for a moment in alarm, enveloped in the warm glow, and disappeared with a whir of wings.

"Must have lost his way," Pavlusha observed. "Now he'll go on flying till he strikes something, and he'll stay until daybreak wherever that may be."

"Are you sure, Pavlusha," Kostya said, "it wasn't just the soul of a saint flying to heaven?"

Pavlusha threw another handful of twigs on the fire. "Perhaps," he said at last.

"But please tell me, Pavlusha," Fedya began, "did you in your village, in Shalamovo, also see the heavenly portents?"*

"You mean when we couldn't see the sun no more?"

"Yes. I expect you too must have been frightened."

"Yes, and we weren't the only ones. The master, who explained to us before it happened that there was going to be a portent, got so frightened himself when it got dark that you would never believe it. And in the servants' cottage, the woman cook, as soon as it got dark, went and broke all the pots in the oven with an oven fork. 'Who is going to eat,' she says, 'now that the end of the world has come?' So the cabbage soup was all spilt. And in our village they were saying that white wolves would run about the earth and eat people up and a bird of prey would fly about, or even that we would see Trishka himself."†

"Who is this Trishka?" asked Kostya.

"Why, don't you know?" Ilyusha cried warmly. "Well, I must say! Not to know about Trishka! Where do you come from? They must all be stay-at-homes in your vil-

* This is what the peasants in our part of the country call an eclipse of the sun. AUTHOR.

† The popular belief about Trishka probably derives from the legend of the Antichrist. AUTHOR.

lage. Yes, stay-at-homes, that's what they are! Trishka is a big magician, and he's going to come one day. And when this magician comes, people won't be able to catch him, and they won't be able to do nothing to him—such an extraordinary man he'll be. If, for instance, some Christians will want to lay hands on him and attack him with sticks and surround him, he'll distract their attention so that they'll start hitting each other. And if, for instance, they put him in prison, he'll ask for a drink of water in a bowl. They'll bring him the bowl, and he'll dive into it, and they'll never see him again. If they put him in chains, he'll clap his hands and the chains will fall off. Well, so this Trishka will be going about from town to town and from village to village, and this same Trishka, clever magician that he is, will tempt the Christian people, and no one won't be able to do nothing to him, such a clever and crafty man he'll be."

"Well, yes," continued Pavlusha in his unhurried voice, "that's the sort of man he'll be, and it was him the people in our village were expecting. The old men said that Trishka would come as soon as ever the heavenly portent started. So the portent started and all the people rushed into the streets and into the fields and waited for what was going to happen next. And, as you know, the country round our village is open, and you can see for miles round. They looked, and suddenly, from the village on the hill, a strange kind of man was coming along, with such an extraordinary head, and everybody started shouting, 'Lord, Trishka's coming! Trishka's coming!' And they all ran away and hid themselves where they could. Our village headman crept into a ditch; his wife got stuck under the gate, and she kept screaming at the top of her voice, giving her own dog in the yard such a fright that he broke his chain, jumped through the fence, and ran off into the forest; and Kuzka's father, Dorofeyich, jumped into a field of oats, squatted down, and started calling like a quail; 'For,' he thought to himself, 'maybe the enemy of man will take pity on a bird!' So scared were they all! And all the time it was our cooper Vavila; he had bought himself a new hooped wooden jug and had put the empty jug on his head!"

All the boys laughed and again fell silent for a moment, as often happens with people who are talking in the open air. I looked round. Solemn and majestic, the night encompassed us on all sides; the damp freshness of late evening had given way to the dry warmth of midnight, which would lie for a long time yet like a soft cloak on the sleeping fields; it was still a long time to the first murmur, the first rustlings and stirrings of the morning, to the first dewdrops of daybreak. There was no moon in the sky: at that time of the year it rose late. The numberless golden stars, twinkling in eager rivalry, seemed to float gently in the direction of the Milky Way; and indeed, looking at them, you seemed to be dimly aware yourself of the headlong and unceasing course of the earth.

A strange, sharp, painful cry suddenly sounded twice in succession over the river, and after a few moments it came again from farther off.

Kostya gave a start. "What was that?"

"It's a heron calling," Pavlusha replied calmly.

"A heron," Kostya repeated. "But what was that I heard yesterday evening, Pavlusha?" he added after a short pause. "Perhaps you know."

"What did you hear?"

"This is what I heard: I was going from the Stone Ridge to Shashkino, and at first I walked along our hazel wood, and then I went across the meadow—you know the place where it turns sharply at the corner of the ravine. There's a pool overgrown with reeds, you know. So I was walking past this pool, boys, when suddenly, from out of that pool, someone groaned, oh, ever so pitifully, 'Whoo-whoo-whoo!' I was frightened, I can tell you. You see, it was late, and the voice sounded so sickly that I nearly started crying myself. What could that have been, do you think?"

"The summer before last," Pavlusha observed, "Akim the forester was drowned there by thieves, so perhaps it was his soul that was complaining."

"I suppose that's what it was, boys," Kostya declared, widening his eyes, which were very big already. "I didn't know Akim was drowned in that pool. Had I known it, I'd have been even more frightened."

"Or else," Pavlusha continued, "they say there are such tiny little frogs which cry pitifully like that."

"Frogs? No! It wasn't frogs. Frogs would never have made a noise like that." A heron called again from over the river. "Oh, get out of it!" Kostya cried involuntarily. "Calling like a wood demon!"

"A wood demon doesn't call," Ilyusha put in. "He's dumb. He can only clap his hands and jabber——"

"Why, have you seen him, the wood demon?" Fedya interrupted sarcastically.

"No, I haven't, and God preserve me from ever seeing him! But other people have. The other day he led one of our peasants astray: he took him round and round in the woods, all round the same clearing. He didn't get home till before dawn."

"Well, did he see him?"

"He did. He said he was a huge, enormous, dark fellow, all muffled up, and he seemed to be hiding behind a tree. He couldn't make him out clearly; he seemed to be hiding from the moon, and he kept staring with his huge eyes, blinking and blinking."

"Lord!" Fedya cried, trembling slightly and shuddering. "Ugh!"

"I wonder why such filthy creatures have spread all over the earth?" Pavlusha observed. "Really!"

"Don't call him names! You'd better be careful or he'll hear you," Ilyusha remarked.

43

There was silence again.

"Look—look, boys!" Vanya's childish voice called suddenly. "Look at God's little stars—swarming like bees!" He poked his fresh little face out from under the matting, leaned on his tiny fist, and slowly raised his big, gentle eyes.

All the boys raised their eyes to the sky and did not lower them for a long time.

"I say, Vanya," Fedya began affectionately, "how is your sister, Anyutka?"

"She's all right," replied Vanya.

"Ask her why she doesn't come and see us! Why doesn't she?"

"Dunno."

"Tell her to come."

"I will."

"Tell her I'll give her a present."

"And me?"

"You too."

Vanya sighed. "Oh, never mind, I don't want one. Better give it to her. She's a good, kind kid." And Vanya put his little head on the ground again.

Pavlusha stood up and picked up the empty pot.

"Where are you going?" Fedya asked him.

"To the river for some water. I want a drink of water."

The dogs rose and went after him. "Mind you don't fall in!" Ilyusha shouted after him.

"Why should he fall in?" said Fedya. "He'll take care."

"Yes, he will, but anything may happen: he may bend down and begin to draw water and then the river demon will seize him by the hand and drag him into the water. Afterwards, I suppose, people will say the poor boy fell into the river, but did he? There, he's gone into the rushes," he added, listening. And true enough, the rushes rustled as they were parted.

"And is it true," asked Kostya, "that Akulina, the fool, went mad after falling into the water?"

"Yes, she's been like that ever since. Just look at her now. Before, they say, she was such a beauty, but the river demon put a spell on her. I expect he didn't think they'd pull her out so soon, so he put a spell on her at the bottom of the river where he lives."

(I had met this Akulina more than once. Covered in rags, terribly thin, with a face as black as coal, bleareyed and with perpetually bared teeth, she would hang about in the same place for hours on end, on the road somewhere, pressing her bony hands tightly to her breast and slowly shifting from one foot to the other like a wild beast in a cage. She did not understand a word of what was said to her and only laughed spasmodically from time to time.)

"But," Kostya went on, "I heard that Akulina threw herself into the river because her lover deceived her."

"Yes, that's why."

"And do you remember Vassily?" Kostya added sadly.

"Which Vassily?" asked Fedya.

"Why, the one who was drowned in this same river," Kostya replied. "Oh, he was such a wonderful boy! Oh, ever such a wonderful boy! How his mother, Feklista, loved him! And she seemed to feel—Feklista, that is—that water would be his undoing. Every time Vassily came with us to bathe in the river in summer she would start trembling all over. The other women didn't mind a bit—they just walked past with their washing in their wooden troughs, swaying from side to side, but Feklista would put her trough down on the ground and would start calling him, 'Come back, come back, my darling!' And the Lord only knows how he got drowned. He was playing on the ground and his mother was there too, raking hay. Suddenly she heard what she thought was someone blowing bubbles in the water. She looked round, and there was only Vassily's cap floating on the water. Since then Feklista isn't right in her mind, either. She comes and lies down at the place where he was

45

drowned. Lies there and starts singing a song—you remember, Vassily used to sing that song too, and it's that
song she sings, and she cries and complains bitterly to
God. . . ."

"Here comes Pavlusha," said Fedya.

Pavlusha came up to the fire with a full pot of water
in his hands. "Well, boys," he began after a pause, "I'm
done for."

"Why? What is it?" Kostya asked hurriedly.

"I heard Vassily's voice."

Everyone gave a start.

"Good Lord, are you sure?" Kostya murmured.

"Of course I'm sure. The moment I started bending
down to the water I heard someone calling me in Vassily's voice, and it seemed as if it came from under the
water. 'Pavlusha, Pavlusha, come here!' I ran back, but
I got the water all the same."

"Dear, oh dear," the boys said, crossing themselves.

"That was the river demon calling you, Pavlusha,"
added Fedya. "We were just talking about him—about
Vassily, I mean."

"Oh, it's a bad omen," Ilyusha said slowly.

"Oh, I don't care, let it!" Pavlusha said resolutely and
sat down again. "No use running away from your fate,
is it?"

The boys fell silent. It could be seen that Pavlusha's
story had made a deep impression on them. They began to settle down before the fire, as if preparing to sleep.

"What's that?" asked Kostya suddenly, raising his
head.

Pavlusha listened hard. "That's snipe flying and
whistling."

"Where are they flying to?"

"Why, to the country where there's no winter."

"Is there such a country?"

"Yes, there is."

"Is it far away?"

"Yes, ever so far away, beyond the warm seas."

Kostya sighed and closed his eyes.

More than three hours had passed since I had joined the company of the boys. At last the moon rose; I did not notice it at once: it was so small and narrow. This moonless night still seemed as magnificent as ever. But many stars, which a short while ago had stood high in the sky, were now sinking to the dark rim of the earth; everything was perfectly still all round, as everything does usually grow still towards the morning: everything was sunk in the deep, immobile sleep before the dawn. There was no longer the same strong scent in the air; once more dampness seemed to pervade it. . . . Oh, the short nights of summer! The boys' talk had died away, together with their fires. Even the dogs were dozing; the horses, as far as I could make out in the faintly glimmering and feebly streaming light of the stars, were lying down too, their heads drooping. A gentle drowsiness came over me, and it passed into a slumber.

A fresh breeze ran over my face. I opened my eyes. The day was breaking. There was still no flush of dawn, but in the east the sky was growing light. Everything became visible, though dimly, round me. The pale grey sky was becoming lighter; it was becoming cold and blue; the stars twinkled feebly, or vanished altogether; the ground had grown damp; the leaves were covered with dew; and from somewhere came the sounds of life, voices, and the light early breeze was already blowing and hovering over the earth. My body responded to it with a light, exhilarating shiver. I rose quickly and went across to the boys. They were all sound asleep round the glowing embers of the campfire; Pavlusha alone half raised himself and stared fixedly at me.

I nodded to him and went my way along the river over which the mist was just beginning to rise. I had not gone two miles when round me, all along the broad water meadow and ahead of me on the hillocks, which were beginning to turn green, from wood to wood, and behind me, over the long dusty road, over the reddened, sparkling bushes and along the river—which was taking on a diffident blue tint as it emerged from the thinning mist —flowed scarlet, then red and golden torrents of new, warm light. . . . Everything stirred, awoke, began to sing, to make a noise, to speak. Everywhere the heavy dewdrops flashed like sparkling diamonds; the sound of church bells, pure and clear—as though they too had been washed in the coolness of the morning—came to meet me; and suddenly, driven by my friends, the boys, the drove of rested horses galloped past me.

I am sorry to have to add that Pavlusha died the same year. He was not drowned: he was killed by a fall from a horse. A pity; he was such a fine lad!

1851

MUMU

In one of the streets on the outskirts of Moscow, in a grey house with white columns, a mezzanine, and a balcony that was all warped and out of shape, there once lived a woman landowner, a widow, surrounded by a multitude of serfs. Her sons were in government service in Petersburg; her daughters were married; she rarely left the house; and she spent the last years of her miserly and weary old age in solitude. Her day, joyless and overcast, had long passed away, but her evening too was blacker than night.

Of all her servants the most remarkable person was the caretaker Gerasim, a man of well over six feet, of immensely strong build, and deaf and dumb from his birth. His mistress had taken him away from his village, where he lived alone in a little hut, apart from his brothers, and was considered to be almost the most punctual peasant to pay his tax to his landowner. Endowed with quite extraordinary strength, he did the work of four men; everything he put his hand to turned out well. It was a sheer delight to watch him ploughing, when, leaning heavily on the plough with his huge hands, he seemed to cut open the yielding bosom of the earth alone and without the help of his poor horse; when, some time at the beginning of August, about St. Peter's Day, he plied his scythe, he did so with a shattering force that might have uprooted a wood of young birch trees; when, swiftly and without stopping for a minute, he threshed the corn with a flail of over two yards long, the elongated and firm muscles of his shoulders rose and fell like levers. His perpetual silence lent a solemn dignity to his unwearying labour. He was a fine peasant and, were it not for his affliction, any girl would have been glad to marry him. But now Gerasim had been brought to Moscow, a pair of boots had been bought for him, a long peasant coat had been made for him for the summer and a sheepskin for winter, a broom and a spade had been put into his hands, and he was assigned the duties of a caretaker.

He took a great dislike to his new life in town at first. He was used to working in the fields and to village life from his childhood. Shut off by his affliction from the society of men, he grew up dumb and powerful, like a tree that grows on fertile soil. Transported to town, he did not know what was happening to him; he pined and was bewildered, as a young healthy bull is bewildered when taken away from a meadow where the lush grass grew up to his belly, put in a railway truck, and whirled along, his well-fed body hidden in smoke and sparks and clouds of steam, whirled along with a clatter and screech of wheels; but where he is whirled to—God only knows! After the heavy work in the fields his new duties seemed a trifling matter to Gerasim; in half an hour he had everything done, and again he either stopped dead in the middle of the yard and stared open-mouthed at the passers-by, as though trying to obtain from them a solution of the mystery of his position, or suddenly retired to some corner and, hurling the broom or spade a long way away, flung himself on the ground face downwards and lay motionless for hours on end, like a wild beast in captivity.

But man gets used to anything, and Gerasim too, in the end, got used to living in town. He had nothing much to do: all his duties consisted in keeping the yard clean, bringing in a barrel of water twice a day, fetching and chopping up logs for the kitchen and the house, keeping out strangers, and keeping watch at night. And it must be said in all fairness that he carried out his duties zealously: there were never any shavings or any litter to be seen lying about in the yard; if the old, jaded mare put at his disposal for fetching water got stuck in the mud in the rainy season, he had only to heave with his shoulder and he would shove aside not only the cart but the horse itself; if he started chopping wood, the axe fairly rang like glass, and logs and chips were sent flying all over the place; as for strangers, after he had one night caught two thieves and knocked their heads together in so rough a fashion that there was no need to take them to the police station afterwards, everyone in the neighbourhood began to show the utmost respect for him; even in the daytime, passers-by, who were not criminals at all but simply strangers, catching sight of the formidable caretaker, would wave him away and shout at him —as though he could hear their shouts.

With all the other servants in the house, who were a little afraid of him, Gerasim was not exactly on friendly, but rather on familiar, terms: he looked upon them as members of his own household. They made themselves understood by signs, and he *did* understand them, and carried out all the orders exactly; but he also knew his own rights, and no one dared sit down in his place at table. Generally speaking, Gerasim was of a strict and serious disposition; he liked order in everything; even the cocks did not dare to fight in his presence—or there would be trouble! The moment he caught sight of them fighting he would seize them by the legs, whirl them round and round in the air a dozen times, and throw them in different directions. His mistress also kept geese in the yard, but a goose, as everyone knows, is a dignified and sober-minded bird, and Gerasim felt a respect for them, looked after them, and fed them; he himself bore a rather striking resemblance to a sedate gander. He was allotted a tiny box-room over the kitchen; he fixed it all up himself, according to his liking, made himself a bedstead out of oak boards on four wooden blocks—a truly Herculean bed! You could put a ton or two on it and it would not have bent under the load. Under the bed was a sturdy chest; in the corner stood a little table of the same strong structure, and beside the table was a three-legged chair, so squat and strongly built that Gerasim himself would sometimes pick it up and drop it with a self-satisfied grin. The little room was locked up by means of a padlock that looked like one of those cottage-loaves that have a hole at the top, except that it was black; the key of this padlock Gerasim always carried about on his belt. He did not like people to come to see him.

So passed a year, at the end of which Gerasim was involved in a little incident.

The old lady in whose house he lived as caretaker was a strict observer of ancient customs in everything and kept a great number of servants: in her house were not only laundresses, sempstresses, carpenters, tailors, and dressmakers, there was even a harness-maker, who also acted as a veterinary surgeon and doctor for the servants; there was also a house doctor for the mistress, and, last, a shoemaker by the name of Kapiton Klimov, an inveterate drunkard. Kapiton was a man with a grudge against the world. He regarded himself as one whose true merits had never been properly appreciated, as a man of metropolitan education, who should not be twiddling his thumbs in some out-of-the-way suburb in Moscow, and if he did drink, he did so—as he himself expressed it with slow deliberation, smiting his breast—because he had to "drown his grief" in drink. One fine day his mistress had a talk about him with her butler Gavrilo, a man whom, to judge only by his little yellow eyes and his nose like a duck's bill, seemed to have been marked out by fate itself to be a person born to command. The old lady was sorry to hear of the depraved morals of Kapiton, who the night before had been picked up somewhere in the street.

"What do you think, Gavrilo?" she said suddenly. "Ought we not perhaps to marry him off? Perhaps he'd settle down then."

"Why not indeed, ma'am?" replied Gavrilo. "Let him get married, ma'am. Sure to be a good thing for him, ma'am."

"Yes, only who'd want to marry him?"

"Aye, that's right, ma'am. Still, just as you please. He might, if I may say so, ma'am, still be of some use for something. Can't throw him out into the street!"

"I believe he likes Tatyana, doesn't he?"

Gavrilo was about to make some reply, but he shut his mouth tightly.

"Yes, let him ask for Tatyana in marriage," the mistress decided, taking a pinch of snuff with relish. "Do you hear?"

"Yes, ma'am," said Gavrilo and went out.

Returning to his own room (it was in a cottage in the yard and was almost entirely filled with iron-bound chests), Gavrilo first of all sent his wife out and then sat down by the window and sank into thought. His mistress's unexpected order had evidently confounded him. At last he got up and sent for Kapiton. Kapiton made his appearance. . . .

But before communicating their conversation to the reader, it would not be out of place to relate in a few words who this Tatyana was whom Kapiton had to marry, and why the butler was embarrassed by his mistress's order.

Tatyana, who was one of the laundresses we mentioned earlier (though as a trained and skilful laundress she was put in charge of the fine linen only), was a woman of twenty-eight, small, thin, fair-haired, with moles on her left cheek. Moles on the left cheek are regarded as an ill omen in Russia, a token of an unhappy life. Tatyana could not boast of her lot. She had been badly treated ever since she was a young girl: she had done the work of two and had never known any affection; she had been poorly clothed and had received the smallest wage; she had practically no relatives—an uncle of hers, an old steward, had been left behind in the country as no longer of any use, and her other uncles were ordinary peasants—and that was all. At one time she was said to have been beautiful, but her good looks were all too soon gone. She was very meek, or rather, cowed; she was completely indifferent about herself and was mortally afraid of others; all she thought of was how to finish her work in good time; she never talked to anyone and trembled at the very mention of her mistress's name, though she scarcely knew her by sight.

When Gerasim was brought from the country she nearly fainted with terror at the sight of his enormous figure. She tried as much as she could to avoid meeting him, and even closed her eyes if she happened to run past him on the way to the laundry. At first Gerasim paid no attention to her; then he started grinning to himself when she crossed his path; then he began to stare at her in admiration; and at last he never took his eyes off her. She had caught his fancy: whether by the gentle expression of her face or by the timidity of her movements—goodness only knows! One day she was walking across the yard, carefully carrying her mistress's starched jacket on her outstretched fingers, when someone suddenly seized her firmly by the elbow. She turned round and uttered a frightened scream: behind her stood Gerasim. Laughing stupidly and grunting affectionately, he held out to her a gingerbread cock with gold tinsel on its tail and wings. She was about to refuse it, but he thrust it into her hand by force, nodded, walked away, and, turning round, again grunted something very affectionately to her. Ever since that day he gave her no peace; wherever she went, he was sure to be there, coming to meet her, smiling, grunting, waving his hands, suddenly producing a ribbon out of the inside of his smock and foisting it on her, or sweeping the dust out of her way with his broom. The poor girl simply did not know how to behave or what to do.

Soon the whole household learnt of the dumb caretaker's extravagant behaviour; Tatyana was overwhelmed with chaffing remarks, broad hints, and innuendoes. But not everyone could pluck up courage to make fun of Gerasim to his face; he did not like jokes; and, as a matter of fact, they left her alone too when he was present. Whether she liked it or not, the girl found herself under his protection. Like all deaf-mutes, he was very quick-witted, and he understood perfectly well when they were laughing at him or her. One day at dinner the maid in charge of linen, Tatyana's superior, began tormenting her and brought her to such a state that the poor girl did not know where to look and was almost bursting into tears from sheer vexation. Gerasim suddenly got up, stretched out his enormous hand, put it on the head of the linen maid, and stared at her with a look of such grim ferocity that she just dropped her hands on the table. Everyone fell silent. Gerasim picked up his spoon again and went on drinking his cabbage soup. "Just look at him, the dumb devil, the wood goblin!" they all muttered in an undertone, while the linen maid got up and went out into the maids' workroom. Another time, noticing that Kapiton, the same Kapiton who has been mentioned earlier, had been chatting a little too amiably with Tatyana, Gerasim beckoned to him to come up, took him to the coach-house, and, snatching up a shaft that was standing in a corner by one end, shook it at him lightly but with unmistakable meaning. After that no one dared say anything to Tatyana. And all this did not get him into any trouble. It is true that as soon as she reached the maids' work-room the linen maid at once fainted and altogether acted so skilfully that Gerasim's rude behaviour was brought to his mistress's knowledge the same day; but the fantastic old woman only laughed, and to the linen maid's great chagrin made her repeat several times how he had pushed her head down with his heavy hand, and next day sent Gerasim a rouble. She regarded him with favour as a strong and faithful watchman. Gerasim was very much afraid of her, but he had great hopes of her favour all the same, and was intending to go to her and ask her for permission to marry Tatyana. He was only waiting for a new coat he had been promised by the butler—for he wished to appear decently dressed before his mistress—when this same mistress suddenly took it into her head to marry Tatyana off to Kapiton.

The reader will now easily understand the reason for the butler Gavrilo's confusion after his conversation with his mistress. "The mistress," he thought to himself as he was sitting at the window, "no doubt favours Gerasim (Gavrilo knew this perfectly well and that was why he himself treated him so well); but, all the same, he is a poor dumb creature. Should I inform the mistress that Gerasim has been courting Tatyana? But, on the other hand, it is quite fair, isn't it? For what kind of husband would Gerasim make? But then again, if that damned wood goblin (God forgive me!) was to find out that Tatyana was being married to Kapiton, he'd be sure to smash up everything in the house. Aye, he would and all. You can't get any sense out of a fellow like him.

Why, a devil like him (God forgive me!) simply can't be got to see reason—— Oh, well . . ."

The appearance of Kapiton interrupted the thread of Gavrilo's thoughts. The shiftless shoemaker came in, put his hands behind him, and, leaning nonchalantly against the projecting angle of the wall near the door, crooked his right foot in front of his left and tossed his head, as much as to say, "Here I am! What do you want?"

Gavrilo looked at Kapiton and drummed with his fingers on the jamb of the window. Kapiton merely narrowed his leaden eyes a little, but did not drop them; he even grinned brightly and passed his hand over his fair hair, which was sticking out in all directions. "Well," he seemed to say, "it's me—see? Me! What are you staring at?"

"A fine fellow," said Gavrilo, and paused. "A fine fellow, I don't think!"

Kapiton merely twitched his slender shoulders.

"Just look at yourself," Gavrilo went on reproachfully. "Have a good look at yourself. Well, what do you think you look like?"

Kapiton cast a serene glance upon his threadbare, torn coat, his patched trousers, examined with particular attention his boots, which were full of holes—especially the one against whose toe his small right foot was leaning so gracefully—and then stared at the butler again. "What about it, sir?"

"What about it?" Gavrilo repeated. "What about it— *sir*? What about it indeed! You're the spitting image of the devil himself, God forgive me! That's what you look like!"

Kapiton blinked rapidly. "You can call me names as much as you like," he thought to himself.

"Drunk again, weren't you?" began Gavrilo. "Again, eh? Answer me, man!"

"Seeing as how I'm in weak health," replied Kapiton,

"I have certainly exposed myself to the influence of alcholic beverages."

"In weak health, are you? You're not flogged enough, that's the trouble! Apprenticed in Petersburg too! You've not learnt a lot during your apprenticeship, have you? All you're good for is to eat the bread of idleness!"

"So far as that is concerned, sir, there's only One Who can judge me, the Lord God Himself and no one else. He alone knows what sort of man I am and whether or not I eats the bread of idleness. As regards the little matter of drunkenness, if you insist, sir, on bringing it up, it's not me but a pal of mine who is to blame for it. It was him who put temptation in my way and it was him who, in a manner of speaking, foxed me—gave me the slip, I mean, while I——"

"While you remained in the street like a fool. Oh, you dissolute fellow! But that's not why I've asked you to come," the butler continued. "What I want to talk to you about is this: the mistress"—here he paused a little —"the mistress wants you to get married. Do you hear? She thinks that you'll—er—settle down when you're married. Understand?"

"Course I understands, sir."

"All right, then. If you ask me, it is about time someone took you in hand properly. However, that's her business. Well? Are you agreeable?"

Kapiton grinned. "Matrimony's an excellent thing for a man, sir. I mean to say, sir, so far as I'm concerned, I'd be only too happy. With the greatest of pleasure, sir, I'm sure."

"Very well, then," said Gavrilo; and he thought to himself, "I suppose the fellow means well." "Only," he went on aloud, "the trouble is, you see, that the wife they've found for you isn't the sort you'd—er—like."

"Oh? And who is she, if I may ask, sir?"

"Tatyana."

58

"Tatyana?" Kapiton detached himself from the wall and stared open-mouthed at Gavrilo.

"Well, why are you so alarmed? Don't you like her?"

"Like her? Of course I like her, sir. She's a good enough girl. A hard-working, quiet girl. But you know perfectly well, sir, that that wood goblin, that damned hellhound of the steppes, is after her himself——"

"I know, my dear fellow, I know all about it," the butler interrupted him with vexation. "But, you see——"

"But, good heavens, sir, he's sure to kill me. Sure to. Swat me like a fly. Why, his hand—have you seen his hand, sir? It's—why, it's simply like Minin's and Pozharsky's.* And he's deaf too. If he hits you, he don't know how hard he's hitting! Swings his enormous fists about without realising what he's doing. And there's no way of stopping him, either. Why? Because, as you knows yourself, sir, he's as deaf as a post. That's why. And he has no more brains, sir, than the heel of my foot. Why, sir, he's just a wild animal, a stone idol, sir, worse'n an idol—in fact, just a block of wood. Why then should I have to suffer because of him now? Not that I care a damn, sir. I've got used to this sort of life; I've lost all I ever possessed; I've got all dirty and greasy like a tramp's kettle; but I'm a man for all that and not some worthless kettle."

"I know, I know. Don't go on about it."

"Dear, oh dear," continued the shoemaker warmly, "when's there going to be an end to all my troubles, O Lord? Oh, I'm a miserable wretch, and there's no end to my misery! What sort of life have I had—what sort of

* Cosmo Minin and Prince Dmitry Pozharsky were two Nizhny-Novgorod patriots who in 1611 raised a people's army and defeated the occupying Polish forces, thus bringing about the union of Russia under the Romanov dynasty. Cosmo Minin was a butcher who offered his property to the national cause of liberation, and Prince Pozharsky was the commander of the national levies. TRANSLATOR.

life—just think of it, sir! When I was a boy I was beaten
by my German master; when in the prime of life I was
beaten by my own kith and kin; and now that I've
reached a ripe age that's the sort of reward I get——"

"Oh, you soul of a bast sponge, you! What are you
carrying on like this for, for goodness' sake?"

"What for, sir? It's not a beating I'm afraid of. Let
my master chastise me in private, but in public I expect
him to give me a civil word, for I'm still a man, am I
not? But who, I ask you, have I got to deal with here?"

"Well, clear out now," Gavrilo interrupted him impatiently.

Kapiton turned round and walked slowly to the door.

"But suppose he didn't come into it," the butler called
after him. "You'd be agreeable yourself, wouldn't you?"

"I give my consent," Kapiton replied and withdrew.
His eloquence did not desert him even in the greatest
emergencies.

The butler paced the room several times. "Well," he
said at last, "call Tatyana now."

A few moments later Tatyana came in very quietly
and stopped on the threshold. "What would you like me
to do, sir?" she said in a soft voice.

The butler looked at her intently. "Well, my dear," he
said, "would you like to get married? The mistress has
found a husband for you."

"Yes, sir. And who has she chosen for my future
husband?"

"Kapiton, the shoemaker."

"Yes, sir."

"He's a shiftless fellow, that's true enough. But the
mistress relies on you to see to that!"

"Yes, sir."

"There's one thing, though. That deaf-mute, Gerasim
—he's courting you, isn't he? How did you manage to be-
witch that bear, I wonder? I shouldn't be surprised if he
killed you, a bear like that."

"He'll kill me all right, sir. Sure to kill me."

"He'll kill you, will he? We'll see about that. But what do you mean—kill you? He has no right to kill you, has he? You see that, don't you?"

"I don't know, sir. I don't know whether he has any right to or not."

"What a funny girl you are! You haven't made him any promise, have you?"

"I beg your pardon, sir?"

The butler was silent and thought to himself, "What a timid creature you are, to be sure!"

"Very well," he said, "I'll have another talk with you later. You can go now, my dear. I can see you're a truly meek creature."

Tatyana turned round, pressed her hand lightly against the frame of the door, and went out.

"Let's hope the mistress will forget all about this wedding tomorrow," thought the butler. "What am I so worried about? As for that mischief-maker, we'll call in the police. Ustinya Fyodorovna," he cried in a loud voice to his wife, "set the samovar on the table, will you, there's a good woman!"

On that day Tatyana hardly left the laundry. At first she cried a little; then she dried her tears and set to work as before. Kapiton stayed in a pub till late at night with some friend of a gloomy aspect and he told him in great detail how in Petersburg he had lived with a gentleman who would have been perfect, had he not been a little too strict about things and had he not suffered just a little bit from a flaw in his character: he was a hard drinker —and as for the fair sex, there was simply no holding him. . . . His gloomy friend merely nodded; but when Kapiton at last declared that because of a certain event he would have to lay hands on himself the next day, his gloomy companion observed that it was time they went to bed. And they parted surlily and in silence.

Meanwhile the butler's expectations were not fulfilled.

The mistress was so taken by the idea of Kapiton's marriage that even in the night she talked only of that to one of her companions who was employed in her house for the sole purpose of distracting her when she suffered from insomnia and who, like a night cabby, slept in the day. When Gavrilo entered her room after breakfast with his report, her first question was, "And what about our wedding? Is it coming off?" He, of course, replied that it was coming off, all right, and that Kapiton would be coming to see her that very day to thank her. The old lady did not feel well, and she did not spend much time in attending to her business affairs.

The butler went back to his room and summoned a council of war. And indeed the matter called for a special discussion. Tatyana of course did not voice any objections, but Kapiton kept announcing in everybody's hearing that he had one head, and not two or three. Gerasim kept casting quick and stern glances at everybody and refused to budge from the steps of the maids' workroom and apparently guessed that some plot was being hatched against him. The people who had answered the butler's summons (among them was an old footman who looked after the sideboard, nicknamed Uncle Tail, whose advice was always respectfully sought by everyone, though all they heard from him was, "So that's how it is! Yes, yes, yes, yes!") began by locking up Kapiton in the little room where the water-filtering plant was kept. This was done as a precaution, in case of an unexpected emergency. They then tried to think what they had better do. It would, of course, have been easy to have recourse to force, but what if—heaven forbid!—there were an uproar and the mistress were upset —that would be a disaster! What then were they to do? They thought and they thought and at last came to a decision. It had been observed repeatedly that Gerasim could not abide drunkards. Sitting at the gates, he would turn away with disgust every time someone who had

had a drop too many passed by with unsteady steps and with the peak of his cap over one ear. They therefore decided to teach Tatyana how to pretend to be drunk and then make her walk past Gerasim, swaying and reeling from side to side. The poor girl would not agree to this for a long time, but she was persuaded in the end; besides, she realised herself that there was no other way of getting rid of her admirer. She went. Kapiton was let out of the little room; for, after all, the matter concerned him closely. Gerasim was sitting on the curbstone at the gates, prodding the ground with a spade. From behind every corner, from behind every window blind, people were watching him.

The stratagem succeeded better than they had hoped. On seeing Tatyana, Gerasim at first, as usual, began nodding at her and grunting affectionately. Then he looked more closely, dropped his spade, jumped to his feet, walked up to her, put his face close to hers. She staggered more than ever from fright and closed her eyes. He seized her by the hand, ran with her across the entire yard, and, going into the room where the council was sitting, pushed her straight towards Kapiton. Tatyana nearly fainted away. Gerasim stood still for several minutes, looked at her, smiled bitterly, and with a wave of the hand went, stepping heavily, straight to his cubbyhole.

He did not come out of it for the whole of the next twenty-four hours. The post-boy Antipka said afterwards that he saw Gerasim through a chink in the door, sitting on his bed, his hand pressed against his face, humming a song quietly and rhythmically, and only from time to time uttering grunts—he was humming, that is, swaying backwards and forwards, closing his eyes, and tossing his head as coachmen or barge-haulers do when they strike up their mournful songs. It gave Antipka the creeps, and he came away from the chink. But when Gerasim came out of his box-room the next day, no particular change could be observed in him. He only seemed to be a little more morose, and he did not take the slightest notice of Tatyana and Kapiton. The same evening both of them, with geese under their arms, went to pay their respects to their mistress, and a week later they were married. On the day of the wedding Gerasim did not show any change in his behaviour, except that he came back from the river without water, having somehow managed to break the barrel on the way; and at night in the stable he cleaned and rubbed down his horse so vigorously that it swayed like a blade of grass in the wind and staggered from one leg to the other under his iron fists.

All this had taken place in the spring. Another year passed, in the course of which Kapiton had at last become an inveterate drunkard and gone completely to seed and as one who was no longer good for anything was sent away with the provision carts to a remote village with his wife. On the day of his departure he did his best to pluck up courage at first, assuring everybody that, send him where they would, even, as the saying is, "where the peasant women wash shirts and throw their carpet flails up into the sky," he would not go under; but later on he lost heart, began complaining that he was being taken to live among uneducated people, and in the end grew so weak that he had not even enough strength to put his own cap on; some compassionate soul pulled it over his forehead, put the peak to rights, and slapped it from above. When everything was ready and the peasants held the reins in their hands and were only waiting for the words of farewell to be said in order to start, Gerasim came out of his box-room, went up to Tatyana, and gave her a parting gift—a red cotton kerchief he had bought for her a year ago. Tatyana, who up to that moment had put up with all the vicissitudes of her life with the utmost indifference, could no longer contain herself, burst into tears, and, before getting into the cart, kissed Gerasim three times, like a good

Christian. He went to see her off to the toll gate, and at
first walked beside her cart, but at the Crimean Ford
he stopped suddenly, dismissed it all with a wave of the
hand, and walked away along the riverbank.

It all happened towards evening. He walked slowly,
looking at the water. Suddenly he thought he saw something floundering in the mud close to the bank. He bent
down and saw a little puppy with white and black spots,
which, in spite of all its efforts, could not scramble out
of the water. It was struggling, slithering, and trembling
with all its little, thin, wet body. Gerasim had a look at
the poor little dog, snatched it up with one hand, thrust
it into the inside of his coat, and walked back home with
long steps. He went into his box-room, put down the
rescued puppy on his bed, covered it with his heavy
peasant overcoat, ran first to the stable for straw and
then to the kitchen for a cup of milk. Carefully remov-
ing the coat and spreading out the straw, he put the milk
on the bed. The poor little dog was not more than three
weeks old, and its eyes had not long been opened; one
eye still seemed a little larger than the other; it did not
know how to drink out of a cup and just kept shivering
and closing its eyes. Gerasim took hold of its head gently
with two fingers and pushed its little nose into the cup.
The little dog suddenly began lapping greedily, sniffing,
shivering, and choking. Gerasim looked and looked at it,
and then suddenly burst out laughing. All through the
night he busied himself with it, kept it covered, rubbed
it dry, and at last fell asleep himself beside it; and his
sleep was quiet and joyful.

No mother could have looked after her baby as
Gerasim looked after his nursling. (The puppy turned
out to be a bitch.) At first she was very weak, feeble,
and rather ugly, but as time passed she put on weight
and improved in looks, and eight months later, thanks
to the unremitting care of the man who had saved her,
she was transformed into a very presentable little dog of

the spaniel breed, with long ears, a feathery, upright tail and large, expressive eyes. She was passionately attached to Gerasim, and never let him out of her sight, always following him about, wagging her tail. He had even given her a name: dumb people know that their inarticulate noises draw the attention of other people, so he called her Mumu. All the servants in the house knew her and also called her Mumu. She was very intelligent and very affectionate with everybody, but she was attached only to Gerasim. Gerasim too was deeply attached to her, and he resented it when other people stroked her. Whether he was afraid for her or jealous— goodness only knows! She would wake him in the morning, tugging at the skirts of his coat; she would bring him by its reins the old horse that drew the water cart and with whom she lived in great amity and would accompany him to the river with an expression of the utmost gravity on her face; she kept watch over his brooms and spades, and never let anyone go near his box-room. He purposely cut a hole in his door for her, and she seemed to feel that only in Gerasim's little room was she complete mistress, and that was why when she went in she at once jumped onto the bed with an air of utter contentment.

She never slept at night, but she did not bark indiscriminately, like some foolish watchdog that, sitting on its hind legs and with its snout in the air and its eyes screwed up, barks just out of boredom, without rhyme or reason, at the stars, and usually three times in succession. No! Mumu's thin little voice was never raised without good reason: either some stranger was coming a little too near the fence, or there was some suspicious sound or rustle somewhere. In a word, she was a most excellent watchdog. It is true, besides her, there was in the yard a sandy-coloured old dog with brown spots, called Volchok, but he was never—not even at night—let off the chain, and indeed he was so decrepit that he never asked for freedom; he just lay curled up in his kennel and only from time to time uttered a hoarse, almost soundless, bark, which he broke off at once, as though realising himself how utterly useless it was. Mumu never went into the mistress's house, and, when Gerasim carried wood into the rooms always stayed behind, waiting for him impatiently at the front steps, pricking up her ears, and at the slightest noise behind the front door turning her head to the right and, suddenly, to the left.

So passed another year. Gerasim carried on with his duties as caretaker and was very satisfied with his lot, when suddenly an unexpected incident occurred. One fine summer day the mistress was walking up and down the drawing room with her lady companions. She was in high spirits; she laughed and joked; her lady companions too laughed and joked, though they did not feel particularly happy: in the house they did not like it very much when the mistress was in a merry mood because, for one thing, she demanded that everyone should respond immoderately and fully to her feelings and was furious when someone's face did not beam with delight, and, for another, because these outbursts did not last long and were usually followed by a sour and gloomy mood. That day she seemed to have got out of bed on the right side. At cards she had four knaves, which meant that her wishes would come true (she always tried to tell her own fortune by cards in the mornings), and her tea seemed to her particularly delicious, for which her maid was rewarded by a few words of praise and twenty copecks in money.

The old lady walked up and down the drawing room with a sweet smile on her wrinkled lips, and then went up to the window. A flower garden had been laid out in front of the window, and in the very middle bed under a little rosebush lay Mumu, busily gnawing a bone. The old lady saw her. "Goodness gracious," she cried suddenly, "what dog is that?"

The lady companion to whom the mistress addressed the question began to dither, overcome, poor soul, by that anguished state of uneasiness which comes upon every person in a dependent position when he is not sure what to make of his master's exclamation.

"I—I d-don't know, ma'am," she murmured. "I believe it belongs to the dumb man——"

"Goodness me," the mistress interrupted, "it's a most charming little dog! Tell them to bring it here. How long has he had it? How is it I haven't seen it before? Tell them to bring it in."

The lady companion at once rushed out into the hall. "You there," she shouted to a servant, "bring Mumu in at once! She's in the flower garden."

"Oh, so her name is Mumu, is it?" said the old lady. "A very nice name."

"Yes, ma'am, a very nice name indeed!" the lady companion was quick to assent. "Make haste, Stepan!"

Stepan, a sturdily built young footman, rushed headlong into the flower garden. He was about to get hold of Mumu, when she cleverly slipped between his fingers and, with her tail in the air, fled as fast as she could to Gerasim, who was at that moment standing outside the kitchen, shaking and scraping out a barrel, turning it round and round in his hands like a child's drum. Stepan ran after her and tried to catch her at her master's feet; but the agile dog would not let a stranger get hold of her and, bounding about, evaded his grasp. Gerasim looked on with a grin at all this commotion; at last Stepan got up, looking very vexed, and quickly explained to him by signs that the mistress wanted to have the dog fetched to her. Gerasim looked a little surprised, but he called Mumu, picked her up from the ground, and handed her to Stepan. Stepan brought her into the drawing room and put her down on the parquet floor. The old lady began calling Mumu to her in a coaxing voice. Mumu, who had never before been in such magnificent rooms, got very frightened and made a rush for the door, but, pushed away by the obliging Stepan, trembled all over and flattened herself against the wall.

"Mumu, Mumu, come to me, come to your mistress," the old lady kept saying. "Come here, you silly little dog—don't be afraid . . ."

"Come, Mumu, come to the mistress," the lady companions kept repeating. "Come along!"

But Mumu looked wistfully round her and did not budge from her place.

"Bring her something to eat," said the mistress. "How stupid she is! Not to come to her mistress! What is she afraid of?"

"She isn't used to you yet, ma'am," one of her lady companions said in a timid, sugary voice.

Stepan brought in a saucer of milk and put it down before Mumu, but Mumu did not even sniff at the milk, and still trembled all over, looking round as before.

"Oh, you stupid little thing!" said the old lady, and, walking up to Mumu, she tried to stroke her.

But Mumu turned her head convulsively and bared her teeth. The old lady quickly drew back her hand.

There was a moment's silence. Mumu gave a faint whine as though complaining or apologising. The old lady moved away and frowned. The dog's sudden movement had frightened her.

"Oh dear," shrieked all the lady companions at once, "she hasn't bitten you, has she?" (Mumu had never bitten anyone in her life.) "Dear, oh dear!"

"Take her away," the old lady said in a changed voice. "She's a bad little dog! Such a spiteful creature!"

And, turning round slowly, she went towards her private office, but she stopped, glared balefully at her lady companions, and saying, "Why are you following me? I haven't called you, have I?" went out.

The lady companions began waving their hands at Stepan frantically. Stepan snatched up Mumu and threw her quickly out of the door straight at Gerasim's feet, and half an hour later a profound silence settled over the house, and the old lady sat on the sofa, looking blacker than a thundercloud.

To think what trifles will sometimes upset a person!

Even when evening came, the old lady was still out of humour. She did not talk to anyone; she did not play cards; and she had a bad night. She took it into her head that the eau de Cologne they gave her was not the same as what they usually gave her, that her pillow smelled of soap, and she made the linen maid smell all the bed linen. In short, she was nervous and in a bad temper.

Next morning she ordered Gavrilo to be summoned an hour earlier than usual. "Tell me, please," she began as soon as the butler, not without some trepidation, stepped over the threshold, "what dog was that barking in our yard all night? It wouldn't let me sleep!"

"A dog, ma'am—what dog, ma'am?" he said in a not-quite-steady voice. "Perhaps the dumb man's dog, ma'am!"

"I don't know whether it was the dumb man's or someone else's, only it wouldn't let me sleep. And I really can't imagine what we want so many dogs for! I'd very much like to know that. We have a yard dog, haven't we?"

"Why, of course we have, ma'am. Volchok, ma'am."

"Well, why another one? What do we want another dog for? Just making a mess of things. There's no one with authority in the house, that's the trouble. And what does that dumb fellow want a dog for? Who gave him permission to keep dogs in my yard? Yesterday I went up to the window and there she was—lying in the flower garden. Had taken some nasty bit of rubbish with her and was gnawing it. And I've had roses planted there!" The old lady paused for a moment. "See that she isn't here today—do you hear?"

"Yes, ma'am."

"Today! You can go now. I'll send for you later for the report."

Gavrilo went out.

Passing through the drawing room, the butler moved a bell from one table to another just to keep things nice and tidy, blew his ducklike nose quietly in the ballroom, and went out into the hall. In the hall Stepan was asleep on a chest in the attitude of a slain warrior in a battle-piece, his bare legs stretched out convulsively from under his coat, which served him for a blanket. The butler shook him by the shoulders and gave him some kind of order in an undertone, to which Stepan replied by something that was between a yawn and a guffaw. The butler went away, and Stepan jumped down from the chest, put on his coat and boots, went outside, and stopped by the front steps. Before five minutes had passed, Gerasim made his appearance with a huge bundle of firewood on his back, accompanied by the inseparable Mumu. (The old lady had given strict orders that her bedroom and study should be heated even in summer.) Gerasim turned sideways towards the door, pushed it open with his shoulder, and pitched into the house with his load, while Mumu, as usual, stayed behind to wait for him. It was then that Stepan, taking advantage of the favourable opportunity, suddenly threw himself on her like a kite on a chick, pressed her to the ground with his chest, snatched her up in his arms, and, without even putting on his cap, rushed out of the yard, hailed the first cab he met, and galloped off to the game market. There he soon found a customer to whom he sold her for fifty copecks, on condition that he keep her tied up for at least a week, and took a cab home at once. But before he reached the house he got out of the cab and, going round the yard, jumped over the fence into the yard from the back lane.

However, he need not have worried: Gerasim was no

longer in the yard. On coming out of the house he had
at once missed Mumu; he could not remember a time
when she failed to wait for him, and he began calling
her in his own way. He rushed into his box-room, up
the hayloft, ran out into the street—this way and that.
She was lost! He turned to the servants, asking about
her with the most despairing signs, pointing about a foot
from the ground, outlining her shape with his hands.
Some of them really did not know where Mumu had
got to and only shook their heads; others did know and
just grinned at him in reply; while the butler assumed
an important air and began shouting at the coachmen.
Then Gerasim just ran out of the yard and disappeared.

Dusk was already falling when he came back. From
his exhausted appearance, his unsteady gait, and his
dusty clothes, one could see that he had been running
over half of Moscow. He stopped in front of the windows of his mistress's house, cast a glance at the front
steps, on which about seven house-serfs were standing
in a group, turned away, uttering once more Mumu's
name in his inarticulate way. But Mumu did not answer.
He went away. They all followed him with their eyes,
but no one smiled or uttered a word. The inquisitive
post-boy Antipka told them next morning in the kitchen
that the dumb man had been groaning all night.

The whole of the following day Gerasim did not put
in an appearance, so that the coachman Potap had to
go for water instead of him, which made the coachman
Potap rather disgruntled. The old lady asked Gavrilo if
her order had been carried out. Gavrilo replied that it
had. The next morning Gerasim came out of his box-
room and began to work. He came in for his dinner, ate,
and went out again without a greeting to anyone. His
face, which, as with all deaf-mutes, looked expression-
less anyway, seemed now turned to stone. After dinner
he went out of the yard again, but not for long. He
came back and went up to the hayloft.

Night came, a clear moonlight night. Gerasim lay, uttering heavy sighs and turning continuously from side to side, when suddenly he felt as though he were being pulled by the skirt of his coat; he trembled all over, but did not raise his head and even shut his eyes tighter; but a moment later he was again pulled by the coat, much more vigorously this time; he jumped up, and there was Mumu spinning round before him with the torn end of a rope round her neck. A drawn-out cry of joy burst from his speechless breast; he seized Mumu and hugged her tightly in his arms; in less than a minute she was licking his nose and eyes, his moustache and beard. He stood pondering for a while; then he climbed cautiously down from the hayloft, looked round, and, having made sure that no one could see him, made his way without incident to his box-room.

Gerasim had realised before that his dog had not got lost by herself and that she must have been taken away by his mistress's orders—the servants had, in fact, explained to him by signs that Mumu had snapped at her —and he decided to take precautionary measures of his own. First he fed Mumu with some bread, fondled her, put her to bed, and then spent the whole night trying to think how best to hide her. At last he decided to keep her in his room all day and only go to see her now and again, and to take her out at night. He stopped up the hole in the door tightly with an old overcoat of his and as soon as it was light he was out in the yard, just as though nothing had happened, even preserving (innocent guile!) the same despondent expression on his face. It never occurred to the poor deaf fellow that Mumu might betray herself by her yelping, and indeed everyone in the house soon knew that the dumb man's dog had come back and was locked up in his box-room, but out of pity for him and his dog, and partly, perhaps, out of fear of him, they did not let him know that they had discovered his secret. The butler alone scratched the back of his head and gave it up. "Well," he seemed to say, "good luck to him! Perhaps it won't come to the mistress's ears!" The dumb man, on the other hand, had never before worked with such a will as on that day: he cleaned and scraped the whole courtyard, pulled out every single weed, got out with his own hand all the stakes from the fence round the flower garden to make sure that they were strong enough and then drove them in again—in a word, he took so much trouble and busied himself so industriously that even his mistress could not help noticing his zeal. Twice in the course of the day Gerasim went to see his prisoner by stealth; when night came, he went to bed with Mumu in his room and not in the hayloft, and only took her out for a walk in the fresh air at two o'clock in the morning. After walking about the yard for quite a long time with her, he was on the point of going back when a faint noise suddenly arose from the lane on the other side of the fence. Mumu pricked up her ears, growled, went up to the fence, sniffed, and started barking, loud and piercingly. Some drunkard had taken it into his head to bed himself down for the night there.

At that very moment the old lady had just dropped off to sleep after a prolonged attack of nerves: these fits always overtook her after a too-hearty supper. The sudden barking woke her; her heart began to beat fast; and she seemed on the point of fainting. "Girls, girls," she moaned, "girls!" The frightened lady companions rushed into her bedroom. "Oh dear, I'm dying!" she cried, spreading her hands in an anguished gesture. "There's that dog again—that dog again! Oh, send for the doctor! They want to kill me! The dog, the dog again! Oh!" And she threw back her head, by which she wished to show that she had fainted. They rushed out for the doctor— that is to say, the household quack, Khariton. This doctor, whose entire skill consisted in wearing boots with soft soles, knew how to feel a pulse with the utmost delicacy; he slept fourteen hours out of twenty-four; and spent the rest of the time sighing and continually regaling his mistress with cherry laurel drops. This quack doctor came at once, waved some burnt feathers under her nose, and, when the old lady opened her eyes, at once offered her a wineglass of the sacred drops on a silver tray. The old lady drank them, but immediately began to complain again in a tearful voice of the dog, Gavrilo, her own fate, of being abandoned by everybody, a poor old woman, of no one's showing any pity for her, of everyone's wishing that she was dead. Meanwhile the luckless Mumu went on barking, Gerasim vainly trying to get her away from the fence. "There—there she goes again—again!" the old lady murmured and once more rolled up her eyes. The doctor whispered to a maid, who rushed into the hall, woke up Stepan, who rushed to waken Gavrilo, who in a fit of temper ordered the whole household to be roused.

Gerasim turned round, saw the lights and shadows moving about in the windows, and, with a foreboding of trouble in his heart, snatched up Mumu under his arm, ran back into his room, and locked himself in. A few minutes later five men were seen trying to break down his door, but, feeling the resistance of the bolt, they gave up. Gavrilo came running in terrible haste and ordered them all to remain there and keep watch till the morning. He himself rushed into the maids' workroom and through Lyubov Lyubimovna, the eldest lady companion, with whom he used to steal and falsify the accounts of the tea, sugar, and other groceries, informed the mistress that the dog had unfortunately come back from somewhere, but that tomorrow she would be done away with, and begged her to be so good as not to be angry with him and compose herself. The old lady would most probably not have composed herself so quickly had not the quack doctor in his haste given her forty instead of twenty drops. It was the strength of the dose of the cherry laurel drops that had its effect: a quarter of an hour later the old lady was already snoring and peacefully asleep. Gerasim was meanwhile lying in bed with a white face, holding Mumu's mouth tightly shut.

Next morning the old lady woke up rather late. Gavrilo was waiting for her to wake up, in order to give the order for a decisive assault on Gerasim's sanctuary, while he prepared himself to resist a violent storm. But the storm did not break. Lying in bed, the old lady sent for the eldest of her lady companions.

"Lyubov Lyubimovna," she began in a soft and weak voice (she sometimes liked to pretend to be a lonely, persecuted martyr, which, needless to say, made all the servants in the house feel very uncomfortable), "you see how I suffer. Please, my dear, go and talk to Gavrilo. Surely some wretched little dog isn't dearer to him than the health and indeed the very life of his mistress! I shouldn't like to believe that," she added with an expression of deep feeling. "Go, my dear, be good enough to go to Gavrilo for me."

Lyubov Lyubimovna went to Gavrilo's room. What they talked about is not known, but a short time after, a whole crowd of people was moving across the yard in the direction of Gerasim's room; Gavrilo advanced in front, holding onto his cap with his hand, although there was no wind; beside him marched the footmen and cooks; Uncle Tail looked out the window and gave orders—that is, just waved his arms about; behind them all, small boys were skipping about and pulling faces (more than half of them were strange boys who had run in from outside). One man was on guard on the narrow staircase leading to the box-room; two more, armed with sticks, stood outside the door. They started climbing the staircase, occupying its entire length. Gavrilo went up to the door, knocked on it with his fist, and shouted, "Open up!"

A stifled bark was heard; but there was no reply.

"Open up, I tell you!" he repeated.

"But he's deaf, sir!" Stepan observed from below. "He can't hear you."

They all laughed.

"What's to be done then?" Gavrilo asked from above.

"He's got a hole in the door," replied Stepan. "You'd better put your stick through it and shake it."

Gavrilo bent down. "He's stopped it up with some coat —the hole, I mean."

"Why not push the coat in, sir?"

Here again a stifled bark was heard.

"See, see, she's answering you," someone observed in the crowd, and again they laughed.

Gavrilo scratched himself behind the ear. "No," he said at last, "you'd better push the coat in yourself, if you like."

"Well, why not?"

And Stepan clambered up the stairs, took the stick, pushed the coat in, and began shaking the stick about in the hole, saying, "Come out! Come out!" as he did so. He was shaking his stick about, when suddenly the door was flung open and the servants, Gavrilo at their head, rushed headlong down the stairs all at once. Uncle Tail shut the window.

"You there," Gavrilo shouted from the yard, "take care, I say! Take care!"

Gerasim stood without moving at his open door. The crowd gathered at the foot of the stairs. Gerasim looked down on all the crowd of puny people in their foreign clothes; with his arms akimbo and in his red peasant skirt he towered like a giant over them.

Gavrilo took a step forward. "Now then, my dear fellow," he said, "don't you play any silly tricks with me!" And he began to explain to him by signs that the mistress demanded that he should hand over his dog to her, and that if he did not give Mumu up at once, there would be trouble.

Gerasim looked at him, pointed to the dog, made a sign with his hand round his neck as if tightening a noose, and glanced inquiringly at the butler.

"Yes, yes," Gavrilo replied, nodding. "Yes, certainly!"

Gerasim dropped his eyes, then suddenly shook himself and pointed again to Mumu, who was all the time standing beside him, wagging her tail innocently and pricking up her ears, as though curious to know what it was all about. He repeated the sign of strangling and smote his chest significantly, as though announcing that he would see to it himself that Mumu was destroyed.

"But you'll deceive us," Gavrilo said, waving his arms at him in reply.

Gerasim looked at him, smiled scornfully, smote his breast again, and slammed the door to.

They all looked at one another in silence.

"What's the meaning of this?" began Gavrilo. "Has he locked himself in?"

"Leave him alone, sir," said Stepan. "He'll do it, if he's promised. He is like that. If he promises something, he'll carry it out for certain. He's different from any of us as far as that's concerned. That's true enough. Yes, sir."

"Yes, sir," they all repeated. "That is so. Yes."

Uncle Tail opened the window and also said, "Yes."

"Very well, we shall see," said Gavrilo. "But the guard is to remain there all the same. Hey, you, Yeroshka," he added, addressing a pale-faced man in a yellow nankeen Cossack coat, who was supposed to be a gardener, "you haven't got anything to do, have you? Take a stick and sit down here. If anything happens, run to me at once!"

Yeroshka took a stick and sat down on the bottom step of the staircase. The crowd dispersed, except for a few men who were curious to see what was going to happen, and the small boys. Gavrilo went back home and informed his mistress through Lyubov Lyubimovna that everything had been carried out as ordered and that he had sent the post-boy for a policeman in case of need. The old lady tied a knot in her handkerchief, sprinkled some eau de Cologne on it, rubbed her temples, had a cup of tea, and, being still under the influence of the cherry laurel drops, fell asleep again.

An hour after all this commotion the door of the box-room opened and Gerasim appeared. He had his Sunday coat on. He was leading Mumu on a string. Yeroshka got out of the way and let him pass. Gerasim went to the gates. All the small boys in the yard followed him with their eyes in silence. He did not even turn round, and only put on his cap in the street. Gavrilo sent Yeroshka after him in the role of an observer. Seeing from a distance that he had gone to an inn with the dog, Yeroshka waited for him to come out again.

In the inn they knew Gerasim and understood his signs. He ordered cabbage soup with boiled meat and sat down, leaning on the table with his arms. Mumu stood beside his chair, watching him calmly with her clever little eyes. Her coat was glossy: it was evident that she had just been thoroughly brushed. They brought Gerasim the cabbage soup. He crumbled some bread into it, cut the meat into very small pieces, and put the plate on the floor. Mumu began to eat with her usual refinement, hardly touching her food with her little muzzle. Gerasim gazed at her for a long time; two big tears suddenly rolled out of his eyes: one fell on the dog's craggy little forehead, the other into the cabbage soup. He covered his face with his hand. Mumu ate up half the meat on the plate and walked away from it, licking her chops. Gerasim got up, paid for the cabbage soup, and went out, accompanied by the somewhat perplexed glances of the waiter. Yeroshka, catching sight of

Gerasim, darted round a corner and, letting him go on, followed him again.

Gerasim walked unhurriedly, without letting Mumu off the string. On reaching the corner of the street he stopped, as though wondering what to do next. Then he set off suddenly straight in the direction of the Crimean Ford. On the way he went into the yard of a house to which a wing was being added and brought away from there two bricks under his arm. At the Crimean Ford he walked along the bank of the river, went up to the place where there were two little rowing boats tied to pegs (he had noticed them before), and jumped into one of them, together with Mumu. A little old man came limping out of a hut, stood in a corner of a kitchen-garden, and shouted at him. But Gerasim just nodded and began rowing so vigorously that, though against the current, he had in no time at all gone two hundred yards. The old man stood there for a few minutes; then he scratched his back, first with his left, then with his right hand, and went limping back to his hut.

Meanwhile Gerasim rowed on and on. Soon Moscow was left behind. Soon meadows, kitchen-gardens, fields, and copses stretched on either side of the bank and peasants' cottages appeared. There came a breath of the open country. He threw down the oars, put his head close to Mumu, who sat before him on a dry cross-seat (the bottom of the boat was full of water), and remained motionless, his powerful hands crossed on her back, while the boat was gradually carried back by the current towards the town. At last Gerasim sat up hurriedly with an expression of painful bitterness on his face, tied the bricks he had taken with a rope, made a running noose, put it round Mumu's neck, lifted her up over the river, and looked at her for the last time. She looked at him trustingly and without fear and wagged her tail slightly. He turned away, shut his eyes, and opened his hands. . . . Gerasim heard nothing, neither the quick,

shrill yelp of the falling Mumu nor the heavy splash of
the water; for him the noisy day was soundless and silent
as no still night is silent to us, and when he opened his
eyes again, little waves as before were hurrying over the
river, as though chasing each other and, as before, rip-
pled against the two sides of the boat, and only far away
behind some wide circles were spreading out towards
the bank.

As soon as Gerasim had disappeared from sight,
Yeroshka returned home and reported what he had seen.

"Well, yes," observed Stepan, "he will drown her.
There's nothing to worry about no more. If he promised . . ."

No one saw Gerasim during the day. He did not have
his dinner at home. Evening came; they were gathered
together to supper, all except him.

"What a funny fellow this Gerasim is, to be sure,"
a fat laundress remarked in a squeaky voice. "Fancy
missing your supper because of some dog! Really!"

"Why, Gerasim has been here!" Stepan cried suddenly, scooping up the porridge with his spoon.

"How? When?"

"Why, two hours ago. Yes, to be sure! I ran across
him at the gates. He was going out again, coming out of
the yard. I was about to ask him about his dog, but he
didn't seem to be in good spirits. I mean, he pushed me
aside. I expect he just wanted to avoid me, for fear I
would pester him, but he caught me such a whack across
the back of the neck—such a terrific wallop—that it hurt,
I can tell you." And he rubbed the back of his neck
with an involuntary grin. "Aye," he added, "he certainly
has got a lucky hand, no doubt about that!"

They all laughed at Stepan, and after supper they
went to bed.

Meanwhile, at that very moment, a giant of a man
with a sack over his shoulder and a big stick in his hand

was briskly walking without stopping along the T——
highway. It was Gerasim. Without looking back, he was
hurrying home to his native village, to the place where
he was born.

After drowning poor Mumu, he ran back to his box-
room, quickly packed some of his belongings in an old
horse-cloth, tied it up in a bundle, hoisted it over his
shoulder, and off he went. He had observed the road
carefully when he was being taken to Moscow; the village from which his mistress had fetched him was only
about fifteen miles off the highway. He walked along it
with a sort of invincible courage, with a desperate and
at the same time joyous determination. He walked on,
his chest thrown out, his eyes fixed eagerly straight before him. He was in a hurry, just as though his old
mother were waiting for him at home, as though she
were calling him to come back to her after long wander-
ings in foreign parts among strangers.

The summer night that had just fallen was still and
warm: on one side, where the sun had set, the rim of
the sky was still white and covered with a faint flush of
the last glow of the vanishing day; and on the other
side a blue-grey twilight was already rising up. The
night was coming from there. The call of quails in their
hundreds could be heard all round; corn crakes were
calling as they chased each other. Gerasim could not
hear them, nor could he hear the delicate, rustling noc-
turnal whisperings of the trees, past which his strong
legs carried him; but he could smell the familiar scent
of the ripening rye, which was wafted from the dark
fields; he could feel the wind, which flew to meet him—
the wind from home—beating caressingly against his face
and playing with his hair and beard; he saw the whiten-
ing road before him, the road that led to his home,
straight as an arrow; in the sky he saw stars without
number, lighting him on his way; and he strode along,
strong and bold like a lion, so that when the rising sun

threw its first rosy light upon the sturdy young fellow who had only just got into his stride, about thirty miles already lay between him and Moscow. . . .

Two days later he was at home in his little cottage, to the great astonishment of the soldier's wife who had been quartered there. After saying a prayer before the icons, he at once went to see the village headman. The headman was at first taken aback; but the haymaking had only just started: Gerasim, a first-class worker, was given a scythe, and he went to mow in his old way, so that the peasants were struck with wonder as they watched his arms sweeping and raking together the hay.

Meanwhile, in Moscow, they discovered Gerasim's flight a day after he had gone. They went to his box-room, ransacked it, and informed Gavrilo. The latter came, had a look round, shrugged his shoulders, and decided that the dumb man had either run away or drowned himself with his silly dog. The police were informed and the old lady was told. The old lady was very angry. She burst into tears and gave orders that he was to be found at all costs. She kept saying that she had never ordered the dog to be destroyed and finally told off Gavrilo so thoroughly that he just kept shaking his head all day, murmuring, "Well!" until Uncle Tail made him see reason by saying to him, "Well *what?*"

At last news of the arrival of Gerasim in the village came from the country. The old lady calmed down a little; at first she gave orders for him to be sent back to Moscow immediately; then she declared that such an ungrateful man was of no use whatever to her. However, she died soon after this, and her heirs had other things to think of beside Gerasim; they let their mother's other servants go free on the payment of an annual tax.

Gerasim is still living, a lonely bachelor in his lonely cottage; he is strong and healthy as before; he does the work of four men as before; and he is grave and staid as before. But neighbours have noticed that since his return from Moscow he completely stopped associating with women—he will not even look at them—nor does he keep a single dog. "Still," the peasants say to each other, "good luck to him! What does he want to get mixed up with women for? As for a dog, what does he want a dog for? No thief will venture into his yard for any money!" Such is the fame of the titanic strength of the dumb man.

1852

ASSYA

1

I WAS twenty-five at the time, began N. N. It happened a long time ago, as you see. I had only just gained my freedom and had gone abroad—not to "finish my education," as people used to say in those days, but simply because I longed to see the world. I was young, in good health and spirits, well provided with money, and, so far, without a care in the world. I lived without worrying about what the next day would bring, and did what I liked—in short, flourished. It never occurred to me at the time that man is not a plant and that he could not flourish long. Youth eats gilt gingerbread and thinks that this is his daily bread; but the time comes when you will be begging for a crust of dry bread. But it's no use talking about it.

I travelled without any aim, without a plan; I stopped where I liked and left the moment I felt a desire to see new faces—yes, faces. I was interested only in people; I hated interesting monuments, remarkable buildings, and the mere sight of a guide aroused in me a feeling of boredom and fury; I was nearly driven mad in the Dresden Grüne Gewölbe. Nature exercised a powerful influence on me, but I did not like her so-called "beauty spots," extraordinary mountains, cliffs, waterfalls. I did not like her to obtrude herself on me, to interfere with me. But faces, living human faces, people's talk, their gestures, their laughter—I simply could not do without them. In a crowd I always felt particularly at ease and happy; I enjoyed going where other people went, shouting when other people shouted, and at the same time I liked to watch other people shouting. It amused me to observe people, and, as a matter of fact, I did not even observe them—I scrutinised them with a kind of joyful and insatiable curiosity. But I am afraid I am digressing again.

Twenty years ago I was staying in the little German town of S., on the left bank of the Rhine. I was seeking solitude: I had just been smitten by a young widow whom I had met at a watering place. She was very pretty and intelligent. She flirted with everyone, and with me too—sinner that I am—at first encouraging me, but later hurting my feelings cruelly, throwing me over in favour of a red-cheeked Bavarian lieutenant. To tell the truth, my heart had not been very deeply wounded. But I thought it my duty to give myself up for a time to sorrow and solitude (the things young people will find amusing!), and went to live in S.

This little town appealed to me greatly because of its situation at the foot of two high hills, because of its crumbling walls and towers, its centuries-old lime trees, its steep bridge over a clear stream, a tributary of the Rhine, and, above all, because of its excellent wine. Very charming fair-haired German girls used to walk about its narrow streets in the evening immediately after sunset (it was June), and on meeting a foreigner said in their delightful voices, *"Guten Abend!"*—and some of them did not go home even when the moon had risen behind the gables of the ancient houses and the small cobblestones in the road were clearly silhouetted in her motionless beams.

I loved to take a walk through the town at that time; the moon seemed to gaze intently at it from the clear sky, and the town felt this gaze and stood there peacefully and imperturbably, bathed in moonlight, that serene light which yet fills the soul with a feeling of soft excitement. The cock on the tall Gothic belfry shone with a pale golden light; the same golden light was reflected in the waves over the black, glassy surface of the stream; thin candles (Germans are a thrifty people!) twinkled modestly in the narrow windows under the slate roofs; vines thrust out their curly tendrils mysteriously from behind stone walls; something darted into the shadow by the ancient well in the three-cornered market place; the drowsy whistle of the night watchman resounded suddenly in the air; a good-natured dog growled in a low voice; while the air simply caressed your face and the lime trees smelt so sweet that your chest unconsciously expanded more and more and the name Gretchen—half exclamation and half question—simply leapt to your lips.

The little town of S. lies a mile and a half from the Rhine. I often went to have a look at the majestic river, and dreaming, not without a certain effort, of the treacherous widow, used to sit for hours on end on a stone seat under a huge, solitary ash tree. A little statue of a Madonna with an almost childlike face and a red heart on the breast, pierced with swords, gazed mournfully out of its branches. On the opposite bank of the river was the town of L., a little larger than the town in which I had taken up my residence. One afternoon I was sitting on my favourite seat and gazing at the river, the sky, and the vineyards. Before me, fair-headed boys clambered over the sides of a boat which had been dragged ashore and turned with its tarred belly upwards. Small sailing boats sailed gently along with their slightly belling sails; the greenish waves glided by gently, swelling and murmuring. All of a sudden sounds of music reached me from a distance. I listened. A waltz was being played in the town of L.: the double bass was booming jerkily, the fiddle was scraping away softly, the flute was tootling pertly.

"What's that?" I asked an old man who came up to me in a velveteen waistcoat, blue stockings, and shoes with buckles.

"That?" he replied, after first moving the mouthpiece of his pipe from one corner of his mouth to the other. "It's the students who arrived from B. for a *Kommersch*."

"Well, let's have a look at this *Kommersch*," I thought, "and besides, I've never been to L. before."

I found the ferryman and was taken across to the other side.

2

Not everybody, perhaps, knows what a *Kommersch* is. It is a special kind of solemn carouse to which students of one and the same district or fraternity (*Landsmannschaft*) come together. Almost all the students who take part in a *Kommersch* wear the traditional costume of German students: a Hungarian tunic, top boots, and little caps with bands of certain colours. The students usually foregather at a dinner presided over by a senior member, and keep up their revels till the morning, drinking, singing songs—"*Landesvater*," "*Gaudeamus*"—smoking, and abusing the Philistines; sometimes they hire a band.

Exactly the same kind of *Kommersch* was taking place in the town of L. before a small inn with the sign of the sun in a garden which fronted the street. Flags were flying over the inn and the garden; the students were sitting at tables under the pollarded lime trees; a huge bulldog was lying under one of the tables; at one side, in a little pergola overgrown with ivy, the musicians were playing zealously, refreshing themselves every now and then with beer. A large crowd of people had collected in the street, in front of the low walls of the garden; the good citizens of the town of L. would not miss the opportunity of staring at their visitors. I also mingled with the throng of spectators. I enjoyed watching the faces of the students; their embraces, exclamations, the innocent affectations of youth, the blazing eyes, the laughter without cause—the best laughter in the world —all this joyous effervescence of young, fresh life, this eager rush forward—anywhere, so long as it is forward —this good-natured freedom moved me and excited me. "Should I join them?" I asked myself.

"Assya, have you had enough?" a man's voice suddenly said behind me in Russian.

"Let's stay a little longer," replied another voice, a woman's, in the same language.

I turned round quickly. My glance fell on a handsome young man in a cap and loose jacket; he had his hand through the arm of a young girl of medium height, in a straw hat which concealed the upper part of her face.

"Are you Russians?" I could not help asking.

The young man smiled and said, "Yes, we are Russians."

"I never expected in—in such a Godforsaken place——" I began.

"We didn't expect to, either," he interrupted me. "Well, so much the better. Let me introduce myself. My name is Gagin, and this is my"—he hesitated for a moment—"my sister. And what is your name, may I ask?"

I told him my name, and we started a conversation. I learnt that Gagin, who, like myself, was travelling for his own pleasure, had arrived the week before in the town of L. and for some reason stayed there. To tell the truth, I do not like striking up an acquaintance with

Russians abroad. I used to recognise them from a distance by their way of walking, the cut of their clothes, and, most of all, by the expression on their faces. Self-satisfied and supercilious, often imperious, this expression would suddenly change to one of the utmost caution and timidity. A man would all of a sudden become watchful, and his eyes would become restless. "Good Lord, I haven't said anything stupid, have I? They're not laughing at me, are they?" his rapid glance seemed to say. A moment later, and once more, the majestic mien was restored, alternating from time to time with one of obtuse bewilderment. Yes, I avoided the Russians, but I liked Gagin at once. There are in the world such lucky faces: everyone likes to look at them, just as though they warmed or stroked you. Gagin had such a face—charming, kind, with large soft eyes and soft curly hair. He spoke in such a way that, even if you did not see his face, you felt by the mere sound of his voice that he was smiling.

The girl whom he had called his sister seemed to me at first glance to be extremely pretty. There was something special, something that belonged only to her, in the cast of her darkish, round face with its small, fine nose, almost childlike cheeks, and bright black eyes. She was gracefully built, but somehow did not seem to be fully developed yet. She did not in the least resemble her brother.

"Would you like to come home with us?" Gagin said to me. "I think we've seen enough of the Germans. Our students, it is true, would have broken a few windows and smashed up the chairs, but these are a little too well behaved. What do you say, Assya? Shall we go home?" The girl nodded.

"We live outside the town," Gagin went on, "in a vineyard, in a little house standing by itself on the top of a high hill. It's a lovely place, you'll see. Our landlady promised to make us some sour milk. It'll soon be dark, and it'll be better for you to cross the Rhine by moonlight."

We set off. Through the low gates of the town—an ancient wall of small cobblestones surrounded it on all sides, and even the embrasures had not all collapsed— we came out into the open country, and after walking about a hundred paces along a stone wall we stopped in front of a narrow gate. Gagin opened it and led us uphill along a steep path. On the slopes on both sides grew the vines. The sun had just set, and a delicate scarlet light lay on the green vines, on the tall poles, on the dry earth strewed all over with big and small stones, and on the white wall of a small house, with slanting black beams and four bright windows, standing on the very top of the hill we were climbing.

"And here's our home!" cried Gagin as soon as we began approaching the little house. "And here's the landlady bringing the milk. *Guten Abend, Madame!* We shall sit down to our meal at once, but before that," he added, "just look round. What a view!"

The view was indeed magnificent. The Rhine lay before us, all silvery between its green banks. In one place it blazed with the purple and gold of the sunset. The little town, which nestled close to the bank of the river, displayed all its houses and streets; the hills and fields stretched for miles round. It was lovely below, but on top it was lovelier still: I was particularly struck by the depth and purity of the sky, the radiant transparency of the air. Fresh and light, it was quivering gently and rolling over in waves, just as though it too felt more free on a height.

"You've chosen a most excellent place to live in," I said.

"It was Assya who found it," replied Gagin. "Well, Assya," he went on, "are you going to see about our meal? Tell them to bring everything here. We'll have supper in the open air. We can hear the music better from here. Have you noticed," he added, turning to me, "near the band a waltz often sounds terrible—a vulgar, coarse tune—but from a distance it's marvellous; it touches every romantic chord in you."

Assya (her real name was Anna, but Gagin called her Assya, and you must let me call her that too) went into the house and soon returned with the landlady. They were carrying together a large tray with a bowl of sour milk, plates, spoons, sugar, strawberries, bread. We sat down and started eating. Assya took off her hat; her black hair, cut short and combed back like a boy's, fell in thick curls on her neck and over her ears. At first she felt shy with me, but Gagin said to her, "Assya, don't be so shy. He won't bite you."

She smiled and a little later began talking to me of her own accord. I had never seen a more mercurial human being. She did not sit still for a moment; she got up, ran off into the house, and ran back again, hummed a tune, often laughed, and in a most curious way: it seemed as if she wasn't laughing at what she heard but at the different thoughts that entered her head. Her big eyes looked straight at you, brightly and boldly, but her eyelids sometimes narrowed slightly, and then her glance at once became deep and tender.

We chatted for about two hours. The day had long faded and the evening, at first all fiery, then clear and scarlet, then pale and dim, was dying away quietly and passing into night while our conversation still went on, as peaceful and gentle as the air round us. Gagin ordered a bottle of Rhenish wine to be fetched, and we drank it unhurriedly. The music, as before, reached us from afar; its sounds seemed more sweet and more tender. Lights were lit in the town and on the river. Assya suddenly lowered her head, so that her curls fell over her eyes; she fell silent and sighed, and then she told us that she felt sleepy, and went into the house; I saw, however, that she stood a long time at an unopened window without lighting a candle. At last the moon rose and began to sparkle all along the Rhine; everything brightened and darkened and was transformed; even the wine in our cut-glass wineglasses glittered with a mysterious light. The wind dropped, just as though it had folded its wings and lay still; the heavy, scented warmth of the night rose from the earth.

"It's time I went!" I exclaimed. "Or else I may not find a ferryman."

"Yes, it's time to go," Gagin repeated.

We walked down the path. Suddenly we heard stones rolling down behind us: it was Assya overtaking us.

"Aren't you asleep?" asked her brother; but she ran past us without answering a word.

The last flickering lamps lighted by the students in the garden of the inn lit up the leaves of the trees from below, which gave them a festive and fantastic look. We found Assya at the bank of the river. She was talking to the ferryman. I jumped into the boat and took leave of my new friends. Gagin promised to look me up next day. I shook his hand and held out my hand to Assya, but she just looked at me and shook her head. The boat cast off and sailed across the rapid river. The ferryman, a hale and hearty old man, plunged his oars and plied them with a great effort in the dark waters.

"You've sailed into a moonlight pillar and you've broken it up!" Assya shouted to me.

I dropped my eyes; all round the boat the waves heaved, looking blacker than ever.

"Good-bye!" her voice resounded again.

"Till tomorrow!" Gagin shouted after her.

The boat reached the other bank. I got out and looked round. There was no one to be seen on the opposite bank. The moonlight pillar again stretched like a golden bridge across the whole of the river. As though in farewell, the strains of an old-fashioned Lanner waltz floated across towards me. Gagin was right: I felt that all the chords of my heart were vibrating in response to those seductive melodies. I made my way back home across the darkened fields, slowly drinking in the scented air, and arrived in my little room, luxuriating in the sensuous languor of endless anticipations. I felt happy. But why was I happy? I wanted nothing; I thought of nothing. . . . I was happy.

Almost laughing from an excess of agreeable and lighthearted feelings, I dived into my bed and was about to shut my eyes when it suddenly occurred to me that during the whole of that evening I had never once remembered my cruel charmer. "What does it mean?" I asked myself. "Am I no longer in love?" But, having put that question to myself, it seems that I immediately fell asleep, like a baby in its cradle.

3

Next morning (I was awake, but had not yet got up) I heard the tapping of a stick on my window, and a voice, which I at once recognised as belonging to Gagin, sang out:

> "Sleepest thou? With my guitar
> I will wake thee. . . ."

I hastened to open the door to him.

"Good morning," said Gagin, coming in. "I'm sorry I got you up so early, but look what a morning it is—fresh dew on the grass, larks singing . . ."

With his wavy, shiny hair, open neck, and rosy cheeks, he was as fresh as the morning himself.

I dressed. We went out into the garden, sat down on a bench and asked my landlady to bring us coffee, and began to talk. Gagin told me his plans for the future: possessing a considerable fortune, and dependent on no one, he wished to devote himself to painting, and he was only sorry to have thought of it so late and to have wasted so much time doing nothing; I too mentioned my future plans and, incidentally, confided to him the secret of my unhappy love. He listened to me indulgently, but, as far as I was able to observe, I did not arouse in him any strong sympathy for my passion. Sighing after me once or twice out of politeness, Gagin suggested that I should go home with him and look at his sketches. I agreed at once.

We did not find Assya at home. The landlady told us that she had gone to the "ruin" (about a mile from the town of L. were the remains of a feudal castle). Gagin opened all his portfolios. There was a great deal of life and truth in his sketches, a certain breadth and freedom, but not a single one of them had been finished, and the drawing struck me as rather careless and uneven. I told him frankly what I thought of them.

"Yes, yes," he agreed with a sigh, "you're right. All this is very poor and immature, but what's to be done? I have not studied as I should, and besides, our confounded Slav lack of discipline always gets the better of us. While you're dreaming of your work you soar aloft like an eagle, you feel you could move heaven and earth, but when it comes to doing something you at once grow weak and tired."

I tried to cheer him up, but he gave a despairing wave of the hand and, gathering up his portfolios, he threw them on the sofa.

"If I have enough patience I shall achieve something," he muttered through his teeth. "If not, I shall remain the sort of failure that is so common among our noblemen. Come, we'd better go and look for Assya."

We went.

4

The path to the ruin twisted and turned down the slope of a narrow, wooded valley; at the bottom ran a stream, leaping noisily over the stones as though hurrying to flow into the great river which was shining quietly beyond the dark ridge of the precipitously broken mountain crests. Gagin drew my attention to some exquisitely lit spots; his words revealed that, if not a painter, he was most certainly an artist. We soon caught sight of the ruin. On the very top of the bare rock rose a square tower, all black and still strong, but as though cleft by a longitudinal crack. Moss-covered walls adjoined the tower; here and there ivy clung to a wall; twisted little trees hung down from the grey embrasures and collapsed arches. A stony path led to the gates, which were still intact. We were on the point of approaching them when suddenly the figure of a girl flashed by in front of us, ran rapidly over a heap of rubble, and sat down on a ledge of a wall straight over the precipice.

"Why, it's Assya!" cried Gagin. "The crazy girl!"

We went through the gates and found ourselves in a small courtyard, half overgrown with crab-apple trees and nettles. Assya, to be sure, was sitting on the ledge. She turned her face to us and laughed, but did not budge from her place. Gagin shook a finger at her, while I loudly reproached her for her recklessness.

"Don't for goodness' sake tease her," Gagin said to me in a whisper. "You don't know her; she may climb on top of the tower if we are not careful. You'd better be admiring the cleverness of the local inhabitants."

I looked round. In a corner, in the shelter of a tiny wooden caravan, an old woman was knitting a sock and looking at us over her spectacles. She was selling beer, honey cakes, and soda water to tourists. We seated ourselves on a little bench and began drinking rather cold beer from heavy pewter mugs. Assya remained seated, motionless, her feet tucked under her and her head wrapped round in a muslin scarf; her graceful figure was clearly and beautifully outlined against the clear sky;

but I kept looking at her with an unfriendly feeling. The evening before, I had already noticed in her something not altogether natural, something forced. "She's trying to surprise us," I thought. "Whatever for? What a childish prank!" As though divining my thoughts, she suddenly threw a rapid, piercing glance at me, laughed again, and, jumping down from the wall in two bounds, went up to the old woman and asked her for a glass of water.

"You think I want a drink?" she said, turning to her brother. "No, I don't. You see, there are flowers on the walls which simply must be watered."

Gagin said nothing to her, and with the glass in her hand she started clambering over the ruins, stopping from time to time, bending down, and with an amusing air of importance pouring a few drops of water, which glistened brightly in the sun. Her movements were very charming, but I still felt vexed with her, though I could not help admiring her lightness and her agility. At one dangerous place she purposely uttered a little scream and then burst out laughing. I felt even more vexed.

"Why, she's clambering like a wild goat," muttered the old woman under her breath, tearing her eyes away from her sock for a moment.

At last Assya emptied her glass and, swaying mischievously, returned to us. A strange smile quivered lightly on her lips, nostrils, and eyebrows; her dark eyes were screwed up half impudently and half gaily.

"You think my behaviour's improper," her face seemed to say. "Well, I don't care; I know you're admiring me."

"Very clever, Assya, very clever," said Gagin in an undertone.

She seemed suddenly to be overcome with shame. She dropped her long eyelashes and sat down beside us modestly, as though she were to blame. Here I was able to examine her face properly for the first time, the most changeable face I had ever seen. A few moments later it went all pale and assumed a concentrated, almost a mournful expression; her very features seemed to me to be larger, more severe, more simple. She grew strangely calm. We walked round the ruin (Assya walked behind us) and admired the views. Meanwhile it was getting near lunch time. As he paid the old woman Gagin asked her for another mug of beer, and, turning to me, he exclaimed with a sly grimace, "To the health of the lady of your heart!"

"Why, has he—have you such a lady?" Assya asked suddenly.

"Who hasn't?" Gagin replied.

Assya fell into thought for a moment; her face changed once more; the defiant, almost insolent smile appeared on it again.

On the way home she laughed more loudly and was more mischievous than before. She broke off a long branch, put it on her shoulder like a gun, and tied a scarf round her head. I remember we met a numerous family of fair-haired and prim-looking English people; all of them, as though at a word of command, followed Assya with their glassy eyes with a look of cold amazement, while she, as though to spite them, began to sing in a loud voice. On returning home she at once went to her room and appeared only a few minutes before lunch dressed in her best clothes, her hair carefully done, her waist pulled in tight, and wearing gloves. At table she conducted herself very decorously, almost primly, scarcely tasting anything, and drinking water out of a wineglass. She quite obviously wished to act a new part before me, the part of a respectable, well-bred young lady. Gagin did not interfere with her; it was clear that he was used to giving in to her in everything. He merely glanced at me good-naturedly from time to time and slightly shrugged a shoulder, as though wishing to say, "She is only a child—don't be hard on her." As soon as lunch was over, Assya got up, curtsied to us, and, putting on her hat, asked Gagin if she might go to see Frau Luise.

"Since when have you begun asking my permission?" he replied with his invariable, though this time somewhat embarrassed, smile. "Are you bored with us?"

"No, but I promised Frau Luise yesterday to visit her. Besides, I thought that you would feel happier by yourselves. Mr. N."—she pointed to me—"will tell you something more about himself."

She went away.

"Frau Luise," began Gagin, trying to avoid meeting my eyes, "is the widow of a former mayor of this town, a good-natured though rather silly old woman. She is very fond of Assya. Assya has a passion for striking up an acquaintance with people of a lower social position. This, I've noticed, is always the result of pride. As you see," he added after a short pause, "I have rather spoilt her, but I'm afraid I couldn't help that. I'm afraid I find it difficult to be exacting with people, and with her, all the more so. I *have* to humour her."

I said nothing. Gagin changed the conversation. The more I got to know him, the more strongly did I get attached to him. I soon understood him. His was a typical Russian nature, truthful, honest, simple, but, unfortunately, a little flabby, without tenacity and inward fire. Youthful energy did not bubble over in him: it shone with a gentle light. He was very charming and clever, but I just could not imagine what he would become when he grew up. To be an artist . . . Without hard, incessant work one can never be an artist. "And as for work," I thought, looking at his soft features and listening to his unhurried speech, "no! You'll never work hard; you're incapable of withdrawing into yourself." But it was impossible not to be fond of him: one's heart was simply drawn to him. We spent four hours together, sometimes sitting on the sofa, sometimes walking slowly up and down in front of the house, and in those four hours we finally became close friends.

The sun had set and it was time for me to go home. Assya had not returned yet.

"What a wilful girl she is!" said Gagin. "Would you like me to see you home? On the way we'll knock at the door of Frau Luise's house and I'll ask whether she is there. We won't have to go far out of our way."

We went down into the town and, turning into a narrow, twisting lane, stopped before a double-fronted four-storied house. The second storey projected into the street, and the third and the fourth projected even farther than the second; the whole house, with its peeling carving, its two thick columns below, steep tiled roof, and the projecting windlass in the shape of a beak in the attic, looked like a huge, hunched-up bird.

"Assya!" shouted Gagin. "Are you there?"

The lighted window on the third floor rattled and opened, and we saw Assya's dark little head. The toothless and weak-sighted face of the old German woman peered from behind her back.

"I'm here," said Assya, leaning out coquettishly with her elbows on the window-sill. "I'm quite happy here. This is for you," she added, throwing a geranium sprig to Gagin. "Imagine that I'm the lady of your heart."

Frau Luise laughed.

"N. is going home," replied Gagin, "and he wants to say good-bye to you."

"Does he?" said Assya. "In that case, give him my geranium and I'll be coming home soon."

She slammed the window to and, I believe, kissed Frau Luise. Gagin held out the geranium sprig to me in silence. I put it in my pocket without uttering a word, walked to the ferry, and crossed over to the other side.

I remember I was walking home without thinking of anything, but with a strange feeling of heaviness in my heart, when suddenly I was struck by a strong, familiar scent which is rare in Germany. I stopped and saw near the road a small bed of hemp. Its fragrance of the steppes instantly recalled my native land to me and aroused a passionate longing for it in my heart. I longed to breathe Russian air, to tread on Russian soil. "What am I doing here? Why am I dragging myself about in a foreign country, among strangers?" I cried, and the dead weight I felt in my heart was instantly transformed into a bitter, burning emotion. I came back home in a totally different mood from that of the evening before. I felt almost angry with myself and could not compose myself for a long time. I was seized with a feeling of vexation which I could not explain. At last I sat down and, remembering my faithless widow (every day concluded with my dutiful recollection of that lady), took out one of her letters. But I did not even open it; my thoughts at once took a different turn. I began thinking —thinking of Assya. It occurred to me that in the course of our talk Gagin hinted at some difficulties which prevented his return to Russia. "Is she really his sister?" I said aloud.

I undressed, went to bed, and tried to get to sleep; but an hour later I was sitting up again in my bed, leaning on the pillow on an elbow and again thinking of that capricious little girl with the affected laugh. "Her figure is like the little Galatea figure by Raphael in the Farnese," I whispered. "Yes—and she is not his sister. . . ."

And the widow's letter lay untouched on the floor, white in the moonlight.

5

Next morning I went again to L. I told myself that I wanted to see Gagin, but secretly I longed to see what Assya would be doing and whether she would behave as eccentrically as she had the day before. I found both of them in the drawing room and, strange to say—possibly because I had been thinking so much of Russia during the night and in the morning—Assya seemed to me a purely Russian girl, and a girl of the common people, almost a lady's maid. She wore an old dress; she had combed her hair back behind her ears; and she was sitting without stirring by the window, embroidering something in a frame, quietly and demurely, just as though she had done nothing else all her life. She scarcely uttered a word, gazing calmly at her work, and her features wore such an ordinary, everyday expression that they reminded me involuntarily of our home-bred Katyas and Mashas. To complete the resemblance, she began humming in an undertone, "Mother, my sweet darling." I looked at her sallow, lacklustre face, recalled my dreams of the previous night, and I felt sorry for something.

The weather was wonderful. Gagin told us that he was going to do a sketch from nature. I asked him whether he would mind if I went with him and whether I would be in his way.

"On the contrary," he replied, "you may give me some good advice."

He put on a round hat *à la* Van Dyke and a blouse, put a portfolio under his arm, and went out; I followed him slowly. Assya stayed at home. Before going out, Gagin asked her to see that the soup was not too thin. Assya promised to look into the kitchen. Gagin went as far as the valley that was already familiar to me, sat down on a stone, and began to sketch an old hollow oak with spreading branches. I lay down on the grass and took out a book. But I did not read even two pages, and he just spoilt a clean sheet of paper. We spent most of the time talking, and, as far as I could judge, we talked rather cleverly and subtly about how one ought to work, what one ought to avoid doing, what rules one ought to observe, and what was the real significance of an artist in our age. Gagin finally decided that he was not "in good form today" and lay down beside me, and from then on, our youthful speeches flowed freely, sometimes passionate, sometimes wistful, sometimes ecstatic, but almost always vague, the sort of conversation in which a Russian so readily engages. Having had our fill of talk and overflowing with a feeling of satisfaction, just as though we had succeeded in doing something, in achieving some sort of success, we returned home. I found Assya exactly the same as I had left her; however much I tried to observe her, I could detect in her not a shadow of coquetry, not a sign of a deliberately assumed role. This time it was quite impossible to reproach her with affectation.

"Aha!" said Gagin. "So she's covered herself with sackcloth and ashes!"

Towards evening she yawned a few times unfeignedly and went early to her room. I myself soon said good-bye to Gagin and on returning home no longer dreamed of anything. That day was remarkable for the sobriety of my sensations. I remember, however, that as I was going to bed I could not help saying aloud, "What a chameleon that girl is!" and after thinking it over a little, added, "All the same, I am sure she is not his sister."

6

Two whole weeks passed. I visited the Gagins every day. Assya seemed to avoid me, but she no longer permitted herself any of those mischievous pranks which had surprised me so much during the first two days of our acquaintance. She seemed secretly aggrieved or embarrassed; she even laughed less. I watched her with interest.

She spoke French and German quite well, but it was perfectly clear that she had not been looked after by women as a child and that she had received a strange and unusual kind of education which had nothing in common with Gagin's upbringing. In spite of his hat *à la* Van Dyke and his blouse, you could not possibly mistake him for anything but a soft, half-effeminate Russian nobleman, while she did not resemble a well-bred young lady at all. In all her movements there was something restless. It was a wild sapling that had been grafted only recently, a wine that was still fermenting. By nature timid and shy, she resented her shyness, and in her resentment tried to force herself to be free and easy and bold, in which she did not always succeed. Several times I tried to talk to her about her life in Russia and about her past, but she replied reluctantly to my questions; I discovered, however, that before her departure abroad she had lived a long time in the country.

One day I found her alone, reading a book. Her head propped up on her hands and her fingers thrust deeply into her hair, she was devouring the lines eagerly. "Bravo," I said, going up to her, "how very studious you are!"

She raised her head and looked gravely and severely at me. "You think that I can only laugh," she said, and was about to go out of the room.

I glanced at the title of the book: it was some French novel. "But I can't commend your choice," I observed.

"What else can I read!" she exclaimed and, throwing the book on the table, added, "I suppose I'd better go and play the fool," and rushed out into the garden.

That evening I read *Hermann und Dorothea* to Gagin. At first Assya kept darting past us; then she suddenly stopped, listened attentively, sat down quietly beside me, and heard the reading through to the end. The following day I again hardly recognised her, until I realised that she had taken it into her head to be as sedate and domestic as Dorothea. In short, she seemed to me to be a sort of enigmatic creature. Touchy in the extreme, she attracted me even when I was angry with her. Of one thing I was becoming more and more convinced: she was not Gagin's sister. He did not treat her as a brother would. He was too affectionate, too indulgent, and at the same time a little constrained.

A strange incident apparently confirmed me in my suspicions.

One evening, on approaching the vineyard where the Gagins lived, I found the gate locked. Without a moment's reflection I walked to the place where the wall was broken down, a spot I had noticed before, and jumped over it. Not far from that place, to one side of the path, there was a small arbour of acacias. I drew level with it and was about to walk past, when I was startled to hear Assya's voice uttering the following words with warmth and through tears: "No, I don't want to love anyone but you! No, no! I want to love only you—and forever!"

"Come, Assya, calm yourself," Gagin said. "You know I believe you."

Their voices came from the arbour. I caught sight of both of them through the thin interlacement of branches. They did not notice me.

"You, you alone," she repeated and, flinging herself on his neck and sobbing convulsively, she began kissing him and clinging to his breast.

"Come, come," he kept repeating, stroking her hair lightly.

For a few minutes I remained motionless. Suddenly I gave a start. "Shall I go up to them? Never!" flashed through my head. I returned quickly to the wall, jumped over it onto the road, and went home almost at a run. I smiled, rubbed my hands, wondered at the chance that had suddenly confirmed my conjectures (I did not for a moment doubt their accuracy)—and yet I felt very bitter at heart. "Good Lord," I thought, "they certainly know how to pretend! But why should they? Why try to fool me? I never expected it of him. And what a sentimental scene!"

7

I slept badly and got up early next morning, slung a rucksack on my back, and, after telling my landlady not to expect me back that night, went walking in the mountains, along the upper part of the stream on which the little town of S. is situated. These mountains, a branch of the range of mountains known as the Dog's-Back (*Hundsrück*), are very interesting from a geological point of view. They are particularly remarkable for the regularity and purity of their basalt deposits; but I did not feel like making any geological observations. I failed to realise what was going on within me; one thing I was quite clear about: I did not want to see the Gagins again. I assured myself that the sole reason for my sudden dislike of them was my annoyance at their duplicity. Who forced them to pass themselves off as brother and sister? However, I tried not to think about them; I walked without hurrying about the mountains and valleys, spent hours in village inns, talking peacefully to the innkeepers and their customers, or lay on a flat, warm stone, gazing at the clouds sailing across the sky, taking full advantage of the wonderful weather. In such pursuits I passed three days, and not without pleasure, either, though my heart did ache at times. The trend of my thoughts seemed to fit in entirely with the peaceful nature of that part of the country.

I gave myself up entirely to the calm play of chance, to fleeting impressions; changing unhurriedly, they flowed through my soul and left there at last one general feeling, a feeling in which everything I had seen, felt, and heard during those three days merged into one—everything: the delicate scent of resin in the woods, the call and tapping of the woodpecker, the unceasing chatter of the clear streams with mottled trout on the sandy bottom, the not-too-bold outlines of mountains, the gloomy cliffs, the spotlessly clean villages with their venerable churches and trees, the storks in the meadows, the cosy windmills with their swiftly turning sails, the welcoming faces of villagers, their blue jackets and grey stockings, the creaking slow carts, drawn by sleek horses and sometimes cows, the young, long-haired hikers trudging along the clean roads, planted with apple and pear trees. . . .

Even now I enjoy recalling my impressions of those days. Greetings to you, unpretentious corner of German soil, with your simple contentment, with the frequent traces of industrious hands and patient though unhurried toil! Greetings to you, and peace!

I returned home at the very end of the third day. I forgot to say that, put out by the Gagins, I tried to revive the image of the cruel-hearted widow; but my efforts were in vain. I remember when I set about to think of her, I saw standing before me a little five-year-old peasant girl with a round face and innocently goggling eyes. She gazed so childishly and artlessly at me that the pure look in her eyes made me feel ashamed. I did not want to lie in her presence and immediately bade a final and everlasting farewell to my former flame.

At home I found a note from Gagin. He was surprised at the suddenness of my decision, upbraided me for not taking him with me, and asked me to come and see them as soon as I returned. I could not suppress my displeasure at reading this note, but the next day I went to L.

8

Gagin welcomed me like an old friend and showered affectionate reproaches on me; but Assya, as though on purpose, burst out laughing without any reason as soon as she saw me and, as she so often did before, at once ran away. Gagin looked embarrassed and muttered after her that she was a "crazy girl" and asked me to excuse her. I confess I was very vexed with Assya. I did not feel particularly at ease, anyway—and now again that unnatural laughter and those strange conceits. However, I pretended not to notice anything and told Gagin about my not very protracted excursion. He told me everything he had done in my absence. But somehow our conversation flagged; Assya kept coming into the room and running out again; I declared at last that I had some urgent business to attend to and that it was time I went home. Gagin at first tried to persuade me to stay a little longer; then, looking intently at me, offered to see me home. In the passage Assya suddenly went up to me and held out her hand. I pressed her fingers lightly and barely bowed to her.

Gagin and I ferried across the Rhine and, passing by my favourite ash tree with the statue of the Madonna, we sat down on the bench to admire the view. A remarkable conversation took place between us.

At first we just exchanged a few words; then we fell silent, gazing at the sparkling river.

"Tell me," began Gagin suddenly, with his usual smile, "what's your opinion of Assya? She seems a little strange to you, doesn't she?"

"Yes," I replied, not without some bewilderment. I did not expect him to start talking about her.

"You have to know her well before passing any judgement on her," he said. "She has a very kind heart, but a mischievous head. She's difficult to get on with. Still, you couldn't really blame her and if you knew her story."

"Her story?" I interrupted. "Isn't she your——"

Gagin glanced at me. "You don't think she's not my sister, do you? No," he went on, without paying any attention to my embarrassment, "she really is my sister. She is my father's daughter. Listen to what I have to say. I feel I can trust you, and I will tell you everything. . . . My father was a very kindly, intelligent, and cultured man, and an unhappy one. Fate treated him no worse than many others, but he could not get over her first blow. He married early, for love; his wife, my mother, died very soon after; I was six months old at the time of her death. My father took me to his estate, and he did not leave it for the next twelve years. He looked after my upbringing himself, and he would never have parted with me if his brother, my uncle, had not come to visit us in the country. This uncle of mine had always lived in Petersburg, where he occupied a very important position. He persuaded my father to let him look after me, because my father would not on any account leave the country. My uncle put it to him that it was not good for a boy of my age to live in complete seclusion; that with such a perpetually gloomy and silent instructor as my father, I would most certainly lag behind other boys of my age; and that, besides, my character itself could be easily spoilt. My father stood out for a long time against his brother's arguments, but gave way at last.

"I cried at parting from my father; I loved him, though I had never seen a smile on his face. But when I got to Petersburg I soon forgot my dark and cheerless home. I entered the Cadet College, and from college I was transferred to a guards regiment. Every year I spent a few weeks on my father's estate and with every year I found my father more and more melancholy, self-centred, and pensive to the point of timidity. He went to church every day and had almost forgotten how to talk. During one of my last visits (I was about twenty at that time), I saw for the first time in our house a thin, black-eyed girl of ten—Assya. My father said that she was an orphan and that he had taken her into the house because 'she would otherwise have starved to death'— that was how he expressed himself. I did not pay any particular attention to her; she was shy, agile, and silent, like a little wild animal, and the moment I entered my father's favourite room, a huge gloomy room in which my mother had died and where, even in daytime, candles were kept burning, she at once hid herself behind his Voltaire chair or behind the bookcase.

"It so happened that for three or four years after that visit I was prevented from visiting my father's estate by my regimental duties. Every month I used to get a short letter from my father; Assya, he mentioned rarely, and only in passing. He was over fifty, but he still looked a young man. Imagine my horror, when suddenly, without suspecting anything, I received a letter from our steward in which he informed me that my father was dangerously ill, and begged me to return home as soon as possible if I wanted to take leave of him. I galloped off at breakneck speed to our estate and found my father still alive but at his last gasp. He was extremely glad to see me, clasped me in his wasted arms, gazed for a long time into my eyes with a sort of half-imploring and half-searching look, and, making me promise that I would carry out his last wish, asked his old valet to fetch Assya. The old man brought her in: she could hardly stand on her feet and was trembling all over.

"'Here,' my father said to me with an effort, 'I bequeath to you my daughter—your sister. You will find everything out from Yakov,' he added, pointing to his valet.

"Assya burst into sobs and flung herself onto the bed with her face downwards. Half an hour later my father died.

"This was what I learnt. Assya was the daughter of my father and a former maid of my mother's, Tatyana. I had a vivid recollection of this Tatyana. I remember her tall, graceful figure, her handsome, stern, intelligent face, with big black eyes. She had the reputation of a proud, unapproachable girl. As far as I could make out from Yakov's respectful though reserved statement, my father had become her lover a few years after my mother's death. At that time Tatyana was no longer living in the manor house, but in the cottage of her married sister, a dairymaid.

"My father became violently attached to her and after my departure from the estate he even wanted to marry her, but she refused to be his wife, in spite of all his entreaties.

" 'The late Tatyana Vlasyevna,' Yakov told me, standing at the door with his hands behind his back, 'was a very sensible woman in everything she did, and she did not want to do anything that would harm your father. "What kind of a wife would I make for you?" she told him. "What kind of a lady am I?" That was how she spoke to your father, sir. She said it in my presence.'

"Tatyana would not even move into our house, and went on living at her sister's, with Assya. As a child I used to see Tatyana only during the holy days in church. With a dark kerchief wrapped over her head and a yellow shawl over her shoulders, she used to stand in the crowd near a window. Her severe profile stood out clearly against the transparent windowpane—and she used to pray humbly and gravely, prostrating herself, in accordance with the old custom. When my uncle carried me off, Assya was only two years old, and at the age of nine she lost her mother.

"When Tatyana died, my father took Assya into his house. He had expressed a wish even before to have her with him, but that too Tatyana had refused him. You can imagine what Assya felt when she was taken into the master's house. To this day she can't forget the moment when she was dressed in a silk dress for the first time and when the servants kissed her hand. Her mother had brought her up very strictly, but in my father's house she enjoyed complete freedom. He was her teacher. She saw no one except him. He did not spoil her—that is to say, he did not make a fuss over her—but he loved her passionately and did not forbid her anything; for in his heart he felt a sense of guilt towards her. Assya soon realised that she was the chief person in the house; she knew that the master was her father; but she also very soon became aware of her false position. Pride developed very strongly in her, as well as mistrustfulness; bad habits took root and simplicity vanished. She wanted—she told me so herself—to make *the whole world* forget her origin: she was ashamed of her mother, and she was ashamed of being ashamed, and she was proud of her. You see, she knew and knows a lot that she should not have known at her age. But who can blame her? She was developing fast; her blood coursed warmly through her veins; and there was not a single hand near her to put her on the right track. Complete independence in everything! It is not an easy thing to bear, is it? She did not want to be worse than other young ladies. She began reading voraciously. What good could come of that! Her life began irregularly and it went on as irregularly, but her heart was not spoilt, and her intelligence remained unharmed.

"And so, there I was, a twenty-year-old youth with a thirteen-year-old girl on my hands! During the first days after my father's death the very sound of my voice threw her into a fever; my caresses plunged her into a state of depression; and it was only little by little and by degrees that she got used to me. It is true that afterwards, when she became convinced that I did acknowledge her as my sister, and loved her as a sister, she became passionately attached to me: she can feel nothing by halves.

"I took her to Petersburg with me, but however much it hurt me to part with her, we could not possibly live together, and I sent her to one of the best boarding schools. Assya understood the necessity of our separation, but she started by falling ill and nearly dying. Then she got used to her new life and spent four years at the boarding school. But, contrary to my expectations, she remained almost the same as she was before. The headmistress of the school often complained to me about her. 'It is impossible to punish her, and she does not respond to affection, either,' she used to say to me. Assya was extremely intelligent, and she got on excellently with her studies, better than anyone else in the school; but she refused to fit in, and she was stubborn and unsociable. I could not blame her very much for it: in her position she had either to fawn upon people or shun them. Of all her school friends she became intimate with only one, a girl of a poor family, unprepossessing and maltreated. The other girls with whom she was being brought up, most of them of good family, did not like her; they taunted her and sneered at her; Assya would not yield an inch to them. Once, at a Scriptures lesson, the teacher was talking about vice. 'Flattery and cowardice are the worst vices,' Assya said aloud. In short, she continued to go her own way; only her manners had improved, though even in that respect I don't think she made much progress.

"At last she was seventeen and she could remain no longer at the boarding school. I found myself in a rather difficult position. Suddenly a happy thought struck me: Why not resign my commission and go abroad for a year or two, taking Assya with me? No sooner thought than done, and now here we are, Assya and myself, on the banks of the Rhine, where I am trying to paint, and she— she carries on in her odd and mischievous way as before. Now I hope you will not judge her too harshly; for though she pretends that she doesn't care a rap about anything, she does value the good opinion of everyone, and yours in particular."

And Gagin smiled again in his gentle way. I pressed his hand warmly.

"It's all very well," said Gagin again, "but I've got a trying time with her. She's terribly quick-tempered. Till now she hasn't shown any liking for anyone in particular, but there's going to be trouble if she does fall in love with someone! Sometimes I am at a loss to know how to deal with her. The other day she suddenly took it into her head to tell me that I was colder to her than I used to be and that she loved only me and would go on loving me forever. And then she burst out crying——"

"Oh, so that's what——" I began, and bit my tongue. "But tell me," I went on, "since we are so frank with one another, has she really cared for no one till now? She must have met lots of young men in Petersburg."

"She did not like them at all. No, what Assya wants is a hero, a man who is out of the ordinary—or a picturesque shepherd on a mountain pass. I'm sorry, though. I'm afraid I have been talking too much to you and detained you," he added, getting up.

"Look here," I began, "let's go back to your place. I don't want to go home."

"But what about your work?"

I made no answer. Gagin smiled good-naturedly and we returned to L. As I caught sight of the familiar vineyard and the little white house on the top of the hill I felt a kind of sweetness—yes, a sweetness in my heart, as though someone had secretly poured some honey into it. I felt lighthearted after what Gagin had told me.

9

Assya met us on the very threshold of the house; I expected laughter again, but she came out to us pale, silent, with downcast eyes.

"Here he is again," said Gagin, "and, observe, he wanted to come back of his own accord."

Assya looked interrogatively at me. It was my turn now to hold out my hand, and this time I pressed her cold fingers warmly. I felt very sorry for her; I understood now a great deal about her which had puzzled me before: her inward restlessness, her lack of social poise, her desire to show off—everything became clear to me. I had had a look into her heart: a secret worry oppressed her constantly; her unsatisfied and misguided ambition was struggling uneasily and in confusion; but she strove with all her being for justice. I understood why this strange girl attracted me; it was not only by her half-wild charm, which pervaded all her slender body, that she attracted me; it was her soul that appealed so strongly to me.

Gagin began to rummage among his drawings; I asked Assya to come out for a walk with me in the vineyard. She agreed at once, with cheerful and almost submissive readiness. We went halfway down the hill and sat down on a wide flagstone.

"Weren't you bored without us?" began Assya.

"Weren't you bored without me?" I asked.

Assya gave me a sidelong look. "Yes," she replied. "Was it nice in the mountains?" she went on at once. "Were they high? Higher than the clouds? Tell me what you saw. You told my brother, but I didn't hear anything."

"You shouldn't have gone away then," I observed.

"I went away—because—— I won't go away now," she added with a confiding caress in her voice. "You were cross today."

"Me?"

"You."

"Why, for goodness' sake?"

"I don't know, but you were cross, and you went away looking cross. I was very sorry that you should have gone away like that and I'm glad you came back."

"I too am glad I came back," I said.

Assya moved her shoulders as children often do when they are happy. "Oh, I'm very good at guessing!" she went on. "From the way father coughed in the next room I could tell whether he was pleased with me or not."

Till that day Assya had never once spoken to me about her father. I couldn't help being struck by that.

"Did you love your father?" I said, and suddenly, to my great annoyance, I felt that I was blushing.

She made no answer, and also blushed. Both of us fell silent. In the distance a steamer was sailing and puffing out smoke on the Rhine. We began watching it.

"Why don't you tell me about your trip?" Assya whispered.

"Why did you laugh today as soon as you saw me?" I asked.

"I don't know myself. Sometimes I feel like crying and I laugh. You must not judge me by—by what I do. Oh, by the way, what a wonderful story that is about the Lorelei! It's her rock we can see from here, isn't it? They say that before she used to drown everyone, but that when she fell in love she threw herself into the river. I like that story. Frau Luise tells me all sorts of fairy tales. Frau Luise has a black cat with yellow eyes . . ." Assya raised her head and shook her curls. "Oh, I'm so happy!" she said.

At that moment we became aware of some monotonous snatches of singing. Hundreds of voices, all at once and at regular intervals, were repeating the refrain of a hymn: a religious procession was winding its way on the road below, with crosses and banners.

"I should have liked to go with them," said Assya, listening to the gradually fading bursts of singing.

"Are you so religious?"

"To go away, far away on a pilgrimage, to do something wonderfully great and difficult," she went on. "As it is, days pass, life passes, and what have we achieved?"

"You're ambitious," I observed. "You don't want to live without doing something; you want to leave some trace behind you."

"Why, is that so impossible?"

Impossible, I nearly repeated, but I gazed into her bright eyes and only said, "Try it."

"Tell me," said Assya after a short pause, in the course

of which a shadow passed over her face, which had already gone pale, "did you love that woman very much? You remember, my brother drank her health at the ruined castle the day after we met for the first time?"

I laughed. "Your brother was joking. I never cared for any woman—at least, I don't care for any now."

"And what is it you like in women?" asked Assya, tossing back her head with an air of innocent curiosity.

"What a strange question!" I exclaimed.

Assya looked a little embarrassed. "I shouldn't have asked you such a question, should I? I'm sorry; I'm used to blurting out everything that comes into my head. That is why I am afraid to speak."

"Do speak, for heaven's sake; don't be afraid!" I cried. "I'm so glad you've stopped being shy at last."

Assya dropped her eyes and laughed a soft and gentle laugh; I had never heard her laugh like that before. "Well, go on, tell me," she went on, smoothing the skirts of her dress and spreading them over her legs as though she were going to sit there for a long time. "Tell me something, or read me something, just as, you remember, you read us something from Pushkin's *Onegin.*"

She sank into thought suddenly.

> "Where now a cross and the branches' shade
> On my poor mother's grave are laid!"

she murmured in an undertone.

"It's not like that in Pushkin," I observed.

"I should like to have been Tatyana," she went on in the same pensive tone of voice. "Tell me something!" she went on animatedly.

But I did not feel like telling stories. I looked at her, all bathed in bright sunshine, so quiet and gentle. Everything round us was so joyously radiant, below, above us—sky, earth, and water; the very air seemed to be saturated with radiance.

"Look how beautiful it is!" I said, lowering my voice involuntarily.

"Yes, it is," she replied, also softly, without looking at me. "If you and I were birds, how we would soar, how we would fly! . . . We would have dissolved in that blue. . . . But we're not birds."

"But we can grow wings," I replied.

"Can we?"

"Live a little longer, and you'll find out. There are feelings which raise us above the earth. Don't worry, you will have wings."

"Have you had them?"

"Well, how shall I put it? I don't believe I have ever flown till now."

Assya pondered again. I bent towards her a little.

"Do you waltz?" she asked me suddenly.

"I do," I replied, a little taken aback.

"Well, come along then—come along. I'll ask my brother to play us a waltz. Let us imagine that we are flying, that we've grown wings."

She ran into the house. I ran after her, and a few moments later we were spinning round in a narrow room to the sweet sounds of a Lanner waltz. Assya waltzed beautifully, with enthusiasm. Something soft and feminine suddenly showed itself through the girlish severity of her profile. For a long time afterwards my hand felt the touch of her yielding waist; for a long time I heard her quickened, close breathing; for a long time I imagined I could see her dark, immobile, almost closed eyes in a pale but animated face, sharply outlined by fluttering curls.

10

The whole of that day was as perfect as one could wish. We were as merry as children. Assya was very sweet and simple. Gagin looked very pleased as he watched her. I went home late. On reaching the middle of the Rhine, I asked the ferryman to let his boat drift down with the current. The old man lifted his oars, and the majestic river carried us along. Looking round, listening, remembering, I suddenly felt my heart seized by a mysterious restlessness. I lifted my eyes to the sky, but there was no rest in the sky, either: spangled with stars, it was all astir, moving, shimmering; I bent over to the river, but there too, in those dark, cold depths, the stars were trembling and flickering; wherever I looked, I seemed to be aware of a disturbing animation, and within me too the feeling of alarm grew. I leaned my elbows on the edge of the boat. The whispering of the wind in my ears, the soft ripple of the water at the tiller, irritated me, and the fresh breath of the waves did not cool me; a nightingale began to sing on the bank and infected me with the sweet poison of its notes. Tears started to my eyes, but they were not the tears of aimless rapture. What I felt was not the vague sense of universal desires I had experienced such a short while ago, when one's soul expands, resounds, when it feels that it understands all and loves all. No! It was the yearning for happiness that was kindled in me. I dared not, as yet, call it by its name, but happiness, happiness to the point of satiety—*that* was what I wanted, that was what I craved for. And the boat was still drifting downstream, and the old ferryman sat dozing as he bent over his oars.

11

On my way to the Gagins' the next day I did not ask myself whether I was in love with Assya, but I thought a lot about her; her life interested me, and I was glad of our unexpected friendship. I felt that it was only since the day before that I had got to know her; till then she had turned away from me. And now, when she at last opened up to me, in what an enchanting light did her image appear; how new it was for me; what secret charms shone shyly through it.

I walked briskly along the familiar road, looking continuously at the little house that gleamed white in the distance; I gave no thought for the future, not even for the morrow; I was very happy.

Assya blushed when I entered the room; I noticed that she had put on her best dress again; but the expression of her face did not suit her dress: it was sad. And I had come feeling so gay! I even thought that she was about to run away as usual, but made an effort and stayed.

Gagin was in that peculiar state of artistic fever and fury which, like a fit, suddenly comes upon amateurs when they imagine that they have succeeded, as they say, in "catching nature by her tail." He was standing all dishevelled and covered with paint before a stretched canvas and, brandishing his brush over it, he nodded almost fiercely to me, then took a few steps back, screwed up his eyes, and pounced on his picture again. I did not attempt to interfere with him and sat down beside Assya. Slowly her dark eyes turned to me.

"You're not the same today as yesterday," I observed, after a vain effort to bring a smile to her lips.

"No, I'm afraid I'm not," she replied in an unhurried and dull voice. "But that's nothing. I haven't slept well. I have been thinking all night."

"What about?"

"Oh, I thought about many things. That's a habit I have had since I was a child, ever since I used to live with my mother."

She uttered the word with an effort and then repeated once more, "Since I lived with my mother. . . . I kept thinking why no one could tell what was going to happen to him. Sometimes you see trouble coming, but there's nothing you can do about it. And why is it that you can never tell the whole truth? Then I kept thinking that I knew nothing and that I ought to study. I have to be re-educated. I'm very badly educated. I can't play the piano, I can't draw, and I can't even sew properly. I have no talent for anything. I expect people must find it very boring to be with me."

"You're unjust to yourself," I objected. "You have read a lot, you are well educated, and with your intelligence——"

"Why, *am* I intelligent?" she asked with such naïve curiosity that I could not help laughing, but she did not even smile. "Am I intelligent?" she asked, turning to Gagin.

He made no answer and went on working, constantly changing his brushes and lifting his hand high.

"Sometimes I don't know myself what's in my head," Assya went on with the same pensive air. "Sometimes I am afraid of myself. I am, really. Oh, I wish . . . Is it true that women ought not to read a lot?"

"No, not a lot, but——"

"Tell me, what ought I to read? Tell me, what ought I to do? I'll do everything you tell me," she added, turning to me with innocent trustfulness.

I did not at once know what to say.

"You don't find it boring with me?"

"Good Lord——" I began.

"Well, thank you," replied Assya. "I thought you would be bored."

And her little hot hand squeezed mine tightly.

"Well," Gagin cried at that moment, "don't you think that background is a little too dark?"

I went up to him. Assya got up and went out of the room.

12

She returned an hour later, stopped in the doorway, and beckoned to me.

"Listen," she said, "would you be sorry for me if I were to die?"

"What ideas you have today!" I exclaimed.

"I can't help imagining that I shall be dead soon. It sometimes seems to me that everything round me is saying good-bye to me. I'd rather be dead than live like this. Oh, don't look at me like that! I'm not pretending, I promise you, or I should be afraid of you again."

"Why, were you afraid of me?"

"If I am strange, it isn't really my fault," she replied. "You see, I can't even laugh any more."

She remained sad and troubled till evening. Something was going on inside her, something I did not understand. Her eyes often rested on me, and my heart sank a little under this enigmatic look. She seemed to be calm enough, but, looking at her, I kept wishing to tell her not to be so agitated. I looked at her with admiration; I found a touching charm in her pale face, in her hesitating, slow movements; but for some reason she imagined that I was out of humour.

"Listen," she said to me, shortly before parting, "I'm worried by the thought that you think me frivolous. Please in future always believe what I tell you; only you too must be frank with me. I will always tell you the truth. I give you my word of honour."

This "word of honour" again made me laugh.

"Oh, don't laugh," she said animatedly, "or I shall say to you today what you said to me yesterday: 'Why do you laugh?'" And after a short pause she added, "Remember, you spoke yesterday of wings? Well, I've grown wings, but I have nowhere to fly."

"Good heavens," I said, "all the ways lie open to you . . ."

Assya looked at me intently, straight into my eyes. "You've a bad opinion of me today," she said, frowning.

"Me? A bad opinion? Of you!"

"What do you look so crestfallen for, the two of you?"

Gagin interrupted me. "Would you like me to play you a waltz, as I did yesterday?"

"No, no," Assya replied, clenching her hands, "not to-day—not for anything in the world!"

"Nobody is forcing you. Please be calm——"

"Not for anything in the world!" she repeated, going pale.

"Is she in love with me?" I thought as I walked to-wards the Rhine and its rapidly rolling dark waves.

13

"Is she in love with me?" I kept asking myself the next morning as soon as I woke up. I did not want to look into myself. I felt that her image, the image of the girl with the affected laugh, had wormed itself into my heart and that I wouldn't be able to rid myself of it for a long time. I went to L. and stayed there for the whole day. But I caught only a few glimpses of Assya. She did not feel well: she had a headache. She came down for a minute with a bandage round her forehead, pale, thin, with almost closed eyes; she smiled weakly and said, "It is nothing; it will pass. Everything will pass, won't it?" and went out of the room.

I felt bored and somehow sad and empty; I would not leave for a long time, though, and went home late, without seeing her again.

The next morning passed in a kind of half-conscious, dreamlike state. I tried to sit down to work, but could not; I tried to do nothing and to think of nothing, but that too I could not manage. I walked aimlessly about the town, went back home, and went out again.

"Are you Mr. N.?" I heard a child's voice ask sud-denly behind me. I looked round. A boy stood before me. "This is from Fräulein Annette for you," he added, handing me a note.

I opened it and recognised Assya's irregular and rapid hand.

"I simply have to see you," she wrote. "Come today at four o'clock to the stone shrine on the road near the ruin. I have done something awful today. Come, for God's sake, and you will find out everything! Say 'Yes' to the messenger."

"Is there an answer, sir?" the boy asked me.

"Say that it is 'Yes.'"

The boy ran away.

14

I went back to my room, sat down, and sank into thought. My heart was beating violently. I read Assya's note through several times. I looked at my watch: it was not even twelve.

The door opened—and Gagin walked in. He looked worried. He seized my hand and pressed it warmly. He seemed very excited.

"What's the matter?" I asked.

Gagin took a chair and sat down opposite me. "Three days ago," he began with a forced smile and with a stammer, "I surprised you with my story. Today I'm going to surprise you even more. With anyone else I don't think I should have made up my mind to speak—so openly. But you are an honourable man, you're my friend, aren't you? Look here, my sister Assya is in love with you——"

I gave a violent start and half raised myself in my chair.

"Your sister, you say——"

"Yes, yes," Gagin interrupted me, "I tell you my sister is crazy, and she'll drive me crazy too. But fortunately she can't tell a lie, and she trusts me. Oh, what a soul that girl has, but she will ruin herself, I'm sure of it!"

"You must be mistaken," I began.

"No, I am not mistaken. Yesterday, as you know, she spent almost the whole day in bed. She ate nothing, but she did not complain. She never complains. I did not worry, although towards evening she had a slight temperature. Today, at two o'clock in the morning, our landlady woke me. 'Go to your sister,' she said, 'there's something wrong with her.' I rushed in to Assya. She had not undressed; she was in a fever, in tears; her head was burning; her teeth were chattering. 'What's the matter with you?' I said. 'Are you ill?' She flung herself on my neck and began imploring me to take her away as soon as possible if I wanted her to remain alive. I couldn't make anything out; I tried to calm her; but she started sobbing even more violently, and through her sobs I heard—well, in short, I heard that she loves you. I assure you, you and I are sensible people, and we can have no idea how deeply she feels and with what an incredible force these feelings express themselves in her; it comes over her as unexpectedly and as irresistibly as a thunderstorm.

"You're a very nice person," Gagin went on, "but why she should have fallen in love with you, I confess I can't understand. She says she has been attracted to you from the first time she saw you. That's why she cried the other day when she assured me she did not want to love anyone but me. She imagines that you despise her, that you probably know who she really is. She asked me whether I had told you the story of her life and, of course, I said that I hadn't. But she's terribly sensitive. She only wants one thing now: to go away, to go away at once. I sat with her till morning. She made me promise that we would not be here tomorrow, and only then did she fall asleep. I thought and thought and decided to talk it over with you. In my opinion Assya is right: I think the best thing for both of us is to go away from here. And I would have taken her away today if something had not occurred to me to stop me. Perhaps—who knows?—you like my sister. If so, why should I take her away? So I made up my mind, putting aside my own personal pride —besides, I noticed something myself. So I made up my mind to—to find out from you——" Poor Gagin looked terribly embarrassed. "You must forgive me, please. I—I'm not used to such—er—awkward situations."

I took his hand. "You want to know," I said in a firm voice, "whether I like your sister, don't you? Yes, I do like her."

Gagin glanced at me. "But," he said with a stammer, "you—you are not going to marry her, are you?"

"How would you like me to answer such a question? You can judge yourself whether I am in a position now——"

"I know, I know," Gagin interrupted me. "I haven't a right to demand an answer from you, and my question is the height of impertinence. But what am I to do? One mustn't play with fire. You don't know Assya. She is quite capable of falling ill, running away, asking you to meet her somewhere. Any other girl would have known how to keep it all dark and bide her time, but not she. It's the first time with her, that's the trouble! If you'd seen how she had sobbed at my feet today, you'd understand my apprehensions."

I pondered. Gagin's words, "asking you to meet her somewhere," had stung me to the quick. I felt it was shameful not to answer his honest candour by being candid in turn.

"Yes," I said at last, "you are right. An hour ago I received a note from your sister. Here it is."

Gagin took the note, glanced through it quickly, and dropped his hands on his knees. The expression of astonishment on his face was very comical, but I did not feel like laughing.

"I repeat, you are an honourable man," he said, "but what are we to do now? I—I just can't make it out: she

herself wants to go away, and she writes to you and reproaches herself with having done something awful. And
when did she manage to write it? What does she want
from you?"

I calmed him, and we began to discuss, as coolly as
we could, what we ought to do.

This is what we decided at last: to avoid disaster, I
should keep my appointment with Assya and explain
the situation to her frankly; Gagin undertook to remain
at home and not to show that he knew about her note.
We arranged to meet again in the evening.

"I rely on you entirely," said Gagin, squeezing my
hand. "Have pity on her and have pity on me. We shall
be leaving tomorrow, all the same," he added, getting
up, "because, you know, you will not marry Assya, will
you?"

"Give me time to think it over till the evening," I said.

"By all means, but you will not marry her."

He went away, and I flung myself on the sofa and
closed my eyes. My head was spinning: too many impressions had swept through it all at once. I was annoyed
with Gagin for his frankness; I was annoyed with Assya,
for her love elated and disturbed me at one and the same
time.

I could not understand what made her reveal everything to her brother. The inevitability of a quick and
almost instantaneous decision tormented me.

"Marry a girl of seventeen with her character? Why,
it's out of the question," I said, getting up.

15

At the appointed hour I had myself ferried across the
Rhine, and the first person to meet me on the opposite
bank was the boy who had been to see me in the morning. He was evidently waiting for me.

"From Fräulein Annette," he said in a whisper, and he handed me another note.

Assya informed me about a change in the place of our rendezvous. I was to come in an hour and a half, not to the shrine, but to Frau Luise's house. I was to knock downstairs and go up to the third floor.

" 'Yes' again?" the boy asked me.

" 'Yes,' " I repeated and walked along the bank of the Rhine.

There was no time to go home, and I did not want to wander about the streets. Outside the town wall there was a small garden with an awning for skittles and a skittle alley, and tables for beer drinkers. I went in there. A few elderly Germans were already having a game of skittles; the wooden balls rolled noisily along, and sometimes cries of approval could be heard. A pretty waitress with eyes red with weeping brought me a tankard of beer. I glanced at her face. She turned round quickly and walked away.

"Yes, yes," a fat, red-faced citizen who was sitting nearby said, "our Hannchen is very upset today: her fiancé has been conscripted into the Army." I looked at her: she had hidden herself away in a corner, her cheek resting on her hand. Tears were rolling one by one over her fingers. Someone called for beer; she brought him a mug and again returned to her place. Her grief affected me; I began to think of the impending rendezvous; but my thoughts were troubled, uncheerful thoughts. It wasn't with a light heart that I was going to this meeting. I was not going to give myself up to the joys of reciprocated love; I had to keep my word, to carry out a difficult duty. "You can't play with her"—those words of Gagin's had gone through my heart like arrows. And only three days ago in that same boat, carried along by the current, I had been thirsting for happiness, hadn't I? It had become possible, and I was hesitating, I was pushing it away, I *had* to push it away. Its suddenness disconcerted me. Assya herself, with her fiery temperament, her past, her upbringing—that fascinating but strange creature, I confess, frightened me. My feelings struggled within me for a long time. The appointed hour approached. "I can't marry her," I decided at last. "She'll never find out that I too have fallen in love with her."

I got up and, putting a thaler in the hand of poor Hannchen (she did not even thank me), went to Frau Luise's. Evening shadows were already falling, and the narrow strip of sky over the dark street crimsoned with the glow of sunset. I knocked quietly at the door. It was opened at once. I stepped over the threshold and found myself in complete darkness.

"This way," I heard an old woman's voice say. "You're expected."

I took two steps, groping my way, and someone's bony hand took mine.

"Is that you, Frau Luise?" I asked.

"Yes, it's me," the same voice replied. "It's me, my handsome young man."

The old woman took me up a steep staircase and stopped on the landing of the third floor. In the dim light that fell from a tiny window I saw the wrinkled face of the mayor's widow. A lascivious, sly smile distended her sunken lips and narrowed her dim little eyes. She pointed to the little door. I opened it with a convulsive movement of the hand and slammed it to behind me.

16

The small room which I entered was rather dark, and I did not at once see Assya. Wrapped in a long shawl, she was sitting on a chair near the window, turning away and hiding her head like a frightened bird. She was breathing rapidly and trembling all over. I felt indescribably sorry for her. I went up to her. She turned away her head still more.

"Miss Anna," I said.

She suddenly drew herself up, tried to look at me, but could not. I grasped her hand. It was cold, and lay like a dead hand in mine.

"I wished——" began Assya, trying to smile, but her pale lips did not obey her, "I wanted—— No, I can't," she said, and fell silent. And indeed her voice faltered at every word she uttered.

I sat down beside her. "Miss Anna," I repeated, and I too found myself unable to add anything more.

We were silent. I continued to hold her hand and to look at her. She shrank into herself as before, drew her breath with difficulty, and quietly kept biting her lower lip softly to prevent herself from crying, to keep back her rising tears. I looked at her: there was something touchingly helpless in her timid immobility: it was as though she had been so exhausted that she had hardly reached the chair and had just collapsed in it. My heart melted within me.

"Assya," I said, scarcely audibly.

She slowly raised her eyes to me. Oh, the look of a woman in love—who can describe it? They implored, those eyes, they threw themselves on my mercy, they questioned, they surrendered. I could not resist their fascination. A thin flame ran through my veins in red-hot needles; I bent down and I pressed my lips to her hand.

There was a tremulous sound, a sound like a broken sigh, and I felt the touch of a weak hand, trembling like a leaf on my hair. I raised my head and saw her face. How it had been suddenly transformed! The expression of fear had gone from it; her eyes seemed to look somewhere far, far away and drew me after them; her lips were slightly parted; her forehead had gone as white as marble; and her curls were tossed back as though the wind had blown them. I forgot everything. I drew her to me—her hand obeyed submissively; her whole body was drawn after her hand; her shawl slipped off her shoulders and her head lay gently on my breast, lay under my burning lips.

"I am yours," she whispered, scarcely audibly.

My hands were already round her waist, but suddenly the recollection of Gagin burst like a flash of lightning before me.

"What are we doing?" I cried and moved away convulsively. "Your brother—— You see, he knows everything. . . . He knows I am with you."

Assya sank down on the chair.

"Yes," I went on, getting up and moving away to the other end of the room, "your brother knows everything. I had to tell him everything."

"Had to?" she murmured faintly. She had evidently not been able to recover herself and hardly understood me.

"Yes, yes," I repeated with a kind of pitiless fury. "And you alone are to blame for it. You alone. Why did you betray our secret? Who forced you to tell everything to your brother? He came to see me today and he told me of what you said to him." Striding up and down the room, I tried not to look at Assya. "Now everything is at an end—everything."

Assya was about to get up from her chair.

"Please stay," I cried, "stay, I beg you! You are dealing with an honourable man—yes, an honourable man. But, for God's sake, why are you so agitated? You haven't noticed any change in me, have you? You see, I could not possibly hide anything from your brother when he came to see me today, could I?"

"What am I saying?" I thought to myself, and the idea that I was an immoral deceiver, that Gagin knew of our meeting, that everything had been misinterpreted, exposed, kept ringing in my head.

"I did not ask my brother to call on you," I heard Assya's frightened whisper. "He came of his own accord."

"See what you've done," I went on, "and now you want to go away . . ."

"Yes, I must go away," she murmured as softly as before. "I only asked you to come here to say good-bye to you."

"And do you think," I said, "that it will be easy for me to part from you?"

"But why did you tell my brother?" Assya repeated, with bewilderment.

"I tell you, I had to. If you had not given yourself away . . ."

"I locked myself in my room. I did not know that the landlady had another key."

This innocent apology on her lips at such a moment almost made me angry at the time, though now I cannot recall it without feeling deeply touched. Poor, honest, candid child!

"And now, now everything is finished!" I began again. "Everything! Now, we shall have to part." I stole a glance at Assya. Her face was colouring rapidly. She was, I sensed it, feeling both ashamed and frightened. I myself was pacing the room and talking as though in a fever. "You did not let the feeling develop which was beginning to ripen; you tore the ties that bound us together yourself; you had no confidence in me, you doubted me . . ."

While I was talking, Assya bent more and more forward, and suddenly she fell on her knees, dropped her head in her hands, and burst into sobs. I rushed up to her and tried to raise her, but she would not let me. I cannot stand women's tears: at the sight of them I at once lose my head.

"Miss Anna—Assya," I kept repeating, "please, I implore you, for God's sake, stop . . ." I took her hand again.

But to my utmost amazement, she suddenly jumped

to her feet, rushed with lightning rapidity to the door, and disappeared.

When, a few minutes later, Frau Luise came into the room, I was still standing in the middle of it, looking absolutely thunderstruck. I could not understand how this meeting could possibly have come to such a quick, such a stupid end, how it could end when I had not said even a hundredth part of what I wanted to say, what I had to say, when I had no idea myself how our meeting might end.

"Has the *Fräulein* gone?" Frau Luise asked me, raising her yellow eyebrows almost to her wig.

I stared at her like a fool—and went out of the room.

17

I got out of the town and struck out straight for the open country. Disappointment, furious disappointment, was gnawing at my heart. I heaped reproaches on myself. How was it I did not understand the reason that made Assya change the place of our meeting? How did I fail to realise what it must have cost her to go to that old woman? How could I let her go? Alone with her in that dimly lit room on the third floor, I had had the heart, I had had sufficient strength, to push her away from me, even to reproach her. . . . And now her image pursued me; I begged her forgiveness; the recollection of that pale face, those moist and timid eyes, the tumbled hair on her bent neck, the light touch of her head on my breast—seared me like red-hot iron. "I am yours," I heard her whisper. "I have acted like an honourable man," I assured myself. . . . It wasn't true! Did I really want such an ending? Was I really capable of parting from her? Could I bear to be without her? "Madman! Madman!" I kept repeating bitterly.

Meanwhile night was falling. I turned in the direction

of the house where Assya lived and began walking swiftly towards it.

18

Gagin came out to meet me. "Have you seen my sister?" he shouted to me while still some distance away.

"Isn't she at home?" I asked.

"No."

"Hasn't she come back?"

"No," Gagin went on, "I'm sorry, I could not restrain myself: I went to the shrine, in spite of our agreement, but she was not there. Didn't she come, then?"

"She was not at the shrine."

"And you haven't seen her?"

I had to admit that I had seen her.

"Where?"

"At Frau Luise's. I parted from her an hour ago," I added. "I was sure she had returned home."

"Let's wait," said Gagin.

We went into the house and sat down beside each other. We were silent. Both of us felt uncomfortable. We kept looking round incessantly, looked at the door, listening.

At last Gagin got up. "This is unheard of!" he exclaimed. "I'm awfully worried. She'll be the death of me, I tell you. Let's go and look for her."

We went out. It was quite dark outside.

"What did you talk to her about?" Gagin asked me, pulling his hat over his eyes.

"I only saw her for five minutes," I replied. "I talked to her as we agreed."

"Do you know what?" he said. "I think we'd better separate. We're sure to run across her much quicker that way. In any case, come back here in an hour."

19

I quickly went down from the vineyard and rushed into the town. I walked hurriedly through all the streets, looking in everywhere, even into Frau Luise's windows, and then went back to the Rhine and ran along the bank. From time to time I ran across women's figures, but Assya was nowhere to be seen. It was not bitter disappointment gnawing at my heart now. I was tormented by a secret fear, and it was not only fear that I felt— no, I was overwhelmed by a feeling of remorse, the most intense regret and love—yes, the most tender love. I wrung my hands; I called Assya by name amid the approaching darkness of the night, first under my breath, then louder and louder. I repeated a hundred times over that I loved her; I vowed never to part from her. I would have given everything in the world to hold her cold hand again, to hear again her soft voice, to see her again before me. She had been so near; she had come to me with her mind absolutely made up, in utter innocence of heart and feelings; she had brought me her untouched youth—and I did not press her to my breast. I had robbed myself of the bliss of watching her sweet face opening like a flower with joy and quiet rapture. This thought was driving me mad.

"Where can she have gone? What can she have done to herself?" I cried in an agony of helpless despair. Something white suddenly flashed by on the bank of the river. I knew the place. There, over the grave of a man who had been drowned seventy years before, stood a stone cross, half buried in the ground, with an old inscription. My heart sank. I rushed up to the cross: the white figure vanished. I shouted, "Assya!" I felt frightened myself by my wild cry—but there was no answer.

I decided to go back and see whether Gagin had found her.

As I hastily climbed up the vineyard path I saw a light in Assya's room. This calmed me a little.

I went up to the house; the front door was locked. I knocked. An unlighted window on the ground floor was cautiously opened and Gagin's head appeared.

"Found her?" I asked him.

"She has come back," he replied in a whisper. "She is in her room, undressing. Everything is all right."

"Thank God!" I cried in an unutterable outburst of joy. "Thank God! Now everything is all right. But, you know, we've still things to talk over."

"Another time," he said, quietly closing the window. "Another time. Now, good-bye."

"Till tomorrow," I said. "Tomorrow everything will be settled."

"Good-bye," Gagin repeated. The window was closed.

I nearly knocked at the window. At that moment I wanted to tell Gagin that I'd like to ask him for his sister's hand. But such a proposal at such a time . . . "Till tomorrow," I thought. "Tomorrow I shall be happy."

Tomorrow I shall be happy. . . . Happiness has no tomorrow; it has no yesterday, either; it does not remember the past; it does not think of the future; it has the present, and that too, not a day, but an instant.

I do not remember how I got to S. It was not my legs that carried me, it was not a boat that took me across: I was being borne by broad, strong wings. I went past the bush where a nightingale was singing; I stopped and listened a long time; I could not help feeling that it sang of my love and my happiness.

When, on the following day, I was approaching the familiar little house I was struck by one circumstance: all its windows were wide open, and the door too was wide open. Bits of paper were lying about in front of the door. A maid with a broom appeared behind the door. I approached her.

"They've gone!" she blurted out, before I had time to ask her whether Gagin was at home.

"Gone?" I repeated. "What do you mean? Where?"

"They went away this morning at six o'clock, sir, and did not say where. But wait a minute—aren't you Mr. N.?"

"I am Mr. N."

"The mistress has a letter for you." The maid went upstairs and returned with a letter. "Here it is, sir."

"Why, it's impossible. . . . How can it be?" I began. The maid stared blankly at me and began to sweep up.

I opened the letter. Gagin had written it to me; there was not a line from Assya. He began by saying that he begged me not to be angry with him at their sudden departure; he was sure that on mature consideration I would approve of his decision. He could find no other solution to a situation which might become difficult and dangerous. "Last night," he wrote, "while we were both waiting in silence for Assya, I became finally convinced of the necessity of separation. There are prejudices I respect; I realise that it's impossible for you to marry Assya. She has told me everything; it was for the sake of her peace of mind that I had to give in to her repeated, emphatic requests."

At the end of the letter he expressed his regret that our acquaintance should have come to an end so quickly, wished me every happiness, shook my hand warmly, and implored me not to attempt to look for them.

"What prejudices?" I cried, as though he could hear me. "What right had he to steal her away from me?" I clutched at my head.

The maid began calling loudly for her mistress; her alarm forced me to take hold of myself. I was seized by one single thought: to find them, to find them at all costs. It was impossible to accept this blow, to resign myself to such an ending. I found out from the landlady that they had embarked on a steamer at six o'clock in the morning and had sailed down the Rhine. I went to the steamship booking office. There I was told that they had taken tickets for Cologne. I went home, intending to pack my things at once and sail after them. I had to walk past Frau Luise's house again. Suddenly I heard someone calling me. I raised my head, and at the window of the same room where I had met Assya the day before, I saw the mayor's widow. She smiled her loathsome smile and called me. I turned away and was about to walk past, but she shouted after me that she had something for me. These words made me stop, and I went into the house. How can I describe my feelings when I saw that little room again? . . .

"Actually," the old woman began, showing me a little note, "I oughtn't to have given you this unless you had come to see me of your own accord, but you're such a nice young man—take it."

I took the note.

On a tiny scrap of paper I read the following words, hastily scribbled in pencil: "Good-bye, we shall not see each other again. It isn't out of pride that I am going away—no, I can't do otherwise. Yesterday when I was crying before you, if you had said one word to me, only one word, I should have remained. You did not say it. It seems it is better so. . . . Good-bye forever!"

One word . . . Oh, madman that I was! That word—I had been repeating it the night before with tears, I had been wasting it on the wind, I had kept saying it

in the empty fields; but I did not say it to her; I did not
tell her I loved her. And indeed I could not have said
it at the time. When I met her in that fateful room I
still had no clear realisation of my love; it had not awakened even when I was sitting with her brother in that
senseless, oppressive, and painful silence. It flared up in
me with irresistible force only a few moments later when,
frightened by the possibility of disaster, I began looking
for and calling her, but then it was already too late.
"Why, that's impossible," I shall be told. I don't know
whether it is impossible or not. I only know that it is
the truth. Assya would not have gone away if there had
been a hint of coquetry about her and if her position
had not been a false one. She could not endure what
every other woman would have endured: I had not understood that. My evil genius had stopped the avowal
on my lips at my last meeting with Gagin at the darkened window, and the last thread I could have caught
at snapped in my hands.

The same day I returned with my packed trunk to
the town of L. and sailed for Cologne. I remember, the
steamer was already leaving the landing stage and I was
bidding farewell to those streets, to all the places which
I should never forget, when I caught sight of Hannchen.
She was sitting on a bench near the bank of the river.
Her face was pale but not sad. A young, handsome lad
was standing beside her, laughing and telling her something; and on the other side of the Rhine my little Madonna was peering as sadly as ever from behind the dark
foliage of the old ash tree.

22

In Cologne I came upon the tracks of the Gagins. I
found out that they had gone to London. I went after
them, but in London all my attempts to find them

failed. I did not want to give in; I persisted in my obstinate search for a long time; but in the end I had to give up the hope of finding them.

And I never saw them again, I never saw Assya. Vague rumours reached me about her brother, but she had disappeared from my life forever. I don't even know whether she is still alive. One day a few years later in a railway carriage abroad I caught a glimpse of a woman whose face reminded me vividly of a face I would never forget, but I was most probably deceived by a chance likeness. Assya remained in my memory the same young girl as I had known her at the best time of my life, as I last saw her, leaning against the back of a low wooden chair.

I must confess, though, I did not mourn long for her; I even found that fate had ordered everything for the best by not uniting me to Assya; I comforted myself with the reflection that I should probably not have been happy with such a wife. I was young then, and the future, the brief, all too swiftly passing future, seemed endless to me. Was it not possible, I thought, that what had happened to me would happen to me again, and that it would be much better and much more beautiful? I knew many women, but the feeling Assya had aroused in me, that intense, tender, deep feeling, was never repeated. No! For me no eyes have taken the place of those which once gazed at me with love; no heart, pressing against my breast, ever awakened such a joyous and sweet emotion in my heart! Condemned to the solitude of an old bachelor, I drag out the last dull years of my life, guarding as a sacred thing her notes and the dried-up flower which she threw me once from the window. It has still a faint fragrance, while the hand which gave it to me, the hand I had only once pressed to my lips, has perhaps been mouldering in the grave for a long time. . . . And I myself—what has become of me? What has been left of me, of those blissful and anxious days, of those winged hopes and aspirations? Even a light exhalation from an insignificant plant outlives all the joys and all the sorrows of man—outlives man himself.

1857

FIRST LOVE

Dedicated to P. V. Annenkov

THE visitors had left long ago. The clock struck half past twelve. Only the host, Sergey Nikolayevich, and Vladimir Petrovich were left in the room.

The host rang and ordered the remains of the supper to be cleared away. "So that's agreed, then," he said, settling himself more deeply in his armchair and lighting a cigar. "Each of us is to tell the story of his first love. It's your turn, Sergey Nikolayevich."

Sergey Nikolayevich, a rotund little man with a chubby face and fair hair, glanced first at his host, then raised his eyes to the ceiling. "I had no first love," he said at last. "I started straight with the second."

"How was that?"

"Quite simple. I was eighteen when I first took an interest in a very charming young girl, but I did this as if it were nothing new to me; and it was just like that that I afterwards flirted with others. Strictly speaking, I fell in love for the first and last time with my nurse when I was six years old. But that was a very long time ago. The details of our relationship have been blotted out from my memory, and even if I remembered them, how could they possibly interest anyone?"

"So what are we to do?" began the host. "There's nothing interesting in my first love, either. I did not fall in love with anyone before I met my wife—and everything went swimmingly with us: our parents arranged the match, we very soon fell in love with each other and got married without wasting much time. My tale is soon told. I don't mind admitting, gentlemen, that when I raised the question of first love, I was relying on you—I won't say old, but not such young bachelors, either. Won't *you*, Vladimir Petrovich, entertain us with some story?"

"My first love certainly cannot be said to be quite ordinary," Vladimir Petrovich, a man of about forty, with greying black hair, replied a little hesitantly.

"Oh," the host and Sergey Nikolayevich cried in one voice, "so much the better! Tell us about it."

"By all means. Or—no! I won't tell it to you; I'm not very good at telling stories. I'm afraid my stories are either too short and dry or too long and unconvincing. If you don't mind, I'd much rather write down all I can remember and read it to you."

At first his friends would not agree, but Vladimir Petrovich insisted on having it his own way. Two weeks later they met again, and Vladimir Petrovich kept his word.

This was what he had written down.

1

I was sixteen at the time. It happened in the summer of 1833.

I was living in Moscow with my parents. They used to take a country house for the summer near the Kaluga

Toll Gate, opposite the Neskoochny Park. I was preparing for the university, but I did very little work and was in no particular hurry.

No one interfered with my freedom. I did what I liked, especially after parting with my last tutor, a Frenchman, who could never get used to the idea that he had dropped like a bomb (*comme une bombe*) into Russia, and he used to lie about in bed for days on end with a resentful expression on his face. My father treated me with good-humoured indifference; my mother scarcely paid any attention to me, although she had no other children: other worries occupied her completely. My father, who was still young and very handsome, had married her for money; she was ten years older than he. My mother's life was far from happy: she was in a state of constant irritation and was always jealous and bad-tempered, though never in my father's presence—she was terrified of him—while his attitude to her was severe, cold, and aloof. I have never seen a man more exquisitely calm, more self-possessed, or more despotic.

I shall never forget the first weeks I spent in the country. The weather was lovely; we left Moscow on the ninth of May, St. Nicholas's Day. I used to go for walks either in the garden of our country house or in the Neskoochny Park or on the other side of the toll gate; I used to take some book with me—Kaydanov's *Primer*, for instance—but I did not open it very often; I preferred much more to recite poetry, and I knew a great many poems by heart; my blood was in a ferment, and my heart ached—so sweetly and so foolishly; I was always expecting something to happen; I was in a state of constant dread of something; and I was full of wonder and seemed always to be seeking something; my imagination fluttered, and the same ideas winged their way swiftly like martins round a bell tower at dawn; I would fall into a reverie, I would be sad, and I would even cry; but through the tears and through the sadness, inspired by some melodious verse or the beauty of the evening, there always shot up, like the grass in springtime, a joyous feeling of young, surging life.

I had a horse; I used to saddle it myself and go for long rides into the country, breaking into a gallop and imagining myself a knight at a tournament (how gaily the wind whistled in my ears!)—or, turning my face towards the sky, received its shining azure light into my wide-open soul.

I remember that at that time the image of woman, the vision of a woman's love, hardly ever took any definite shape in my mind; but in everything I thought, in everything I felt, there was hidden a half-conscious, shy presentiment of something new, unutterably sweet, feminine.

This presentiment, this expectation, pervaded my whole being: I breathed it; it ran through my veins with every drop of blood. . . . It was soon to be fulfilled.

Our country place consisted of a wooden manor house with columns and two one-storied cottages; in the cottage on the left was a very small factory for the manufacture of cheap wallpaper; I used to go over there quite frequently to watch about a dozen thin and dishevelled boys with pinched faces, in long greasy smocks, who kept jumping onto wooden levers and pressing them down onto the square blocks of the presses and in this way by the weight of their feeble bodies, stamp the brightly coloured patterns on the wallpaper. The cottage on the right stood empty and was to let. One day, three weeks after the ninth of May, the shutters of this cottage were opened and women's faces appeared in the windows. Some family must have moved in. I remember that that same day at dinner my mother asked the butler who our new neighbours were, and hearing the name of Princess Zasyekin first remarked, not without a certain note of respect, "Oh, a princess," and then added, "A poor one, I expect."

"They arrived in three cabs, ma'am," observed the butler, handing her a dish deferentially. "I don't think they have a carriage of their own, ma'am. Their furniture is of the cheapest kind."

"I see," said my mother. "So much the better."

My father gave her a cold look, and she fell silent.

And indeed Princess Zasyekin could not have been a rich woman; the cottage she had rented was so dilapidated, so small, and so low that people who were even moderately well off would not have consented to live in it. However, at the time I paid no attention to it. The princely title had little effect on me; I had just been reading Schiller's *The Robbers*.

2

I was in the habit of wandering about our garden every evening with a gun, looking for crows. I had for a long time felt a detestation for these wary, predatory, and cunning birds. On the day I am speaking of I also went into the garden, and, having walked through all the avenues without result (the crows knew me and only cawed harshly from afar), I chanced to come near the low fence which separated *our* property from the narrow strip of garden which ran to the right behind the cottage and which belonged to it. I was walking along with my eyes fixed on the ground. Suddenly I heard voices. I looked across the fence and stood rooted to the spot. A curious sight met my eyes.

A few paces from me, in a clearing among the green raspberry bushes, stood a tall, slender girl in a striped pink dress with a white kerchief on her head; she was surrounded by four young men and she was tapping them in turn on the forehead with those small grey flowers whose name I do not know, though they are very well known to children: these flowers form little bags and burst with a pop when struck against anything hard.

The young men presented their foreheads so eagerly, and there was in the movements of the young girl (I saw her in profile) something so fascinating, imperious, caressing, mocking, and charming, that I nearly cried out with wonder and delight and would, I believe, have given everything in the world at that moment to have those lovely fingers tap me on the forehead too. My gun slipped to the grass; I forgot everything; my eyes devoured this graceful figure, the slender neck, the beautiful arms, the slightly untidy fair hair under the white kerchief, and the half-closed, intelligent eye, the eyelashes, the delicate cheek beneath them.

"I say, young man," said a voice suddenly near me, "is it proper to stare like that at young ladies you do not know?"

I started, thunderstruck. Near me, on the other side of the fence, stood a man with close-cropped black hair, looking ironically at me. At that very moment the young girl too turned towards me. I saw a pair of enormous grey eyes in a vivacious, lively face, and this face suddenly quivered and laughed; her white teeth flashed and her eyebrows lifted in a rather amusing fashion. I flushed, snatched up my gun from the ground, and, pursued by ringing though not unkind laughter, fled to my room, flung myself on the bed, and covered my face with my hands. My heart leapt inside me; I was very ashamed and happy; I felt tremendously excited.

After a short rest I brushed my hair, tidied myself, and went downstairs to tea. The image of the young girl floated before me; my heart was no longer leaping but seemed to contract delightfully.

"What's the matter with you?" my father asked me suddenly. "Shot a crow?"

I was about to tell him everything, but stopped short and merely smiled to myself. As I was going to bed, without knowing myself why, I spun round three times on one foot, put pomade on my hair, got into bed, and

slept soundly all night. Before morning I woke up for a
moment, raised my head, looked round me in ecstasy,
and—fell asleep again.

3

"How can I get to know them?" was my first thought
when I woke in the morning.

Before breakfast I went for a walk in the garden, but
did not go too near the fence and saw no one. After
breakfast I walked several times up and down the street
before the cottage and peered into the windows from a
distance. I thought I could see *her* face behind the curtain, and I walked away quickly in a panic. "Still, I
must get to know them," I thought, walking aimlessly
about the sandy stretch before the Neskoochny Park.
"But how? That is the question." I recalled the minutest
details of yesterday's meeting: for some reason I had a
most vivid recollection of the way she had laughed at
me. But while I worried and made all sorts of plans, fate
was already doing her best to gratify my desire.

While I was out, my mother had received from her
new neighbour a letter on grey paper, sealed with the
sort of brown wax that is used only in official post-office
notices and on the corks of bottles of cheap wine. In
this letter, illiterate and written in a slovenly hand, the
princess begged my mother to do her a great favour: my
mother, the princess wrote, was on very intimate terms
with people in high positions on whom depended the
fortunes of herself and her children, for she was engaged
in a number of very important lawsuits. "I rite to you,"
she wrote, "as one noblewoman to another, and becos
of that I am pleesed to make use of this oportunity." In
conclusion she asked my mother's permission to call on
her. I found my mother in a disagreeable mood: my
father was not at home, and she had no one to consult.
Not to reply to a "noblewoman," and a princess into the

bargain, was impossible. But my mother was at a loss as to how to reply. To write a note in French was, she thought, inappropriate, while she was not particularly good at Russian spelling herself. She knew this and did not want to compromise herself. She was therefore glad of my return and at once told me to go round to the princess and explain to her by word of mouth that she was always ready to be of service to Her Highness as far as was in her power and she asked the princess to do her the honour of calling on her at one o'clock. The unexpectedly rapid fulfilment of my secret desires both delighted and frightened me; however, I did not show any sign of the confusion that overcame me and went first to my room to put on my new cravat and frock coat: at home I still went about in a tunic and a turned-down collar, although I was sick and tired of them.

4

In the narrow and untidy passage of the cottage, which I entered shaking nervously all over, I was met by a grey-headed old servant with a face the colour of dark copper, surly little pig's eyes and deep furrows on his forehead, and temples such as I had never seen in my life before. He was carrying a plate with a clean-picked herring bone on it, and, shutting the door leading into another room with his foot, said in an abrupt tone of voice, "What do you want?"

"Is Princess Zasyekin at home?" I asked.

"Vonifaty!" a woman's cracked voice screamed from behind the door.

The manservant turned his back on me without a word, revealing the extremely threadbare back of his livery, with a solitary rusty crested button, and, putting the plate down on the floor, went away.

"Have you been to the police station?" the same

woman's voice repeated. The man muttered something in reply. "What? Someone's come?" I heard her say again. "The young gentleman from next door? Well, ask him in."

"Will you step into the drawing room, sir?" said the servant, reappearing before me again and picking up the plate from the floor.

I put myself to rights and went into the "drawing room."

I found myself in a small and not particularly tidy room with rather shoddy furniture which seemed to have been arranged in a hurry. By the window, in an armchair with a broken arm, sat a woman of about fifty, bare-headed and rather plain, in an old green dress with a striped worsted kerchief round her neck. She glanced at me with her small black eyes.

I went up to her and bowed.

"Have I the honour to address Princess Zasyekin?"

"I am Princess Zasyekin. Are you the son of Mr. W.?"

"Yes, ma'am, I am. I have come to you with a message from my mother."

"Sit down, please. Vonifaty, where are my keys? You haven't seen them, have you?"

I told Princess Zasyekin my mother's reply to her note. She listened to me, drumming on the window-sill with her thick, red fingers, and when I had finished, she stared at me once more.

"Very good, I shall certainly call," she said at last. "But, gracious me, how young you are! How old are you, may I ask?"

"S-sixteen," I replied with an involuntary stammer.

The princess pulled out of her pocket some greasy papers covered with writing, raised them to her nose, and began looking through them. "An excellent age," she said suddenly, turning to me and fidgeting in her chair. "Please make yourself at home. We're ordinary people here."

"A bit too ordinary," I thought to myself, glancing with a feeling of involuntary disgust at her unprepossessing person.

At that moment another door was flung open and in the doorway there appeared the girl I had seen in the garden the previous evening. She raised her hand, and a mocking smile appeared for a moment on her face.

"And here's my daughter," said the princess, pointing to her with her elbow. "Zeena, darling, this is the son of our neighbour, Mr. W. What's your name, may I ask?"

"V-Vladimir," I replied, getting up and stuttering in my excitement.

"And your patronymic?"

"Petrovich."

"I see. I used to know a police commissioner once. He was also called Vladimir Petrovich. Vonifaty, don't look for the keys—they are in my pocket."

The young girl continued to look at me with the same mocking smile, screwing up her eyes slightly and putting her head a little on one side.

"I've already met M'sieu Woldemar," she began. (The silvery sound of her voice ran through me with a kind of delightful shiver.) "You don't mind me calling you that, do you?"

"Why, of course not," I murmured.

"Where was that?" asked the princess.

The young princess did not answer. "You haven't got anything special to do now, have you?" she asked, without taking her eyes off me.

"Why, no, ma'am."

"Would you like to help me wind some wool? Follow me, please. This way—to my room." She nodded to me and left the drawing room. I followed her.

In the room we entered, the furniture was a little better and arranged with more taste. At that moment, though, I was quite unable to notice anything: I moved as though in a dream and was overwhelmed by an intense feeling of happiness verging on imbecility.

The young princess sat down, took a skein of red wool, and, motioning me to a chair opposite, carefully untied the skein and put it across my hands. All this she did in silence with a kind of amused deliberation and with the same bright, sly smile on her slightly parted lips. She began to wind the wool round a bent card and then suddenly dazzled me with so swift and radiant a glance that I could not help dropping my eyes. When her eyes, mostly half closed, opened wide, her face was completely transformed, as though flooded with light.

"What did you think of me yesterday, M'sieu Woldemar?" she asked, after a short pause. "I expect you must have thought me dreadful."

"Why, I—er—Princess—I—I—didn't think anything—how—could—I?" I replied in confusion.

"Listen," she said. "You don't know me yet. I'm an awfully strange person. I want people to tell me the truth always. You are sixteen, I hear, and I am twenty-one. You see, I'm very much older than you, and that is why you must always tell me the truth—and," she added, "do what I tell you. Look at me! Why don't you look at me?"

I was more confused than ever, but I did raise my eyes and look at her. She smiled, not as before, but approvingly.

"Look at me," she said, dropping her voice caressingly. "I do not mind it at all. I like your face. I have a feeling we shall be friends. And do you like me?" she added slyly.

"Princess——" I began.

"First of all, you must call me Zinaida Alexandrovna, and, second, what a strange habit children"—she quickly corrected herself—"young men have of not saying frankly what they feel. That's all very well for grown-ups. You do like me, don't you?"

Though I was very pleased that she should be talking so frankly to me, I was a little hurt. I wanted to show her that she was not dealing with a mere boy, and, assuming as serious and nonchalant an air as I could, I said, "Of course I like you very much, Zinaida Alexandrovna. I have no wish to conceal it."

She shook her head slowly. "Have you a tutor?" she asked suddenly.

"No, I haven't had one for ages." I was telling a lie: it was not a month since I had parted with my Frenchman.

"Oh, I see, you're quite grown up." She rapped me lightly over the fingers. "Hold your hands straight!"

And she busily began winding the ball of wool. I took advantage of the fact that she did not raise her eyes to examine her at first stealthily and then more and more boldly. I thought her face was even more lovely than on the previous day: everything in it was so delicate, intelligent, and charming. She was sitting with her back to the window, which was covered with a white blind: the sunshine streaming through the blind shed a soft light on her fine, golden hair, her virginal throat, her sloping shoulders, and her calm, tender bosom. I gazed at her—and how dear and near she was already to me! I couldn't help feeling that I had known her a long, long time and that before her I had known nothing and had not lived. She was wearing a dark, rather old and worn dress with an apron; I would gladly have caressed every fold of that dress and that apron. The tips of her shoes peeped from under her skirt: I could have knelt in adoration to those shoes! "And here I am, sitting in front of her," I thought. "I have made her acquaintance. God! What happiness!" I almost leapt from my chair in ecstasy, but, in fact, all I did was to swing my legs a little, like a child eating a sweet.

I was as happy as a fish in water. I could have stayed in that room forever. I could have never left it.

Her eyelids were slowly raised and once more her bright eyes shone caressingly upon me, and again she smiled. "How you do look at me!" she said slowly, and she shook a finger at me.

I blushed. "She understands everything; she sees everything," flashed across my mind. "And how could she fail to understand it all and see it all?"

Suddenly there was a clatter in the next room—a sabre clanked.

"Zeena," the old princess cried from the drawing room, "Belovzorov has brought you a kitten!"

"A kitten!" cried Zinaida, and, rising impetuously from her chair, she threw the ball of wool into my lap and ran out of the room.

I too got up and, leaving the skein and the ball of wool on the window-sill, went out into the drawing room and stopped dead in amazement: a tabby kitten was lying in the middle of the room with its paws in the air; Zinaida was on her knees before it, cautiously lifting up its tiny head. Near the old princess, almost filling the entire space between the two windows, I saw a fair-haired and curly-headed stalwart young hussar officer, with a pink face and protruding eyes.

"What a funny little thing!" Zinaida was saying. "And its eyes aren't grey—they're green—and what enormous ears he's got! Thank you, Victor! How sweet of you."

The hussar, whom I recognised as one of the young men I had seen the previous evening, smiled and bowed, clicking his spurs and clinking the chain of his sabre.

"You were pleased to say yesterday that you'd like to have a tabby kitten with large ears, so I—I got one. Your word is law." And he bowed again.

The kitten miaowed feebly and began to sniff the floor.

"It's hungry!" cried Zinaida. "Vonifaty, Sonia, bring some milk."

The maid, in an old yellow dress and with a faded kerchief round her neck, came in with a saucer of milk in her hands and set it before the kitten. The kitten gave a start, screwed up its eyes, and began to lap.

"What a pink little tongue it's got!" observed Zinaida, bending her head almost to the floor and looking at the kitten sideways under its very nose.

The kitten drank its fill and began purring and moving its paws up and down finickingly. Zinaida got up and, turning to the maid, said in an indifferent voice, "Take it away."

"Allow me to kiss your hand in return for the kitten," said the hussar, flashing his teeth and flexing his whole powerful frame, tightly encased in a new uniform.

"Both of them," replied Zinaida, and she held out her hands to him.

While he kissed them, she looked at me over his shoulder.

I stood stock-still and did not know whether to laugh, to say something, or to remain silent. Suddenly I caught sight of our footman, Fyodor, through the open passage door. He was making signs to me. Mechanically I went out to him.

"What are you doing here?" I asked.

"Your mother has sent for you," he said in a whisper. "She is angry because you haven't come back with the answer."

"Why, have I been here long?"

"Over an hour, sir."

"Over an hour!" I repeated involuntarily and, returning to the drawing room, I began to take my leave, bowing and scraping my feet.

"Where are you off to?" asked the young princess, glancing at me from behind the hussar.

"I'm afraid I have to go home. . . . So I am to say," I added, turning to the old woman, "that you will call on us about two o'clock?"

"Yes, do say that, dear boy." The old princess hurriedly reached for a snuffbox and took the snuff so noisily that it almost made me jump. "Yes, do say that," she repeated, blinking tearfully and groaning.

I bowed once more, turned, and walked out of the room with that uncomfortable sensation in my back which a very young man feels when he knows he is being watched from behind.

"Mind you come and see us again, M'sieu Woldemar!" cried Zinaida, and laughed again.

"Why is she always laughing?" I thought as I was returning home, accompanied by Fyodor, who said nothing to me, but walked behind me with a disapproving air. My mother scolded me and wondered what I could have been doing so long at the princess's. I made no answer and went off to my room. Suddenly I felt very sad. I tried hard not to cry. I was jealous of the hussar.

5

The old princess paid a visit to my mother as she had promised. My mother did not like her. I was not present at their interview, but at dinner my mother told my father that this Princess Zasyekin struck her as *"une femme très vulgaire,"* that she had wearied her out with her requests to intercede on her behalf with Prince Sergey, that she seemed to be involved in some lawsuits and shady business deals—*des vilaines affaires d'argent* —and that she must be a thoroughly unpleasant woman. My mother, however, added that she had asked her and her daughter to dinner the next day (hearing the words "and her daughter," I buried my nose in my plate), because she was, after all, a neighbour and a titled woman. Upon which my father informed my mother that he now remembered who this lady was; that when he was a young man he had known the late Prince Zasyekin, a highly cultured but frivolous and ridiculous man; that in society he was known as *"le Parisien"* because he had lived in Paris for a long time; that he had been very rich but had gambled away his entire fortune, and for some unknown reason, probably for money—"though he could have made a much better choice," my father added with a cold smile—married the daughter of some departmental clerk and after his marriage had begun speculating and completely ruined himself.

"I do hope she's not going to ask for a loan," observed my mother.

"I should not be in the least surprised," my father said calmly. "Does she speak French?"

"Very badly."

"I see. However, that doesn't matter. I think you said you'd also asked her daughter? Someone was telling me that she was a very charming and well-educated girl."

"Oh? Then she can't take after her mother."

"No, nor after her father," said my father. "He was cultured too, but a fool."

My mother sighed and sank into thought. My father was silent. I felt very uncomfortable during this conversation.

After dinner I went into the garden, but without my gun. I vowed not to go near the "Zasyekin garden," but an irresistible force drew me there, and I was not disappointed. For I had hardly reached the fence when I caught sight of Zinaida. This time she was alone. She had a book in her hand and was walking slowly along the path. She did not notice me.

I nearly let her pass by, but suddenly recollected myself and coughed. She turned round but did not stop. With her hand she pushed back the broad blue ribbon of her round straw hat, looked at me, smiled gently, and again dropped her eyes to the book.

I took off my cap and, after hesitating a little, walked away with a heavy heart. *"Que suis je pour elle?"* I thought (goodness only knows why!) in French.

Familiar footsteps sounded behind me: I looked

round—my father was coming towards me with his light, quick step. "Is that the young princess?" he asked me.

"Yes."

"Do you know her?"

"I saw her this morning at the old princess's."

My father stopped and, turning sharply on his heels, went back. Drawing level with Zinaida, he bowed to her courteously. She too bowed to him—not without some surprise, though—and lowered her book. I saw how she followed him with her eyes. My father always dressed very exquisitely and simply and in a style all his own; but never before had his figure struck me as more elegant, and never before had his grey hat sat more handsomely on his barely perceptibly thinning hair.

I walked towards Zinaida, but she did not even glance at me. She raised her book again and walked away.

6

I spent the whole of that evening and the following morning in a state of stunned misery. I remember I tried to work and opened Kaydanov, but the clearly printed lines and pages of the celebrated textbook flashed before my eyes in vain. A dozen times over I read the words: "Julius Caesar was distinguished for martial valour," but did not understand a word and threw the book down. Before dinner I pomaded my hair again and again put on my new coat and cravat.

"What's this for?" asked my mother. "You're not a university student yet, and heaven knows whether you'll ever pass your examinations. Besides, how long is it since I bought you your tunic? You're not going to throw it away, are you?"

"We're going to have visitors," I whispered almost in despair.

"What nonsense! Visitors indeed!"

I had to give in. I changed the coat for my tunic, but I did not take off the cravat.

The princess and her daughter arrived half an hour before dinner. The old woman had thrown a yellow shawl over the green dress in which I had seen her before and put on an old-fashioned bonnet with flame-coloured ribbons. She began talking at once about her bills of exchange, sighing and complaining about her poverty, and went on and on about it without apparently feeling in the least humiliated: she took snuff as noisily as before and fidgeted and turned about on her chair as freely as ever. It never seemed to occur to her that she was a princess. Zinaida, on the other hand, carried herself very gravely, even haughtily, like a true princess. An expression of cold immobility and dignity appeared on her face, and she seemed quite a different person to me; I could discover no trace of the glances, the smiles I knew so well, though in this new guise, too, she seemed beautiful to me. She wore a light *barège* dress with a pale blue pattern; her hair fell in long curls down her cheeks, in the English fashion. This way of doing her hair went well with the cold expression on her face. My father sat beside her during dinner and entertained his neighbour with his usual exquisite and calm courtesy. From time to time he glanced at her, and she too looked at him now and again, but so strangely, almost with hostility. Their conversation was carried on in French; I remember I was surprised by the purity of Zinaida's pronunciation. The old princess was, as before, not in the least put out at dinner, eating a lot and praising the dishes. My mother was obviously bored by her and answered her with a sort of melancholy disdain. Now and then my father frowned a little.

My mother did not like Zinaida either. "Very proud, isn't she?" she said the next day. "And what has she to be so proud about, I wonder—*avec sa mine de grisette?*"

"You've evidently never seen any grisettes," observed my father.

"No, I haven't, thank God!"

"Yes indeed, thank God—only how on earth can you form an opinion of them?"

Zinaida had paid no attention whatsoever to me. Soon after dinner the old princess began to take her leave.

"I shall count on your good offices, madam, and on yours too, sir," she said in a singsong voice to my mother and father. "I'm afraid there's nothing we can do about it. We've had our good times, but they're gone, so here I am, a Highness," she added with an unpleasant laugh, "but what's the use of a title if you're starving?"

My father bowed to her respectfully and saw her off to the front door. There I stood, in my short tunic, staring at the floor as though under sentence of death. Zinaida's treatment of me had crushed me completely. Imagine my surprise when, as she passed by me, she said in a rapid whisper and with the former affectionate look in her eyes, "Come and see us at eight o'clock. Do you hear? Without fail!"

I did not know what to make of it, but she was already gone, throwing a white scarf over her head.

7

Punctually at eight o'clock, in my tail coat, with a raised quiff of hair, I entered the passage of the cottage where the princess lived. The old servant scowled at me and got up unwillingly from the bench. I could hear gay voices in the drawing room. I opened the door and stepped back in astonishment. In the middle of the room, on a chair, stood the young princess, holding a man's hat in front of her; about half a dozen men crowded round the chair. They were trying to put their hands into the hat, while she kept raising it and shaking it violently.

On seeing me she cried, "Wait, wait, another visitor!

I must give him a ticket too," and, jumping lightly off the chair, she took me by the cuff of my coat. "Come along," she said. "What are you standing there for? Gentlemen, let me introduce you: this is M'sieu Woldemar, our neighbour's son. And these," she added, turning to me and pointing to each one of her guests in turn, "are Count Malevsky, Dr. Lushin, the poet Maydanov, retired Captain Nirmatsky, and Belovzorov, the hussar, whom you have met already. I hope you will all be good friends."

I was so overcome with confusion that I did not even bow to anyone; in Dr. Lushin I recognised the same dark man who had put me to shame so mercilessly in the garden; the others I did not know.

"Count," Zinaida went on, "write out a ticket for M'sieu Woldemar."

"That's not fair," the count replied with a slight Polish accent. "He did not play forfeits with us."

The count was a very handsome and fashionably dressed, dark-haired young man with expressive brown eyes, a small, narrow white nose, and a thin moustache above a tiny mouth.

"It's not fair," repeated Belovzorov and the gentleman who had been introduced as a retired captain, a man in his forties, hideously pock-marked, with frizzy hair like a Negro's, bandy-legged, and dressed in a military coat without epaulettes, which he wore unbuttoned.

"Write out the ticket, I tell you," repeated the princess. "What is this? A mutiny? M'sieu Woldemar is here for the first time, and today the rules do not apply to him. Don't grumble, and write it out! That is my wish."

The count shrugged his shoulders, but, bowing his head obediently, picked up a pen in his white, beringed fingers, tore off a scrap of paper, and began writing on it.

"Let me at least explain to M'sieu Woldemar what this is all about," began Lushin in a sarcastic voice, "or else he'll be completely at a loss. You see, young man, we are playing a game of forfeits. The princess has to pay a forfeit, and he who draws the lucky ticket will have the right to kiss her hand. Do you understand what I have told you?"

I just glanced at him and continued to stand like one in a trance, while the young princess again jumped on a chair and once more began shaking the hat. They all moved up to her, and I with the rest.

"Maydanov," said the princess to the tall young man with a thin face, shortsighted little eyes, and extremely long black hair, "you, as a poet, ought to be magnanimous and give up your ticket to M'sieu Woldemar so that he may have two chances instead of one."

But Maydanov shook his head and tossed back his hair. I put my hand into the hat after all the others and unfolded my ticket. Good Lord, what did I feel when I saw on it the word *kiss!*

"Kiss!" I cried involuntarily.

"Bravo, he won!" the young princess cried. "I am so glad!" She got off the chair, looked into my eyes, and gave me such a bright and sweet look that my heart turned over within me. "Are you glad?" she asked me.

"Me?" I murmured.

"Sell me your ticket," Belovzorov suddenly blurted out in my ear. "I'll give you a hundred roubles."

I answered the hussar with so indignant a look that Zinaida clapped her hands, while Lushin cried, "Stout fellow! But," he added, "as master of ceremonies, I am obliged to see that all the rules are kept. M'sieu Woldemar, go down on one knee! That's our rule."

Zinaida stood in front of me with her head a little on one side, as though she wished to get a better look at me, and held out her hand to me with an air of great solemnity. Everything went black before my eyes; I was about to go down on one knee, but sank on both and touched Zinaida's fingers so awkwardly with my lips that I scratched the tip of my nose on her nail.

"Splendid!" cried Lushin, and helped me to get up.

The game of forfeits went on. Zinaida made me sit down beside her. The forfeits she thought of! She had, among other things, to represent a statue, and she chose the hideous Nirmatsky as her pedestal, told him to lie down on the floor and to lower his head to his chest. The laughter never ceased for a moment. All this noise and uproar, all this unceremonious, almost riotous gaiety, all this strange relationship with unknown persons, simply went to my head, for I had been brought up soberly, in the seclusion of a staid country house. I was intoxicated, as though with wine. I began laughing at the top of my voice and talking a lot of nonsense more loudly than the others, so that even the old princess, who was sitting in the next room with some pettifogging lawyer's clerk from the Iversky Gate, who had been invited for a consultation, came out to have a look at me. But I felt so intensely happy that I did not care for anyone's sarcastic remarks or anyone's disapproving looks.

Zinaida continued to show a preference for me, and would not let me leave her side. For one forfeit I had to sit beside her, both of us covered with the same silk kerchief: I had to tell her *my secret*. I remember how both our heads were suddenly plunged in a close, semi-transparent, fragrant darkness and how near and how softly her eyes shone in this darkness, and I remember the burning breath of her parted lips and the glint of her teeth and how her hair tickled and scorched me. I was silent. She smiled mysteriously and slyly and at last whispered to me, "Well, what is it?" but I only blushed and laughed and turned away, hardly able to breathe. We got tired of forfeits and began playing a game with string. Heavens, how delighted I was when, in a moment of absent-mindedness, I received a sharp and painful blow on my fingers and how I afterwards purposely tried to pretend that I was not paying attention and she

teased me and refused to touch the hands that I held out
to her!

The things we did that evening! We played the piano,
we sang and danced, and we acted a gipsy encampment.
Nirmatsky was dressed up as a bear and made to drink
salt water. Count Malevsky showed us all sorts of card
tricks and finished up by shuffling the cards and dealing
himself all the trumps at whist, upon which Lushin "had
the honour" to congratulate him. Maydanov recited passages from his poem "The Murderer" (all this took place
at a time when the romantic movement was at its
height), which he intended to publish in a black cover
with the title printed in blood-red letters; we stole the
lawyer's clerk's cap off his knee and made him dance a
Cossack dance by way of ransom; we dressed up old
Vonifaty in a bonnet, and the young princess put on a
man's hat. . . . It is impossible to enumerate everything
we did that evening. Belovzorov alone skulked in a corner, looking cross and frowning. Sometimes his eyes
would become bloodshot, he flushed all over, and it
seemed as though he would at any moment hurl himself upon us all and scatter us in all directions; but the
young princess would glance at him, shake her finger,
and he would once more slink back to his corner.

We were quite worn out at last. Even the old princess,
who, as she expressed it, could "put up with anything"
—no amount of noise seemed to trouble her—felt tired
and declared that she would like to have a little rest. At
midnight, supper was served. It consisted of a piece of
stale, dry cheese and some cold ham patties which
seemed more delicious to me than any pies; there was
only one bottle of wine, and that too was a rather
strange one: a dark-coloured bottle with a blown-out
neck, and the wine in it smelt of pink paint: however, no
one drank it. Tired and exhausted with happiness, I left
the cottage: at parting, Zinaida pressed my hand warmly
and again smiled enigmatically.

The night air was heavy and damp against my burning face. A storm seemed to be gathering. Black clouds grew and crept across the sky, changing their smoky outlines even while one looked at them. The breeze quivered restlessly in the dark trees, and somewhere far beyond the horizon thunder was growling angrily and hollowly, as though to itself.

I made my way to my room by the back door. The old manservant who looked after me was asleep on the floor, and I had to step over him; he woke up, saw me, and told me that my mother had again been angry with me and had again wanted to send for me, but that my father would not let her. (I never went to bed without saying good night to my mother and asking her blessing.) However, there was nothing to be done about it now!

I told my manservant that I would undress and get myself to bed, and put out the candle. But I did not undress and I did not go to bed.

I sat down on a chair and sat there a long time, like one enchanted. What I felt was so new and so sweet. I sat still, hardly looking around and without moving, breathing slowly, and only at times laughing silently at something I remembered or turning cold inwardly at the thought that I was in love and that that was *it*, that was love. Zinaida's face floated slowly before me in the darkness—floated, but did not float away; her lips still wore the same enigmatic smile; her eyes still looked at me a little sideways, questioningly, dreamily, tenderly, as at the moment when I had parted from her. At last I got up, tiptoed to my bed, and without undressing carefully laid my head on the pillow, as though afraid to disturb by an abrupt movement that which filled my whole being.

I lay down but did not even close my eyes. Soon I noticed faint glimmers of light continually lighting up my room. I sat up and looked at the window. The window bars showed up against the mysteriously and dimly lit panes. "A thunderstorm," I thought, and I was right. It was a storm, but it was very far away, so that the thunder could not be heard; only the faint, long, branching-out forks of lightning flashed uninterruptedly across the sky: they did not flash so much as quiver and twitch, like the wing of a dying bird. I got up, went to the window, and stood there till morning. The lightning did not cease for a moment; it was what is known among the peasants as a "sparrow night," or a night of uninterrupted storm with thunder and lightning. I looked at the silent stretch of sand and the dark mass of the Neskoochny Park, at the yellowish façades of distant buildings, which also seemed to quiver with each faint flash. I looked and could not tear myself away: this silent lightning, these restrained gleams of light, seemed to respond to the mute and secret fires which kept blazing up in me too. Morning began to break; the dawn came up in crimson patches. As the sun rose higher in the sky, the flashes of lightning grew fainter and less frequent: they quivered more and more seldom and at last vanished, drowned in the tempering and clear light of the rising day.

And the lightning within me vanished too. I felt a great weariness and silence. But Zinaida's image continued to hover triumphant over my soul. Only this image too seemed more at peace; like a swan rising from the reeds of a marsh into the air, it detached itself from the unseemly figures which surrounded it, and as I fell asleep I clung to it for a last time in a parting and trusting adoration.

Oh, gentle feelings, soft sounds, the goodness and the growing calm of a heart that is deeply moved, the melting gladness of the first tender raptures of love—where are you? Where are you?

Next morning when I came down to breakfast my mother scolded me—not as much as I had expected, however—and made me tell her how I had spent the previous evening. I answered her in a few words, leaving out many details and trying to make everything appear most innocent.

"All the same, they're not *comme il faut*," observed my mother, "and you have no business to be hanging about there instead of working for your examinations."

Knowing that my mother's concern for my studies would be confined to these few words, I did not consider it necessary to take exception to what she had said; but after breakfast my father put his arm through mine, and, going into the garden with me, made me give him a full account of all I had seen at the Zasyekins'.

My father had a strange influence on me—and strange indeed were our relations towards one another. He took practically no part in my education, but he never hurt my feelings; he respected my freedom; he even was, if I may put it this way, polite to me; but he never let me come near him. I loved him and I admired him. He seemed to me to be a paragon of a man—and, dear me, how passionately attached to him I should have grown if only I had not constantly felt his restraining hand! Yet he could, whenever he wanted to, arouse in me an absolute trust in him almost instantaneously, by one single movement, as it were. My heart opened up to him and I chatted to him as I would to an intelligent friend or an indulgent teacher; then he would desert me with the same suddenness, and his hand would push me away again—gently and tenderly, but push me away it did for all that.

Occasionally a gay mood would come upon him, and then he would be ready to play with me as though he were a little boy himself (he was fond of all strong physical exertions); once—only once!—he caressed me with such tenderness that I nearly burst into tears. But his gaiety and tenderness vanished without a trace, and what had passed between us gave me no hope for the future; it was as though it had all been happening in a dream. Sometimes as I gazed at his handsome, clever, bright face my heart would leap up and all my being would rush towards him. . . . He seemed to feel what was going on inside me, and he would give me a casual pat on the cheek and go away and do something, or he would suddenly turn cold as only he knew how to turn cold, and I would shrink back within myself at once and go cold too. His rare fits of friendliness towards me were never caused by my mute but unmistakable entreaties: they always came quite unexpectedly. Reflecting on my father's character afterwards, I came to the conclusion that he could not be bothered with me—or with his family; it was other things he cared for, and he derived full satisfaction from them. "Grab all you can, but never allow yourself to be caught; to belong to yourself alone is the whole trick of living," he said to me once. Another time, like the young democrat I was, I began discussing freedom in his presence (that day he was, as I called it, "good," and it was possible to talk to him about everything).

"Freedom," he repeated, "but do you know what can give a man freedom?"

"What?"

"His will, his own will: that will give him power, which is better than freedom. Know how to want something, and you will be free and you will be able to command."

My father wanted to live above everything else and more than everything else, and he *did* live: perhaps he had a premonition that he was not going to enjoy the trick of living long: he died at forty-two.

I gave my father a detailed account of my visit to the Zasyekins'. He listened to me half attentively and half absently, sitting on a bench and drawing in the sand with the end of his riding crop. From time to time he would chuckle, look at me in a sort of bright and amused way, and he egged me on with short questions and rejoinders. At first I could not pluck up sufficient courage even to utter Zinaida's name, but I could not contain myself and began extolling her to the skies. My father continued to smile; then he sank into thought, stretched himself, and got up.

I remembered that as he was going out of the house he ordered his horse to be saddled. He was an excellent horseman and he could break in the wildest horse long before Rarey.*

"May I come with you, Father?" I asked him.

"No," he replied, and his face assumed its usual half-indifferent, half-affectionate expression. "Go alone, if you like, and tell the groom that I shall not be going."

He turned his back on me and walked rapidly away. I followed him with my eyes—and he disappeared behind the gates. I saw his hat moving along above the fence: he went into the Zasyekins' cottage. He did not stay there more than an hour and then left at once for the town and did not return home till evening.

After dinner I myself called on the Zasyekins. In the drawing room I found only the old princess. On seeing me, she scratched her head under her bonnet with the end of a knitting needle and suddenly asked me whether I would copy out a petition for her.

"With pleasure," I replied, sitting down on the edge of a chair.

"Only, mind, make your letters as big as you can," said the old princess, handing me a sheet of paper scrib-

* John S. Rarey (1828–1866) was an American horse trainer who introduced a system of throwing down vicious or unruly horses, so as to train them. TRANSLATOR.

bled over with her writing. "You couldn't do it today, could you, my boy?"

"Yes, ma'am, I'll copy it out today."

The door to the adjoining room was slightly open, and Zinaida's face appeared in the opening—pale, pensive, with her hair carelessly tossed back: she looked at me with big, cold eyes and softly closed the door.

"Zeena! I say, Zeena!" said the old woman.

Zinaida made no answer. I carried away the old woman's petition and sat the whole evening over it.

9

My passion began from that day. What I felt at that time, I remember, was something similar to what a man must feel on entering government service: I had ceased to be simply a young boy: I was someone in love. I have said that my passion began from that day; I might have added that my suffering began on that day too. Away from Zinaida, I languished: I could not think of anything, I had not the heart to do anything, and for days on end all my thoughts revolved round her. I languished . . . but in her presence I did not feel any happier. I was jealous; I realised my own insignificance; I sulked stupidly and cringed stupidly; and yet an irresistible force drew me towards her, and every time I stepped over the threshold of her room I was seized by an uncontrollable tremor of happiness. Zinaida guessed at once that I had fallen in love with her, and indeed I never thought of concealing it; she amused herself with my passion; she made a fool of me, petted me, and tormented me. It is sweet to be the only source, the despotic and arbitrary cause, of the greatest joys, the greatest sorrows, in another human being, and I was like soft wax in Zinaida's hands.

However, I was not the only one to have fallen in love with her: all the men who visited the house were madly

in love with her, and she kept them all on leading strings
—at her feet. It amused her to arouse their hopes one
moment and their fears another, to twist them round her
little finger (she used to call it "knocking people's heads
together"); and they never dreamt of offering any resistance and were only too glad to submit to her. Her
whole being, so beautiful and so full of vitality, was a
curiously fascinating mixture of cunning and carelessness, artificiality and simplicity, calmness and vivacity;
there was a subtle, delicate charm about everything she
did or said, about every movement of hers; in everything
a peculiar, sparklingly vivacious force was at work. Her
face too was vivacious and always changing: it expressed
almost at one and the same time irony, pensiveness, and
passionateness. The most various emotions, light and
swift like shadows of clouds on a windy, sunny day,
chased each other continuously over her lips and eyes.

Every one of her admirers was necessary to her.
Belovzorov, whom she sometimes called "my wild
beast," and sometimes simply "mine," would gladly have
flung himself into the fire for her; placing little confidence in his own intellectual abilities and other accom-
plishments, he kept proposing marriage to her, hinting
darkly that the others only talked. Maydanov responded
to the poetic chords of her soul: a rather cold man, like
nearly all writers, he kept assuring her strenuously, and
perhaps himself too, that he adored her; he extolled her
in endless verses and read them to her with a kind of affected yet sincere enthusiasm. She sympathised with him
and at the same time made fun of him a little; she had no
great faith in him, and, after listening to his effusions,
made him read Pushkin—in order, as she said, to "clear
the air." Lushin, the sarcastic doctor, who was so cynical
in speech, knew her better than any of them—and loved
her more than any of them, though he scolded her to
her face and behind her back. She respected him but
paid him back in his own coin, and occasionally used to

make him feel with particularly malicious pleasure that he was completely in her power. "I am a flirt, I'm heartless, I am an actress by nature," she said to him once in my presence. "Oh, all right, then! Give me your hand and I will stick a pin in it and you'll be ashamed before this young man. It will hurt you, but all the same you will be good enough to laugh, Mr. Truthful Man." Lushin flushed, turned away, bit his lips, but in the end held out his hand to her. She pricked him, and he did begin to laugh—and she laughed too, driving the pin in quite deep, and kept peering into his eyes, with which he tried in vain not to look at her.

Least of all did I understand the relations which existed between Zinaida and Count Malevsky. He was good-looking, adroit, and intelligent, but even I, at sixteen, felt that there was something equivocal, something false about him, and I was surprised that Zinaida did not notice it. But possibly she did notice this falseness and felt no aversion to it. Her irregular education, strange acquaintances and habits, the constant presence of her mother, poverty and disorder in the house—everything, beginning with the very freedom which the young girl enjoyed, and with the consciousness of her superiority over the people round her, had developed in her a sort of half-disdainful carelessness and a lack of fastidiousness. Whatever happened, whether Vonifaty came in to announce that there was no sugar left, or whether some unsavoury piece of scandal came to light, or her guests began to quarrel, she would only shake her curls, say, "Nonsense," and take no notice of it.

On the other hand, my blood used to boil every time Malevsky went up to her, swaying cunningly like a fox, leaned elegantly against the back of her chair, and began whispering into her ear with a self-satisfied and ingratiating little smile, while she would fold her arms over her bosom, look attentively at him, and smile herself and nod her head.

"What do you want to receive Count Malevsky for?" I asked her one day.

"Oh, but he has such a lovely little moustache," she replied. "But I'm afraid that is something you don't understand. . . .

"You don't think I'm in love with him, do you?" she said to me another time. "Oh no, I couldn't possibly be in love with people whom I have to look down on. I want someone who will master me. But, thank goodness, I shall never come across any man like that! I will never fall into any man's clutches—never!"

"You'll never be in love, then?"

"And what about you? Don't I love you?" she said and flicked me on the nose with the tips of her glove.

Yes, Zinaida amused herself a great deal at my expense. For three weeks I saw her every day, and what didn't she do to me! She visited us seldom, and I was not sorry for it: in our house she became transformed into a young lady, a princess, and I was shy of her. I was afraid of betraying myself in front of my mother; she was not at all kindly disposed towards Zinaida, and watched us with an unfriendly eye. I was not so much afraid of my father: he did not seem to notice me and spoke very little to her, but whatever he said to her seemed somehow particularly brilliant and significant.

I stopped working and reading; I even stopped going for walks in the neighbourhood and riding. Like a beetle tied by the leg, I circled constantly round my beloved little cottage: I would have stayed there forever if I could. But that was impossible. My mother grumbled at me, and sometimes Zinaida herself used to drive me away. Then I would shut myself up in my room, or go to the end of the garden, climb onto the very top of the ruin of a high brick greenhouse, and, with my legs dangling from the wall that looked onto the road, sit there for hours, staring and staring and seeing nothing. White butterflies fluttered lazily on the dusty nettles near me;

a cheeky sparrow settled not far off on a half-broken red brick, twittering irritably, incessantly turning with its whole body and preening its little tail; now and then the still mistrustful crows cawed, sitting very high up on the bare top of a birch; the sun and the wind played gently in its sparse branches; the sound of the bells of the Donskoy monastery came floating across at times, tranquil and melancholy, while I sat there, gazing and listening, filled to overflowing with a kind of nameless sensation which had everything in it: sadness and joy, a premonition of the future, and desire, and fear of life. But just then I understood nothing of it and could not have given a name to anything that was seething within me, or I should have called it all by one name—the name of Zinaida.

And Zinaida continued to play with me like a cat with a mouse. Sometimes she would flirt with me, and I was all agitated and melting with emotion; at other times she would suddenly push me away, and I dared not go near her, dared not look at her.

I remember she was very distant with me for several days. I was completely abashed and, dropping in timidly at the cottage, tried to keep close to the old princess, in spite of her being particularly loud-voiced and abusive just at that time: her financial affairs had been going badly and she had already had to give two statements to the police.

One day as I was walking in the garden past the familiar fence I caught sight of Zinaida: she was sitting on the grass, her head propped up on both her hands, and did not stir. I was about to retreat cautiously, but she suddenly raised her head and signalled to me imperiously to come up to her. I was rooted to the spot: I failed to understand what she meant at first. She signalled to me again. I jumped over the fence at once and rushed joyfully up to her, but she stopped me with a glance and pointed to a path two paces away from her.

Overcome with confusion and not knowing what to do, I knelt at the edge of the path. She was so pale, and such bitter grief, such profound weariness were manifest in every feature of her face that my heart contracted and I murmured involuntarily, "What's the matter?"

Zinaida stretched out her hand, tore off a blade of grass, bit it, and flung it from her as far as she could. "Do you love me very much?" she asked at last. "Do you?"

I made no answer, and what need was there for me to answer?

"You do," she said, looking at me as before. "That is so. The same eyes," she added; then sank into thought and buried her face in her hands. "I'm sick and tired of it all," she whispered. "I wish I could go away somewhere, far, far away. I can't bear it; I can't do anything about it. And what sort of future can I hope for? Oh, I am so miserable! God, I am so miserable!"

"Why?" I asked timidly.

Zinaida did not reply, and only shrugged her shoulders. I remained on my knees, looking at her with blank despondency. Every word of hers cut me to the heart. At that moment I would, I believe, gladly have given up my life, if only she would have no more cause to grieve. I gazed at her, and, still not understanding why she was so unhappy, I vividly pictured to myself how, suddenly, in a fit of irrepressible sorrow, she had gone into the garden and collapsed on the ground as though felled by a blow. All round us everything was bright and green; the wind rustled in the leaves of the trees, now and again swinging a long raspberry cane over Zinaida's head. Somewhere doves were cooing and bees were buzzing, flying low over the sparse grass. Overhead the sky was blue and tender—but I felt terribly sad.

"Read me some poetry, please," said Zinaida softly, raising herself on an elbow. "I like the way you read poetry. You speak it in a singsong way, but that doesn't matter; that is because you are so young. Read me 'On the Hills of Georgia,' only first sit down."

I sat down and recited "On the Hills of Georgia."

" 'Which it cannot choose but love,' " Zinaida repeated. "That's why poetry is so good: it speaks to us of what does not exist and which is not only better than what exists but even more like the truth. . . . 'Which it cannot choose but love'—it would like not to, but cannot!"

She fell silent again and suddenly started and got up. "Come along. Maydanov is in the house with Mother. He's brought me his poem, but I left him. His feelings too are hurt now, but it can't be helped. You'll find out someday—only don't be angry with me!" Zinaida pressed my hand hurriedly and ran on ahead.

We went back to the cottage. Maydanov began reading to us his "Murderer," which had just been published, but I did not listen to him. He shouted his four-foot iambics in a singsong voice; the rhymes alternated, ringing like harness bells, loud and hollow, while I kept looking at Zinaida, trying to grasp the meaning of her last words.

> "Or perchance some secret rival
> Hath without warning conquered thee?"

Maydanov cried suddenly in a nasal tone—and my eyes and Zinaida's met. She dropped them and blushed slightly. I saw her blush, and froze with terror. I had been jealous of her before, but it was only at that moment that the thought that she was in love flashed through my mind. "Good Lord, she is in love!"

10

From that moment my real torments began. I racked my brain, thought it over again and again, and kept a relentless, though as far as possible secret, watch on Zinaida. It was quite clear that a change had come over her. She went for walks alone and was away for hours. Sometimes she refused to see her visitors; she sat for hours in her room. This had never happened to her before. I had suddenly become—or imagined that I had become—extremely perspicacious. "It isn't he, or is it?" I asked myself in alarm as I went over her different admirers in my mind. Count Malevsky (though for Zinaida's sake I was ashamed to admit it to myself) I secretly regarded as more dangerous than the others.

My powers of observation did not go farther than the end of my nose, and my secrecy most likely deceived no one; Dr. Lushin, at least, soon saw through me. He too, though, had changed of late. He had grown thinner; he laughed just as often, it is true, but his laughter somehow sounded more hollow, more spiteful, and much shorter, and in place of his former light irony and affected cynicism he now displayed a nervous irritability.

"Why are you always hanging about here, young man?" he said to me one day when we were left alone together in the Zasyekins' drawing room. (The young princess had not yet returned from her walk, and the shrill voice of the old princess could be heard on the first floor: she was having words with her maid.) "You ought to be studying, working, while you're young, and what on earth do you think you're doing?"

"You can't tell whether I work at home or not," I replied, not without haughtiness, though not without some embarrassment, either.

"Working indeed! You've something else on your mind. Well, I won't argue with you about it. At your age it's what one would expect. Except that you've been terribly unlucky in your choice. Don't you see what sort of house this is?"

"I don't know what you're talking about," I said.

"Don't you? So much the worse for you. I consider it my duty to warn you. It's all right for old bachelors like me to go on coming here: nothing much could hap-

pen to us, could it? We've been hardened in the battle
of life. Nothing can hurt us now. But you've still got a
tender skin. The atmosphere here is bad for you. Believe
me, you might become infected."

"What do you mean?"

"You know what I mean. Are you well now? Are you
in a normal condition? Is what you feel now healthy for
you? Is it good for you?"

"Why, what am I feeling?" I said, while in my heart
I realised full well that the doctor was right.

"Oh, young man, young man," the doctor went on,
looking as though there was something highly insulting
to me in those two words, "you can't deceive me! For,
thank God, one can still read your face like an open
book. However, what's the use of talking? I wouldn't be
coming here myself if"—the doctor gritted his teeth"—if
I hadn't been as big a fool as you. What I'm really surprised at, though, is how, with your intelligence, you
can't see what is going on round you."

"Why, what *is* going on?" I said, all ears.

The doctor looked at me with a sort of mocking pity.
"I'm a fine one too," he said, as though to himself. "Why
should I be telling him this? In short," he added, raising
his voice, "let me tell you again: the atmosphere here
is no good for you. You like it here, but what does that
matter? It smells sweet in a hothouse too, but you can't
live in it, can you? Now you'd better listen to me and
go back to Kaydanov again."

The old princess came in and began to complain to
the doctor about her toothache. Then Zinaida appeared.

"Please, Doctor," added the old princess, "you'd better tell her off properly. She's been drinking iced water
all day long. Is that good for her with her weak chest?"

"Why do you do that?" asked Lushin.

"Why, what effect can it have on me?"

"What effect? You might catch cold and die."

"Could I really? Are you sure? Well, so much the better!"

"I see," muttered the doctor.

The old princess went out.

"I see," repeated Zinaida. "Do you think life is so gay? Just look round you! Well, is it so nice, or do you think that I don't understand it, that I don't feel it? I get pleasure from drinking water with ice, and do you seriously tell me that such a life as mine is not worth risking for a moment's pleasure? I don't speak of happiness."

"Oh well," observed Lushin, "caprice and independence—those two words sum you up: your whole nature is contained in those two words."

Zinaida laughed nervously. "You're too late, my dear doctor. You're not a good observer. You're not abreast of the times. Put on your glasses. This is no time for caprices. To make a fool of you, to make a fool of myself —there's not much fun in that any more. And as for independence—— M'sieu Woldemar," Zinaida added suddenly, stamping her foot, "don't pull such a melancholy face. I can't stand it when people pity me." She went quickly out of the room.

"This atmosphere is very bad for you, young man, very bad," Lushin said again.

11

That same evening the usual visitors gathered at the Zasyekins'; I was among them.

The conversation turned on Maydanov's poem; Zinaida expressed genuine admiration for it.

"But," she said to him, "let me tell you this. If I were a poet, I would choose different subjects. Perhaps it's all nonsense, but all sorts of strange thoughts sometimes come into my head, especially when I can't sleep, at daybreak when the sky begins to turn pink and grey. I would, for instance—— You won't laugh at me, will you?"

"No! No!" we all cried in one voice.

"I would describe," she went on, crossing her arms and looking away, "a whole company of young girls in a large boat on a quiet river at night. The moon is shining and they are all in white, with garlands of white flowers, and they are singing, you know, something like a hymn."

"I understand, I understand, go on," Maydanov said dreamily and meaningfully.

"All of a sudden there's an uproar—loud laughter, torches, tambourines on the bank. . . . It's a troupe of bacchantes running, with songs and cries. It's your business, Mr. Poet, to paint this picture, only I'd like the torches to be red and smoking a lot and the eyes of the bacchantes to gleam under their wreaths, and the wreaths to be dark. Don't forget the tiger skins and the goblets and the gold, lots and lots of gold."

"Where should the gold be?" asked Maydanov, tossing back his lank hair and dilating his nostrils.

"Where? On their shoulders, arms, legs, everywhere! In ancient times, they say, women wore gold bracelets on their ankles. The bacchantes call to the girls in the boat. The girls have stopped singing their hymn. They cannot continue it, but they do not stir: the river is carrying them to the bank. Suddenly one of them gently rises. . . . This has to be beautifully described—how she gently rises in the moonlight, and how her companions are frightened. She steps over the edge of the boat; the bacchantes surround her; they whirl her off into the night, into the dark. Here you must describe the smoke rising in clouds and everything becoming confused. All one can hear is their shrill cries, and her wreath is left lying on the bank."

Zinaida fell silent. ("Oh, she is in love!" I thought again.)

"And is that all?" asked Maydanov.

"That's all," she replied.

"That can't be the subject of a whole epic poem," he remarked pompously, "but I shall make use of your idea for a lyric poem."

"In the romantic style?" asked Malevsky.

"Of course, in the romantic style. The Byronic."

"Well, in my opinion Hugo is better than Byron," the young count declared nonchalantly. "More interesting."

"Hugo is a first-rate writer," replied Maydanov, "and my friend Tonkosheyev, in his Spanish novel *El Trovador——*"

"Oh," interrupted Zinaida, "is that the book with the question marks upside down?"

"Yes. That is the rule with the Spaniards. What I wanted to say was that Tonkosheyev——"

"Oh dear, you'll be arguing again about classicism and romanticism," Zinaida interrupted him a second time. "Come, we'd better play a game."

"Forfeits?" Lushin asked.

"No. Forfeits is boring. Let's play comparisons." (Zinaida had invented this game herself. Some object was mentioned, and everyone tried to compare it with something else, and the one who chose the best comparison got the prize.)

She went up to the window. The sun had just set; long red clouds stood high in the sky.

"What are those clouds like?" asked Zinaida, and, without waiting for an answer, said, "I think they are like the purple sails on the golden ship in which Cleopatra sailed to meet Antony. Remember, Maydanov, you were telling me about it not long ago?"

All of us, like Polonius in *Hamlet*, declared that the clouds were exactly like those sails and that not one of us could find a better comparison.

"And how old was Antony then?" asked Zinaida.

"He was certainly a young man," observed Malevsky.

"Yes, a young man," Maydanov affirmed emphatically.

"I'm sorry," cried Lushin, "but he was over forty!"

"Over forty," repeated Zinaida, giving him a quick glance.

I went home soon. "She's in love," my lips whispered involuntarily. "But with whom?"

12

Days passed. Zinaida became stranger and stranger and more and more incomprehensible. One day I went into her room and saw her sitting on a wicker chair with her head pressed against the sharp edge of the table. She sat up—her face was wet with tears. "Oh, it's you!" she said with a cruel smile. "Come here."

I went up to her. She put her hand on my head and, seizing me by the hair, suddenly began to twist it.

"It hurts!" I said at last.

"Oh, it hurts, does it? And do you think it doesn't hurt me? Me?" she repeated. "Oh, dear!" she cried suddenly, seeing she had pulled a little tuft of hair out of my head. "What have I done? Poor M'sieu Woldemar!" She carefully smoothed the hair she had torn out, wrapped it round her finger, and twisted it into a ring. "I'll put your hair in a locket and wear it round my neck," she said, tears still glistening in her eyes. "This will perhaps comfort you a little, and now good-bye."

I returned home to discover a disagreeable state of affairs. My mother was having words with my father, she was reproaching him for something; and he, as was his habit, responded with a polite and frigid silence, and soon left the house. I could not hear what my mother was saying, and, anyway, I had other things on my mind; I remember only that after her talk with my father, she sent for me to the study and told me that she was very displeased with my frequent visits to the old princess, who, in her words, was *"une femme capable de tout."* I kissed her hand (this was what I always did when I wanted to cut short a conversation) and went

up to my room. Zinaida's tears had completely bewildered me. I simply did not know what to think and
was about to burst into tears myself: I was a child, after
all, in spite of my sixteen years.

I was no longer thinking of Malevsky, though Belovzorov was assuming more and more menacing attitudes
every day and kept looking at the shifty count like a
wolf at a sheep. As for me, I had no longer any thought
of anyone or anything. I was lost in all sorts of speculations and was always trying to find some secluded spots.
I became particularly fond of the ruins of the hothouse.
I used to climb onto the high wall, sit on top of it, and
remain sitting there, an unhappy, solitary, and melancholy youth, so that in the end I felt sorry for myself.
And how sweet were those mournful sensations! How I
revelled in them!

One day I was sitting on the wall, looking into the
distance and listening to the ringing of the church bells;
suddenly something passed over me—it wasn't a wind,
it wasn't a shiver, but something like a hardly perceptible breath, like a sensation of someone's presence. I
looked down. Below, on the road, in a light grey dress
with a pink parasol on her shoulder, Zinaida was walking
rapidly. She saw me, stopped, and turning back the brim
of her straw hat, raised her velvety eyes to me.

"What are you doing up there at such a height?" she
asked me with a strange sort of smile. "Now," she went
on, "you keep telling me that you love me. Jump down
into the road to me, if you really love me."

Zinaida had scarcely uttered those words when I was
falling headlong towards her just as though someone
had pushed me from behind. The wall was about fifteen
feet high. I reached the ground on my feet, but the im-
pact was so strong that I could not keep my balance. I
fell down and for a moment lost consciousness. When I
came to, I felt, without opening my eyes, Zinaida beside me.

"My sweet boy," she was saying, bending over me, and there was a note of alarmed tenderness in her voice, "how could you do it? How could you listen to me—you know I love you. Please get up."

Her bosom rose and fell close to me; her hands were touching my head; and suddenly—oh, what became of me then?—her soft fresh lips began to cover my face with kisses—they touched my lips—but at that moment, Zinaida probably guessed from the expression on my face that I had regained consciousness, though I still did not open my eyes, and, rising quickly, she said, "Well, get up, you naughty boy, you crazy young lunatic. Why are you lying in the dust?"

I got up.

"Give me my parasol," said Zinaida. "See where I have thrown it! And don't stare at me like that! Really! You're not hurt, are you? Stung by the nettles, I expect. I tell you, don't keep staring at me. . . . Why, he doesn't understand a word, he doesn't answer," she added, as though to herself. "Go home, M'sieu Woldemar, and brush yourself, and don't you dare follow me, or I shall be angry and will never again——"

She did not finish the sentence and walked rapidly away, while I sat down by the side of the road. My legs would not support me. My arms throbbed from the stings of the nettles, my back ached, my head swam, but the feeling of bliss I experienced at that moment I never again felt in my life. It spread like a sweet pain through all my limbs and resolved itself at last in rapturous leaps and shouts. Yes, indeed, I was still a child.

13

I was so gay and proud all that day, I retained so vividly the sensation of Zinaida's kisses on my face, I recalled her every word with such a shudder of delight, I cherished my unexpected happiness so much, that I felt absolutely terrified, and did not even want to see her who was the cause of all these new sensations. It seemed to me that I had no right to demand anything more of fate, that all I had to do now was "go, take a deep breath for the last time, and die." Yet the next day, on my way to the cottage, I felt greatly embarrassed and I tried in vain to conceal my embarrassment by assuming a modestly nonchalant air, such as is proper for a man who wishes to convey that he knows how to keep a secret.

Zinaida received me very simply, without betraying any emotion. She merely shook a finger at me and asked whether I had any bruises on my body. All my modest nonchalance and air of mystery vanished instantly, and with them my embarrassment. Of course I had never expected anything in particular, but Zinaida's composure made me feel as though someone had poured cold water over me: I realised that I was a child in her eyes —and I felt very unhappy! Zinaida walked up and down the room, giving me a quick smile every time she glanced at me; but her thoughts were far away—I saw that clearly enough. "Shall I speak to her about what happened yesterday," I thought, "and ask her where she was going in such a hurry and find out once and for all?" But I just dismissed it all as hopeless and sat down quietly in a corner.

Belovzorov came in; I was glad to see him.

"I couldn't find you a quiet horse," he said in a hard voice. "Freitag says he can answer for one, but I'm not so sure. I am afraid."

"What are you afraid of, may I ask?" asked Zinaida.

"What am I afraid of? Why, you don't know how to ride. Goodness knows what might happen! And what a fantastic idea has come into your head suddenly!"

"Well, that's my affair, my dear wild beast. In that case, I'll ask Peter." (My father's name was Peter, and I was surprised that she mentioned his name in so free and easy a manner, just as though she were sure of his readiness to do her a service.)

"I see," replied Belovzorov, "so it's with him you mean to go out riding."

"With him or someone else—what difference does it make to you? Not with you, at any rate."

"Not with me," repeated Belovzorov. "As you wish. Oh, all right. I'll get you a horse."

"Only mind it isn't some old cow. I warn you, I want to gallop."

"Gallop, by all means. But with whom? You won't go riding with Malevsky, will you?"

"And why not with him, O Great Warrior? Now please calm down and don't glare at me like that. I'll take you too. You know that for me Malevsky is now— ugh!" She tossed her head.

"You say that to console me," growled Belovzorov.

Zinaida narrowed her eyes. "Does that console you? Oh, oh, oh, Great Warrior!" she said at last, as though unable to find another word. "And you, M'sieu Woldemar, would you come with us?"

"I shouldn't like to—not in—in a crowd," I murmured without raising my eyes.

"You prefer tête-à-tête? Well," she added with a sigh, "freedom to the free; heaven—to the saints! Go along, Belovzorov, and do your best. I must have a horse for tomorrow."

"Yes, but where are you going to get the money?" the old princess put in.

Zinaida wrinkled her brow. "I'm not asking you for it: Belovzorov will trust me."

"Trust you, trust you," growled the old princess and suddenly shouted at the top of her voice, "Dunyashka!"

"Mother, I've given you a bell," the young princess observed.

"Dunyashka!" the old woman shrieked again.

Belovzorov took his leave; I left with him. Zinaida made no attempt to detain me.

14

Next day I got up early, cut myself a stick, and went out for a walk beyond the toll gate. "I'll go for a walk," I thought to myself, "and get rid of my grief." It was a beautiful day, sunny and not too hot; a gay, fresh wind roamed the earth, playing and murmuring away gently, setting everything astir but disturbing nothing. I wandered a long time, over hills and through woods; I did not feel happy; I had left home with the intention of giving myself up to melancholy thoughts; but youth, the glorious weather, the fresh air, the fun of rapid walking, the delight of lying on thick grass away from everyone, got the better of me: the recollection of those unforgettable words, of those kisses, again invaded my soul. I was glad to think that Zinaida could not but recognise my resolution, my heroism. "Others may please her better than I," I thought, "let them! They will only tell her what they will do, while I have done it. . . . And that is not the only thing I could do for her!" I gave full rein to my imagination. I imagined how I would save her from the hands of enemies; how, covered with blood, I would drag her out of a dark dungeon; how I would die at her feet. I remembered a picture which hung in our drawing room: Malek-Adel carrying off Matilda— and at that very moment became absorbed in the appearance of a large, brightly coloured woodpecker, busily climbing up the slender trunk of a birch tree and peeping nervously from behind it, first to the right and then to the left, just like a double-bass player behind the neck of his instrument.

Then I began singing, "Not white the snows," and finished up with the at-the-time-popular song, "For you I wait when Zephyr wanton," and so on. Then I began reciting aloud Yermak's invocation to the stars from Khomyakov's tragedy, attempted to compose something myself in a sentimental vein, and even thought of a line with which the whole of my poem was to conclude: "Oh, Zinaida, oh, Zinaida!" but nothing came of it.

Meanwhile it was getting near dinnertime. I went down into the valley; a narrow, sandy path wound its way through it towards the town. I walked along that path. The dull thud of horses' hooves sounded behind me. I looked round, stopped involuntarily, and took off my cap: I saw my father and Zinaida. They were riding side by side. My father was saying something to her, bending right over her and leaning with his hand on the neck of his horse. He was smiling; Zinaida listened to him in silence, her eyes severely cast down and her lips tightly pressed together. At first I saw only them; a few moments later I caught sight of Belovzorov round a bend in the valley in his hussar's uniform with a short cloak, on a foaming black horse. The gallant steed tossed its head, snorted, and pranced. The rider was holding him back and at the same time spurring him on. I stepped aside. My father gathered up the reins, moved away from Zinaida; she raised her eyes to him slowly and they galloped off. Belovzorov raced after them, his sabre rattling. "He's as red as a lobster," I thought, "while she . . . why is she so pale? Out riding the whole morning and—pale?"

I redoubled my steps and got home just before dinner. My father was already sitting, washed and fresh and dressed for dinner, beside my mother's chair, and was reading to her in his even and rich voice an article from *Journal de Débats;* but my mother listened to him without attention and when she saw me asked where I had been all day long, adding that she didn't like it when people ran about goodness knows where and with whom. "But I have been taking a walk by myself," I was about to reply, but I looked at my father and for some reason said nothing.

15

During the next five or six days I scarcely saw Zinaida: she appeared to be unwell, which, however, did not prevent the usual visitors of the cottage from calling—in order, as they put it, to "keep watch by the patient's bedside"—all except Maydanov, who immediately lost heart and looked bored whenever there was no chance for going into ecstasies. Belovzorov sat dejectedly in a corner, all buttoned up and red in the face; a kind of evil smile constantly hovered over Count Malevsky's refined face. He really had fallen out of favour with Zinaida and was waiting with special zeal on the old princess, drove with her in a hired carriage to call on the Governor General; this visit, however, turned out to be a failure, and Malevsky was even involved in some unpleasantness, for he was reminded of an unsavoury incident with some officers of a sapper regiment and in explaining it away he had to plead his inexperience at the time. Lushin used to come twice a day, but he did not stay long; I was a little frightened of him after our last talk, and yet at the same time I felt genuinely attracted to him. One day he went for a walk with me in the Neskoochny Park, was very amiable and friendly, told me the names and the properties of various herbs and flowers, and suddenly, as they say, "out of the blue," cried, striking himself on the forehead, "And I, fool that I am, thought that she was a flirt. It seems some people find it sweet to sacrifice themselves."

"What do you mean by that?" I asked.

"I don't want to say anything to you," Lushin replied brusquely.

Zinaida avoided me: my presence—I could not help noticing it—made an unpleasant impression on her. She turned away from me involuntarily—involuntarily. It was that that was so bitter, so crushing, but I could do nothing about it. I did my best to keep out of her sight and merely watched her from a distance, which I did not always succeed in doing. As before, something I could not understand was happening to her: her face had changed; she was quite a different person.

The change that had taken place in her struck me particularly one warm, quiet evening. I was sitting on a low seat under a spreading elder bush; I was very fond of that place, for from it I could see the window of Zinaida's room. I sat there; in the dark foliage over my head a little bird was busily moving about; a grey cat, its back arched, was creeping stealthily into the garden, and the early beetles were droning heavily in the air which was still clear, though no longer bright. I sat there looking at her window and waiting to see whether it would open: it did open, and Zinaida appeared in it. She was wearing a white dress, and she was pale: her face, shoulders, and arms were pale, almost white. She stayed there a long time without moving, and for a long time gazed straight before her from under her knitted brows. I had never seen her look like that. Then she clasped her hands tight, very tight, raised them to her lips, her forehead, and suddenly pulled her fingers apart and thrust her hair back from her ears, tossed it and nodded her head with an air of determination, and slammed the window to.

Three days later she met me in the garden. I was about to turn away, but she stopped me herself. "Give me your hand," she said to me in her old affectionate tone of voice. "It's a long time since I've had a talk with you."

I looked at her: her eyes shone softly and her face was smiling as though through a haze. "Are you still not well?" I asked her.

"No, that's all over now," she replied and picked a

small red rose. "I'm a little tired, but that too will pass."

"And you'll be the same as before?" I aked.

Zinaida held the rose up to her face, and it seemed to me as if her cheeks had caught the reflection of its bright petals. "Why, have I changed?" she asked me.

"Yes, you have," I answered in a low voice.

"I've been cold to you, I know," began Zinaida, "but you shouldn't have paid any attention to it. I'm afraid I couldn't help it—but why talk about it?"

"You don't want me to love you, that's what it is!" I exclaimed darkly, in an uncontrollable outburst.

"No, do love me, but not as before."

"How then?"

"Let us be friends—that's how!" Zinaida said, giving me the rose to smell. "Listen," she said, "you know I am much older than you, don't you? I might be your aunt, mightn't I? Well, perhaps not your aunt, but your elder sister. And you——"

"And I am a child so far as you're concerned," I interrupted.

"Well, yes, a child, but a sweet, good, clever child whom I love very much. Do you know what? I'm going to make you my page from today, and please don't forget that pages should never be very far from their ladies. And here's the token of your new dignity," she added, sticking the rose in the buttonhole of my tunic, "a sign of our gracious favour."

"I used to get other favours from you before," I murmured.

"Oh!" Zinaida said, giving me a sidelong look. "What a memory he has. Oh well, I'm just as ready now." And bending over me, she imprinted a chaste, calm kiss on my forehead.

I just looked at her, but she turned away and saying, "Follow me, my page," went towards the cottage. I followed her, but still in a state of bewilderment. "Can this gentle sensible girl," I could not help thinking, "be the

Zinaida I used to know?" I thought that she walked more quietly now and that her whole figure was more stately and more graceful.

And, good Lord, with what fresh force my love flared up in me!

16

After dinner the visitors gathered again at the cottage —and the young princess came out to them. The entire company was there in full force, as on that first unforgettable evening. Even Nirmatsky dragged himself to the party to see her; this time Maydanov arrived before anyone else and brought a new poem with him. The game of forfeits began again, but this time without the strange pranks, without the horseplay and noise—the gipsy element had gone. Zinaida gave a new tone to our gathering. I sat beside her, as her page. Among other things, she proposed that anyone who had to pay a forfeit should tell his dream; but this was not a success. The dreams were either uninteresting (Belovzorov had dreamt that he fed carp to his mare and that she had a wooden head), or unnatural and made-up. Maydanov regaled us with a long, long story; there were sepulchres in it, angels with lyres, talking flowers, and mysterious sounds coming from afar.

Zinaida did not let him finish. "If we have to have fiction," she said, "then let everyone tell something he has made up."

It was Belovzorov again who had to begin. The young hussar looked embarrassed. "I can't think of anything!" he exclaimed.

"What nonsense!" Zinaida cried. "Well, imagine, for instance, that you are married and tell us how you would spend your time with your wife. Would you lock her up?"

"Yes, I should."

"And would you stay with her yourelf?"

"Yes, I should most certainly stay with her myself."

"Excellent. But what if she got tired of it and was unfaithful to you?"

"I'd kill her."

"And if she ran away?"

"I'd catch up with her and kill her all the same."

"I see. Well, and suppose I were your wife, what would you do then?"

Belovzorov was silent for a minute. "I'd kill myself."

Zinaida laughed. "I can see that your tale is quickly told."

The next forfeit was Zinaida's. She lifted her eyes to the ceiling and sank into thought. "Now listen," she began at last, "this is what I have thought of. Imagine a magnificent palace, a summer night, and a wonderful ball. The ball is being given by a young queen. Everywhere is gold, marble, crystal, silk, lights, diamonds, flowers, burning joss-sticks, all the wild extravagances of luxury."

"You like luxury?" Lushin interrupted her.

"Luxury is beautiful," she replied, "and I love everything beautiful."

"More than the beautiful?" he asked.

"That sounds a little too clever," she replied. "I don't understand it. Please don't interrupt. And so, the ball is magnificent. Lots and lots of guests, and all of them are young, handsome, and brave, and all are head over heels in love with the queen."

"Are there no women among the guests?" Malevsky asked.

"No, or wait—there are."

"Are they all unattractive?"

"No, they're lovely. But the men are all in love with the queen. She is tall and graceful, and she has a little gold diadem on her black hair."

I looked at Zinaida, and at that moment she seemed

to me so much above us all, there was such bright intelligence and such power about her white forehead and
her motionless eyebrows, that I could not help thinking,
"You are that queen yourself!"

"They all crowd round her," Zinaida went on, "they
all lavish the most flattering speeches upon her."

"Why, does she like flattery?" asked Lushin.

"What an insufferable creature you are! You *will* interrupt. Who doesn't like flattery?"

"Just one last question," Malevsky observed. "Has the
queen a husband?"

"I hadn't thought of that. No, why a husband?"

"Naturally," Malevsky put in. "Why should she?"

"*Silence!*" cried Maydanov in French, which he spoke
badly.

"*Merci,*" Zinaida said to him. "And so," she went on,
"the queen listens to these speeches, listens to the music,
but does not look at any of the guests. Six windows are
open from top to bottom, from floor to ceiling, and beyond them is a dark sky with big stars and a dark garden
with big trees. The queen looks out into the garden.
There, near the trees, is a fountain: it is white in the
darkness, and it is tall, tall like a ghost. The queen hears
through the talk and the music the soft plashing of its
waters. She looks and thinks, 'You, gentlemen, are all
noble, intelligent, rich, you crowd round me, you treas-
ure every word I utter, you are all ready to die at my
feet, I have you all in my power. But there, near the
fountain, near that plashing water, he whom *I* love and
who holds me in his power awaits me. He wears neither
costly garments nor precious stones, no one knows him,
but he waits for me, certain that I will come—and I
will come, and there is no power on earth which can
stop me when I want to go to him, stay with him, and
lose myself with him there in the darkness of the garden, with the whispering trees and the plashing of the
fountain. . . .'"

Zinaida fell silent.

"Is this—fiction?" Malevsky inquired cunningly.

Zinaida did not even look at him.

"And what should we have done, gentlemen," Lushin suddenly said, "if we had been among the guests and had known of the lucky fellow at the fountain?"

"Wait, wait," Zinaida interrupted. "I will myself tell you what each of you would have done. You, Belovzorov, would have challenged him to a duel; you, Maydanov, would have written an epigram on him—though, no, you don't know how to write epigrams: you would have written a long poem on him in iambics, something in the style of Barbier, and would have published it in the *Telegraph*. You, Nirmatsky, would have borrowed —no, you would have loaned him money at high interest. You, Doctor . . ." She stopped. "I'm sorry, but I really don't know what you would have done."

"As her court physician," replied Lushin, "I should have advised the queen not to give balls when she was not in the mood for entertaining guests."

"Perhaps you'd have been right. And you, Count?"

"And I?" Malevsky repeated with his evil smile.

"You would have offered him a poisoned sweet."

Malevsky's face became slightly twisted and for a moment assumed a villainous look, but he burst out laughing immediately.

"As for you, Woldemar . . ." Zinaida went on. "But I suppose that's enough. Let's play another game."

"M'sieu Woldemar, as the queen's page, would have carried her train as she ran into the garden," Malevsky remarked venomously.

I flushed, but Zinaida quickly laid a hand on my shoulder and, getting up, said in a slightly trembling voice, "I never gave your lordship the right to be insolent, and I must ask you to leave." She pointed to the door.

"Good Lord, Princess," murmured Malevsky, turning very pale.

"The princess is right," cried Belovzorov and he too rose.

"Good Lord, I never expected——" Malevsky went on. "I—I believe there was nothing in my words—I had never intended to insult you. . . . Forgive me."

Zinaida looked him up and down very coldly and smiled coldly. "You may stay, if you like," she said, with a careless gesture of the hand. "M'sieu Woldemar and I have no real cause to be angry. You seem to enjoy stinging people—much good may it do you."

"Forgive me," Malevsky repeated.

But I, recalling Zinaida's gesture, could not help reflecting once more that no real queen could have shown an impertinent man the door with greater dignity.

After this little scene the game of forfeits went on for only a short time; everyone felt rather ill at ease, not so much because of the scene itself as because of another, vague but oppressive feeling. No one spoke of it, but everyone was conscious of it in himself and in his neighbour. Maydanov read us his poem, and Malevsky praised it with exaggerated warmth.

"How keen he is to show us now what a good fellow he is," Lushin whispered to me.

We soon left. Zinaida suddenly became thoughtful; the old princess sent word that she had a headache; Nirmatsky started complaining of his rheumatism.

I could not sleep for a long time. I was very much struck by Zinaida's story. "Can there have been a hint in it?" I asked myself. "And at whom and at what could she have been hinting? And if there really is something to hint at, what am I going to do about it?

"No, no, it can't be," I whispered, turning from one hot cheek to the other; but I recalled the expression on Zinaida's face as she told her story; I remembered the exclamation that had escaped Lushin in the Neskoochny

Park, the sudden changes in her behaviour to me, and I was lost in conjectures. "Who is he?" These three words seemed to stand before my eyes, traced clearly in the darkness; it was as though a low, ominous cloud hung over me and I felt its pressure and was waiting for it to burst at any moment. I had got used to many things during the last few weeks, and I had seen as much as I wanted at the Zasyekins': their disorderly life, the tallow candle-ends, the broken knives and forks, the gloomy Vonifaty, the slatternly maids, the manners of the old princess herself—all this strange mode of life no longer surprised me. But what I seemed to be dimly discerning now in Zinaida I could never become used to. . . . "An adventuress," my mother had once described her. An adventuress—she, my idol, my goddess! That word stung me. I tried to escape from it into my pillow. I was indignant and, at the same time, what would I not have agreed to do, what would I not have given, to be that lucky fellow at the fountain!

My blood was on fire and coursing through my veins. "The garden—the fountain," I thought. "I'll go to the garden." I dressed quickly and slipped out of the house. The night was dark. The trees scarcely whispered; a gentle chill fell from the sky; the scent of fennel came from the kitchen-garden. I walked through all the avenues; the light sound of my own footsteps disturbed and at the same time emboldened me; every now and then I stopped dead, waited, and listened to my heart beating fast and heavily. At last I went up to the fence and leaned against a stake. Suddenly—or did I imagine it? —a woman's figure flashed by a few paces from me. I stared intently into the darkness; I held my breath. . . . What was that? Did I hear steps, or was it again the beating of my heart? "Who is there?" I murmured, almost inaudibly. What was that again? A smothered laugh? Or the rustling of leaves? Or a sigh close to my ear? I felt frightened. "Who is it?" I repeated, still more softly.

A slight breeze came and went in a moment; a streak of fire flashed across the sky—a falling star. "Zinaida?" I was about to ask, but the sound died on my lips. And suddenly everything became profoundly still all round me, as often happens in the middle of the night. Even the cicadas ceased whirring in the trees—only a window was slammed to somewhere. I stood and stood and then went back to my room, to my bed, which had grown quite cold by then. I felt a strange excitement, as though I had gone to a rendezvous and had been left out in the cold, passing by another man's happiness.

17

The next day I only caught a glampse of Zinaida: she was driving somewhere with the old princess in a cab. I did see Lushin, though, who barely acknowledged my greeting, and Malevsky. The young count grinned and began talking to me very amiably. Of all the visitors to the cottage, he alone had managed to worm himself into our house. My mother took a liking to him. My father was not particularly friendly with him and treated him with almost offensive politeness.

"Ah, *Monsieur le page,*" began Malevsky. "Very glad to meet you. What is your beautiful queen doing?"

His fresh, handsome face was so detestable to me at that moment and he was looking at me with such a playfully contemptuous expression at that moment that I did not answer him at all. "Are you still angry with me?" he went on. "You shouldn't be, you know. It wasn't I who called you a page. Besides, queens usually have pages. But I hope you won't mind my telling you that you are performing your duties very badly."

"Oh?"

"Pages should never be far away from their mistresses.

Pages should know everything their mistresses do; they should even watch them," he added, lowering his voice, "day and night."

"What do you mean by that?"

"What do I mean? I believe I've made myself perfectly clear. Day—and night. In the daytime it doesn't matter very much. It is light by day, and there are lots of people about. But by night—ah, that's when you should expect trouble. I advise you not to sleep at night and watch, watch with all your might. Remember? At night, in the garden, by the fountain—that's where you must keep watch. You'll thank me for it."

Malevsky laughed and turned his back on me. I don't suppose he attached any great importance to what he had said to me. He had the reputation of a man who was very good at mystifying people, and he was famed for his ability to make fools of people at fancy-dress balls, greatly enhanced by his almost unconscious mendacity, which permeated his whole being. . . . He just wanted to tease me, but every word he uttered ran like poison through my veins. The blood rushed to my head. "Oh, so that's what it is," I said to myself. "Very well, it was not for nothing that I felt drawn into the garden! Well then, it shall not be!" I exclaimed loudly, striking myself on the chest with my fist, though I had no clear idea what exactly it was that was not to be. "Whether it is Malevsky himself who goes into the garden," I thought (he might have let the cat out of the bag; he certainly was impudent enough for that), "or whether it was someone else" (the fence of our garden was very low, and there was no difficulty in climbing over it), "whoever I happen to come across will be sorry for it! I should not advise anyone to cross my path! I'll prove to all the world and to her, the traitress"—I actually called her a traitress—"that I know how to be revenged!"

I went back to my room, took out of the writing desk an English penknife I had recently bought, felt the sharp edge, and, knitting my brows, thrust it into my pocket with a look of cold and concentrated determination, just as though I was quite used to such things and had done them many times before. My heart was full of malice and turned to stone; I kept frowning all day and from time to time would walk up and down with compressed lips, my hand in my pocket clutching the knife, grown warm in my grasp, while I was preparing myself beforehand for something terrible. These new and never-before-experienced sensations absorbed me and even delighted me so much that I scarcely thought of Zinaida herself. All the time I imagined I could see Pushkin's Aleko, the young gipsy—"Where are you going, my handsome youth—lie still . . ." And then: "You're all bespattered with blood! Oh, what have you done? . . . Nothing!" With what a cruel smile I kept repeating this "Nothing!"

My father was not at home; but my mother, who had for some time past been in a state of almost continual wild exasperation, noticed my look of desperate determination and said to me at supper, "What are you sulking for, like a bear with a sore head?"

I just smiled condescendingly to her in reply and thought, "If they only knew!" It struck eleven; I went to my room but did not undress; I was waiting for midnight; at last it struck. "Time I went!" I muttered through my teeth, and buttoned my coat up to the top, and even rolled up my sleeves. I went into the garden. I had already selected the spot from which to keep watch: at the end of the garden, where the fence separating our part of the grounds from the Zasyekins' joined the common wall, grew a solitary pine tree. Standing under its low, thick branches, I could see quite well, as far as the darkness of the night permitted, everything that went on round me; nearby ran a path which always seemed full of mystery to me; like a snake, it crept under the fence which, at that spot, bore the marks of climbing feet and led up to a round summer house of thickly growing acacias. I made my way to the pine tree, leaned against its trunk, and began my watch.

The night was still and quiet, like the night before; but there were fewer clouds in the sky, and the outlines of the bushes and even of tall flowers could be seen more clearly. The first moments of waiting were full of agonizing suspense and almost of terror. I was determined to stop at nothing; all I was uncertain of was what I had to do. Was I to thunder out, "Where are you going? Stop! Confess, or die!" Or should I simply strike? Every sound, every rustle and whisper, seemed extraordinarily significant. . . . I was getting ready. . . . I leaned forward. . . . But half an hour passed, an hour passed: my blood grew calmer, colder; the realisation that I was doing it all for no reason, that I was even a little ridiculous, that Malevsky had pulled my leg began to dawn on me. I left my hiding place and walked all round the garden. As though on purpose, not the slightest noise could be heard; everything was at rest; even our dog was aleep, curled up by the gate. I climbed up on the ruins of the hothouse, saw the open countryside stretching far into the distance, recalled my meeting with Zinaida, and sank into a reverie. . . .

I gave a start; I thought I heard the creak of an opening door, then the faint crack of a snapping twig. In two bounds I got down from the ruin and—stood rooted to the spot. I could clearly hear the sound of rapid, light, but cautious footsteps in the garden. They were coming towards me. "Here he is—here he is at last!" raced through my heart. I pulled the knife out of my pocket convulsively, opened it convulsively—red sparks whirled round before my eyes, my hair stood on end from terror and fury. The footsteps were coming straight towards me. I stooped and crouched forward to meet them. A man came into view—— Good heavens, it was my father!

I recognised him at once, although he was all muffled

in a dark cloak and his hat was pulled down over his
face. He walked past me on tiptoe. He did not notice
me, though nothing concealed me, shrunk into myself
and huddled up so that I seemed to be almost level with
the ground. Jealous Othello, ready for murder, was suddenly transformed into a schoolboy. I became so terrified
by my father's unexpected appearance that for the first
few moments I did not notice where he had come from
or in what direction he had disappeared. It was only
when everything was quiet again that I got up from the
ground and thought to myself, "Why is my father walking about in the garden at night?" In my panic I dropped
my knife in the grass, but I did not even try to look for
it: I was so terribly ashamed of myself. I became quite
sober all at once. On my way back, however, I went up
to my seat under the elder bush and looked up at the
window of Zinaida's bedroom. The small, slightly curved
windowpanes showed dimly blue in the faint light that
fell from the night sky. Suddenly their colour began to
change. Behind them I saw—saw quite clearly—a whitish
blind pulled down cautiously and gently to the window-
sill—and it remained like that, absolutely still.

"What does this mean?" I said aloud, almost involuntarily, when I found myself once more in my room. "A
dream, a mere coincidence, or——" The suppositions
which suddenly came into my head were so new and
disturbing that I did not dare even consider them.

18

I got up in the morning with a headache. The excitement of the previous day had gone. It was replaced
by an oppressive feeling of bewilderment and a strange
sadness I had never experienced before. It was as though
something were dying inside me. "Why are you looking like a rabbit who has had half its brain removed?"
said Lushin as he met me. At lunch I kept glancing

stealthily first at my father and then at my mother. My father was, as usual, composed; my mother, also as usual, secretly irritated. I waited to see whether my father would say something friendly to me, as he sometimes did, but he showed not even a sign of his ordinary cold affection. "Shall I tell Zinaida everything?" I thought. "It really can't make any difference—it is all over between us, anyway." I went to see her, but not only told her nothing; I did not even succeed in talking to her, much as I wanted to. The old princess's son, a twelve-year-old cadet, had arrived from Petersburg for his holidays and Zinaida at once asked me to take him under my wing.

"Here," she said, "my dear Vladimir (she called me that for the first time), is a companion for you. His name is Vladimir too. Please be friends. He is still very shy, but he has a kind heart. Show him the Neskoochny Park, take him for walks, take him under your protection. You will do so, won't you? You're so kind too!" She laid both her hands affectionately on my shoulders, and I was completely lost. The arrival of this boy turned me into a boy too. I looked in silence at the cadet, who stared silently back at me.

Zinaida burst out laughing and pushed us towards each other. "Come on, children," she said, "embrace."

We embraced.

"Want me to take you round the garden?" I asked the cadet.

"If you like," he replied in a hoarse, regular cadet-like voice.

Zinaida laughed again. I had time to notice that never before had the colour in her face been so lovely. The cadet and I set off for our walk. There was an old swing in our garden. I sat him down on the thin plank and began swinging him. He sat motionless in his small new uniform of thick cloth with wide gold braiding, and held on tightly to the ropes.

"Why don't you unbutton your collar?" I said to him.

"It's all right, I'm used to it," he said, and cleared his throat. He was like his sister. His eyes especially recalled her. I was glad to be of some use to him, and at the same time an aching sadness was gnawing at my heart. "Now," I thought, "I really am a little boy, whereas yesterday . . ." I remembered where I had dropped my knife the night before, and found it. The cadet asked me for it, broke off a thick stalk of wild parsley, cut himself a whistle out of it, and began whistling. Othello whistled a little too.

But, that very evening, how he wept, this same Othello, in Zinaida's arms, when, finding him in a corner of the garden, she asked him why he was so sad? My tears gushed out of my eyes with such force that she was frightened.

"What's the matter? What's wrong with you, Vladimir?" she kept repeating, and seeing that I neither replied to her nor stopped weeping, she bent down to kiss my wet cheek. But I turned away from her and whispered through my sobs, "I know everything. Why did you play with me? What did you want my love for?"

"I'm sorry, dear, dear Vladimir," said Zinaida. "Oh, I am very much to blame," she said, clasping her hands tightly. "There's so much in me that is evil, dark and wicked. . . . But now I am not playing with you. I do love you. I don't think you even suspect why and how much I love you. . . . But—what is it you know?"

What could I tell her? She stood before me and looked at me, and I belonged to her entirely from head to foot the moment she looked at me. . . . A quarter of an hour later I was running races with the cadet and Zinaida: I was no longer crying, I was laughing, though, as I laughed, my swollen eyelids dropped tears; Zinaida's ribbon was tied round my neck instead of a cravat, and I screamed with joy every time I succeeded in catching her by the waist. She did what she liked with me.

19

I should have found it very difficult if someone had asked me to describe in detail what was going on within me during the week after my unsuccessful midnight expedition. It was a strange, feverish time, a kind of chaos, in which the most conflicting feelings, thoughts, suspicions, hopes, joys, and pains whirled about madly within me. I was afraid of looking into myself, if a boy of sixteen can ever look into himself. I was afraid of giving an account to myself of anything; I simply tried to live through the day as fast as I could, but at night I slept —the lightheartedness of childhood came to my aid. I did not want to know whether I was loved, and I did not want to admit to myself that I was not loved. I avoided my father, but avoid Zinaida I could not. In her presence I burnt as in a fire, but what did I care what kind of fire it was in which I burnt and melted, so long as I felt happy to burn and melt? I gave myself up to all my sensations and tried to cheat myself by turning away from my memories and shutting my eyes to what I felt was going to happen. . . . This state of sweet anguish would probably not have lasted long in any case. A thunderbolt cut it all short at one blow and flung me onto an altogether new path.

One day when I came back to dinner after a rather long walk I learnt with astonishment that I was to dine alone, that my father had gone away and my mother was not well and did not want any dinner and had shut herself up in her bedroom. I could see by the faces of the footmen that something unusual had happened. I did not dare to question them, but I had a friend among them, a young pantry-boy, Phillip by name, who was passionately fond of poetry and an excellent performer on the guitar, and it was to him that I turned. From him I learnt that a terrible scene had taken place be-

tween my father and my mother (every word of it had
been overheard in the maids' room; much of it had been
spoken in French, but Masha, our parlourmaid, had
lived for five years with a dressmaker in Paris and understood every word); that my mother had accused my
father of infidelity, of being on intimate terms with the
young lady next door; that my father had at first tried
to justify himself, but afterwards had lost his temper
and, in his turn, said something brutal, "something
about Madam's age," which had made my mother cry;
that my mother too had alluded to some loan given to
the old princess, and spoken very unfavourably of her
and of the young lady also, and that then my father had
threatened her.

"And the whole trouble arose," continued Phillip,
"from an anonymous letter, and no one knows who wrote
it. Otherwise there's no reason why anything should have
come out at all."

"Why, was there anything?" I managed to bring out
with difficulty, while my hands and feet went cold, and
something began to tremble deep inside me.

Phillip winked significantly. "There was. There's no
hiding these things. However careful your father was
this time, he had, you see, to hire a carriage. Besides,
you can't do nothing without servants' knowing, neither."

I dismissed Phillip and flung myself on my bed. I did
not sob; I did not give myself up to despair; I did not
ask myself when and how all this had happened; I did
not wonder how it was I had not guessed it all before,
long ago; I did not even harbour any ill will against my
father. What I had learnt was more than I could cope
with: this sudden revelation crushed me utterly. All was
at an end. All my flowers were torn out by the roots
at one fell swoop and they lay about me, strewn all
over the place and trampled underfoot.

20

Next day my mother announced that she was moving back to town. In the morning my father went into her bedroom and remained with her a long time alone. No one heard what he said to her, but my mother cried no more. She grew calm and asked for food, but did not show herself, nor did she change her decision. I remember I wandered about all day, but did not go into the garden and did not once glance at the cottage. In the evening I was the witness of a most extraordinary scene: my father led Count Malevsky by the arm through the drawing room into the hall and, in the presence of the footman, said to him coldly, "A few days ago your lordship was shown the door in a certain house. I shall not enter into any kind of explanation with you, but I should like to make it quite clear to you that if you ever do me the honour of calling on me again I shall throw you out of the window. I don't like your handwriting."

The count bowed, gritted his teeth, shrank into himself, and disappeared.

Preparations began for our removal to town, to the Arbat, where we had a house. I expect my father himself did not want to stay in the country any longer, but he had evidently succeeded in persuading my mother not to make any more scenes; everything was done quietly, without haste; my mother even sent her compliments to the old princess and expressed regret that she was not able to see her before she left because of ill health.

I wandered about the place like one distraught and longed for it all to be over as quickly as possible. One thought kept running through my head: How could she, a young girl and a princess, have made up her mind to do such a thing when she knew that my father was not free and when she had the opportunity of marrying

Belovzorov, for instance? What did she hope for? How was it that she was not afraid of ruining her whole future? "Yes," I thought, "this is love, this is passion, this is devotion." And I remembered Lushin's words: *Some people find it sweet to sacrifice themelves. . . .* One day I managed to catch sight of something white in one of the windows of the cottage. "Can it be Zinaida's face?" I thought. Indeed, it was her face. I could bear it no longer. I could not part with her without a final good-bye. I took advantage of a favourable moment and went over to the cottage.

In the drawing room the old princess met me with her usual slovenly and careless greeting. "Why are your people so anxious to leave the country so soon, my boy?" she said, stuffing snuff into both her nostrils.

I looked at her, and a load was lifted from my heart. The word *loan* which Phillip had used had been torturing me. But she did not seem to suspect anything, at least I thought so at the time. Zinaida came in from the next room, pale, in a black dress, and her hair hanging loose. She took me by the hand in silence and led me away with her.

"I heard your voice," she began, "and came out at once. And do you find it so easy to leave us, you bad boy?"

"I've come to say good-bye to you, Princess," I said, "probably forever. I expect you must have heard we are going away."

Zinaida looked intently at me. "Yes, I have heard. Thank you for coming. I had thought that I would not see you again. Don't think badly of me. I've tortured you sometimes, but all the same I'm not the sort of person you imagine me to be." She turned away and leaned against the window. "No, I really am not like that. I know that you have a bad opinion of me."

"Me?"

"Yes—you."

208

"Me?" I repeated mournfully, and my heart trembled as it always did under the influence of her irresistible, inexpressible fascination. "Me? Believe me, Princess, that I would love and adore you to the end of my life, whatever you did and however much you tortured me."

She turned to me quickly and, flinging her arms wide, put them round my head and kissed me warmly and passionately. God knows for whom that long farewell kiss was meant, but I eagerly tasted its sweetness—I knew that it would never be repeated.

"Good-bye, good-bye," I kept repeating.

She tore herself away and went out of the room. I too went away. I am not able to describe the feelings with which I left. I would not wish them ever to be repeated; but I would have considered myself unfortunate had I never experienced them at all.

We moved back to town. It was some time before I could shake off the past and it was some time before I could sit down to work again. My wound healed slowly; but I bore no ill will against my father. On the contrary, he seemed to have risen in my estimation. Let psychologists explain this contradiction as best they can.

One day I was walking along a boulevard and, to my indescribable joy, ran into Lushin. I liked him for his straightforward and unhypocritical character, and, besides, he was dear to me because of the memories he awoke in me. I rushed up to him.

"Aha," he said, frowning, "so it's you, young man. Come, let's have a look at you. You're still as sallow as ever, but there's no longer any silly nonsense in your eyes. You look like a man and not like a lap-dog. That's good. Well, what are you doing? Working?"

I heaved a sigh. I did not want to tell a lie, but I was ashamed to tell the truth.

"Well, never mind, don't lose heart. The main thing is to lead a normal life and not to give in to every passing fancy. For what's the use of it? Wherever the tide may carry you, it will all be no good. A man must stand on his feet, even if he has to stand on a rock. As you see, I've got a bad cough. . . . And Belovzorov—have you heard?"

"No. What is it?"

"Vanished without a trace. They say he's gone off to the Caucasus. Let it be a lesson to you, young man, and it's all because people don't know how to part in time, how to break out of the net. You seem to have got out of it unscathed. Mind you don't get caught again. Good-bye."

"I shan't be caught," I thought. "I shall never see her again."

But I was destined to see Zinaida once more.

21

My father used to go riding every day. He had an excellent roan English mare, with a long slender neck and long legs, an indefatigable and vicious animal. She was called Electric. No one could ride her except my father. One day he came into my room in a good humour, something which had not happened to him for a long time: he was about to go for his ride and had already put on his spurs. I began to beg him to take me with him.

"I'd rather have a game of leapfrog with you," my father replied, "for you'll never keep up with me on your pony."

"I will. I'll wear spurs too."

"Oh, all right."

We set off. I had a black, shaggy pony, sturdy and very spirited; it is true he had to gallop at full speed when Electric was in full trot, but all the same I did not lag behind. I have never seen a horseman who could ride as well as my father; he sat on his horse so beautifully and with such effortless ease that it seemed that the horse herself felt it and took pride in him. We rode through all the boulevards, rode across Devichy Square, took several fences (at first I used to be afraid of the jumps, but my father despised timid people, and I stopped being afraid), crossed the Moskva River twice, and I was beginning to think that we were returning home, particularly as my father himself remarked that my horse was getting tired, when suddenly he turned away from me at the Crimean Ford and galloped off along the bank. I rode after him. On reaching a high pile of stacked-up old timber, he jumped nimbly off Electric, told me to dismount, and, giving me his bridle to hold, asked me to wait for him there at the stack, while he himself turned into a small back-street and disappeared.

I began to walk up and down along the bank of the river, leading the horses and scolding Electric, who kept tossing her reins, shaking herself, snorting, and neighing; whenever I stopped, she kept pawing the ground and biting my pony in the neck, whinnying—in short, she behaved like the spoilt thoroughbred she was. My father did not come back. An unpleasant dampness came drifting from the river; a fine rain began to fall softly, covering with tiny dark spots the stupid grey timber logs which I kept walking past backwards and forwards and which, by that time, I was heartily sick of. I was beginning to feel depressed, but still my father did not come. A Finnish policeman, who was also grey all over, with a huge, old-fashioned shako like a pot on his head and with a halberd (why on earth a policeman in such an old-fashioned attire should be patrolling the bank of the river Moskva is quite beyond me!) approached me, and turning his face, wrinkled like an old woman's, towards me, said, "What are you doing here with them horses, sir? Come, let me hold them for you."

I made no answer; he asked me for some tobacco. To get rid of him (besides, I was getting very impatient),

I took a few steps in the direction in which my father had disappeared, walked down to the end of the lane, turned the corner, and stopped dead. In the street, about forty paces from me, stood my father in front of the open window of a small wooden house; he had his back to me and was leaning with his chest over the window-sill; inside the house, half hidden by a curtain, sat a woman in a dark dress, talking to my father; the woman was Zinaida.

I was thunderstruck. That, I confess, I had not expected. My first impulse was to run away. "Father will look round," I thought, "and I shall be done for." But a strange feeling, a feeling stronger than curiosity, stronger even than jealousy, stronger than fear, stopped me. I began to watch. I did my best to hear what they were saying. My father seemed to be insisting on something. Zinaida would not agree. I can see her face just as if it were all happening now—sad, serious, beautiful, and with an indescribable imprint of devotion, sadness, love, and a kind of despair—I can find no other word for it. She uttered words of one syllable; she did not raise her eyes but just smiled—submissively and obstinately. It was by this smile alone that I recognised my Zinaida as I used to know her. My father shrugged and set his hat straight on his head, which was always a sign of impatience with him. Then I heard the words: *"Vous devez vous separer de cette . . ."* Zinaida drew herself up and stretched out her hand. . . . Suddenly something quite unbelievable took place before my very eyes: my father all of a sudden raised his riding crop, with which he had been flicking the dust from the skirts of his coat, and I heard the sound of a sharp blow across her arm, which was bared to the elbow. I just managed to restrain myself from crying out, while Zinaida gave a start, looked at my father without uttering a word, and, raising her arm to her lips, kissed the scar that showed crimson on it. My father flung away the crop and, running up the steps rapidly, rushed into the house. Zinaida turned round, tossed back her head, and, with arms outstretched, also moved away from the window.

Faint with fright, and my heart gripped with a kind of bewildered horror, I rushed back, and running down the lane, nearly letting go of Electric, returned to the bank of the river. I simply did not know what to make of it. I knew that my cold and reserved father was sometimes given to fits of fury, but for all that I could not possibly make any sense of what I had just seen. But at the same time I felt sure that however long I lived, I could never forget Zinaida's gesture, her look, her smile; and that image of her, this new image which had so suddenly arisen before me, was forever imprinted on my memory. I gazed vacantly at the river and did not notice that tears were streaming down my cheeks. "They are beating her," I thought, "beating, beating . . ."

"Hello there, what are you doing? Give me the horse!" I heard my father's voice behind me.

Mechanically I gave him the bridle. He leapt on Electric's back. The horse, chilled with standing, reared on its hind legs and leapt forward about six feet, but my father soon curbed her; he drove the spurs into her sides and hit her on the neck with his fist.

"Damn, no crop," he murmured.

I recalled the swish and the blow from the same crop a short while before, and shuddered.

"Where have you put it?" I asked my father after a short pause.

My father made no answer and galloped on. I overtook him. I simply had to see his face.

"You weren't bored waiting for me, were you?" he muttered through his teeth.

"A little. Where did you drop your crop?" I asked him again.

My father glanced quickly at me. "I did not drop it," he said. "I threw it away."

He sank into thought and lowered his head, and it was then that I saw for the first and almost for the last time how much tenderness and pity his stern features could express.

He galloped on again, and this time I could not over-take him; I arrived home a quarter of an hour after him.

"This is love," I again said to myself, sitting at night at my writing desk on which my books and exercise books had begun to make their appearance. "This is passion. How was it possible not to feel resentment, to suffer a blow from any hand—even the dearest! But it seems one can if one is in love . . . and I—I imagined . . ."

I had grown much older during the last month—and my love, with all its excitements and sufferings, struck me as something very small and childish and trivial beside that other, unknown something which I could scarcely grasp and which frightened me like an unfamiliar, beautiful, but menacing face one tries in vain to make out in the gathering darkness.

That night I had a strange and terrible dream. I dreamt that I went into a low, dark room. My father, whip in hand, was standing there and stamping angrily with his feet; Zinaida was crouching in a corner, and there was a red scar, not on her arm, but on her forehead, and behind them both rose Belovzorov, covered with blood, and he opened his pale lips and shook his fist angrily at my father.

Two months later I entered the university, and six months after that my father died (of a stroke) in Petersburg, where he had just moved with my mother and me. A few days before his death he received a letter from Moscow which upset him greatly. He went to beg some favour from my mother and, I was told, he even wept, he—my father! On the morning of the day he had his stroke, he had begun a letter to me in French. "My son," he wrote, "fear the love of woman, fear that ec-

FIRST LOVE

stasy, that poison . . ." My mother, after his death, sent a considerable sum of money to Moscow.

22

Four years passed. I had just left the university and had not quite made up my mind what to do with myself, at what door to knock; for the time being, I just did nothing. One fine evening I met Maydanov at the theatre. By that time he had got married and joined the civil service, but I found him quite unchanged. He still went into raptures for no obvious reason and grew depressed just as suddenly.

"You know," he said to me, "Mrs. Dolsky is here."

"What Mrs. Dolsky?"

"Why, you've not forgotten, have you? The former Princess Zasyekin. The girl we were all in love with —and you, too. Remember, in the country near the Neskoochny Park?"

"Is she married to a Dolsky?"

"Yes."

"And is she here, in the theatre?"

"No, she's in Petersburg. She arrived a few days ago. She's going abroad."

"What sort of man is her husband?"

"Oh, a splendid fellow. A man of property. He's a colleague of mine in Moscow. You understand, after that affair—I expect you must know all about it"—Maydanov smiled significantly—"it was not so easy for her to make a match. There were consequences—but with her brains, nothing is impossible. Go and see her. I am sure that she'll be very pleased to see you. She is prettier than ever."

Maydanov gave me Zinaida's address. She was staying in the Hotel Demuth. Old memories stirred in me. . . . I made up my mind to call on my former flame.

215

But all sorts of things prevented me from calling on her. A week passed, then another; and when at last I went to the Hotel Demuth and asked for Mrs. Dolsky I was told that she had died four days before, quite suddenly, in childbirth.

I felt a sudden stab in my heart. The thought that I could have seen her and did not, and would never see her again—that bitter thought drove its sting into me with all the force of an irrepressible reproach. "She is dead," I repeated, staring vacantly at the hotel porter, and, going out into the street quietly, I walked on without knowing myself where I was going. All my past suddenly rose up and stood before me. So that was the end of this young, passionate, and brilliant life! That was the goal to which, in its haste and agitation, it aspired. When I thought of this, I conjured up those dear features, those eyes, those curls—in the narrow box, in the dank underground darkness, quite near, not far from me who was still living, and perhaps only a few paces from my father. I thought of all this; I exerted my imagination; and meanwhile—

> From lips indifferent, the tidings
> Of death I heard, and, indifferent
> To it, I listened—

sounded in my heart. Oh, youth, youth! You don't care for anything, you seem to own all the treasures of the world; even sorrow amuses you, even grief becomes you; you are self-confident and insolent; you say, "I alone am alive—look at me!"—even while your days pass away and vanish without trace and without number, and everything in you melts away like wax in the sun, like snow. . . . And perhaps the whole secret of your charm lies not in your ability to do everything, but in your ability to think that you will do everything—lies just in the way you are scattering to the winds the powers which you could never have used for anything else—in the fact that each of us seriously considers himself to have been a spendthrift, seriously believes that he has a right to say, "Oh, what could I not have done if I had not wasted my time!"

So I too—what did I hope for? What did I expect? What rich promise did the future hold out to me when —with scarcely a sigh, with no more than a feeling of bleak despondency—I bade farewell to the phantom of my first love, risen for a fleeting moment?

And what came of it all—of all I had hoped for? Now, when evening shadows are beginning to fall on my life, what have I left that is fresher, that is dearer to me than the memories of the storm that came and passed over so swiftly one spring morning?

But I am not quite fair to myself. Even then, in those thoughtless days of my youth, I did not remain deaf to the mournful voice which called to me, to the solemn sound which came to me from beyond the grave. I remember how a few days after I had learnt of Zinaida's death, I myself, in response to an irresistible impulse, was present at the death of a poor old woman who lived in the same house with us. Covered with rags, lying on hard boards, with a sack for a pillow under her head, she was dying a hard and painful death. All her life had been spent in a bitter struggle with daily want. She had known no joy; she had not tasted the honey of happiness; and one would have thought that she of all people would have been glad to die, and thus to gain freedom and rest. And yet, so long as her frail body held out, so long as her breast was still rising and falling in agony under the icy hand that weighed upon her, so long as there was still strength left in her body, the old woman kept crossing herself and kept whispering, "Lord, forgive me my sins," and only after the last spark of consciousness had gone did the look of fear and terror of death

disappear from her eyes. . . . And I remember that
there, by the deathbed of that poor old woman, I felt
terrified for Zinaida, and I longed to say a prayer for
her, for my father—and for myself.

1860

KNOCK...KNOCK...KNOCK

A STUDY

1

... We all settled down in a circle, and Alexander Vassilyevich Ridel, a good friend of ours (his surname was German, but he was a Russian born and bred), began as follows.

I am going to tell you a story, gentlemen, something that happened to me in the thirties—that is, about forty years ago. I shall be brief, and you must not interrupt me.

I was living in Petersburg at the time and had only just left the university. My brother was a lieutenant in the horse-guard artillery. His battery was stationed in Krasnoye Selo—it all happened in the summer. My brother was quartered, not in Krasnoye Selo, but in one of the nearby villages; I stayed with him more than once, and made the acquaintance of all his fellow officers. He was living in a fairly clean and tidy peasant's cottage with another officer of his battery. The name of that officer was Ilya Stepanych Teglyov. I became particularly friendly with him.

Marlinsky is considered old-fashioned now and nobody reads him; people even make fun of his name. But in the thirties he was regarded as a great literary genius, and no one, not even Pushkin, could compare with him, according to the views of the young people of that time. He not only enjoyed the reputation of being the foremost Russian writer, but, what is much harder to achieve and which happens much less frequently, he left his mark on his own generation. Heroes à la Marlinsky were to be found everywhere, but especially in the provinces and especially among infantry and artillery officers; they conversed and corresponded in his language; they held themelves aloof in society, glaring darkly at everyone—"with a storm in the heart and a fire in the blood"—like Lieutenant Belozor in *The Frigate Hope*. Female hearts were "devoured" by them. It was about them that the nickname "fatal" was invented. This type, as we all know, lasted a long time, up to the time of Pechorin.* It was composed of all sorts of elements: Byronism, romanticism, memories of the French Revolution, of the Decembrists, and—worship of Napoleon, faith in one's destiny, in one's lucky star, in the strength of one's character, a pose and a fine phrase, and—the depression that comes from the sense of the futility of things, uneasy alarms of petty vanity, and real strength and daring, noble aspirations, and bad education and ignorance, aristocratic airs, and ostentatious parade of gewgaws. But, no more philosophising. . . . I promised to tell you a story.

2

Second Lieutenant Teglyov belonged to the number of just such "fatal" men, though he did not possess the personal appearance commonly associated with such in-

* Pechorin is the hero of Lermontov's famous romantic novel, *A Hero of Our Time*. TRANSLATOR.

dividuals; he did not, for instance, in any way resemble Lermontov's "fatalist." He was a man of medium height, rather thickset, round-shouldered, with fair hair, almost white eyelashes and eyebrows; he had a round, fresh, rosy-cheeked face, a turned-up nose, a low forehead with the hair growing thick over the temples, and full, regular, always immobile lips: he never laughed; he did not even smile. Only occasionally when he got tired and out of breath did he show his square teeth, white as sugar. The same sort of artificial immobility was spread over all his features: but for it he would have looked quite good-humoured. In the whole of his face only his eyes were not quite ordinary. They were small, with green irises and yellow eyelashes: his right eye was a little higher than his left and the eyelid of his left eye lifted less than the eyelid of his right eye, which made his eyes look somewhat odd and somnolent. Teglyov's face, which was not by any means unattractive, almost always wore an expression of dissatisfaction with an admixture of bewilderment, as though he were chasing within himself after some gloomy thought which, try as he might, he was never able to catch. For all that, he did not give you the impression of a proud man; he would rather be taken for an aggrieved than a proud person. He spoke very little, stammeringly, in a hoarse voice, repeating his words unnecessarily. Unlike the majority of "fatalists," he did not use particularly florid expressions, resorting to them only in writing; his handwriting was absolutely childlike.

His superiors regarded him as an officer who was "so-so," not too capable and not particularly zealous. "Punctuality he has, but no punctiliousness," the brigadier general, a man of German extraction, used to say of him. The soldiers too regarded Teglyov as "so-so," neither fish nor flesh nor good red herring. He lived modestly within his means. He was left an orphan at the age of nine; his father and mother were drowned when they were being ferried across the Oka in the spring floods. He had been educated at a private boarding school, where he was regarded as one of the dullest and quietest of pupils. He obtained a commission in the horse-guard artillery at his own urgent desire and at the recommendation of a great-uncle, and, though with some difficulty, passed his examination first as an ensign and then as a second lieutenant.

His relations with his fellow officers were rather strained. He was not liked, and his fellow officers did not visit him often, and he himself hardly ever visited anyone. The presence of strangers made him feel uncomfortable; he at once became unnatural and awkward. There was nothing of a comradely nature in him, and he was not on familiar terms with anyone. But he was respected; and he was respected, not for his character, nor for his intelligence and education, but because he was generally acknowledged to possess that special stamp which is considered to be the hall-mark of all "fatal" men. "Teglyov will go far, Teglyov will distinguish himself in some way or other"—*that* none of his fellow officers expected, but that "Teglyov will do something extraordinary" or that "Teglyov will suddenly become a Napoleon"—*that* was not regarded as impossible; for in this sort of thing it is one's "lucky star" that matters, and he was "a man of destiny," just as there are "men of sighs" and "men of tears."

3

Two incidents which marked the beginning of his service as an officer contributed a great deal to the consolidation of his "fatal" reputation. On the very first day after receiving his commission, about the middle of March, he was walking with some other newly commissioned officers in full-dress uniform along the Neva embankment. The spring had come early that year; the ice on the Neva had broken up: the large ice floes had gone, but the whole river was one solid mass of small pieces of ice. The young men were talking and laughing. Suddenly one of them stopped: he had caught sight of a little dog on the slowly moving surface of the river, about twenty paces from the bank. Perched on a projecting piece of ice, it was trembling all over and whining. "Why, it's sure to drown," one officer muttered through his teeth. The little dog was slowly being carried past one of the ramps constructed along the embankment. Suddenly Teglyov, without uttering a word, ran down the ramp and, jumping over the thin ice, falling through, and leaping out again, made his way to the little dog, seized it by the scruff of the neck, and, getting safely back to the bank, threw it down in the road. The danger which Teglyov had run was so great, and his action was so unexpected, that his fellow officers seemed petrified with horror, and it was only when he hailed a cab to take him home that they started talking all at once; his uniform was soaking wet. In reply to their exclamations Teglyov remarked coolly that no one could ever escape what was written in the book of fate, and told the cabman to drive on.

"You might at least take the dog with you in memory of your exploit!" cried one of the officers, but Teglyov declined the suggestion by a wave of the hand, and his fellow officers looked at each other in silent amazement.

The other incident occurred a few days later at a card party at the battery commander's. Teglyov was sitting in a corner. He took no part in the game. "Oh, if only I had a grandmother to tell me beforehand what cards will win, as in Pushkin's *Queen of Spades!*" cried one ensign, who was just losing his third thousand. Teglyov went up silently to the table, picked up a pack of cards, cut it, and saying, "The six of diamonds!" turned the pack up: the bottom card was the six of diamonds. "The ace of clubs," he announced and cut again: the bottom card was the ace of clubs. "The king of diamonds!" he said in an angry whisper and through clenched teeth, and he was right the third time—and suddenly he blushed to the roots of his hair. He probably had not expected it himself. "An excellent trick!" observed the battery commander. "Show us some more." "I don't go in for tricks," Teglyov replied dryly and went into the other room.

How it happened that he guessed a card right, I am not in a position to say, but I saw it with my own eyes. Many of the players present tried to do the same, but not one succeeded: one or two did guess *one* card, but no one could guess two cards in succession. And Teglyov had guessed three! This incident strengthened still further his reputation as a mysterious, "fatal" individual. It has often occurred to me afterwards that, but for his trick with the cards, goodness only knows what a different turn his reputation might have taken and how he would have regarded himself; but this unexpected success settled the matter once and for all.

4

Teglyov of course did not hesitate to get all the advantages he could out of this reputation. It lent him a certain prestige, a special glamour—"*Cela le posait,*" as the French say—and for a man of his small intelligence, scanty education, and enormous vanity, such a reputation was just what he wanted. It was difficult to acquire it, but to keep it up required no effort: all he had to do was to be silent and shun people.

But it was not on the strength of this reputation that I made friends with Teglyov and, I might say, grew fond of him. I grew fond of him, first, because I was not a very sociable fellow myself and I saw in him a kindred spirit; and, second, because he was a good-natured fellow and a very simple-hearted one at bottom. He inspired a sort of compassion in me; I could not help feeling that, apart from his affected "fatality," a tragic fate, which he did not himself suspect, really hung over him. *That* feeling, needless to say, I did not speak to him about: could there be any worse insult for a "fatalistic" person than to inspire compassion?

Teglyov, too, was well disposed to me: he felt at ease with me, he liked to talk with me, and in my presence he felt he could come down from the strange pedestal on which he had either climbed up himself or just happened to have got there by means of some outside agency. Agonizingly, morbidly vain as he was, he probably realised at heart that there was no justification whatever for his vanity and that other people might very well look down upon him. But I, a boy of nineteen, did not embarrass him; the fear of saying something stupid, something inappropriate, did not oppress his oversensitive heart. He sometimes even became quite talkative, and lucky for him that no one ever heard his speeches except me! He would not have enjoyed his reputation long. He not only knew very little; he practically never read anything, and he confined himself to collecting a number of anecdotes and stories of a suitable kind. He believed in presentiments, predictions, omens, meetings, lucky and unlucky days, in the persecution or the benevolence of fate—in the significance of life, in short. He even believed in certain "climacteric" years, which someone had mentioned in his presence, and the meaning of which he did not understand very well himself. To "fatal" men of the true stamp one should not express such beliefs; they should inspire them in others. . . . But I was the only one who knew that side of Teglyov's character.

5

One day—I remember, it was July 20, St. Elijah's Day —I went to stay with my brother and did not find him at home: he had been sent off on regimental business for a whole week. I did not want to go back to Petersburg; I went snipe-shooting in the nearby marshes, shot a brace of snipe, and spent the evening with Teglyov under a lean-to of an empty barn in which, as he expressed it, he had "set up his summer quarters." We chatted about all sorts of things, though mostly drank tea, smoked pipes, and talked sometimes to the landlord, a Russianised Finn, and to the pedlar who used to hang about the battery, selling, "Oranges and lemons, fine juicy ones!"—a nice man who was fond of cracking jokes and who, in addition to his other talents, played the guitar and used to tell us of the unhappy attachment which "in the days of [his] youth" he formed for the daughter of a policeman. Now that he had reached years of maturity, this Don Juan in a striped red and white shirt had no more unhappy attachments.

In front of the doors of our barn stretched a wide plain which gradually disappeared into the distance; a small stream gleamed here and there in the winding hollows, and low-lying woods could be seen farther away on the very edge of the horizon. Night was falling, and we were left alone. A thin damp vapour descended upon the earth with the night, and, growing more and more dense, at last turned into a thick mist. The moon rose in the sky: its light penetrated through the mist and seemed to invest it with a golden radiance. Everything moved about, became mixed and wrapped up in a strange way; distant objects seemed to be close and close objects distant, large things small and small things large—everything became bright and blurred. We seemed to have been carried off into a fairyland kingdom, a kingdom of whitish golden haze, profound stillness, and light sleep. . . . And how mysteriously, with what silvery flashes of light, did the stars filter through the mist. Both of us fell silent. The fantastic nature of that night had its effect on us; it put us into the mood for the fantastic.

6

Teglyov was the first to break the silence. He spoke with his usual stutter, omissions, and repetitions about premonitions—about ghosts. On exactly such a night, according to him, one student he knew, who had a short while before obtained the post of tutor to two orphan children and had been lodged with them in a pavilion in the garden, saw a woman's figure bending over their beds and the next day recognised the figure in a portrait of the mother of the orphans he had not noticed before. Then Teglyov told me that his parents had heard the sound of running water a few days before they were drowned; that his grandfather had apparently been saved from death in the Battle of Borodino by catching sight of an ordinary grey pebble on the ground, bending down suddenly to pick it up at the very moment when a piece of shrapnel flew over his head and sliced off his long black plume. Teglyov even promised to show me the very pebble which had saved his grandfather and which he had had set into a medallion. Then he spoke of the high calling of every man, and of his own in particular, adding that he still believed in it, and that if he had ever had any doubts about it, he would know how to make an end of them and of his life, for life would then lose all meaning for him.

"You think," he said, looking askance at me, "I won't have the courage to do it, don't you? You don't know me; I have a will of iron!"

"Well said," I thought to myself.

Teglyov sank into thought, heaved a deep sigh, and, dropping his long pipe out of his hand, told me that that day was a very important one for him. "It's St. Elijah's Day—my name day. . . . It is always a very difficult time for me."

I said nothing and merely looked at him as he sat be-

fore me, bent, round-shouldered, clumsy, with his somnolent, sullen eyes fixed on the ground.

"An old beggarwoman" (Teglyov did not let a single
beggar pass without giving alms) "told me today," he
went on, "that she would pray for my soul. Don't you
think it's strange?"

"Why on earth does he always worry about himself?"
I thought again. I must, however, add that lately I had
begun to notice an unusual look of worry and alarm on
Teglyov's face, and it was not a "fatal" melancholy; he
really was worried and upset about something. This time
too I was struck by the gloom that was spread all over
his features. Had the doubts that he had just spoken to
me about already begun to arise in his mind? Teglyov's
fellow officers had told me that a short while before, he
had sent to the authorities a suggestion about some im-
provements of parts of the gun carriage, and that this
had been returned to him with "a comment"—that is, a
reprimand. Knowing his character, I had no doubt that
such a contemptuous treatment on the part of his superiors had hurt his feelings badly. But what I felt I
saw in Teglyov was more like grief and had more of a
personal character.

"It's getting damp, though," he said suddenly, hunching his shoulders. "Let's go back to the cottage. Besides,
it's time to turn in."

He had a habit of hunching his shoulders and turning
his head from side to side as though his necktie were
too tight, and when he did that he usually clutched at
his throat with his right hand. Teglyov's character, so at
least it seemed to me, found expression in this nervous
and moody gesture. He too felt cramped in the world.

We returned to the cottage and lay down on benches
covered with hay, he in the corner with the icons and
myself on the opposite side.

7

Teglyov tossed and turned on his bench for a long time, and I could not go to sleep, either. Whether his stories had excited my nerves or this strange night excited my blood, I do not know—only I could not fall asleep. Indeed, every desire for sleep disappeared at last, and I lay with my eyes open, thinking, thinking intensely, goodness only knows about what, about the most stupid trifles, as is always the case when one cannot go to sleep. Turning from side to side, I stretched out my hand. One of my fingers knocked against one of the beams of the wall. A faint but hollow and, as it were, drawn-out sound was heard. I must have happened to strike a hollow place.

I knocked for a second time, this time on purpose. The sound was repeated. I knocked again.

Suddenly Teglyov raised his head. "Ridel," he said, "do you hear? Someone's knocking under the window."

I pretended to be asleep. It suddenly occurred to me to pull the leg of my "fatal" friend. I could not sleep, anyway.

He let his head fall on the pillow. I waited a little and again knocked three times in succession.

Teglyov again raised his head and began to listen.

I knocked again. I was lying with my face turned towards him, but he could not see my hand. I put it behind me under the bedclothes.

"Ridel!" Teglyov cried.

I made no answer.

"Ridel!" he repeated in a loud voice. "Ridel!"

"Oh? What is it?" I said as though half awake.

"Don't you hear? Someone keeps knocking under the window. Wants to come in, I suppose."

"Some passer-by," I muttered.

"We must let him in, or find out who he is."

But I did not reply and again pretended to be asleep. Several minutes passed. I was at it again.

Knock . . . knock . . . knock . . .

Teglyov sat up at once and began to listen.

Knock . . . knock . . . knock! Knock . . . knock . . . knock . . . !

Through my half-closed eyelids, by the whitish light of the night, I could distinctly see every movement he made. He kept turning his face to the window and then to the door. And, again, it was difficult to say where the sound came from; it seemed to fly round the room as though gliding along the walls. I seemed to have accidentally lighted upon a spot which possessed acoustic properties.

Knock . . . knock . . . knock . . .

"Ridel!" Teglyov shouted at last. "Ridel! Ridel!"

"What's the matter?" I said, yawning.

"Don't you hear anything? Someone's knocking!"

"Well, let him!" I replied, and again pretended to fall asleep. I even began to snore.

Teglyov quietened down.

Knock . . . knock . . . knock . . . !

"Who's there?" cried Teglyov. "Come in!"

No one answered, of course.

Knock . . . knock . . . knock . . . !

Teglyov jumped out of bed, opened the window, and, poking his head out, asked in a wild voice, "Who's there? Who's knocking?" Then he opened the door and repeated the question. A horse neighed in the distance; that was all.

He went back to bed.

Knock . . . knock . . . knock . . . !

Teglyov immediately turned over and sat up.

Knock . . . knock . . . knock . . . !

Teglyov quickly put on his boots, threw his greatcoat over his shoulders, and, unhooking his sword from the wall, went out of the cottage. I heard him go round it twice, asking all the time, "Who is there? Who is there? Who goes there? Who's knocking?" Then he suddenly fell silent, stood still for some time not far from the corner where I was lying, and, without uttering another word, came back into the cottage and lay down without taking his things off.

Knock . . . knock . . . knock . . . ! I began again. Knock . . . knock . . . knock . . . !

But Teglyov did not stir, did not ask who was knocking, only propped his head on his hand.

Seeing that *this* had no effect any longer, I pretended a few minutes later to wake up and, after looking intently at Teglyov, assumed an air of amazement. "Have you been out?" I asked.

"Yes," he said unconcernedly.

"Have you heard the knocking all the time?"

"Yes."

"And you met no one?"

"No."

"And did the knocking stop?"

"Don't know. I don't care now."

"Now? Why now?"

Teglyov made no answer.

I was beginning to feel a little ashamed and a little annoyed with him. I could not, however, bring myself to confess that I had played a trick on him.

"Do you know what?" I began. "I am convinced that it was just your imagination."

"Oh, you think so, do you?"

"You say you heard a knocking——"

"It wasn't only knocking I heard," he interrupted me.

"What else?"

Teglyov leaned forward and bit his lips. He was apparently hesitating. "I was called!" he said at last in an undertone and turned away his face.

"Called? Who called you?"

"A woman . . ." Teglyov still looked away. "A being

whom till now I had only believed to be dead, but now I know it for certain."

"I swear, Teglyov, this is all your imagination!"

"Imagination?" he repeated. "Do you want me to prove it to you?"

"I do."

"Very well, let's go outside."

8

I dressed hurriedly and went out of the cottage with Teglyov. Opposite the cottage, on the other side of the road, there were no houses, but a low wattle fence, broken down in places, and beyond it began a rather steep descent into the valley. The mist shrouded everything as before and it was practically impossible to see anything twenty paces ahead. Teglyov and I walked up to the fence and stopped dead.

"Here," he said and lowered his head. "Stand still, keep quiet, and—listen!"

I pricked up my ears like him, and except for the usual, very faint noises of the night, which seemed to come from every direction, the breathing of the night, I could hear nothing. Glancing at one another from time to time, we stood there without moving for a couple of minutes, and were just about to resume our walk. . . .

"Ilya darling!" I thought I heard a faint whisper from behind the fence.

I glanced at Teglyov, but he apparently had heard nothing, and still stood there with a lowered head.

"Ilya darling . . . Ilya darling . . ." the voice repeated more distinctly than before, so distinctly indeed that it was possible to tell that the words were uttered by a woman.

We both gave a start simultaneously and stared at one another.

"Well?" Teglyov asked me in a whisper. "You won't doubt it now, will you?"

"Wait," I replied just as softly, "that doesn't prove anything. Let's see if there is anybody there. Someone may be playing a trick on us."

I jumped over the fence and walked in the direction from which, as far as I could judge, the voice had come.

I felt the soft, yielding earth under my feet; long furrows stretched before me and disappeared in the mist. I was in a kitchen-garden. But nothing stirred, neither round me nor in front of me. Everything seemed to be dead still in the stupor of sleep. I took a few more steps.

"Who's there?" I cried, no less wildly than Teglyov.

"Prrrr!" A flushed quail leapt out almost from under my feet and flew away as straight as a bullet. I could not help starting back. . . . What nonsense!

I looked behind and I could see Teglyov at the same spot where I left him. I walked up to him.

"You needn't bother to call again," he said. "That voice has come to me—from far away."

He passed his hand over his face and walked back home across the road with slow steps. But I did not want to give in so quickly and I went back to the kitchen-garden. That someone had really called "Ilya darling!" three times, I had no doubt whatever; that there was something plaintive and mysterious in that call—that too I had to admit to myself. But—who knows?—perhaps all this only appeared to be inexplicable, but could be explained as simply as the knocking which had excited Teglyov so much.

I walked along the wattle fence, stopping from time to time and looking round. Close to the fence, not far from our cottage, grew an old, leafy willow tree: it loomed, a big black patch, in the general whiteness of the mist, the dim whiteness which dulls and blinds your sight more than if you were in a confined space. Suddenly I fancied I saw something rather big and alive stirring on the ground near that willow. With a cry of: "Stop! Who is it?" I rushed forward. I heard the sound of light, harelike footfalls, and a crouching figure darted quickly past me, whether man or woman, I could not tell. I tried to grab it, but I was too slow; I stumbled, fell, and stung my face against some nettles. As I was getting up I leaned on the ground with a hand and felt something hard under it: it was a chased brass comb on a cord, such as our peasants wear on their belts.

My further investigations led to nothing, and with the comb in my hand and cheeks smarting from the nettles, I went back to the cottage.

9

I found Teglyov sitting on the bench. A candle was burning on the table before him, and he was writing something in a small notebook which he always carried about with him. Seeing me, he quickly put the notebook in his pocket and started filling his pipe.

"Look, my dear fellow," I began, "what a trophy I've brought from my expedition." I showed him the comb and told him what had happened to me by the willow tree. "I expect I must have frightened away a thief," I added. "You must have heard that a horse was stolen from our neighbour yesterday."

Teglyov smiled coldly and lit his pipe. I sat down beside him. "And are you as sure as before," I said, "that the voice we heard came from the unknown?"

He stopped me with an imperious gesture of his hand. "Ridel," he began, "I'm in no mood for jokes now, and I would therefore thank you not to joke, either."

And indeed Teglyov was in no mood for jokes. His face was changed. It looked paler, more expressive, and —longer. His strange "odd" eyes wandered slowly from one object to another.

"I never thought," he began again, "that I should ever

tell anyone else—any other man—what you are about to hear, and what should have died—yes, died—in my breast. But it seems it is to be, and besides, I have no choice. Fate! Listen."

And he told me a long story.

I have told you already, gentlemen, that he was not very good at telling stories, but it was not only his lack of skill in relating the events that had happened to him that struck me that night; the very sound of his voice, his looks, the movements he made with his fingers and his hands—everything about him, in short, seemed unnatural, unnecessary, and, indeed, false. I was still very young and inexperienced at the time and I did not know that the habit of expressing oneself rhetorically, that the falsity of intonation and manner, can become so much a part of a man that he is no longer able to rid himself of it: it is a kind of curse. Long afterwards I happened to meet a woman who, in the same florid language, with the same theatrical gestures, with the same melodramatic shaking of her head and rolling of her eyes, told me of the impression her son's death had made on her, of her "boundless" grief, of her fears for her reason, and I could not help thinking to myself, "How affected and untruthful this grand lady is! She didn't love her son at all!" And a week later I learnt that the poor woman had really gone mad. After that I became much more careful in my judgements and have had much less confidence in my own impressions.

10

The story which Teglyov told me was, briefly, as follows.

In addition to his high-ranking uncle, he had living in Petersburg an aunt, a woman who, though not of high rank, was extremely well to do. Having no children of her own, she had adopted a young girl, an orphan of the artisan class, given her a good education, and treated her like a daughter. Her name was Masha. Teglyov saw her almost every day. It ended in their falling in love with one another, and Masha gave herself to him. Their affair became known. Teglyov's aunt was furious, turned the unhappy girl out of her house in disgrace, and went to live in Moscow, where she adopted a young girl of noble birth and made her her heiress. On her return to her relations, poor people given to drink, Masha suffered terribly. Teglyov had promised to marry her, but did not keep his promise. At his last meeting with her he was forced to declare his intentions. She wanted to know the truth, and she got it. "Well," she said, "if I'm not to be your wife, then I know what there is left for me to do." More than two weeks had passed since that last meeting.

"I never for a moment deceived myself as to the meaning of her last words," added Teglyov. "I'm sure that she has done away with herself and that was *her* voice, that it was *she* calling me to follow her—there. I *recognised* her voice. Well, I'm afraid there's only one thing left for me to do!"

"But why did you not marry her?" I asked. "Have you fallen out of love with her?"

"No. I still love her passionately!"

Here, gentlemen, I just stared at Teglyov. I remembered another friend of mine, a very sensible fellow, who, being married to a highly unattractive, unintelligent woman with no fortune of her own, and being very unhappy in his marriage, when asked why he had married and whether it was for love, said, "For love? Of course not. I just did it for no reason at all." And yet here Teglyov was passionately in love with a girl and did not marry her. Well, was that too—for no reason?

"Why then don't you marry her?" I asked for a second time.

Teglyov's strange, somnolent eyes shifted over the

table. "That I—I can't put in—er—a few words," he began, stammering. "There are reasons. Besides, she—er
—belongs to the artisan class, and, well, there's my uncle,
and I have to take him into consideration too."

"Your uncle?" I cried. "What the devil do you want
your uncle for? You only see him at the New Year when
you go to offer him the compliments of the season. You
don't count on getting his money, do you? Why, he has
a dozen children of his own!" I spoke with warmth.

Teglyov winced and blushed—blushed unevenly, in
patches. "Please don't lecture me," he said in a hollow
voice. "However, I'm not trying to justify myself. I've
ruined her life, and now I shall have to repay my debt."

He dropped his head and fell silent. I could find nothing to say, either.

11

We sat like that for a quarter of an hour. He kept
looking away, but I looked at him and noticed that the
hair over his forehead seemed to stand up and curl in an
odd way, which, as an army doctor who had had a great
deal of practice among wounded soldiers observed, is always a sign of intense overheating of the brain. . . . It
again occurred to me that the hand of fate really did
weigh heavily on this man and that his fellow officers
had good reason in seeing something "fatal" in him. At
the same time, I could not help inwardly blaming him.
"A girl of the artisan class indeed!" I thought to myself. "A fine aristocrat you are!"

"Perhaps you blame me, Ridel," Teglyov began suddenly, as though guessing my thoughts. "I—er—am very
unhappy myself. But what can I do? But what can I do?"

He propped his chin on his hand and began to bite the
broad, flat nails of his stubby red fingers, hard as iron.

"I'm of the opinion," I said, "that you must first make
sure whether your fears are justified. Perhaps the girl

you're in love with is in excellent health." ("Shall I tell him the real cause of the knocking?" flashed through my head. "No, later.")

"She has not written to me once, ever since we have been in camp here," replied Teglyov.

"That doesn't prove anything, my dear fellow."

Teglyov waved his hand in despair. "No! I'm sure she's no longer among the living. She called me . . ." He suddenly turned his face to the window. "Someone's knocking again!"

I could not help laughing.

"I'm very sorry, my dear fellow, but this time it's your nerves. You see, it is getting light. In ten minutes the sun will rise. It's past three o'clock, and ghosts have no power in the daytime."

Teglyov cast a gloomy look at me, and saying through his teeth, "Good-bye, sir," lay down on the bench and turned his back to me.

I too lay down, and before I fell asleep I remember thinking to myself, "Why does Teglyov always go on hinting that he is going to—commit suicide? What ridiculous nonsense! He refused to marry the girl of his own free will, he jilted her, and now, all of a sudden, he wants to kill himself! It makes no sense! He can't help showing off!"

With these thoughts I fell asleep and I slept like a log. When I opened my eyes the sun was already high in the sky—and Teglyov was not in the cottage.

He had, his servant told me, gone to town.

12

I spent a very wearisome and dull day. Teglyov did not return to dinner or to supper; I was not expecting my brother, either. Towards evening a thick mist, worse than that of the day before, came on once again. I went to bed rather early. I was awakened by a knocking under the window.

It was now *my* turn to start!

The knocking was repeated, and so clearly and insistently that I could not possibly doubt that it was real. I got up, opened the window, and saw Teglyov. Wrapped in his greatcoat and with his cap pulled over his eyes, he stood there motionless.

"Is that you?" I cried. "I'm sorry we couldn't wait up for you. Come in, or is the door locked?"

Teglyov shook his head. "I have no intention of coming in," he said in a hollow voice. "I only wanted to ask you to give this letter to the battery commanding officer tomorrow."

He held out to me a large envelope sealed with five seals. I was dumfounded, but I took the envelope mechanically. Teglyov at once walked off to the middle of the road.

"Wait, wait!" I began. "Where are you going? Have you only just come? And what is this letter?"

"Do you promise to deliver it to the right address?" said Teglyov, stepping back a few paces. The mist blurred the outlines of his figure. "Promise?"

"I promise. But first——"

Teglyov stepped back still farther and became a dark, long blur. "Good-bye!" I heard him say. "Good-bye, Ridel! Don't think badly of me and don't forget Semyon . . ."

And the dark blur, too, vanished.

That was too much. "Oh, the damned phrase-monger!" I thought. "Always trying to show off!" However, I could not help feeling uneasy; involuntary fear clutched at my heart. I threw my greatcoat over my shoulders and rushed out into the road.

13

Yes, but where was I to go? The thick mist enveloped me on every side. I could still make something out five or six steps ahead, but farther on, the mist stood like a wall, white and soft like cotton wool. I turned to the right along the village street, which came to an end just there. Our cottage was the last but one in the village, and farther on was nothing but a wasteland overgrown here and there with bushes. Beyond it, about a quarter of a mile from the village, was a birch copse, through which flowed the stream that skirted the village a little lower down. I knew that very well, because I had seen it many times in daylight. But now I saw nothing, and it was only because of the greater thickness and whiteness of the mist that I could guess where the ground sloped and the stream flowed. The moon hung in the sky like a pale blur, but its light, as on the night before, had no power to pierce through the dense mist, and hung high up in a broad, opaque canopy. I got out into the field and listened. There was not a sound anywhere: all I could hear was the whistling of snipe.

"Teglyov!" I cried. "Teglyov!"

My voice died away all round me without any answer. It seemed as if the mist did not let it carry any farther.

"Teglyov!" I repeated.

No one answered.

I walked straight ahead at random. Twice I ran into the fence. Once I nearly plunged into a ditch and nearly stumbled against a peasant's horse lying on the ground.

"Teglyov! Teglyov!" I shouted.

Suddenly, close behind me, I heard a low voice, "Well, here I am. What do you want of me?"

I turned round quickly.

Before me stood Teglyov with his arms hanging down and with no cap on his head. His face was pale, but his eyes seemed brighter and larger than ever. He was breathing heavily and slowly through his parted lips.

"Thank God!" I cried in an outburst of joy and seized both his hands. "Thank God! I had almost given up hope of finding you. Aren't you ashamed of frightening me like that! Really, Teglyov!"

"What do you want of me?" Teglyov repeated.

"I want—— First of all, I want you to come back home with me, and, secondly, I—er—I want, I demand of you as a friend, that you should at once explain to me what is the meaning of this letter to the colonel! Has anything you did not expect happened to you in Petersburg?"

"I found in Petersburg exactly what I expected," said Teglyov, still without moving.

"That is—you mean to say—your—er—friend— Masha——"

"She committed suicide," Teglyov put in hurriedly and as though with fury. "She was buried the day before yesterday. She did not even leave me a note. She took poison." Teglyov uttered these terrible words hurriedly, himself standing motionless, as if turned to stone.

I threw up my arms in horror. "Did she? How awful! Your premonition has come true. Oh, it's dreadful!"

In my confusion, I fell silent. Teglyov folded his hands slowly and as though in triumph.

"But," I said, "what are we standing here for? Let's go home."

"Yes, let's. But how are we going to find the way in this fog?"

"There's a light in the window of our cottage and we'll make straight for it. Come along."

"You go ahead," replied Teglyov. "I'll follow you."

We set off. We walked for about five minutes, and the light which should have served us as a beacon did not appear; at last it gleamed in the distance in two red points. Teglyov walked slowly behind me. I was terribly anxious to get home as quickly as possible and find out from him all the details of his unhappy trip to Petersburg. Struck by what he had told me, I confessed to him on the way back to the cottage, in a fit of remorse and a sort of superstitious fear, that it was I who was responsible for the mysterious knocking the other night—and what a tragic turn my jest had taken!

Teglyov confined himself to remarking that I had had nothing to do with it, that something else had guided my hand, and that this only proved how little I knew him. His voice, strangely composed and even, sounded at my very ear.

"But you will get to know me," he added. "I saw how you smiled yesterday when I mentioned the strength of my will. You will get to know me—and you will remember my words."

The first cottage of the village, looking like some dark monster, loomed out of the mist in front of us. A minute later the second, our cottage, appeared and my pointer started barking, probably because it scented me.

I knocked at the window. "Semyon!" I shouted to Teglyov's servant. "Hey, Semyon, open the gate for us quickly!"

The gate opened wide with a clatter; Semyon stepped over the threshold.

"After you, Teglyov," I said, looking back.

But there was no Teglyov behind me. He had vanished just as though the ground had swallowed him up.

I went into the cottage like one distraught.

14

Annoyance with Teglyov and with myself replaced the astonishment which had come over me at first.

"Your master is mad!" I shouted, pouncing on Semyon. "Stark, raving mad! He galloped off to Petersburg, then came back, and now he's running about without rhyme or reason. I got hold of him, brought him to the gate, and now suddenly he's taken to his heels again! Not to stay at home on a night like this! Found a nice time to go for a walk!

"And why did I let him out of my hands?" I reproached myself.

Semyon kept looking at me in silence, as though about to say something, but, as was the custom with men-servants in those days, he merely stood shuffling his feet in one place.

"When did he leave for town?" I asked.

"At six o'clock in the morning, sir."

"And what was he like? Worried? Sad?"

Semyon dropped his eyes. "Master's a strange man, sir," he began. "Who can make him out? Before going to town, he asked me to get him his new uniform and —well—waved his hair."

"Waved his hair?"

"Yes, sir. I got the curling tongs ready for him."

That, I admit, I had not expected.

"Do you know a young lady," I asked Semyon, "a friend of your master's? Her name is Masha."

"Why, yes, sir. Of course, I know Maria Anempodistovna. A nice young lady."

"I understand your master is in love with her, with this young lady, and—and so on."

Semyon sighed. "That young lady will be my master's undoing, and why, sir? Because he loves her terribly but can't make up his mind to marry her. And he can't give her up, either. Why is that, sir? Because he is faint-hearted, he is. Loves her too much, he does."

"What is she like? Is she pretty?" I asked, unable to overcome my curiosity.

Semyon assumed a grave air. "She's the sort that gentlemen like, sir."

"And do you like her?"

"No, sir, she isn't our sort at all."

"Why not?"

"Because she's too scrawny."

"If she died," I began again, "do you think your master would not survive her?"

Semyon sighed again. "Afraid, sir, it's not for me to say. It's for my master to say. Only my master's a strange one, he's that and all."

I picked up the large and rather thick letter Teglyov had given me from the table and turned it over in my hands. The address to "Commanding Officer of the Battery, Colonel ——" followed by the name, patronymic and surname, was very clearly and distinctly written. In the top corner of the envelope, twice underlined, was written the word *Urgent*.

"Listen, Semyon," I began, "I'm worried about your master. I believe he may be thinking of doing something awful. We simply must find him."

"Yes, sir," replied Semyon.

"It's true there's such a fog outside that it's impossible to make anything out a few yards ahead, but that doesn't matter: we must try our best. Let's take a lantern each and light a candle in each window—just in case."

"Yes, sir," Semyon repeated. He lit the lanterns and candles and we set off.

15

It is impossible to describe how we wandered and how we kept losing our way in the fog. The lanterns were of no use to us at all; they did not disperse the white, almost luminous haze which surrounded us. Semyon and I lost each other several times, in spite of the fact that we kept shouting and hallooing to each other and every now and again called out: I—"Teglyov! Ilya!" He—"Mr. Teglyov, sir!" The fog confused us so much that we wandered about as though in a dream; soon we both grew hoarse: the damp penetrated deep down into one's chest.

Somehow, however, we managed, thanks to the candles in our windows, to meet again at the cottage. Our combined searches had led to nothing; we were only hampering each other, and that is why we decided not to worry any more about getting separated, but to go each our own way. He went off to the left and I to the right. Soon I stopped hearing his voice. The fog seemed to have made its way into my brain, and I wandered about in a daze, only shouting from time to time, "Teglyov! Teglyov!"

"Here!" someone suddenly cried in answer to my call.

Heavens, how relieved I was! I rushed to the spot from where the voice came. A human figure loomed out in front of me. I rushed up to it. At last!

But instead of Teglyov I saw another officer of the same battery whose name was Telepnyov.

"Was it *you* who answered me?" I asked him.

"Was it you calling me?" he asked in his turn.

"No, I was calling Teglyov."

"Teglyov? Why, I've just met him. What an idiotic night! I can't find my way home."

"You saw Teglyov? Which way did he go?"

"That way, I think!" The officer waved his hand in the air. "But it's quite impossible to be sure of anything now. Do you, for instance, know where the village is? The only hope is that a dog may start barking. What a confoundedly idiotic night! Do you mind if I light a cigarette? Helps to light the way a little."

The officer was, as far as I could make out, a little drunk.

"Did Teglyov say anything to you?" I asked.

"Why, of course he did. I said to him, 'Good evening, my dear fellow!' and he said to me, 'Good-bye, my dear fellow!' 'Why good-bye?' 'Why? Because,' he says, 'I'm going to shoot myself in a minute.' Funny fellow!"

My breath failed me. "You say he told you——"

"Funny fellow!" the officer repeated and walked away.

I had barely time to recover from what the officer had

told me when my own name, shouted a few times with an effort, caught my ear. I recognised Semyon's voice.

I called back. He came up to me.

16

"Well," I asked him, "have you found your master?"

"Yes, sir."

"Where?"

"Why, sir, not far from here."

"How—have you found him? Is he alive?"

"Why, of course, sir. I've been talking to him." (I felt greatly relieved.) "He was sitting under a birch tree, sir, in his greatcoat, and he seemed all right. I said to him, 'Won't you come back home, sir? Mr. Ridel is very worried about you, sir.' And he says to me, he says, 'What does he want to worry about me for? I want to be in the open air. I have a headache. You go home,' he says. 'I'll be coming along later.'"

"And you went?" I cried, clasping my hands.

"Of course I did, sir. He told me to go. How could I stay?"

All my apprehensions returned to me at once. "Take me to him this very minute—do you hear? This very minute! Oh, Semyon, Semyon, I didn't expect that of you! Did you say he wasn't far from here?"

"Very near, sir. Just where the copse begins. He's sitting there, sir. A couple of yards from the river, from the bank. I walked along the river and there he was."

"Very well, take me to him, take me!"

Semyon walked on ahead of me. "Follow me, sir; we have only to get down to the river, and from there it's only a minute."

But instead of getting down to the river, we found ourselves in some hollow in front of an empty shed.

"Sorry, sir!" Semyon cried. "I'm afraid I've gone too far to the right. We'll have to keep to the left—that way."

We went to the left and found ourselves in such tall weeds in the middle of a field that we could hardly get out. As far as I could remember, there were no such weeds anywhere near our village. A few minutes later we felt the squelching of water under our feet as we suddenly found ourselves in a swamp, and I caught sight of round moss-covered mounds, which I had never seen before, either. We turned back: a steep hillock loomed out in front of us, and on the hillock was a hut, and someone was snoring in it. Semyon and I shouted several times to the man in the hut; something began turning over inside it, the straw rustled, and a hoarse voice muttered, "I'm the night—watchman!"

We turned back again. Fields, fields, endless fields . . .

I nearly cried. The words of the fool in King Lear came to my mind: "This cold night will turn us all to fools and madmen."

"Where are we to go now?" I said to Semyon in despair.

"The wood demon must have led us astray, sir," the bewildered servant replied. "There's something behind this. I'm sure, sir, the devil is mixed up in it."

I was about to scold him, but at that very moment my ear caught a sound, isolated and not very loud, which at once attracted my attention. Something popped faintly, just as though someone had pulled out a stiff cork from the narrow neck of a bottle. Why that sound seemed strange and peculiar to me, I cannot say, but I at once went in its direction.

Semyon followed me. A few moments later something tall and broad loomed out of the fog.

"The copse! There it is! The copse!" Semyon cried joyfully. "Why, look there, sir, there! There's the master sitting under the birch. Sitting where I left him. It's him, all right!"

I looked intently and indeed, hunched up awkwardly on the ground near the birch tree with his back towards us, a man was sitting. I went up to him quickly and recognised Teglyov's greatcoat, recognised his figure, his head bowed on his breast.

"Teglyov!" I called, but he did not answer.

"Teglyov!" I repeated, and put my hand on his shoulder. Then he suddenly lurched forward, quickly and obediently, just as though he were expecting me to push him, and fell onto the grass. Semyon and I raised him at once and turned him over with his face upwards.

It was not pale, but lifeless and motionless; his clenched teeth gleamed white, and his eyes, also motionless and not closed, preserved their habitual somnolent and "odd" look.

"Good Lord!" Semyon cried suddenly and showed me his hand, which was stained with blood. The blood was oozing out from under Teglyov's unbuttoned greatcoat, from the left side of his chest.

He had shot himself with a small, single-barrelled pistol which was lying beside him. The faint sound I had heard was the report made by the fatal shot.

17

Teglyov's suicide did not surprise his fellow officers very much. I have told you already that, according to their ideas, as a "fatal" man he had to do something extraordinary, though they had not, perhaps, expected that from him. In the letter to the commanding officer he asked him, first of all, to order that the name of Second Lieutenant Ilya Teglyov be struck off the list of officers, as he had died by his own hand, adding that in his money box they would find more than sufficient cash to pay his debts; secondly, to forward to the important personage who had at that time been commanding the whole corps of guards an unsealed letter, which was in the same envelope. This second letter, of course, we all read, and some of us made a copy of it. It was clear that Teglyov had taken great pains over the composition of this letter.

"Just as you, sir"—that was, I believe, how it began—"are so strict and impose penalties for the slightest incorrectness in dress and for the least infringement of the rules of conduct, when a pale, trembling officer appears before you, so I am now about to appear before our universal, incorruptible, noble-minded Judge, before the Supreme Being, before the Being of infinitely greater importance than you, sir; and I appear before Him without formality, in my greatcoat and even without a cravat round my neck. . . ."

Oh, what a painful and unpleasant impression that phrase made on me, every word, every letter of which was so painstakingly written in the childish hand of the dead man! Was it really worth while, I asked myself, to concoct such nonsense at such a moment? But Teglyov had evidently liked that phrase; for in it he had used all the accumulated epithets and amplifications *à la* Marlinsky that were fashionable at that time. He went on to mention his "fate," his persecution, his vocation which remained unfulfilled, a mystery which he would take to his grave with him, the people who did not want to understand him; he had even quoted the verses of a certain poet who referred to the mob as wearing life "like a dog-collar" and clinging to vice "like a burdock" —and all that not without spelling mistakes. To tell the truth, this last letter of poor Teglyov's was rather vulgar, and I can imagine the disdainful look of perplexity of the high personage to whom it was addressed; I can imagine the tone of voice in which he uttered the words, "A worthless officer! Clear the weeds out of the field!" It was only at the very end of the letter that a sincere cry escaped Teglyov's heart. "Oh, sir"—so his letter concluded—"I am an orphan. I had no one to love since I was a child and everyone shunned me and I myself destroyed the only heart which gave itself to me!"

Semyon found in the pocket of Teglyov's greatcoat the little notebook from which his master never parted. But almost all the pages had been torn out. Only one page remained, on which there was the following calculation:

Napoleon was born on August 15, 1769

Ilya Teglyov was born on the 7th of January, 1811

1769		1811	
15		7	
8	(August—the 8th month of the year.)	1	(January—the 1st month of the year.)

Total: 1792

Total: 1819

1	1
7	8
9	1
2	9

Total: 19!

Total: 19!

Napoleon died on the 5th of May, 1825

Ilya Teglyov died on the 21st of July, 1834

1825		1834	
5		21	
5	(May—the 5th month of the year.)	7	(July—the 7th month of the year.)

Total: 1835

Total: 1862

1	1
8	8
3	6
5	2

Total: 17!

Total: 17!

Poor fellow! Was that why he joined an artillery regiment?

As a suicide, he was buried outside the cemetery and he was immediately forgotten.

18

On the day after Teglyov's funeral (I was still in the village, waiting for my brother) Semyon came into the cottage and announced that Ilya wanted to see me.

"Which Ilya?" I asked.

"Why, our pedlar."

I told Semyon to call him.

He came in. He said he was sorry about the death of the second lieutenant and expressed his surprise that he should have done such a thing.

"He doesn't owe you anything, does he?" I asked.

"No, sir, he paid for everything he took. Paid regular-like for everything. What I've come to see you about, sir, is this." The pedlar grinned. "I see you've got a little thing of mine."

"What little thing?"

"Why, sir, that." He pointed to the chased comb which lay on my dressing table. "It's an unimportant little thing," the jester went on, "but as it was given me as a present——"

I suddenly raised my head. Something dawned on me. "Is your name Ilya?"

"Yes, sir."

"Was it you then I saw the other night under—the willow tree?"

The pedlar winked at me and gave me even a bigger grin. "It was me, sir."

"And it was *you* someone was calling?"

"Yes, sir, it was me," the pedlar repeated with play-ful modesty. "There's a young girl here," he went on in a falsetto voice, "who, on account of the great strictness of her parents——"

"All right, all right," I interrupted him, gave him back his comb, and got rid of him.

So that was who "Ilya darling" was, I thought, sinking into philosophic speculations, which, however, I will not bore you with, for I do not want to prevent anyone from believing in fate, predestination, and other fatalities.

On my return to Petersburg I gathered some information about Masha. I even found the doctor who had treated her. To my amazement I heard from him that she had died not of poisoning but of cholera! I told him what I had heard from Teglyov.

"I see!" the doctor exclaimed suddenly. "Is Teglyov an artillery officer of medium height, with a stoop, and speaks with a lisp?"

"Yes."

"Well, that's what it is, then. That gentleman came to see me—that was the first time I ever saw him—and began insisting that that girl had poisoned herself. 'Cholera,' I said. 'Poison,' he said. 'No,' I said, 'it was cholera.' 'Oh no,' he said, 'it was poison.' I could see that the man was behaving like a lunatic. He had a broad back to his head, which meant that he was a stubborn fellow. Kept pestering me. 'Very well,' I thought, 'what does it matter? The girl's dead, anyway.' 'Well,' I said, 'she poisoned herself, if that makes you happy.' He thanked me, even shook hands—and disappeared."

I told the doctor how that officer had shot himself on the same day.

The doctor didn't turn a hair, merely observing that there were all sorts of eccentric fellows in the world.

"So there are," I agreed.

Yes, someone has said truly about suicides: when they do not carry out their intention, no one believes them; when they do, no one is sorry for them.

Baden-Baden, 1870

LIVING RELICS

O land of long-suffering—
Land of the Russian people!
F. TYUTCHEV

A FRENCH proverb says: "A dry fisherman and a wet sportsman are a sorry sight." Never having had a predilection for fishing, I cannot say what a fisherman feels on a fine, clear day and how much, in a downpour, the pleasure he gets from a good catch offsets the unpleasantness of getting wet. But for the sportsman rain is a real disaster. A disaster of this kind befell Yermolay and myself on one of our black-cock shoots in the district of Belevo. From the very early morning the rain had not stopped. What had we not done to escape it! We had put rubber capes practically over our heads; we had stood under trees to avoid being drenched. Our waterproof capes, besides hindering us when shooting, had let the water through in the most shameless fashion; and under the trees at first, it is true, it seemed quite dry, but afterwards the water which had collected in the leaves suddenly broke through and from every branch it poured down on us as from a rain pipe—a cold stream penetrating under the cravat and running down the spine. That was "the last straw," as Yermolay put it. "No, sir," he cried at last, "we can't go on like this! We can't shoot today. The dog's scent is drowned and the guns are misfiring. Hang it! What a problem!"

"What shall we do?" I asked.

"Well, sir, let's go to Alexeyevka. You may not know of it, sir, but it's a hamlet belonging to your mother. About five miles from here. We'll spend the night there and tomorrow——"

"Come back here?"

"No, sir, not here. I know some places beyond, on the other side of Alexeyevka. Much better than here, sir, for black-cock."

I did not start inquiring of my faithful companion why he had not taken me straight to those places, and the same day we reached my mother's farm, whose exist-ence, I confess, I had not suspected till then. There was a little cottage on this farm, a very dilapidated one, but uninhabited and for that reason clean; I passed a fairly peaceful night there.

The next day I woke up very early. The sun had just risen; there was not a cloud in the sky. Everything round sparkled with a double radiance: the radiance of the early morning sunshine and of the heavy downpour of the day before.

While my two-wheeled cart was being harnessed I went for a stroll in the small orchard, now overgrown, which surrounded the cottage on all sides with its fra-grant, lush thicket. Oh, how wonderful it was in the open air, under a clear sky, in which larks quivered and from which their ringing voices fell in silver beads. They must have carried off dewdrops on their wings, and their songs seemed drenched in dew. I even took off my hat and breathed joyously—to the full capacity of my lungs. On the slopes of a shallow ravine, close beside a wattle fence, I saw an apiary; a narrow path led to it, meandering between the unbroken walls of tall weeds and nettles over which towered—brought there goodness only knows from where—the pointed stalks of dark green hemp.

I walked along the path and came to the beehives. Beside them stood a little wattle shed where the hives were put in winter. I looked through the half-open door: it was dark, quiet, dry; there was a smell of mint and balsam. In a corner a small platform had been erected, and on it, covered by a blanket, there was a sort of small figure. I was about to go away . . .

"Sir, sir!" I heard a voice, weak, slow, and husky, like the rustling of sedge in a marsh.

I stopped.

"Sir, come closer, please," repeated the voice. It seemed to come from the corner where I had noticed the platform.

I came closer and was struck dumb with amazement. Before me lay a living human being, but who on earth could it be?

A head completely dried up, all one colour, the colour of bronze, exactly like an ancient icon; a nose as thin as the blade of a knife; lips almost invisible—only the white glint of teeth, and eyes, and a few thin strands of yellow hair on the forehead coming out from under the kerchief. Beside the chin, on the folds of the blanket, slowly twisting their twiglike fingers, two tiny hands of the same bronze colour. I looked closer. The face was far from ugly—it was beautiful, even, but extraordinary and terrifying. And that face seemed all the more terrifying to me because on it, over its metallic cheeks, I could see a smile trying hard, very hard, to break, but all in vain.

"Don't you recognise me, sir?" the voice whispered

again. It seemed to come like an exhalation from the scarcely moving lips. "But how could you recognise me? I'm Lukerya, sir. Don't you remember, I used to lead the round dances at your mother's at Spasskoye? I used to lead the singing too. Remember, sir?"

"Lukerya!" I cried. "Is it you? Is it possible?"

"Yes, sir, it's me. I am Lukerya."

I did not know what to say and I gazed dumfounded at that dark, motionless face with its bright and death-like eyes fixed on me. Was it possible? This mummy—Lukerya, the most beautiful girl of all our house-serfs —tall, plump, pink and white—always laughing, dancing, singing! Lukerya, clever Lukerya, whom all our young lads were chasing after, for whom I too had sighed in secret, I, a sixteen-year-old boy!

"Good heavens, Lukerya," I said at last, "what has happened to you?"

"Oh, sir, I've had such terrible trouble! But please, sir, don't mind me and don't be afraid to come near because of my misfortune. Sit down on this small tub. A little nearer, or you won't be able to hear me. . . . See what a strong voice I've got, sir! I'm so glad to see you, sir. So glad. How did you happen to turn up at Alexeyevka?" Lukerya spoke very softly and weakly, but without faltering.

"Yermolay the huntsman brought me here. But tell me——"

"About my trouble, sir? As you wish, sir. It happened some time ago. Six or seven years back. I had just been promised to Vassily Polyakov. Remember what a fine-looking, curly-headed lad he was, sir? Pantry-boy at your mother's house, he was. But you had left the country by then, hadn't you, sir? You had gone to Moscow to study. . . . Vassily and I were very much in love. He was never out of my thoughts. It all happened in the spring, sir. One night—it was not long before dawn—I couldn't go to sleep: a nightingale in the garden was

singing so sweetly, sir, so wonderfully! I just couldn't
stay in bed, sir. So I got up and went out on the front
steps to listen to it. The song kept pouring out of it—and
suddenly it seemed to me that someone was calling me
in Vassily's voice. Very quiet-like. Very quiet-like.
"Lusha!" I looked round. I was half asleep, sir, and I
slipped and fell off the top step. I went flying down and
—smack!—hit the ground. It wasn't that I had hurt myself badly—oh no, sir. I got up at once and went back to
my room. Only I felt as though something inside me, in
my womb, had broken loose. . . . I'm sorry, sir, just a
minute, please. . . . Must get my breath . . ."

Lukerya fell silent, and I looked at her in amazement.
What so amazed me was that she told her story almost
gaily, without groans or sighs, never complaining or asking for sympathy.

"Ever since that accident, sir," Lukerya went on, "I
began to pine and waste away. A blackness came over
me. At first I found it hard to walk, and a little later I
couldn't use my legs at all. I could neither stand nor sit.
Had to lie down all the time. Didn't want to eat or drink;
got worse and worse. Your mother, sir, out of the goodness of her heart, showed me to the doctors and sent me
to a hospital. But it was no good at all, sir. There was
not a single doctor who could say what my illness was.
They did everything they could think of to me: burnt
my back with red-hot irons; made me sit in chopped ice;
but it was no good. In the end I grew so stiff I couldn't
move. So then the mistress decided that it was no use
trying to cure me and that she could not afford to keep
a cripple in her house in the country. Well, sir, so they
sent me over here, because I have relations here. And
that's how I live, as you see, sir."

Lukerya paused once more and again tried to smile.

"But," I cried, "your condition must be terrible!" And,
not knowing what to add, I asked, "And what about
Vassily Polyakov?"

It was a very stupid question. Lukerya looked away a little.

"What about Polyakov, sir? He grieved and grieved and then married someone else. A girl from Glinnoye. Do you know Glinnoye, sir? It isn't far from us. Her name is Agrafena. He loved me very much, sir, but he was a young man and he couldn't very well stay a bachelor, could he? And what kind of wife could I have been to him? He found himself a good wife. She is very kind-hearted, she is, sir. And they have children. He lives on a neighbouring estate, sir. He is a clerk in the estate office. Your mother let him go with a passport, and, thank God, he is happy."

And so I asked again, "So you just lie and lie?"

"Yes, sir. I have been lying like this for more than six years. In summer I lie here—in this wattle hut. When it gets cold they move me to the bath-house. And I lie there."

"And who looks after you? Who keeps an eye on you?"

"There are good people here too, sir. They don't leave me without help. Besides, sir, I don't need much looking after. I hardly eat anything, and as for drinking—there's water in that mug there. There's always some clear spring water kept by me. I can reach the mug myself. One of my hands still works, you see, sir. There's a little girl here, an orphan child, sir, and she comes in here now and again, bless her, to see whether I want anything. She was here just now. Didn't you meet her? A pretty little thing she is—fair-skinned. She brings me flowers. I'm very fond of flowers, I am, sir. There are no garden flowers here—they're all gone. But wild flowers are lovely too. They smell even better than garden ones. Take the lily of the valley, sir. Could anything be sweeter?"

"But don't you get bored? Aren't you frightened to be here by yourself, my poor Lukerya?"

"There's nothing to be done about it, is there, sir? But

mind you, sir, I don't want to tell you a lie. At first it was very depressing, but I settled down. Got used to it. It's not so bad now. There are people who're even worse off."

"Oh?"

"Yes, sir. There are people who haven't a roof over their heads, and some people are blind or deaf. But, thank God, I can see beautifully and can hear everything—everything. A mole burrows underground, and I can hear it. I can smell every smell, sir, be it ever so faint! If buckwheat blossoms in the field or lime in the garden—you needn't tell me—I'm always the first to know. Provided, of course, sir, that a breath of wind comes from there. No, sir, why anger the Lord? Lots of people are worse off than me. And another thing, sir, someone who is well can easily commit a sin. But I can sin no more. The other day, sir, Father Alexey, the priest, came to give me Communion and he says to me, he says, 'I need not confess you, for how can you sin, in your condition?' 'What about sinning in my thoughts, Father?' I said. 'Well,' he said at last, 'that isn't a big sin, is it?'

"But I don't think, sir, I could even be much of a sinner in my thoughts," Lukerya went on, "for I've trained myself not to think, and, which is more important still, not to remember. Time passes quicker like that."

I confess I was surprised. "You're quite alone all day long, Lukerya; how then can you prevent thoughts from coming into your head? Or do you sleep all the time?"

"Good Lord, no, sir. You see, sir, I can't always sleep. I have no great pains, but I've always a nagging pain inside, sir. In my bones too. It doesn't let me sleep as I ought to. I just lie by myself. I lie and lie and—I do not think. I can feel I'm alive, that I'm breathing, and that's all there is of me. I look and listen. The bees in the bee-garden are buzzing and droning away; a pigeon will sit on the roof and start cooing; a mother hen will come in with her chicks to peck up the crumbs; or else a sparrow will fly in, or a butterfly—and I am happy. Why, sir, the year before last some swallows even built a nest over there in the corner and hatched their fledglings. Oh, that was interesting, sir. One of them would fly in, drop into the nest, feed the fledglings, and fly out again. Before you knew where you was, the other one would come to take her place. Sometimes they wouldn't fly in but just swoop past the open door, and all at once the fledglings would start squeaking and opening their beaks. . . . I was waiting for them to come next year too, but they say some sportsman from the neighbourhood shot them with his gun—and what use were they to him? Why, a swallow, sir, is no bigger than a beetle. How wicked you sporting gentlemen are, sir!"

"I don't shoot swallows," I hastened to observe.

"And once," Lukerya began again, "I had such a big laugh! A hare ran in. Yes, sir, a hare! I suppose the hounds must have been after him. Only he came hopping straight in at the door! He sat very close to me, he did. Sat there for hours, twitching his nose and moving his whiskers up and down—a regular Army officer! Looked at me too, he did. Must have realised he had nothing to fear from me. At last he got up, hop-hopped to the door, looked round from the threshold—and was gone! Such a funny one!"

Lukerya glanced at me, as if wondering whether I too found it amusing. To please her, I laughed. She moistened her dried lips.

"Well, sir, in winter, of course, I'm worse off, because it's dark, you see. To light a candle would be such a waste, and besides, what for? It's true, I know how to read and write. I was always fond of reading. But what is there to read? There are no books here, and even if there were, how am I going to hold one? The book, I mean. Father Alexey brought me a calendar to keep me occupied, but he saw that it was no good and took it away again. Still, even if it's dark, there's always something to listen to: a cricket whirs, or a mouse starts scratching somewhere. I feel happy then: I don't have to think, you see. . . .

"Or else I say prayers," Lukerya went on after a short rest. "Only I don't know many of them. Many prayers, I mean, sir. And why should I bore the Lord? What can I ask Him? He knows better than I what I need. He has sent me a cross to bear, which means that He must love me. That is how we are taught to understand it. I say 'Our Father,' 'Mother of God,' and a prayer for all who suffer. Then I just go on lying without ever thinking of anything. And it's all right!"

Two minutes passed. I did not break the silence and did not stir on the narrow tub which served me for a seat. The cruel stony immobility of the unhappy living creature lying before me communicated itself to me: I too seemed to go stiff and numb.

"Listen, Lukerya," I began at last, "listen to what I am going to suggest to you. Would you like me to arrange for you to be taken to a hospital? To a good city hospital? Perhaps they may still cure you. In any case, you won't be alone there."

Lukerya moved her eyebrows slightly. "Oh no, sir," she said in a worried whisper, "don't move me to a hospital. Please, don't touch me. I'm sure I'll feel much worse there. I'm past curing now. Once a doctor came to see me here. Wanted to examine me, he said. I told him, 'Don't disturb me, for Christ's sake.' But it was no use, sir. He started turning me over, stretching my arms and legs, bending them—doing it, he says to me, 'for the sake of science.' 'You see,' he says, 'I'm a scientist. I'm in government service,' he says, 'and you must not oppose me, because I've been awarded an order for my work, and I try to do the best for fools like you.' He pulled me about and pulled me about, told me the name of my illness—an odd sort of name it was, sir—and went away. Had a gnawing pain in my bones for a whole week after that, I had. You say, sir, I'm alone, always alone. No, not always. All sorts of people come to see me. I'm a quiet one, you see. I don't interfere with no one. Peasant girls come to see me to exchange village gossip. A pilgrim woman will wander in, start telling me of Jerusalem, Kiev, and other holy cities. Besides, sir, I'm not afraid to be alone. I prefer it, sir. Yes, I do. So please, sir, don't touch me and don't take me to a hospital. . . . I thank you, sir. You are so kind. Only please, dear sir, don't touch me."

"Well, just as you like, Lukerya. I just suggested it for your benefit, you know."

"I know, sir. But, sir, who can help someone else? Who can get into someone else's soul? A man must know how to help himself. You won't believe me, sir, but sometimes I lie alone here like this and it is as if I was the only living soul left in the whole world. I'm the only one to be alive, and it seems to me as if I am about to find out something—I start thinking then—and it really is too funny for words!"

"Why, what do you think about then, Lukerya?"

"I'm afraid, sir, I just can't tell you. I can't explain it properly. Besides, I forget it afterwards. It just comes on me like a little cloud. It bursts over me, and I feel so refreshed, so happy! But what it is, I simply can't understand! Only I can't help thinking that if there were people near me, none of this would happen, and I shouldn't feel anything except my own unhappiness."

Lukerya sighed painfully. Her chest did not obey her any more than the rest of her body.

"I can see, sir, by looking at you," she began again, "that you're very sorry for me. Well, don't be too sorry for me, sir. Please don't. Let me tell you this, for instance: even now I sometimes—well, you remember how gay I used to be in the past? A regular tomboy. Well, you won't believe me, sir, but even now I sing songs."

"Songs? You?"

"Yes, sir. Songs, old songs, roundelays, drinking songs, carols. All sorts of songs. I used to know lots of them, you see, sir. And I've not forgotten them. I don't sing dancing songs, though. In my present condition that wouldn't be appropriate, would it?"

"How do you sing them? To yourself?"

"To myself and aloud. I can't sing very loud, but loud enough to understand. I told you about the little girl who comes to see me, didn't I, sir? An orphan child, she is, and intelligent. So I have taught her to sing too. She's already learnt four songs from me. Don't you believe me, sir? Wait, I'm going to——"

Lukerya braced herself. The thought that this half-dead creature was getting ready to sing aroused an involuntary feeling of horror in me. But before I could utter a word I heard a trembling, drawn-out, scarcely audible, but pure and true note. Another followed, and then another. "In the meadows," Lukerya was singing. She sang with no change of expression on her petrified face, her eyes fixed on one point in the room, but this poor, forced little voice, wavering like a puff of smoke, rang so touchingly. She tried so hard to pour out her whole soul. . . . It was no longer horror that I felt: my heart was gripped by an indescribable pity.

"Oh, I can't!" she said suddenly. "I have no more strength. Oh, sir, I've been so pleased to see you." She closed her eyes.

I put my hand on her tiny, cold fingers. She looked at me and her dark eyelids, edged with golden lashes like those of an ancient statue, closed again. A moment later they glittered in the half-darkness. A tear had moistened them.

I did not stir, as before.

"What an awful creature I am!" Lukerya said suddenly with unexpected force and, opening her eyes wide, tried to blink away a tear. "Oughtn't I to be ashamed? What am I crying for? This hasn't happened to me for a long time. Not since Vassily Polyakov came to see me last spring. While he was sitting and talking to me I— well, I was all right, but after he had gone, I did cry a lot by myself! I don't know where all my tears came from! But then, tears come easy to a woman. I expect, sir," Lukerya added, "you must have a handkerchief. I hope you won't mind, sir, wiping my eyes."

I hastened to carry out her wish and left her the handkerchief. At first she would not accept it. What did she want with such a present? she kept saying. It was a very ordinary handkerchief, but clean and white. Then she seized it with her weak fingers and did not unclench them again. Having grown used to the darkness, I could make out her features clearly. I could even notice the faint blush that showed through the bronze of her face; I could—at least, so it seemed to me—discern the traces of its former beauty in that face.

"Now you asked me, sir," Lukerya began again, "if I sleep. I don't sleep a lot, but every time I do, I dream —such good dreams! In my dreams I am never an invalid. I'm always young and healthy. But the only trouble is, sir, that when I wake up and want to stretch myself properly, it's as if I was tied up. . . .

"Once I had such a lovely dream. Would you like me to tell you it, sir? Well, listen. I dreamt I was standing in a rye field and all round me the rye was so tall and ripe and golden! And there was a little red dog with me, ever such a fierce, cross-tempered dog—trying all the time to bite me. And in my hands I had a sickle. Not an ordinary sickle. Just like the moon when it is like a sickle. And it was with that same moon that I had to cut down the rye to the very last stalk. Only I was very weak from the heat, and the moon dazzled me, and I felt very lazy. All round me cornflowers were growing. Ever such big ones! And they all turned their heads to me. And I thought, 'I'll pick these cornflowers. Vassily promised to come, so I'll make a wreath for myself first and there'll be plenty of time left for reaping.' I began picking the cornflowers, but they just melted away between my fingers and I could do nothing about it. And so I couldn't make my wreath. Then I heard someone coming towards me quite near and calling, 'Lusha! Lusha!' 'Oh,' I thought, 'what a shame I haven't finished! Never mind, I'll put the moon on my head instead of the cornflowers.' So I put the moon on, just like the embroidered headdress with artificial pearls our peasant women wear. And I began to shine all over and I lit up the whole field all round. I looked, and, over the very tops of the ears of rye there came walking swiftly towards me—no, not Vassya, not Vassily, but Christ Himself! How I knew it was Christ I can't say, but it was Him! He wore no beard. He was tall and young and all in white, except for His belt, which was golden—and He stretched out his hand to me. 'Be not afraid,' He says, 'my well-adorned bride, but follow me. You will lead the rounds in my heavenly mansions and sing the songs of paradise.' And, dear Lord, how I clung to His hand! My little dog went for my legs, but at that moment we soared upwards! He was in front of me. His wings spread all over the sky, long ones like a sea gull's—and I went after Him! And the dog had to stay behind. It was only then that I realised that this dog was my illness, and that in the kingdom of heaven there would be no place for it."

Lukerya paused for a minute. "And then," she began again, "I had another dream—or perhaps this one was a vision—I just don't know. It seemed to me, sir, that I was alone in this hut, and my dead parents came to see me—my father and mother. They bowed low to me but said nothing. And I asked them, 'Why are you bowing to me?' 'Why,' they said, 'because you have suffered so much in this world that you've lightened not only the burden of your soul, but removed a big burden from ours. And we find things much easier now in the other world. You've already finished with your own sins, and

now you're overcoming ours.' And, having said that, my
parents bowed to me again and I didn't see them any
more: all I could see was the walls. I was not sure afterwards what exactly had happened to me. I even told the
priest about it in my confession. But he thinks that it
could not have been a vision, because visions come only
to people in holy orders.

"And then I had another dream," Lukerya went on.
"I dreamt that I was sitting under a willow tree at the
side of a highway, holding a peeled stick with a bundle
on my shoulders, and my hair was covered with a kerchief—a regular pilgrim woman! And I had to go somewhere far, far away on a pilgrimage. And all the time
pilgrims kept going past me. They walked quietly, as
though against their will, and always the same way.
They all had gloomy faces and they were all very much
like one another. And I saw a woman among them. She
was a head taller than the others, and she was rushing
about, weaving in and out among them. She was wearing
a peculiar dress, not like ours, not Russian, and her face
too was peculiar, a stern, Lenten face. And all the others
seemed to keep away from her. Suddenly she turned
round quickly and came straight for me. She stopped
and looked at me, and her eyes were like a falcon's, yellow, large, and ever so bright. And I asked her, 'Who are
you?' And she said to me, 'I am your death.' I ought
to have been afraid but, on the contrary, I was terribly
glad, and I crossed myself. And this woman, my death,
she says to me, 'I'm sorry for you, Lukerya, but I'm
afraid I can't take you with me. Good-bye!' Lord, how
awfully sad I was just then! 'Take me,' I said, 'Mother
dearest, take me!' And my death turned to me and began to tell me something. I understood that she was fix-
ing my appointed hour, but it was all hard to understand, it was so indistinct. . . . 'After St. Peter's Day,' I
understood her to say. I woke up then. Yes, sir, that is
the kind of strange dreams I have."

Lukerya raised her eyes and sank into thought.

"Only you see, sir, my trouble is that for a week at a time I cannot go to sleep. Last year a lady drove by, saw me, and gave me a little bottle of medicine against sleeplessness. She told me to take ten drops at a time. It helped me a lot and I slept. Only now the bottle has been finished long ago. . . . Do you know, sir, what kind of medicine that was and how to get it?"

The lady must have given Lukerya opium. I promised to get her just such a bottle and again could not help expressing my amazement at her patience.

"Good Lord, sir," she said, "what are you saying? My patience indeed! Now St. Simon on the pillar, he really had great patience. He stood on his pillar for thirty years. And another saint ordered himself to be buried in the ground up to his chest and the ants ate his face. And this is what a man who had read many books told me: there was a certain country, and that country had been conquered by the heathen, and they tortured and put to death many of its inhabitants. And the people of that country could not free themselves, whatever they did. And then there appeared among the people a holy virgin, and she took a great sword and put armour weighing eighty pounds on herself and she went out against the heathen and drove them all out beyond the sea. Only after she had driven them out she said to them, 'Now you burn me because that was my promise, to die at the stake for my people.' And the heathen took her and burnt her and the people have been free ever since. There's a great deed for you! And what have I done?"

And I could not help marvelling to myself how far and in what a strange form the legend of Joan of Arc had reached us. After a short pause I asked Lukerya how old she was.

"Twenty-eight or twenty-nine. I don't think I am thirty yet. But why count the years? Let me tell you something more, sir——"

Lukerya suddenly coughed hollowly and groaned.

"You're talking too much," I said to her. "It is bad for you."

"That's true, sir," she whispered in a scarcely audible voice. "It's the end of our talk. Well, so be it! When you've gone I shall have as much silence as I like. At least I've unburdened my heart."

I started saying good-bye to her, repeated my promise to send her the medicine, asked her to think carefully and tell me if there was anything she wanted.

"I want nothing, sir," she replied with a great effort, but with emotion. "I'm well satisfied, thank God. May the Lord grant health to everyone. You, sir, ought to try to persuade your mother—the peasants here are poor— to reduce their rent a little. They haven't enough land, you see, not enough pastures. . . . They would say a prayer to God for you. But I—I want nothing. I am well satisfied."

I promised Lukerya to carry out her request. I was walking to the door when she called me back. "Do you remember, sir," she said, and there was a flash of something beautiful in her eyes and on her lips, "what a wonderful plait I had? Do you remember? Right down to my knees! I couldn't make up my mind for a long time —such wonderful hair! But how could I comb it? In my condition! So I just cut it off. Yes, sir. Well, I'm sorry, sir, I can't . . . any more . . ."

The same day, before going off for the shoot, I had a talk about Lukerya with the village constable. I found out from him that they called her "living relics" in the village and that she gave no trouble at all. She never grumbled or complained. "She asks for nothing herself. On the contrary, she is grateful for everything. She is a quiet one. Aye, a quiet one, I must say that. A bit touched in the head, I'm afraid," the constable concluded. "For her sins, I suppose—but we don't go into that. But as for condemning her, sir—no, sir, we do not condemn her. Let her be!"

A few weeks later I heard that Lukerya was dead. Death had come for her after all, and—"after St. Peter's Day." It was said that on the day of her death she kept hearing the sound of church bells, though it is more than three miles from Alexeyevka to the church, and it was on a weekday. But then, Lukerya said that the tolling did not come from the church but "from above." I suppose she did not dare to say—"from heaven."

1874

CLARA MILICH

(After Death)

1

In the spring of 1878 there lived in Moscow in a small wooden house in Shabolovka a young man of twenty-five, Yakov Aratov by name. His aunt, Platonida Ivanovna, his father's sister, an old maid of over fifty, lived with him. She looked after his house, did all the shopping for him, and paid all his bills, all of which Aratov was quite incapable of doing himself. He had no other relations. A few years earlier his father, a small landowner in the Province of Tula, had moved to Moscow together with him and Platonida Ivanovna, whom he always, however, called familiarly, "Platosha"; her nephew too used the same name.

Having left the village in which they had been living continuously till then, the elder Aratov settled in the old capital with the aim of sending his son to the university for which he had himself prepared him; he bought a little house in one of the outlying streets of the city for an absurdly low price, and established himself there

with all his books and "preparations." He had a multitude of books and preparations, for he was a man of
considerable learning—"a natural, born eccentric," as his
neighbours called him. He even passed among them for
a magician. Indeed, he was nicknamed an "insectorator."
He studied chemistry, mineralogy, entomology, botany,
and medicine; he treated patients who came to him, of
their own free will, with herbs and metallic powders of
his own invention, after the method of Paracelsus. It was
with these same powders that he brought to the grave
his pretty, young, but a little too delicate wife, whom
he loved passionately and by whom he had an only son.
With the same metallic powders he also almost ruined
his son's health, which he had had every intention of im-
proving, having diagnosed anæmia and a disposition
to consumption in his constitution inherited from his
mother. He was called "magician" partly because he
considered himself to be a descendant—not in the di-
rect line, of course—of the famous James Bruce, in
honour of whom he had called his son Yakov. He was
what is called a most kindhearted fellow, but given to
melancholy, sluggish and timid, with a propensity for
everything mysterious and occult. His usual exclamation
was a half-whispered "Ah!" He actually died with that
exclamation on his lips, two years after he had moved
to Moscow.

His son Yakov did not resemble in appearance his father, who had been far from handsome, clumsy, and
awkward; he was more like his mother. He had the
same delicate, comely features, the same soft ash-grey
hair, the same aquiline nose, the same pouting, childish
lips and large, greenish-grey, languishing eyes and silky
eyelashes. But in his character he resembled his father;
and his face, so unlike his father's, bore the stamp of
his father's expression; and he had the angular hands
and the hollow chest of the old Aratov—who could, however, scarcely be called an old man, because he did not

live even to the age of fifty. It was during his lifetime that Yakov entered the university, in the faculty of physics and mathematics. He did not, however, complete his course, not because he was lazy, but because, according to his opinion, one did not learn more at the university than one could studying at home; he was not anxious to obtain a degree because he did not intend to join the civil service. He shunned his fellow students, was acquainted with scarcely anyone, kept away from women especially, and lived a very solitary life, immersed in books. He kept away from women, although he had a very tender heart and was deeply affected by beauty. . . . He had even acquired a magnificent English keepsake, and (oh, shame!) kept admiring the "beautifully engraved" pictures of all sorts of ravishing Gulnaras and Medores; but his innate shyness constantly held him in check. At home he occupied his father's former study, which he also used as his bedroom. His bed too was the same in which his father had died.

The chief support of his whole existence, his unfailing friend and companion, was his aunt, the same Platosha with whom he scarcely exchanged a dozen words a day but without whom he could not take a single step. She was a long-faced, long-toothed creature, with pale eyes set in a pale face, and with an invariable expression that was a mixture of melancholy, worry, and fear. She always wore a grey dress and a grey shawl, which smelt of moth balls. She wandered about the house like a shadow with noiseless steps; she sighed, whispered prayers—one especially, a favourite of hers, of three words only: "Lord, help me!"—and looked after the household in an extremely businesslike manner, watched over every penny, and did all the shopping herself. She adored her nephew, was constantly worried about his health, afraid of everything—not for herself but for him; and the moment she suspected anything wrong, she would immediately walk up softly to his writing table and put a cup of herb tea on it or stroke his back with her hands, which were as soft as cotton-wool. Yakov did not resent these attentions, though he did not drink the herb tea, merely nodding approvingly.

Still, his health was nothing to boast about. He was too sensitive, nervous, and fastidious, suffered from palpitations of the heart, and sometimes from shortness of breath; like his father, he believed that there existed in nature and in the soul of man mysteries which one could sometimes divine but which one could never grasp; he believed in the presence of certain powers and influences, sometimes beneficent but more often hostile, and he also believed in science, in its dignity and importance. During recent months he had acquired a passion for photography. His old aunt was greatly worried by the smell of the different chemicals he used for his photographic experiments, and, again, she was not worried about herself but about Yakov, because of his chest; but for all the softness of his character, he had not a little stubbornness in his make-up, and he persisted in his new hobby. Platosha had to give in and merely sighed more than ever and whispered, "Lord, help me!" as she looked at his iodine-stained fingers.

Yakov, as I have already said, shunned his colleagues; with one of them, however, he became rather friendly, and he used to see him often, even after his friend, on graduating from the university, obtained a post in the civil service, which, however, did not take up too much of his time: he had, to quote his own words, "got himself a job" in the building of the Church of Our Saviour, without, needless to say, knowing anything about architecture.

Strange to say, this only friend of Aratov's, whose surname was Kupfer, a German who had become so Russianised that he did not know one word of German and even used to call people he disliked "Germans"—this friend apparently had nothing in common with him. He was a black-haired, red-cheeked young fellow, merry, talkative, and a great admirer of the female society which Aratov so much avoided. It is true, Kupfer lunched and dined at his place very often, and even, being far from rich, used to borrow small sums from him; but it was not this that induced the free and easy little German to visit the modest little house in Shabolovka so often. He came to like the spiritual purity and idealism of Yakov, perhaps as a contrast to what he was seeing and meeting every day; or perhaps his German blood showed itself in this very desire for the company of the "idealist" youth. Yakov, for his part, liked Kupfer's good-natured candour; besides, his accounts of the theatres, concerts, and balls where he was always to be found, and generally all that alien world which Yakov dared not enter, secretly interested and even excited the young recluse, without rousing in him any desire to learn about it by his own experience. Platosha too liked Kupfer; it is true, she found him a little too unceremonious at times, but, instinctively feeling and realising that he was sincerely attached to her precious Yakov, she not only put up with the noisy visitor but also regarded him with favour.

2

At the time we are speaking of there lived in Moscow a certain widow, a Georgian princess, a rather ambiguous, almost suspicious character. She was a woman of about forty. In her youth she had probably bloomed with that special Oriental beauty which fades so quickly; now she powdered, rouged, and dyed her hair yellow. All sorts of not altogether favourable and not altogether definite rumours about her were current; no one had ever known her husband, and she had never stayed long in any one town. She had neither children nor money, but she kept open house, whether on borrowed money or by some other means, nobody knew. She kept a *salon,* as it is called, and received a rather mixed society, mostly young people. Everything in her house, from her own dress, furniture, and table to her carriage and her servants, bore the stamp of something shoddy, spurious, ephemeral; but neither the princess nor her guests apparently expected anything better. The princess was reputed to be greatly fond of music and literature, a patroness of actors and artists, and indeed she was interested in all these "problems" even to the point of enthusiasm, and enthusiasm not altogether affected. There was no doubt that she possessed a natural bent for the fine arts. Besides, she was very approachable, amiable, without any affectation or vanity, and—what many people did not suspect—she was intrinsically very goodnatured, softhearted and indulgent—rare qualities, and all the more precious in people of that kind in particular! "A silly goose," a clever man said about her, "but she's quite sure to get to heaven, for she forgives everything and everything will be forgiven her!" It was also said of her that when she disappeared from some town she always left as many people owing her money as people she owed money to. A soft heart turns in any direction you like.

Kupfer, as may have been expected, found his way into her house and became an intimate—a little too intimate—friend of hers, evil tongues even asserted. He himself always spoke of her not only affectionately but also with respect; he described her as a woman with a heart of gold, whatever people might say about her; and he firmly believed in her love for art and her understanding of art.

One day, after dinner at the Aratovs' and after talking at length about the princess and her parties, he tried to persuade Yakov to break away for once from his life as a hermit and allow him, Kupfer, to introduce him to his friend. At first Yakov would not hear of it.

"Why," Kupfer exclaimed at last, "what are you thinking of? What kind of introduction do you imagine I mean? I'll simply take you just as you are now, in your coat, and go with you to the party she is giving this evening. There's no need for official invitations there, my dear fellow! You see, you are a scholar and you're fond of literature and music" (in Aratov's study there was, in fact, a piano on which he sometimes struck a few minor chords) "and there's plenty of these things in her house. You'll find lots of sympathetic people there too, people with no pretensions! And besides, at your age and with your good looks"—Aratov dropped his eyes and waved his hand deprecatingly—"yes, yes, with your good looks, you mustn't keep away from society and the world like this! After all, I'm not taking you to call on some generals. Anyway, I don't know any generals myself. Don't be obstinate, my dear fellow. Morality is an excellent thing, a most honourable thing, but why lead the life of an ascetic? You're not going to become a monk, are you?"

Aratov, however, continued to be obstinate, but Platosha unexpectedly came to Kupfer's aid. Though she did not quite grasp the meaning of the word *ascetic*, she too was of the opinion that it would do her darling Yakov no harm if he enjoyed himself a little, saw people, and showed himself—"Particularly," she added, "as I have absolute confidence in Mr. Kupfer. I'm sure he'll never take you to a bad place."

"I shall bring him back to you in all his purity!" cried Kupfer, which, in spite of all her confidence, made Platosha cast rather uneasy glances at him. Aratov blushed to the roots of his hair, but he no longer objected.

It ended by Kupfer's taking him the next day to one of the princess's evening parties. But Aratov did not stay there long. In the first place, he found about twenty visitors there, men and women, sympathetic people, no doubt, but still strangers, and that embarrassed him,

though he did not have to talk a great deal to them: that
he feared most of all. Secondly, he had taken a dislike
to their hostess herself, though she received him very
graciously and simply. He disliked everything about her:
her painted face, her fluffed-up curls, her husky, sugary
voice, her shrill laughter, her manner of rolling her eyes,
her over-deep neckline, and those chubby, shiny fingers
of hers with their multitude of rings! Hiding in a corner,
he sometimes threw rapid glances at the faces of all the
visitors without even distinguishing among them and
sometimes stared obstinately at his own feet. When at
last a foreign pianist with a sallow face, long hair, and
a monocle under a contracted eyebrow sat down at the
piano and, with a crash of hands on the keys and a foot
on the pedal, began thumping away at Liszt's *Fantasia
on a Theme by Wagner,* Aratov could stand it no longer
and slipped away, carrying away in his heart a vague
and painful impression through which, however, there
broke something which he himself could not understand,
but which struck him as significant and even alarming.

3

The next day Kupfer came to dinner. He did not, however, enlarge upon the party of the night before and did
not even reproach Aratov for his hurried flight, merely
expressing his regret that he had not stayed to supper,
at which they had served champagne (of a Nizhny-
Novgorod brand, let us observe in parenthesis!). Kupfer
probably realised that he had made a mistake in wishing
to rouse his friend and that Aratov was a person who
was least of all suited to that society and way of life.
For his part, too, Aratov did not mention the princess
or the party of the previous evening.

Platosha did not know whether to be glad of the failure of that first attempt to get her nephew out into
society or to regret it. She decided at last that her dar-

ling Yakov's health might suffer from such visits, and
did not worry any more. Immediately after dinner Kupfer went away and did not show himself again for the
whole of the next week. It was not that he was cross
with Aratov for the failure of his introduction—he was
too good-natured a man to be capable of that—but he
had evidently found some occupation that took up all
his time and all his thoughts, because even afterwards
he appeared very rarely at the Aratovs', and when he
did, he looked preoccupied, spoke little, and soon disappeared.

Aratov continued to live as before, but a kind of—if
one may put it this way—little hook stuck into his heart.
He was always trying to remember something without
himself having any clear idea what it was, and that
"something" had to do with the evening he had spent
at the princess's. For all that, however, he had no desire
whatever to go back there again; high society, a part of
which he had seen at her house, repelled him more than
ever. So passed six weeks.

One fine morning Kupfer again came to see him, this
time looking somewhat embarrassed. "I know," he began with a forced laugh, "that you were far from pleased
with your visit to the princess that evening, but I hope,
all the same, that you will agree to my proposal, and
that you won't refuse my request."

"What is it?" asked Aratov.

"You see," Kupfer went on, growing more and more
animated, "we have here a Society of Friends of Actors, which from time to time organises readings, concerts, and even theatrical performances in aid of some
charity——"

"And is the princess also a member of it?" Aratov interrupted.

"The princess always takes part in charitable affairs,
but that's neither here nor there. We have organised a
literary and musical matinee, and at this matinee you

can hear a girl—an extraordinary girl! We are not yet quite sure whether she is a second Rachel or a second Viardot, for she sings beautifully, and recites and acts. A first-class talent, my dear fellow. I'm not exaggerating. Well, are you going to take a ticket or not? Five roubles for a seat in the front row."

"And where has this remarkable girl sprung from?" asked Aratov.

Kupfer grinned. "I'm afraid I can't say. During the last few weeks she has been living with the princess. The princess, you know, likes to patronise all such artists. Why, I expect you must have seen her at that party!"

Aratov gave a faint start, but he said nothing.

"I believe she has even acted somewhere in the provinces," Kupfer went on, "and, as a matter of fact, she seems to have been created for the theatre. You'll see for yourself."

"What's her name?" asked Aratov.

"Clara."

"Clara?" Aratov interrupted a second time. "Impossible!"

"Why impossible? Clara—Clara Milich. It's not her real name, but that is what she is called. She is going to sing a love song by Glinka, and a—er—er—by Tchaikovsky, and then she'll read the letter from *Eugene Onegin*. Well, taking a ticket?"

"When is it going to be?"

"Tomorrow—tomorrow at half past one, in a private ballroom in Ostozhenka. I'll come for you. A five-rouble ticket? Here—no, that's a three-rouble one. This is it, and here is the programme. I'm one of the stewards."

Aratov pondered, and at that moment Platosha came into the room and, glancing at his face, suddenly looked worried. "Yakov dear," she exclaimed, "what's the matter with you? Why do you look so upset? What have you been telling him, Mr. Kupfer?"

But Aratov did not let his friend answer his aunt's

279

question and, hastily snatching the ticket Kupfer held out to him, told Platosha to give Kupfer five roubles at once.

His aunt blinked in surprise. However, she gave Kupfer the money in silence. Her darling Yakov had shouted at her a little too peremptorily.

"I tell you, she's a wonder of wonders!" Kupfer exclaimed and rushed to the door. "Wait for me to-morrow!"

"Has she black eyes?" Aratov called after him.

"Black as coal!" Kupfer shouted gaily and vanished.

Aratov went back to his room, while Platosha stood rooted to the spot, repeating in a whisper, "Lord, help me! Lord, help me!"

4

The large ballroom in the private house in Ostozhenka was already half full of visitors when Aratov and Kupfer arrived. In this room theatrical performances were sometimes given; but this time there was no sign of any scenery or curtain. The organisers of the matinee had confined themselves to putting up a platform at one end of the room, placing a grand piano on it as well as a pair of music stands, a couple of chairs, a table with a decanter of water and a glass; in addition, they had concealed the door leading to the artists' room with a red curtain. The princess was already sitting in the front row, wearing a bright green dress; Aratov sat down at some distance from her, after exchanging a very curt greeting with her. The audience was what is known as "mixed"; it consisted mostly of young men from various educational establishments. Kupfer, as one of the stewards, with a white ribbon on the lapel of his coat, fussed and bustled about busily; the princess was quite unmistakably excited, and she kept looking round and sending

smiles in all directions, talking to the people beside her
—there were only men sitting near her.

The first to appear on the platform was a flautist of
consumptive appearance, who most painstakingly spluttered—I'm sorry, I mean, of course, *piped* a piece also
of a consumptive nature; two persons shouted, "Bravo!"
Then a stout gentleman in glasses, of a very solid, even
surly aspect, read in a bass voice a sketch by Shchedrin;
it was the sketch, not he, that was applauded; then the
pianist, who was already known to Aratov, came on and
strummed the same Liszt *Fantasia;* the pianist was
deemed worthy of taking a call. He bowed, leaning with
his hand on the back of a chair, and after each bow he
tossed back his hair exactly like Liszt!

At last, after a rather long interval, the red curtain
over the door behind the platform stirred, was flung back,
and Clara Milich appeared. The room resounded with
applause. She walked up to the front of the platform
with irresolute steps, stopped, and stood motionless,
clasping her large, beautiful, ungloved hands in front of
her; she did not curtsey, or incline her head, or smile.

She was a girl of about nineteen, tall, rather broad-
shouldered, but well built. Her face was dark, either of a
Jewish or a gipsy type. Her eyes were small and black,
under thick eyebrows, which almost met in the middle;
her nose was straight and slightly turned up; her lips
were thin, with a beautiful though strongly marked
curve; her hair was black and hung down in a heavy
plait; her forehead was low and immobile, as though
made of stone; her ears were tiny—her whole face
looked pensive, almost stern. A nature passionate, wilful,
hardly very intelligent, hardly good-tempered, but gifted
—everything showed that.

For some time she did not raise her eyes, but suddenly
she gave a start and ran an intent but inattentive and
as though self-absorbed glance over the rows of spectators. "What tragic eyes she has!" observed a man who

was sitting behind Aratov, a grey-haired dandy with the face of a Revel cocotte, notorious all over Moscow as an unscrupulous gossip writer. The dandy was stupid and he wanted to say something stupid, but he spoke the truth. Aratov, who had kept his eyes fixed on Clara ever since she appeared on the platform, only at that moment remembered that he had seen her at the princess's; and he had not only seen her but had even noticed that she had several times looked at him with her dark, intent eyes, with particular persistence. And now too— or was he imagining it?—on seeing him in the front row, she seemed pleased, seemed even to colour—and again looked persistently at him. Then, without turning round, she took a few steps backwards in the direction of the piano, at which her accompanist, the long-haired foreigner, was already sitting. She was to sing Glinka's love song "The Moment I Knew You." She began to sing at once, without changing the position of her hands and without looking at the music. She had a rich and soft contralto voice, and she enunciated the words distinctly and with emphasis; she sang monotonously, without nuances but with intense expression. "The wench sings with conviction," said the dandy sitting behind Aratov, and again he spoke the truth. Shouts of "Encore!" "Bravo!" resounded from all parts of the room, but she threw a quick glance at Aratov, who neither shouted nor clapped—he did not particularly care for her singing —gave a slight bow, and went out, without accepting the crooked arm of the long-haired pianist.

She was called back. She did not appear for some time, and when she did, she walked up to the piano with the same irresolute steps and, whispering a few words to her accompanist, who had to find and put in front of him a piece of music he had not got ready beforehand, began to sing Tchaikovsky's song "None But the Lonely Heart." This song she sang differently from the first—in a low voice, as though she were tired, and only at the line before the last "can know my sadness" a ringing, ardent cry burst from her. The last verse, "And how I suffer," she almost whispered, drawing out the last word mournfully.

This song did not make as big an impression on the audience as had the Glinka song; however, there was a great deal of applause. Kupfer was particularly enthusiastic; putting his hands together at each clap in a special way, in the shape of a little cask, he produced an extraordinarily booming sound. The princess handed him a large, battered bouquet to offer to the singer; but she did not seem to notice Kupfer's bowing figure, his outstretched hand with the bouquet, and turned and went out again, without waiting for the pianist, who jumped to his feet more rapidly than before, to escort her to the door and, being left with his task unaccomplished, he tossed his hair back so violently—probably Liszt himself had never tossed his quite like that.

Aratov had watched Clara's face during the whole time of the singing. It seemed to him that her eyes, through her drooping eyelashes, had again been directed at him; but he was particularly struck by the immobility of the face, the forehead, the eyebrows, and only at her passionate cry did he notice a row of white and closely spaced teeth flash warmly through the barely parted lips.

Kupfer came up to him. "Well, my dear chap, what do you think of her?" he asked, beaming with pleasure.

"She has a good voice, but she doesn't yet know how to sing. She hasn't had any proper training." (Why he said this and what his idea of "training" was—goodness only knows!)

Kupfer looked surprised. "Training?" he repeated slowly. "Well, she can still get that. But what wonderful feeling! You'd better wait, though. You shall hear her in Tatyana's letter."

He ran off, and Aratov thought, "Feeling! With such a motionless face!" He thought that she carried herself and moved about just as if she were hypnotised, like a sleepwalker. And at the same time she was undoubtedly —yes, undoubtedly looking at him.

Meanwhile the matinee continued. The stout man in spectacles appeared again; in spite of his serious exterior, he fancied himself as a comic actor and read a scene from Gogol, this time without arousing a single sign of approval. The flautist came and went again; the pianist thumped the keys once more; a twelve-year-old boy, his hair oiled and waved, but with traces of tears on his cheeks, scraped out some variations on a violin. It was certainly strange that in the intervals between the reading and the music there occasionally came from the artists' room the abrupt sounds of a horn, and yet the player of this instrument made no appearance on the platform. Afterwards it turned out that the amateur who had volunteered to perform on it had got stage fright at the moment he had to come out before the public.

At last Clara Milich made her appearance again. She held in her hand a small volume of Pushkin's poems, but she never glanced at it once during her reading. She was obviously nervous. The little book trembled slightly in her fingers. Aratov noticed also an expression of despondency which now spread all over her severe features. The first verse, "I write to you, what more?" she spoke very simply, almost naïvely, and she stretched out both her hands in front of her with a naïve, sincere, helpless gesture. Then she began to hurry a little; but beginning with the lines

> "Another! No, my heart I give
> To no one in the world!"

she regained her self-control, grew animated; and when she came to the words

> "My whole life a pledge has been
> Of a meeting true with you—"

284

her hitherto rather hollow voice rang out boldly and rap-
turously, while her eyes were fixed as boldly and directly
on Aratov. She continued with the same fervour and only
towards the end did she lower her voice again, and her
former despondency was again reflected in her face. The
last quatrain she made a complete "hash" of, as the saying is; the little volume of Pushkin's poems suddenly
slipped out of her hands and she withdrew hurriedly.

The audience began applauding desperately and calling for her. One Ukrainian seminarist bellowed, "Mylych!
Mylych!" in so thunderous a voice that his neighbour
asked him politely and with unmistakable concern to be
careful "not to ruin [his] future career as a deacon!"
But Aratov got up at once and made for the door.

Kupfer overtook him. "Good heavens, where are you
off to?" he cried. "Would you like me to introduce you
to Clara?"

"No thanks," said Aratov hastily and almost ran all
the way home.

<hr/>

5

He was troubled by strange feelings he could not himself explain. As a matter of fact, he did not like Clara's
reading, either, though he could not tell why. It had
made him feel uneasy, this reading: it seemed harsh and
inharmonious to him; it seemed to disturb something in
him, to be a kind of outrage. And those intent, persist-
ent, almost importunate glances—what were they for?
What did they mean?

Aratov's modesty did not permit him to imagine for
one moment that he might have turned the head of this
strange girl, that he might have inspired in her a feeling
akin to love, to passion! And besides, she was not the
type of girl whom he fancied he would one day meet,
to whom he would give himself up entirely and who
would also be in love with him and become his fiancée,

his wife. He seldom dreamt of it—he was a virgin both in soul and body—but the pure image which arose at those moments in his imagination had been evoked by a different image, the image of his dead mother, whom he scarcely remembered but whose portrait he preserved as something sacred. This portrait was a water colour, painted rather unskilfully by a woman who had been a friend and neighbour of his mother's; but the likeness, as everyone told him, was a striking one. The woman, the girl whom he dared not as yet hope for, would have just such a tender profile, just such kind, bright eyes, just such silken hair, just such a smile and serene expression.

But this swarthy dark girl with coarse hair and a little moustache on her upper lip—why, she was certainly bad, unbalanced. "A gipsy!" (Aratov could not think of a worse description.) What was she to him?

And yet Aratov was unable to get this swarthy gipsy girl out of his mind, much as he disliked her singing, her reading, and her very appearance. He was bewildered; he was angry with himself. A short while before, he had read Sir Walter Scott's *St. Ronan's Well* (there was a complete edition of Sir Walter Scott's works in the library of his father, who had a great regard for the English novelist as a serious, almost scientific writer). The heroine of this novel is named Clara Mowbray. A certain poet of the forties, called Krasov, wrote a poem on her, ending with the words

> "Unhappy Clara, poor crazy Clara!
> Unhappy Clara Mowbray!"

Aratov knew that poem also . . . and now these words kept coming to his mind continuously: "Unhappy Clara, poor crazy Clara!" (That was why he was so surprised when Kupfer had told him the name of Clara Milich.) Platosha herself noticed not so much a change in Yakov's mood—there was really no change in it—but something wrong in his looks and his words. She questioned him

cautiously about the literary matinee at which he had
been present; muttered to herself, sighed, gazed at him
from the front, gazed at him from the side and from behind, and suddenly, slapping her thighs, she exclaimed,
"Well, my dear, I see now what's the matter with you!"

"What's the matter with me?" Aratov echoed.

"I expect you must have met one of those bustle-
carrying creatures at the matinee." (Platosha spoke of
all fashionably dressed ladies this way.) "I daresay she
has a pretty but silly face, and goes mincing *like this*
and pulling a face *like that*"—Platosha mimicked the
supposed expressions of their faces—"and rolls her eyes
like *that.*" This too she mimicked, drawing large circles
in the air with her forefinger. "I suppose that not being
used to this sort of thing you imagined . . . But, my
dear boy, that means nothing, n-nothing at all! Have a
cup of tea before going to bed and it will pass! Lord,
help me!"

Platosha fell silent and left the room. She had never
before made such a long and animated speech. And
Aratov thought to himself, "I suppose Auntie's right. I'm
not used to it." (And indeed it was the first time that
he had aroused an interest in a person of the fair sex—
at least, he had never noticed it before.) "One mustn't
let one's conceit get the better of oneself."

And he sat down to his books and before going to bed
had some lime-flower tea and indeed slept well that night
and had no dreams. The next morning he applied himself to his photography again as though nothing had
happened.

But towards evening his peace of mind was again
disturbed.

6

What happened was that a messenger brought him
the following note, written in a large, irregular, woman's
hand.

"If you can guess who it is who writes to you, and if that does not bore you, please come tomorrow after dinner to the Tversky Boulevard—about five o'clock—and wait there. You will not be kept long. But it is very important. Do come."

There was no signature. Aratov at once guessed who his correspondent was, and it was this that disturbed him. "What nonsense!" he said, almost aloud. "This is the last straw! Of course I shan't go." He did, however, send for the messenger, but all he learnt from him was that the letter had been given to him by a servant girl in the street. Having dismissed him, Aratov read the letter again and threw it on the floor. But a few minutes later he picked it up and read it again; for the second time he exclaimed, "What nonsense!" but this time he did not throw the letter on the floor but hid it in a drawer. Aratov went on with his usual occupations, starting one thing and then another, but nothing he did turned out to his satisfaction. Suddenly he caught himself wishing that Kupfer would come. He might want to ask him something, or even tell him something. . . . But Kupfer did not appear. Then Aratov got Pushkin's works, read Tatyana's letter, then once again satisfied himself that the "gipsy girl" did not have an inkling of the real meaning of that letter. "And that idiot Kupfer shouts, 'Rachel! Viardot!'" Then he went up to his piano, raised its lid without apparently realising what he was doing, and tried to play from memory the melody of Tchaikovsky's song; but he almost immediately closed it in vexation with a crash, and went to see his aunt in her private room, which was always very hot, smelled of mint, sage, and other medicinal herbs, and was so cluttered up with so many little rugs, whatnots, footstools, cushions, and all sorts of soft furniture that anyone coming there for the first time would have found it difficult to turn round and hard to breathe.

Platosha was sitting at the window with knitting needles in her hand (she was knitting her darling Yakov a scarf, the thirty-eighth in the course of his life!) and was greatly surprised to see him. Aratov seldom went to see her in her room, for whenever he wanted something he used to call in a high-pitched voice from his study, "Aunt Platosha!" However, she made him sit down and pricked up her ears in expectation of his first words, looking at him through her round spectacles with one eye and over them with the other. She did not ask him how he was or offer him tea, for she could see he had not come for that. Aratov hesitated a little; then he began to talk. He talked of his mother, of what her life with his father had been like and how his father had met her. All this he knew very well, but he just longed to talk about it. Unfortunately for him, Platosha did not know at all how to carry on a conversation; she replied shortly, as though she suspected that was not what her darling Yakov had come for.

"Well," she kept repeating, moving her knitting needles about hurriedly, almost with vexation, "we all know your mother was an angel. An angel. Yes, an angel. And your father loved her as a husband should, truly and faithfully to the day of her death. And," she added, raising her voice and taking off her glasses, "he never loved another woman in his life."

"But—er—was she a timid woman?" Aratov asked after a pause.

"Yes, of course she was. As a woman should be. It's only quite recently that women have grown bold."

"Why, weren't there any bold ones in your day?"

"Of course there were! There were bold ones in our time too. But who were they? Why, sluts, shameless hussies! Hitched up their skirts and went gadding about. What did they care? Why should they worry? If some poor wretch of a man was fool enough to fall into their clutches, it was all the better for them. Respectable people would have nothing to do with them. Try to remember—have you ever seen a girl like that in our house?"

Aratov made no reply, and went back to his study. Platosha followed him with her eyes, shook her head, put on her spectacles again, and picked up her knitting once more, but she would now and again sink into thought and drop her knitting needles in her lap.

Aratov, much against his will, kept thinking all day long with the same exasperation and the same bitterness about the note, the "gipsy girl," and the appointed meeting, to which he was quite certain he would not go. At night too she gave him no rest. All the time he seemed to see her eyes, half closed at one time and wide open at another, and their unflinching look fixed straight on him—and those motionless features with their imperious expression.

The next morning he again, for some reason, kept expecting Kupfer to turn up; he nearly wrote a note to him, but did nothing, and kept pacing up and down his study. Not for a moment would he go so far as to admit to himself that he would go to that stupid rendezvous —and at half past four, after a hastily swallowed dinner, he suddenly put on his overcoat, pulled his cap over his forehead, dashed out into the street without being observed by his aunt, and set off for the Tversky Boulevard.

7

Aratov found few passers-by there. It was damp and rather cold. He tried not to think about what he was doing, forced himself to turn his attention to everything that crossed his path, and tried to persuade himself that he had simply gone out for a walk, like the other people in the street. The letter he had received the day before was in his breast pocket, and he was constantly conscious of its presence. He walked twice up and down the boulevard, looking intently at every woman who approached him, and his heart beat violently. He felt tired and sat down on a bench.

Suddenly it occurred to him, "And what if that letter was not written by her at all, but by someone else, by some other woman?" Actually, that should have been all the same to him, and yet he had to admit to himself that he did not want it to be so. "That would be too silly," he thought. "Even sillier than this!" A feeling of nervous excitement was taking hold of him; he began to shiver, not outwardly but inwardly. He took his watch out of his waistcoat pocket several times, looked at the face, put it back, and each time forgot how many minutes it was to five. It seemed to him that the people who were passing by looked at him in a peculiar way, with a kind of sarcastic astonishment and curiosity. A stray dog ran up to him, sniffed at his legs, and began to wag its tail. He waved it away angrily. He was most of all exasperated by a young factory hand in a workday smock who sat down on a bench on the other side of the boulevard and kept staring at him, whistling or scratching himself or swinging his legs in huge, torn boots. "I'm sure," thought Aratov, "his master is waiting for him, and yet there he sits, doing nothing, the lazy lout!"

But at that very moment he felt that someone had walked up and was standing close behind him. He felt a breath of something warm coming from that direction.

He looked round. It was she!

He recognised her at once, though a thick dark blue veil covered her face. He at once leapt from the seat and remained standing like that, unable to utter a single word. She too was silent. He felt greatly embarrassed, but her embarrassment was no less. Even through the veil Aratov could not help noticing how deathly pale she had gone.

It was she, however, who was the first to speak. "Thank you," she began in a broken voice. "Thank you for coming. I hardly dared to hope . . ." She turned away a little and walked along the boulevard. Aratov followed her. "I hope you don't think too harshly of me," she went on, without turning her head. "I'm afraid you must think my behaviour very strange, but I have heard so much about you—no, no! I—that isn't the reason. If only you knew—— Oh dear, there was so much I wanted to tell you, but how am I to do it? How am I to do it?"

Aratov walked beside her, a little behind. He could not see her face: all he saw was her hat and a bit of her veil and her long, black, rather threadbare cloak. All his annoyance both with her and with himself suddenly came back to him; he became suddenly aware how utterly ridiculous, how absurd this meeting was, these explanations between perfect strangers on a boulevard.

"I have come at your invitation," he began in his turn. "I have come, my dear lady"—her shoulders gave a little twitch; she turned off into a bypath, and he followed her—"simply to find out—to—to discover what strange misunderstanding made you turn to me, a complete stranger, who—er—only *guessed*, as you put it in your letter, that it was you writing to him—guessed it because during that literary matinee you took it into your head to show him—er—a little—er—too-obvious attention."

The whole of this short speech was delivered by Aratov in that loud but unsteady voice in which very young men answer questions at an examination on a subject in which they have been thoroughly prepared. He was cross; he was angry. And it was this anger that loosened his tongue, which at any ordinary time was not particularly ready.

She continued to walk along the path with somewhat slower steps. Aratov, as before, walked behind her and, as before, saw only her old cloak and her hat, which was not new, either. His vanity suffered from the thought that she must now be thinking, "I had only to make a sign and he came running at once!"

Aratov was silent. He waited to hear what she had

to say to him, but she did not utter a word. "I'm quite ready to hear what you have to say," he began again. "Indeed, I'd be very glad if I could be of some assistance to you in any way, though I—I must confess the whole thing is a great surprise to—to me. I mean, when you consider the solitary life I lead . . ."

But at these last words of his Clara suddenly turned to him and he saw such a terrified, such a deeply grieved face, with such large, bright tears in her eyes, such a mournful expression about her parted lips, and that face was so lovely that he involuntarily stopped short and himself felt something like panic—and compassion and tenderness.

"Oh why, why are you like that," she said, with an irresistible, sincere, and candid force, and her voice rang out so movingly! "Could my appeal to you have possibly offended you? Have you really understood nothing? Oh, yes! I see you understood nothing; you did not understand what I said to you. You imagined goodness only knows what about me. It never even occurred to you what it cost me—to write to you! You were only worried about yourself, about your own dignity, your peace of mind! Why, do you really believe that I——" She clenched her hands she had raised to her lips so violently that he could hear her knuckles crack. "As if I made any demands on you, as if explanations were necessary first. . . . 'My dear young lady . . . I can't help being surprised . . . if I can be of any assistance to you . . .' Oh, I am mad! I was mistaken in you, in your face. . . . When I saw you for the first time—— You stand here and not a word from you! Not a single word?" She implored him. Her face suddenly flushed and as suddenly assumed an angry and arrogant expression. "Good Lord, how stupid all this is!" she cried suddenly with a harsh laugh. "How stupid our meeting is! How stupid I am! And you too! Ugh!"

She waved her hand in a contemptuous gesture, as

though pushing him out of her way, and, running past him, rushed off down the boulevard and disappeared.

This gesture of her hand, this insulting laugh, this last exclamation, at once made Aratov regain his original frame of mind and smothered the feeling which had arisen in his heart when she turned to him with tears in her eyes. He grew angry again and almost shouted after the retreating girl, "You may make a good actress, but what gave you the idea that you could fool me?"

He went back home, walking fast, and though he continued to be vexed and ill-tempered all the way, yet these hostile and evil feelings could not suppress the recollection of the wonderful face he had seen for a moment only. He even asked himself why he hadn't answered her when she asked only one word of him. "I didn't have time," he thought. "She didn't let me utter that word, and what word could I have uttered?" But he shook his head at once and said with reproach, "What an actress!"

And at the same time the vanity of the inexperienced, nervous young man, injured at first, seemed now to be flattered at having, anyhow, inspired such a passion.

"On the other hand," he went on with his reflections, "at this very moment, all this is, of course, over and done with. She must have thought me ridiculous. . . ."

This thought displeased him and again he was angry—with her and with himself. On returning home, he locked himself up in his study. He did not want to see Platosha. The good old lady came to his door twice, put her ear to the keyhole, but only sighed and murmured a prayer.

"It's begun!" she thought. "And he's only twenty-five. Oh, it's early, it's early!"

8

On the following day Aratov was not in a good mood. "What's the matter, dear?" Platosha said to him. "You seem to be all topsy-turvy today!" In the peculiar language of the old lady this expression defined rather correctly Aratov's state of mind. He could not work; besides, he did not know himself what exactly he wanted. One moment he would be waiting for Kupfer (he suspected that it was from Kupfer that Clara had got his address, and who else could have told her "So much about him?"); another moment he would wonder whether his acquaintance with her was to end this way. Then he imagined that she would write to him again; then he asked himself whether he ought not to write her a letter in which he would explain everything, for he certainly did not want to leave an unfavourable opinion of himself. But what exactly was he to explain? Then he aroused in himself almost a feeling of revulsion for her, especially for the way she had thrown herself at his head, and for her arrogance; then again he saw that ineffably moving face and heard her irresistible voice; then he recalled her singing, her reading, and wondered whether he was right in his sweeping condemnation of it. In short, he was all topsy-turvy!

At last he got tired of it all and decided to "take himself in hand," as the saying is, and to *expunge* the whole of this incident; for there could be no doubt that it was interfering with his work and ruining his peace of mind. But it was not so easy to carry out his decision. More than a week passed before he got back to his old accustomed mode of life. Fortunately, Kupfer did not turn up at all, just as though he had left Moscow. Shortly before this "incident" Aratov had turned to painting, which he hoped would be of some assistance to his photographic hobby; he now took it up with redoubled zeal.

So, imperceptibly, with some—as doctors put it—"relapses," consisting, for instance, in his once almost deciding to pay a call on the princess, two, three months passed and Aratov was his old self again. Only deep inside him, under the surface of his life, something dark and painful secretly accompanied him wherever he went. So a great fish, caught on a hook but not yet landed, swims along the bottom of a deep river under the very boat in which the fisherman sits with a strong line in his hand.

And so, one day looking through a not-quite-new number of the *Moscow News*, Aratov came upon the following news item.

"With great regret," wrote the Kazan correspondent of the paper, "we enter into our theatrical annals the news of the sudden death of our talented actress, Clara Milich, who during the brief period of her engagement had succeeded in becoming the favourite of our discerning public. Our grief is all the greater in view of the fact that Miss Milich herself put an end to her young life, so full of promise, by taking poison. And this is all the more dreadful because the actress took poison in the theatre itself. She had scarcely been taken home when, to our general regret, she passed away. There are rumours in the town that it was unrequited love that drove her to this terrible act."

Aratov quietly put down the copy of the paper on the table. He seemed to be perfectly calm, but he felt as though someone had struck him a violent blow in the chest and on the head, and this feeling spread slowly all over his body. He got up, stood still for a moment and sat down again, and again read the news item. Then he got up again, lay down on the bed, and, folding his hands behind his head, stared for a long time at the wall, as though in a daze. Gradually this wall seemed to fade away and then to disappear, and he saw before him the boulevard beneath a grey sky and her in a black cloak, and then her on the platform, even saw himself beside her. The thing that hit him so violently in the chest at first was beginning to rise now, rise up to his throat. . . . He tried to clear his throat; he tried to call someone; but his voice failed him, and to his own amazement tears gushed irrepressibly from his eyes. What provoked these tears? Pity? Remorse? Or were his nerves simply unable to stand the sudden shock? For she was nothing to him, or was she?

"But," it suddenly dawned on him, "perhaps it's not true. I must find out! But from whom? From the princess? No, from Kupfer. But they say he's not in Moscow. Never mind! I must go and see him first!" With these thoughts in his mind Aratov hastily dressed himself, hailed a cab, and drove to Kupfer's.

9

He had not expected to find Kupfer at home, but he did find him after all. Kupfer had, as a matter of fact, been away from Moscow for some time, but he had returned a week ago and was again on the point of paying a visit to Aratov. He received him with his usual cordiality, and was about to say something to him, but Aratov at once interrupted him with the impatient question, "Have you heard? Is it true?"

"Is what true?" Kupfer, taken aback, said.

"About Clara Milich?"

An expression of regret appeared on Kupfer's face. "Yes, yes, my dear fellow, it's true. She poisoned herself! What a terrible thing!"

Aratov was silent. "Did you also read it in the paper, or have you perhaps been to Kazan yourself?"

"I have been in Kazan, yes. You see, the princess and I took her there. She got a stage engagement there and was a great success. But I did not stay up there to the time of the catastrophe. I was in Yaroslav."

"In Yaroslav?"

"I escorted the princess there. She has settled now in Yaroslav."

"But is your information correct?"

"Absolutely. I have it at first hand. You see, I made the acquaintance of her family in Kazan. But look here,

my dear fellow, does this news upset you very much?
Why, I remember, you did not like Clara very much at
that matinee, did you? You were wrong, you know. She
was a marvellous girl, only what a temper! What a wilful
girl! Oh, I was very distressed over her!"

Aratov did not utter a word. He sank into a chair
and after a short pause asked Kupfer to tell him——
He stopped short.

"What?" asked Kupfer.

"Why, everything," Aratov replied slowly. "Tell me
all about her family, and the rest of it. Everything you
know!"

"Does it interest you? By all means!"

And Kupfer, whose face did not convey the impression of his having been so terribly distressed over Clara,
began his story.

From his account Aratov learnt that Clara Milich's
real name was Katerina Milovidov; that her father, now
dead, had been a drawing master in a school in Kazan,
that he had painted bad portraits and regulation icons
and that he had, besides, the reputation of a drunkard
and a domestic tyrant and an *iconoclast* too! (here Kupfer laughed self-complacently, hinting at the pun he had
just made); that he had left behind him, first, a widow
of the merchant class, a very stupid woman, a character
straight out of an Ostrovsky comedy, and, secondly, a
daughter much older than Clara and not at all like her
—a very intelligent girl, only rather too gushing, a sick,
remarkable girl, and "highly advanced, my dear fellow!";
that both of them—the widow and her daughter—"are
quite well off and are living in a decent house, bought
from the proceeds of the bad icons; that Clara, or Katya,
if you like, had from childhood amazed everybody by her
talent, but was constantly at daggers drawn with her
father; that having an inborn passion for the theatre, she
had run away from home at the age of sixteen with an
actress——"

"With an actor?" Aratov interrupted.

"No, not with an actor, with an actress, to whom she became attached. It's true the actress had a protector, a rich, elderly nobleman, who did not marry her only because he was married already, and besides, the actress too, I believe, was a married woman."

Kupfer further told Aratov that Clara had already, before her arrival in Moscow, acted and sung on the provincial stage; that having lost her friend the actress (the nobleman too, it seems, had died or had returned to his wife—Kupfer could not quite remember this), she had made the acquaintance of the princess—"that wonderful woman whom you, my friend," he added with feeling, "failed to appreciate as she deserved"—that at last Clara had been offered an engagement in Kazan, though before that she kept saying that she would never leave Moscow. The Kazan public, though, made so much of her that it was really astonishing. Bouquets and presents, bouquets and presents after every performance! A corn-chandler, the richest man in the province, even presented her with a gold inkstand.

Kupfer told it all with great animation, without, however, displaying any great emotion and even interrupting his narrative with such questions as, "What do you want to know all this for?" or, "What is it to you?" when Aratov, who listened to him with rapt attention, demanded to be told more and more details. At last Kupfer had told him everything he knew, and he fell silent, lighting a cigar as a reward for his labours.

"And why did she poison herself?" asked Aratov. "It said in the paper——"

Kupfer waved his hands. "Well, that I'm afraid I can't say. Don't know. But the paper is talking nonsense. Clara's conduct was most exemplary. No love affairs of any kind. And how could she have had any with her pride? She was as proud as Satan himself, and unapproachable. A wilful girl. Hard as stone. I tell you, I knew her as intimately as anyone and yet I never saw a tear in her eyes!"

"But I have," Aratov thought to himself.

"There's one thing, though," Kupfer went on. "I noticed a great change in her during the last few months: she became so sad, so silent. Couldn't get a word out of her for hours. I kept asking her whether anyone had hurt her feelings. For, you see, I knew her character; she could not swallow an insult. But she wouldn't say a word. Not a word! Even her successes on the stage did not cheer her up. Bouquets were showered on her, but she didn't even smile. She gave one look at the gold inkstand and put it aside. She used to complain that no one had written a real part for her, as she understood it. And she gave up singing altogether. I'm afraid, my dear fellow, that must have been my fault. I told her that you thought she had no musical training. All the same, why she poisoned herself is an absolute mystery. And the way she poisoned herself!"

"In what part was she most successful?" Aratov asked. He wanted to find out in what part she had appeared for the last time, but for some reason he asked a different question.

"In Ostrovsky's *Gruna*, I believe. But I tell you again, she had no love affairs. None whatever. Don't forget, she lived in her mother's house, and you know what merchants' houses are like—in every corner an icon case and a lamp burning before it, the rooms terribly stuffy, a sour smell, nothing but chairs in the drawing room along the walls, geranium pots in the windows; and if anyone comes to see them, the woman of the house gets into such a state that you'd think an enemy were attacking it. What sort of flirting or lovemaking could there be in such a house? Why, sometimes they wouldn't even let me in. The maid, a big, strapping woman in a red calico dress, with pendulous breasts, would stand right across the passage and growl, 'Where are you going?' . . . No,

I simply can't understand why she poisoned herself. I expect she just got tired of living," Kupfer concluded his discourse philosophically.

Aratov sat with a bowed head. "Can you give me the address of that house in Kazan?" he said at last.

"I can, but what do you want it for? You're not going to send a letter there, are you?"

"Perhaps."

"Well, just as you like. Only the old woman won't answer your letter, because she's illiterate. The sister may, though. Oh, the sister's a clever girl. But again I can't help being surprised at you, my dear fellow. So indifferent at first and now—such an interest! I'm afraid, old man, it's all because of the secluded life you lead!"

Aratov made no reply to this remark and went away after taking down the Kazan address.

When he had gone to see Kupfer his face had expressed excitement, consternation, expectation. Now he walked home with measured steps, with lowered eyes, with a hat pulled over his forehead. Almost every person he passed in the street followed him with a searching look—but he did not notice the passers-by. His behaviour was quite unlike his behaviour on the boulevard.

"Unhappy Clara, poor, crazy Clara!" it resounded in his mind.

10

The next day, however, Aratov spent fairly calmly. He was even able to pursue his usual occupations. Except for one thing, though: during both his work and his leisure he thought constantly of Clara and of what Kupfer had told him the day before. It is true that his thoughts too were of a fairly placid character. It seemed to him that this strange girl interested him from the psychological point of view as a kind of mystery which it is worth while racking one's brains over. "Ran away with an actress who was a kept woman," he thought. "Put herself under the protection of that princess, at whose house she seems to have lived—and no love affairs? Highly improbable! Kupfer says, 'Pride!' But, in the first place, we know"—Aratov should have said, "We have read in books"—"that pride and flighty behaviour can exist side by side, and, secondly, how could it happen that a proud girl like her should arrange a meeting with a man who might have treated her with contempt and, in fact, *did* treat her with contempt—in a public place too—on the boulevard!" At this point Aratov recalled the whole scene on the boulevard and he asked himself whether he had really treated Clara with contempt. "No," he decided. "That was a different feeling, a feeling of bewilderment—of mistrust, in fact!" "Unhappy Clara!" was again ringing in his head. "Yes, unhappy," he decided again. "That's the right word. But if so, then I was unjust to her. She was quite right in saying that I did not understand her. A pity! Such a remarkable human being, perhaps, passed so close to me and I took no advantage of it; I pushed her away. . . . Well, it can't be helped! My life is still all before me. I expect there will be other, much more interesting meetings!

"But why on earth should she have chosen me of all people?" He glanced into a looking-glass he was passing just then. "What is there so special about me? I'm not even handsome, am I? An undistinguished face, like lots of other faces. Still, she wasn't a beauty, either.

"Not a beauty, but what an expressive face! Immobile —but how expressive! I've never come across such a face. And she has talent—that is, she *had* quite incontestable talent. Untrained, undeveloped, even coarse, but incontestable. In that regard too, I was unjust to her."

Aratov went back in his mind to the literary and musical matinee, and could not help noticing how extraordinarily clear was his recollection of every word she had sung and recited, every intonation of her voice; and that would not have happened if she had had no talent.

"And now it is all in the grave into which she threw herself of her own free will. . . . But I had nothing to do with it. It was not my fault! Why, it would be absurd even to think that it was my fault."

It occurred to Aratov that even if she had felt "anything of the sort," his conduct during their meeting must most certainly have disillusioned her. That was why she had laughed so cruelly when parting from him. "And what proof is there that she poisoned herself because of an unhappy love affair? That's just the newspaper correspondents, who ascribe every death of that kind to an unhappy love affair. People with a character like Clara's often get to hate it, get tired of it—yes, they get tired of life. Kupfer was right: she was simply sick of life.

"In spite of her successes, in spite of the ovations?" Aratov pondered. He was rather enjoying the psychological analysis he was giving himself up to. Having had till now no contact with women, he did not even suspect how important this close analysis of a woman's soul was to him.

"It follows," he went on with his reflections, "that art did not satisfy her, did not fill the void in her life. Real artists exist only for art, for the theatre. Everything else pales before what they consider to be their vocation. She was a dilettante!"

Here Aratov again sank into thought. No, the word *dilettante* did not fit that face, the expression of that face, the expression of those eyes.

And once more there arose before him Clara's image with her eyes fixed upon him and filled with tears, with clenched hands raised to her lips.

"Oh, don't, don't," he whispered. "What's the good of it?"

So passed the whole day. At dinner Aratov talked a great deal to Platosha, questioned her about the old days, which she remembered but described very badly, because she was not able to express herself properly and, except for her darling Yakov, had scarcely noticed anything in her life. She was only glad he was so kind and affectionate today! Towards evening Aratov calmed down to such a degree that he played several games of cards with his aunt.

So passed the day—but the night!

11

It began well: he soon fell asleep and when his aunt tiptoed into his room to make the sign of the cross three times over her sleeping nephew—she did so every night—he lay breathing as quietly as a child. But before daybreak he had a dream.

He dreamt that he was walking in a bare steppe, strewn with big stones, beneath a lowering sky. Between the stones meandered a path; he walked along it.

Suddenly there arose before him something like a thin cloud. He peered at it and the small cloud turned into a woman in a white dress with a bright sash round her waist. She was hurrying away from him. He could not see her face or her hair—they were covered by a long shawl. But he felt he simply had to overtake her and look into her eyes. Only however much he hurried after her, she walked much faster than he.

On the path lay a broad, flat stone like a tombstone. It barred her way. The woman stopped. Aratov ran up to her. She turned to him, but still he could not see her eyes—they were closed. Her face was white, white as snow; her arms hung motionless. She was like a statue.

Slowly, without bending a single limb, she leaned backwards and sank down on the tombstone. . . . And now Aratov was lying beside her, stretched out like a statue on a tomb, his hands too folded like a dead man's hands.

But at this point the woman suddenly rose and walked away. Aratov tried to get up too . . . but he could neither move nor unclasp his hands—all he could do was look after her in despair.

Then the woman suddenly turned round and he saw bright, living eyes on a living but unfamiliar face. She laughed, she beckoned to him—and still he could not move.

She laughed once more and went away rapidly, gaily nodding her head, on which he could see a wreath of small red roses.

Aratov tried to cry out, he tried to shake off this terrible nightmare. . . .

Suddenly everything round him grew dark and the woman returned to him. But it was no longer the unfamiliar statue. It was Clara. She stopped before him, crossed her arms, and looked sternly and intently at him. Her lips were compressed, but Aratov imagined that he could hear words.

"If you want to know who I am, go there!"

"Where?" he asked.

"There!" he heard the moaning answer. "There!"

Aratov woke up.

He sat up in bed, lighted the candle on his bedside table, but did not get out of bed. He sat like this a long time, chilled through and through and looking slowly round him. He couldn't help feeling that something had happened to him since he went to bed, that something had taken root in him, that something had taken possession of him. "But is it possible?" he whispered unconsciously. "Does such a power exist?"

He could not stay in bed. He dressed himself quietly and kept pacing his room till the morning. And, strange to say, he never thought of Clara for a moment, and he did not think of her because he had made up his mind to go the next day to Kazan.

He thought only of the journey, of how to arrange it

and what to take with him and how he would investigate and find everything there and regain his peace of mind. "If I don't go," he reasoned with himself, "I shall most probably go off my head!" He was afraid of that, afraid of his nerves. He was absolutely certain that as soon as he saw everything there with his own eyes, all his delusions would vanish like the nightmare of the night before. "And I won't have to spend more than a week on the trip," he thought to himself. "What is a week? Otherwise I shall never shake it off."

The rising sun lighted his room, but the light of day did not disperse the shadows of the night that encompassed him and did not make him change his mind.

Platosha nearly had a stroke when he informed her of his decision. She literally collapsed on the floor—her legs gave way under her. "To Kazan? Why to Kazan?" she whispered, peering at him with shortsighted eyes. She would not have been more surprised if she had been told that her darling Yakov was going to marry the baker's daughter from next door, or that he was going to America. "And how long will you be in Kazan?"

"I shall be back after a week," replied Aratov, standing with his body half turned to his aunt, who was still sitting on the floor.

Platosha was about to object, but Aratov screamed at her in an unexpected and quite extraordinary way.

"I'm not a child!" he shouted, turning pale, and his lips trembled and his eyes flashed with fury. "I'm twenty-five and I know what I'm doing. I'm free to do as I like. I shall not allow anyone—— Let me have the money for the journey, pack my trunk with my clothes and linen, and—don't torture me! I'll be back in a week, Plastosha," he added in a more gentle voice.

Platosha got up groaning from the floor and without protesting any more staggered off to her room. Yakov had frightened her. "It isn't a head I've got on my shoulders," she said to the cook, who was helping her to pack

Yakov's things, "not a head but a hive, and what kind of bees are buzzing there I don't know! Going to Kazan, my dear, to Ka-a-zan!"

The cook, who the day before had seen their caretaker having a long talk with the policeman about something, would have liked to report this circumstance to her mistress, but did not dare and merely thought, "To Kazan? I hope he's not going somewhere much farther than that!" Platosha was so upset that she did not even mutter her usual prayer. In such trouble even the good Lord could not help her!

Aratov left for Kazan the same day.

12

No sooner had he arrived in that town and taken a room in a hotel than he rushed off to find the house of the widow Milovidov. During the whole journey he had been in a state of insensibility, which, however, had not prevented him from taking all the necessary steps, such as changing from the train to a steamer at Nizhny-Novgorod, having his meals at the stations, and so on. He was quite certain that there everything would be solved, and, for that reason, banished all memories and reflections, contenting himself with rehearsing in his mind the speech in which he would explain to Clara Milich's family the real reason for his trip. Now at last he got to his destination and asked the servant to announce him. He was admitted—with bewilderment and alarm, but he was admitted.

The widow Milovidov's house turned out to be exactly as Kupfer had described it; and indeed the widow herself looked like one of Ostrovsky's merchants' wives, though she was the widow of a civil servant with the rank of a collegiate assessor. Not without a certain embarrassment, Aratov, who first apologised for his boldness and the strange nature of his visit, made his prepared speech in which he explained his anxiety to gather all the necessary information about a talented actress who had died so early; that it was not idle curiosity that prompted him in this case but profound sympathy for her talent, of which he was an admirer (he actually used the word *admirer*); and, finally, that it would be a great pity to leave the public in ignorance of what it had lost and why its hopes had not been fulfilled.

Mrs. Milovidov did not interrupt Aratov; it is doubtful if she understood what the stranger was saying to her; all she did was stare goggle-eyed at him, finding, however, that he looked a quiet, well-dressed person and not a rogue, and had not come to beg.

"Is it Katya you are speaking of?" she asked as soon as Aratov was silent.

"Yes, of your daughter."

"And have you come from Moscow for that?"

"Yes, from Moscow."

"Only for that?"

"Yes."

Mrs. Milovidov suddenly gave a start. "Are you a writer? Do you write for the newspapers?"

"No, I'm not a writer and till now I've never written for the newspapers."

The widow lowered her head. She was completely at a loss. "So I suppose you've come on your own account?" she asked suddenly.

Aratov did not at once know what to say in reply. "Because of my sympathy, and respect for talent," he said at last.

The word *respect* made a good impression on Mrs. Milovidov. "Well," she said with a sigh, "I may be her mother, and I'm terribly grieved—for, you see, it was such a sudden blow. But I must say she always was a crazy girl, and she finished the same way. Oh, the disgrace of it! You can easily imagine, sir, what a mother must feel when such a thing happens, but I suppose I must be thankful they gave her a Christian burial." Mrs. Milovidov crossed herself. "Even as a child she would not listen to anyone—left her parents' house and in the end—I'm ashamed to say—became an actress. Everyone knows that I never forbade her the house, for, you see, I loved her. I was her mother, after all! I couldn't let her live with strangers and go begging, could I?" Here the widow burst into tears. "And if you, sir," she went on, wiping her eyes with the ends of her kerchief, "really mean to do what you say and you don't intend anything dishonourable to us, but, on the contrary, wish to do us a courtesy, then you'd better have a talk with my other daughter. She'll tell you everything much better than I can.

"Anna," cried Mrs. Milovidov, "Anna, darling, come here! Here's a gentleman from Moscow who wants to talk to you about Katya." There was the sound of a movement in the next room, but no one appeared. "Anna," the widow called again, "Anna, my dear, come here, I tell you."

The door opened softly and in the doorway appeared a girl no longer young, looking ill—and rather plain—but with very sad and gentle eyes. Aratov got up from his chair and introduced himself, adding that he was a friend of Mr. Kupfer.

"Oh," the girl said softly and sank softly into a chair.

"Well, you'd better have a talk with the gentleman," said Mrs. Milovidov, rising heavily from her chair. "He's taken the trouble to come from Moscow and he wants to gather information about Katya. And you, sir, will have to excuse me. I'm afraid I have to go. Must look after the house. You will get all the information you want from Anna. She will tell you all about the theatre and everything else. She's a clever girl. Speaks French and reads books as well as her sister did. You see, she really brought her up. She was older and so she looked after her."

Mrs. Milovidov went out of the room. Left alone with Anna, Aratov repeated his speech to her, but realising at the first glance that he was dealing with a girl who really was well educated, and not an ordinary merchant's daughter, he expatiated a little and used different expressions; towards the end he grew agitated, flushed, and felt that his heart was pounding. Anna listened to him in silence, one hand on top of the other; the sad smile never left her face—a bitter, still aching grief could be detected in that smile.

"Did you know my sister?" she asked Aratov.

"No, I didn't really know her," he replied. "I met her and heard her once, but it was quite enough to see and hear your sister once to——"

"Do you want to write her biography?" Anna asked.

Aratov did not expect that question. However, he replied at once, "Why not?" But, above all, he explained, he wanted to acquaint the public——

Anna stopped him with a movement of her hand. "What do you want to do that for? The public caused her a great deal of grief as it is, and besides, Katya had only just begun to live. But if you yourself"—Anna looked at him and smiled the same sad but now more friendly smile, as if she had thought to herself, "Yes, you do inspire confidence in me"—"if you yourself are so interested in her, I'd like you to come and see us this evening —after dinner. I can't now—so suddenly—— I'll feel much stronger then, and I'll do my best. . . . Oh, I loved her so much!" Anna turned away: she was on the point of bursting into tears.

Aratov rose quickly from his chair, thanked her for her suggestion, and said that he would most certainly come—most certainly!—and left the house, carrying away with him an impression of a soft voice and gentle and sad eyes—and full of suspense.

13

Aratov returned the same day to the Milovidovs' and spent three whole hours there talking to Anna. Mrs. Milovidov went to bed immediately after dinner—at two o'clock—and "rested" till evening tea at seven. Aratov's talk with Clara's sister was not, properly speaking, a conversation: she did almost all the talking, first hesitatingly, with embarrassment, then with irrepressible warmth. She quite obviously worshipped her sister. The confidence Aratov had inspired in her grew and strengthened; she was no longer diffident, and once or twice she even cried silently in his presence. She thought him worthy of her outspoken communications and she did not hesitate to pour out her heart to him: in her own dull life nothing of the kind had ever happened. And he—he drank in every word she uttered.

This is what he found out—a lot of it, of course, not from what she told him but from what she kept back, and a lot he filled in for himself.

Clara had undoubtedly been a very difficult child, and as a girl she had not been much better: wilful, hottempered, proud, she had not got on with her father, whom she despised for his drunkenness and his mediocrity. He felt it and could not forgive her for it. She showed an early aptitude for music, but her father would not let it develop, recognising no art except painting, in which, however, he was not particularly successful himself, though it provided a living for himself and his family. Clara loved her mother, but in a rather matter-of-fact sort of way, as one does a nurse; her sister she adored, though she had fights with her and had even bit her. It is true that afterwards she fell on her knees before her and kissed the places she had bitten. She was all fire, all passion, and all contradiction: vindictive and kindhearted, generous and full of rancour. She believed in fate—and did not believe in God (these words Anna whispered with horror); she loved everything beautiful but took no trouble over her own looks or her dresses; she could not bear to have young men make love to her, but in books she read only the pages which described love; she did not want to be liked and she did not care for caresses, but she never forgot a caress just as she never forgot an insult; she was afraid of death and killed herself! She used to say sometimes, "The man I want I shall never meet, and I don't want any others!" "But what if you do meet him?" Anna would ask. "If I meet him I'll take him!" "But if he won't let you?" "Well then—I'll kill myself. For it means I am no good."

Clara's father (he used sometimes, when drunk, to ask his wife, "Who gave you this swarthy little she-devil? It wasn't me!")—Clara's father tried to get rid of her as soon as possible by marrying her off to a young son of a rich merchant, a very stupid young fellow of the "educated" sort. Two weeks before the wedding (she was only sixteen at the time) she went up to her betrothed, her arms folded and her fingers drumming on her elbows (a favourite pose of hers), and suddenly slapped his rosy cheek with her large, powerful hand. He leapt to his feet and just gaped at her—he was, as a matter of fact, head over heels in love with her. "What's that for?" he asked. She laughed and walked away.

"I was there in the room," Anna said. "I was present at the scene. I ran after her and I said to her, 'Good heavens, Katya, why did you do that?' She answered, 'If he'd been a real man he would have given me a beating, but he's just a milksop! Fancy asking me, *What's that for?* If he loves me and does not hit back, he ought to put up with it and not ask, *What's that for?* He won't be anything to me—never, never in my life!' So, of course, she did not marry him. Soon after that she made the acquaintance of the actress and left our house. Mother cried, but Father only said, 'A black sheep should be kept out of the fold!' And he did not even bother to look for her. My father did not understand Clara. . . . She nearly smothered me in her arms the night she ran away," Anna added. "She kept repeating, 'I can't, I can't do otherwise! Even if my heart breaks, I can't. Your cage is too small—there's no room for my wings in it! Besides, you can't escape your fate.'

"After that," Anna observed, "we did not often see each other. When my father died, she came for two days, took nothing of her inheritance, and disappeared again. She did not feel happy here. I could see that. The next time she came to Kazan, she was already an actress."

Aratov began questioning Anna about the theatres and the parts in which Clara had appeared, about her successes. Anna told him about it all in detail, but with the same sad, though animated, eagerness. She even showed Aratov a photograph in which Clara appeared in the costume of one of her parts. In the photograph she was looking away, as though turning away from the spectators; her thick plait of hair, twined with a ribbon, fell in a coil over her bare arm. Aratov examined the photograph a long time, found that it was like her, asked whether Clara had taken part in public readings and learnt that she had not; that she had to have the excitement of the theatre, the stage.

But another question was burning on his lips. "Tell me," he exclaimed at last with special force, though not in a loud voice, "tell me, I beg you, what—what made her do such a terrible thing?"

Anna dropped her eyes. "I don't know," she said after a few moments. "I swear I don't know," she went on impulsively, noticing that Aratov spread out his hands in a gesture of disbelief. "From the very first day of her arrival she looked, it is true, wistful and depressed. Something must certainly have happened to her in Moscow, but what it was, I could not find out. On that

terrible day she seemed to be, on the contrary—well,
if not more cheerful, then at least more composed than
usual. Even I had no presentiment of what was going to
happen," Anna added with a bitter smile, as though reproaching herself for it.

"You see," she said again, "Katya seems to have been
predestined to be unhappy. She was convinced of it ever
since her childhood. She used to prop up her face on her
hand, like this, look thoughtful, and say, 'I haven't got
long to live!' She used to have premonitions. Just imagine, sometimes in a dream, and sometimes when
awake, she would foresee what was going to happen to
her! 'If I can't live as I want to live, then I don't want to
live at all,' was another of her sayings. 'You see, our life
is in our hands!' And she has proved it!" Anna buried
her face in her hands and fell silent.

"I expect," Aratov began after a short pause, "you
must have heard what the papers wrote about the
cause——"

"An unhappy love affair?" Anna interrupted, snatching her hands away from her face. "It's a libel! A libel,
an invention! My untouched, unapproachable Katya!
Katya—and unhappy, unrequited love! And me not know
of it? Everyone fell in love with her, but she—— And
whom could she have fallen in love with here? Who of
all the people here was worthy of her? Who could have
reached her ideal of honesty, truthfulness, purity—yes,
above all, purity, which, with all her shortcomings, she
always aspired to? To reject her—her . . ."

Her voice failed her. Her fingers trembled lightly. She
flushed suddenly all over, flushed with indignation, and
at that moment—and only for a moment—she looked like
her sister.

Aratov began to apologise.

"Listen," Anna interrupted him again, "I'd be very
glad if you did not believe that libellous story yourself
and, if possible, tried to contradict it. You want to write

an article about her, don't you? Well, here's your chance
to defend her memory. That is why I'm speaking so
frankly to you. Listen, Katya left a diary——"

Aratov gave a start. "A diary!" he whispered.

"Yes, a diary. Just a few pages, though; Katya did not
like writing. For months on end she would not write anything down, and her letters too were so short. But she
was always, always truthful. She never told a lie. With
her pride—tell a lie! I—I will show you this diary. You'll
see for yourself whether there was any hint in it of an
unhappy love affair!"

Anna hurriedly pulled out of a table drawer a thin
notebook of no more than a dozen pages and held it out
to Aratov. He snatched it from her eagerly, recognised
the irregular, sprawling handwriting, the handwriting of
that anonymous letter, opened it at random, and his eyes
at once fell on the following lines:

"Moscow. Tuesday, June ——. Sang and recited at a
literary matinee. Today is an important day for me. *It
must decide my fate.*" (These words were twice underlined.) "I saw again . . ." Here followed a few carefully
crossed out lines. And then: "No! No! No! Must take up
my old work again, if only . . ."

Aratov dropped the hand in which he held the notebook and his head slowly sank upon his breast.

"Read it!" cried Anna. "Why don't you read it? Read
it from the beginning. You can read it all in five minutes, though the diary covers two years. She didn't write
anything more in Kazan."

Aratov slowly rose from his chair and flung himself
on his knees before Anna. Anna was simply petrified with
surprise and alarm.

"Give me—give me that diary," Aratov said in a faltering voice, stretching out both hands to Anna. "Give it to
me, and—and—the photograph. You—you must have another one. The diary I promise to return to you. But I
must—I must have it——"

315

In his entreaty, in his contorted features, there was such despair that it looked like fury, like suffering. And he really did suffer. It was as though he could not have foreseen that such a calamity would befall him and begged petulantly to be spared, to be saved.

"Give it to me!" he repeated.

"Why—you—were you in love with my sister?" Anna brought out at last.

Aratov was still on his knees. "I saw her only twice —believe me—and if I were not driven to this by reasons I can neither understand nor properly explain myself, if there had not been some power over me stronger than myself, I should not be begging you; I should not have come here. I must, I ought to have it! You said yourself that I have to show people what she really was like!"

"And were you not in love with my sister?" Anna asked.

Aratov did not at once reply, and he turned away a little, as though in pain. "Well, yes! I was! I was! I'm still in love with her!" he cried with the same note of despair in his voice.

There was the sound of footsteps in the next room.

"Get up, get up!" Anna said quickly. "Mother's coming."

Aratov got up.

"And take the diary and the photograph, please. Poor, poor Katya! But you must return the diary to me," she added quickly. "And if you do write something, promise to send it to me. Do you hear?"

The appearance of Mrs. Milovidov saved him from the necessity of answering. He had time, however, to whisper, "You're an angel! Thank you. I will send you anything I write."

Mrs. Milovidov was still not awake enough to suspect anything.

So it was that Aratov left Kazan with the photograph in the breast pocket of his coat. He returned the notebook to Anna, but, unperceived by her, tore out the page with the underlined words.

On the way back to Moscow he again sank into a state of torpor. Though he was secretly glad that he had obtained what he had gone for, he put off all thoughts of Clara till his return home. He was thinking much more of her sister Anna. "What a wonderful, charming creature!" he thought. "What a subtle understanding of everything, what a loving heart, what an absence of egoism! And how girls like that come to be in our provinces, and in such surroundings too! She is delicate and plain and far from young, but what an excellent wife she would make for a decent, cultivated man! That's the girl I should have fallen in love with!" Aratov was thinking on those lines, but on his arrival in Moscow the affair took quite a different turn.

14

Platosha was overjoyed at the return of her nephew. The things she had imagined while he was away! "He'll be sent to Siberia, at least!" she whispered, sitting motionless in her little room. "For a year at least!" In addition, the cook too frightened her by telling her all sorts of most well-authenticated stories about the disappearance of one or another young man in the neighbourhood. Her darling Yakov's perfect innocence and political reliability did not in the least reassure the old lady. "For —any excuse will do—he is interested in photography— and that's quite enough. Arrest him!" And here was her darling Yakov back again, safe and sound! It is true, she noticed that he seemed to be a little thinner and that his dear face had grown a little pinched, but what else could you expect, with no one to look after him! But she dared not question him about his trip. All she asked at dinner was, "Is Kazan a fine city?" "Yes, it is," Aratov replied. "I expect there are all Tartars living there?" "Not only Tartars." "And you didn't bring a Tartar dressing-gown from there, did you?" "No, I didn't." And that was the end of their conversation.

But as soon as Aratov found himself alone in his study he felt all at once as though something had gripped him, that he was again *in the power*—yes, in the power of another life, another being. Though he had said to Anna—in a fit of sudden frenzy—that he was in love with Clara, that expression seemed to him now utterly senseless and wild.

No, he was not in love, and how could he be in love with a girl who was dead and whom he had not particularly liked even while she was alive, whom he had almost forgotten? No! But he was in the power of—in *her* power; he did not belong to himself any more. He was *taken*. So much so, that he did not even attempt to free himself by sneering at his own idiocy or by arousing, if not a feeling of confidence, then at least some hope in himself that it would all pass, that it was only his nerves, or by looking for some proofs, or by anything! "If I meet him I'll take him!" He remembered Clara's words as Anna had repeated them to him. So now he was taken. But surely she was dead, wasn't she? Yes, her body was dead—but her soul? Was not her soul immortal? Did it require any earthly organs to show its power? Has not magnetism proved to us the influence of one living soul on another living human soul? Why should not this influence go on after death also, if the soul remains living? For what purpose? What could come of it? But then, did we, as a rule, comprehend the purpose of everything that was going on round us? These ideas absorbed Aratov so much that he suddenly asked Platosha at tea whether she believed in the immortality of the soul. Platosha at first did not understand his question; then she crossed herself and replied that she should think so—a soul—and not be immortal!

"But if so, can it have any influence after death?"

Aratov asked again. The old lady replied that it could—that is to say, it could pray for us; but that too only after it had gone through all the ordeals and in the expectation of the Last Judgement. Only during the first forty days did it hover over the place where its death had occurred.

"The first forty days?"

"Yes, and then it has to undergo its ordeals."

Aratov was astonished at his aunt's knowledge, and went back to his room. And once more he felt the same thing, the same power over him. This power showed itself in the fact that Clara's image appeared before him continuously and that he could see it in its minutest details, the sort of details he did not seem to have noticed while she was alive: he saw—yes, saw her fingers, her nails, the strands of hair over her cheeks, beneath her temples, the little mole under her left eye; he saw the movements of her lips, her nostrils, her eyebrows—and the way she walked and the way she held her head a little on the right side—he saw everything! There was no question of his admiring any of it; he just could not help thinking of it and seeing it.

But during the first night after his return he did not dream of her. He was very tired and slept like a log. But as soon as he woke up, she returned to his room again and remained in it all the time, just as though she owned the place, just as though she had bought this right by her voluntary death, without asking him and without requiring his permission. He picked up her photograph and began reproducing it, enlarging it. Then it occurred to him that he would try to adapt it for the stereoscope. He gave a violent start when through the glass he saw her figure, which had become three-dimensional. But the figure was grey, as though covered with dust, and besides, her eyes were averted, just as though turning away. He gazed at them a long, long time, as though expecting them to turn round towards him at any moment. He even screwed up his eyes on purpose, but the eyes remained immovable and the whole figure assumed the aspect of some sort of doll. He moved away and flung himself in an armchair, took out the torn-off page of her diary with the underlined words, and thought, "Lovers, they say, kiss the words written by the hand of their beloved, but I don't feel like doing it, and besides, I think the handwriting is far from beautiful. But my sentence of death is in that line."

At this point he remembered the promise he had made Anna about the article. He sat down at the table and began to write it, but everything he wrote was so false, so rhetorical—but, above all, so false, as if he did not believe in what he was writing or in his own feeling. Besides, Clara herself seemed unknown and incomprehensible to him. She seemed to evade him. "No," he thought, throwing down the pen, "either writing is not in my line at all, or I must wait a little longer!" He began recalling his visit to the Milovidovs' and the whole story that Anna, that good, wonderful Anna, had told him. . . . The word *untouched* which she had uttered suddenly struck him. It was just as though something had burnt him and made everything clear to him.

"Yes," he said aloud, "she was untouched, and I'm untouched. That's what gave her this power over me!"

He was thinking again about the immortality of the soul, about life beyond the grave. Was it not said in the Bible, "Death, where is thy sting?"; and in Schiller, "And the dead too shall live!—*Auch die Todten sollen leben!*" And also he believed in Mickiewicz: "I will love to the end of time—and after the end of time!" And an English writer had said: "Love is stronger than death!"

The Biblical saying affected Aratov in quite a special way. He tried to find the passage where the words occurred. He had no Bible, and he went to ask Platosha for it. Platosha was surprised. However, she produced a very old book in a warped leather binding with copper clasps, covered with candle wax, and handed it to Aratov. He carried it to his room, but could not find the text for a long time; but he did find another one: "Greater love hath no man than this, that a man lay down his life for his friends." (John 15:13.)

He thought, "It should have been said differently. It should have said, 'Greater power hath no man . . . !'

"But what if she did not die for me at all? What if she committed suicide simply because life had become an unbearable burden to her? What, in fine, if she did not come to that meeting for any declaration of love?"

But at that moment he saw Clara as she was before their parting on the boulevard; he remembered the mournful expression on her face; he remembered the tears and the words, *Oh, you understood nothing!*

No! He could no longer doubt why and for whom she had given up her life.

So passed the whole day, till nightfall.

15

Aratov went to bed early, without any particular desire to go to sleep; but he hoped to find rest in bed. The strained condition of his nerves made him feel very tired, a feeling infinitely more unbearable than the physical fatigue caused by his journey. But in spite of his exhaustion, he could not fall asleep. He tried to read, but the lines swam before his eyes. He put out the candle, and his room was plunged into darkness. But he continued to lie with closed eyes, unable to sleep. Presently he imagined that someone was whispering in his ear. "It's the beating of my heart, the pounding of my blood," he thought. But the whisper soon turned into coherent speech. Someone was talking in Russian, hurriedly, plaintively, indistinctly. He could not make out a single separate word—but it was the voice of Clara!

Aratov opened his eyes, sat up, and leaned on his elbow. The voice became fainter, but carried on with its plaintive, hurried, and, as before, indistinct speech. It was unmistakably Clara's voice.

Someone's fingers ran light arpeggios over the keys of the piano. . . . Then the voice began to speak again. More drawn-out sounds could be heard, like moans, and all indistinguishable one from another. And then single words began to stand out.

"Roses . . . roses . . . roses . . ."

"Roses," Aratov repeated in a whisper. "Ah yes! It's the roses I saw in my dream on that woman's head!"

"Roses . . ." he heard again.

"Is that you?" Aratov asked in the same whisper.

The voice suddenly fell silent.

Aratov waited—waited—and dropped his head on the pillow. "Auditory hallucinations," he thought. "But what if she were really here, near me? If I saw her, should I be frightened? Or glad? But what should I be frightened of? What should I be glad of? Why, of this: it would be a proof that another world does exist, that the soul is immortal. But then, even if I did see something—it too might be a visual hallucination."

However, he lighted the candle and glanced round the room quickly, not without a touch of panic, but he could see nothing unusual in it. He got up, went to the stereoscope—again the same grey doll with its eyes averted. The feeling of panic turned to one of annoyance. He seemed to have been cheated in his expectations, and besides, those very expectations seemed to him ridiculous. "Why," he murmured, "this is just silly!" He lay down in his bed again and blew out the candle. The room was again plunged into profound darkness.

This time Aratov made up his mind to go to sleep. But a new sensation arose in him. It seemed to him that someone was standing in the middle of the room not far from him and breathing scarcely audibly. He turned round quickly, opened his eyes. But what could he see in that impenetrable darkness? He began groping for the matches on his bedside table, when suddenly he imagined that a sort of soft, noiseless whirlwind was rushing through the whole room, passing over him, through him, and the word *I!* sounded clearly in his ears.

"I! I!"

A few moments passed before he managed to light the candle. Again there was no one in the room, and he heard nothing except the violent pounding of his own heart. He drank a glass of water and remained motionless, his head propped up on his hand. He waited.

He thought, "I'm going to wait. Either all this is just nonsense, or she is here. She wouldn't play cat and mouse with me like this!" He waited, waited a long time, so long that the hand on which he had propped up his head went to sleep. But none of his former sensations was repeated. Twice he could hardly keep his eyes open. . . . He opened them immediately—at least, he believed that he opened them. Gradually they became fixed on the door and kept staring at it. The candle guttered and nearly went out, and again it grew dark in the room. But in the half darkness the door showed up like a white patch. Then suddenly this patch began to stir. It diminished in size, vanished, and in its place, in the doorway, a woman's figure appeared. Aratov peered intently at it. . . . Clara! And this time she was looking straight at him; she was coming towards him. On her head was a wreath of red roses. He trembled all over. He sat up.

Before him stood his aunt in a nightcap with a large red ribbon and a white jacket.

"Platosha!" he pronounced her name with difficulty. "Is it you?"

"It's me," replied Platosha. "Me, Yakov, my darling, me!"

"What have you come for?"

"Why, because you wakened me. At first you kept

moaning and then you suddenly screamed, 'Help! Save me!'"

"I screamed?"

"Yes, you did, and in such a hoarse voice too: 'Save me!' I thought, 'Goodness, he's not ill, is he?' So I came in. Are you all right?"

"I'm quite all right."

"Well, in that case you must have had a bad dream. Would you like me to burn a little incense?"

Aratov again peered intently at his aunt and burst into loud laughter. The figure of the good-natured old lady in her nightcap and jacket, with a long, frightened face, really was very comic. Everything that was mysterious and that had surrounded and oppressed him—all that witchcraft was dispelled in a twinkling.

"No, Platosha, dear, that's quite unnecessary," he said. "I'm very sorry to have troubled you unwittingly. Go back to bed and have a good night's sleep. I too will go to sleep!"

Platosha remained standing a little longer in the same place, pointed to the candle, grumbled, "Why don't you blow it out? You might set the whole house on fire!" and as she went out could not refrain from making the sign of the cross over him, though only from a distance.

Aratov fell asleep at once and slept till morning. He got up in a good humour, though he seemed to be sorry for something. He felt lighthearted and free from care. "Come to think of it, what absurd, romantic ideas!" he said to himself with a smile. He did not look even once at the stereoscope or at the torn-out page. After breakfast, however, he went at once to see Kupfer. He was only dimly aware of what drew him there.

16

Aratov found his sanguine friend at home. He chatted a little to him, reproached him for having quite forgotten his aunt and him, listened to new praises of the "wonderful woman," the princess, who had just sent Kupfer from Yaroslav a skullcap embroidered with fish scales—and suddenly, sitting down before Kupfer and looking him straight in the face, declared that he had just returned from Kazan.

"You've been to Kazan? Whatever for?"

"Well, you see, I—er—wanted to collect some facts about that—er—Clara Milich."

"You mean the girl who poisoned herself?"

"Yes."

Kupfer shook his head. "So that's the sort of fellow you are! A quiet one too! You must have covered a thousand miles there and back—and for what? Eh? If you had shown any interest in a woman! Then I could understand anything! Anything! Any folly!" Kupfer ruffled his hair. "But just to collect material, as it's called, among you— among you scholars—— Not for anything in the world! For this sort of thing we have a statistical committee! Well, did you meet the old woman and the sister? A wonderful girl, isn't she?"

"Yes, wonderful," Aratov confirmed. "She told me lots of interesting things."

"Did she tell you how Clara poisoned herself?"

"What do you mean, *how?*"

"I mean, in what way."

"No. . . . She was still very upset. I dared not question her too much. Why, was there anything special about it?"

"Of course there was. Just imagine, she had to appear on the stage on the same day, and she did appear. She took a bottle of poison to the theatre with her, drank it before the first act, and played all through the first act. With the poison inside her! What strength of will, eh? What character! And I'm told she never acted her part with such feeling, with such passion! The audience did not suspect anything. They clapped, called for her. But as soon as the curtain fell, she collapsed on the stage. She was writhing, writhing with pain, and an hour later she was dead. Didn't I tell you about it? Why, it was in the papers too!"

Aratov's hands suddenly went cold, and something trembled in his breast. "No, you did not tell me that," he said at last. "And do you know what play it was?"

Kupfer thought hard. "They did tell me the title of the play. . . . There's a betrayed girl in it. Must have been some kind of drama. Clara was created for dramatic parts. Her very appearance—— But where are you off to?" Kupfer interrupted himself, seeing that Aratov had reached for his hat.

"I'm afraid I don't feel well," Aratov replied. "Goodbye. I'll come another time."

Kupfer stopped him and peered into his face. "What a nervous fellow you are. Just look at yourself: you're as white as chalk."

"I'm sorry, I'm not well," Aratov said, freed himself from Kupfer's grasp, and went home. Only at that moment did he realise clearly that he had gone to see Kupfer for one reason only: to have a talk about Clara, about "unhappy Clara, poor crazy Clara!"

However, on arriving home he soon regained his composure—to a certain extent, at least.

The circumstances attending Clara's death had at first made a shattering impression on him, but afterwards this acting "with the poison inside her," as Kupfer had expressed it, seemed a sort of monstrous gesture to him, a "bravura" piece—and he tried not to think of it, afraid of arousing in himself a feeling not unlike disgust. And at dinner, sitting opposite Platosha, he suddenly recalled her midnight appearance, recalled her short bed-jacket, that nightcap with the high ribbon (and what is a ribbon doing on a nightcap?), the whole of that comic figure at which, as at the property man's whistle in a fantastic ballet, all his visions crumbled to dust. He even made Platosha repeat how she had heard his scream, got frightened, jumped out of bed, and could not at once find either his door or her own, and so on. In the evening he played a game of cards with her and then retired to his room, feeling a little sad, but again quite composed.

Aratov did not think about the coming night and was not afraid of it: he was certain that he would pass it in the best possible way. The thought of Clara did awaken in him from time to time, but he at once remembered how "flamboyantly" she had killed herself and turned away from it. This "disgraceful" act interfered with his other memories of her. Glancing in passing into the stereoscope, he even imagined that she looked away because she was ashamed. Directly on the wall over the stereoscope hung the portrait of his mother. Aratov took it off the nail, looked at it for a long time, kissed it, and carefully put it away in a drawer. Why did he do that? Was it because he did not think the portrait should be anywhere near that woman, or for some other reason? Aratov did not bother to ask himself. But his mother's portrait made him think of his father—of his father, whom he had seen dying in that very room, on that very bed. "What do you think of all this, Father?" he addressed him in his mind. "You understood it all; you too believed in Schiller's world of spirits. Advise me what to do."

"Father would have advised me to dismiss all these foolish things," said Aratov aloud and picked up a book. But he could not read for long, and feeling a sort of heaviness all over, he went to bed earlier than usual in the firm belief that he would fall asleep immediately.

And so it was, but his hopes of a peaceful night did not materialise.

17

Midnight had not yet struck when he had a dream which was both extraordinary and full of menace.

He dreamt that he was in a rich country mansion of which he was the owner. He had bought the house and the estate belonging to it only recently, and all the time he kept thinking, "It's all right, it's all right now, but there's going to be trouble!" A little man kept bustling about beside him. It was his agent. He kept laughing, bowing, and trying to show Aratov that everything in his house and on his estate was in excellent condition. "This way, sir, this way," he kept saying, sniggering at every word. "Look how wonderful everything here is! Look at the horses—what splendid horses!" And Aratov saw a great number of enormous horses. They were standing in their stalls with their backs to him; they had magnificent manes and tails. But as soon as Aratov walked past, the horses turned their heads towards him and bared their teeth viciously. "It's all right, but there's going to be trouble," thought Aratov. "This way, this way," the agent kept saying. "Please come into the orchard. See what wonderful apples you have." The apples were indeed wonderful, red and round. But as soon as Aratov looked at them they shrivelled up and fell off the trees. "There's going to be trouble," he thought. "And here's the lake, sir," gabbled the agent. "Look how smooth and blue it is! And here's a golden boat; would you like to have a sail in her? She will sail by herself." "I'm not going to get into it! There's going to be trouble!" But he got into the boat all the same. At the bottom a little creature looking like a monkey lay all huddled up; it held in its paws a bottle full of a dark liquid. "Don't worry, sir!" the agent shouted from the bank. "It's nothing! It's death! Happy journey!" The boat scudded along rapidly, but all of a sudden a hurricane came swooping down on it, not like the whirlwind of the night before, gentle and noiseless—no: a black, terrible, howling hurricane! Everything round grew confused and amid the whirling darkness Aratov saw Clara in her stage costume. She was raising a bottle to her lips; from a distance the cries of "Bravo! Bravo!" could be heard, and someone's coarse voice shouted in Aratov's ear, "Oh, you thought everything would end as in a comedy, did you? No! It's a tragedy! A tragedy!"

Trembling all over, Aratov woke up. It was not dark in the room. From somewhere came a faint, unflickering light, lighting up all the things in the room mournfully. Aratov did not try to find out where that light was coming from; he was aware of one thing only: Clara was there, in that room—he felt her presence—he was again and forever in her power!

A cry was wrested from his lips. "Clara, Clara, are you here?"

"Yes!" he clearly heard a voice saying from the middle of the room bathed in that unflickering light.

Aratov repeated his question soundlessly.

"Yes!" he heard again.

"Then I want to see you!" he cried and jumped out of bed.

For a few moments he stood still in one place, his bare feet pressed against the cold floor, his eyes roving all over the room. "Where, where?" his lips murmured.

There was nothing to be seen, nothing to be heard.

He looked round and noticed that the faint light that filled the room came from the night-light screened with a sheet of paper and put in a corner, probably by Platosha, while he was asleep. He even became aware of the smell of incense, for which Platosha too was probably responsible.

He dressed hurriedly. To stay in bed, to sleep, was out of the question. Then he stood still in the middle of the room and folded his arms. The sense of Clara's presence was stronger in him than ever.

And presently he began to speak in a loud voice, but with the solemn, slow deliberation of one who intones an incantation.

"Clara"—so he began—"if you really are here, if you see me, if you hear me—show yourself! If the power which I feel over me is really your power—show yourself! If you realise how bitterly I regret that I did not understand you, that I rejected you—show yourself! If what I've heard was really your voice, if the feeling that has taken possession of me is love, if you are now convinced that I love you—I who till now have never been in love and never known any woman—if you know that after your death I have fallen passionately, deeply in love with you, if you don't want me to go mad—show yourself, Clara!"

Aratov had scarcely uttered the last word when suddenly he felt that someone had come up to him quickly from behind, as that day on the boulevard, and put a hand on his shoulder. He turned round—and saw no one. But the feeling of *her* presence became so real, so unmistakable, that he again looked round quickly.

What was that? In his armchair, two paces from him, sat a woman, all in black. Her head was turned away, as in the stereoscope. It was she! It was Clara! But what a stern, what a despondent face.

Aratov slowly sank on his knees. Yes, he had been right: he felt neither panic nor joy—not even surprise. Even his heart began to beat more calmly. He felt he was conscious of one thing only. *Oh, at last! At last!*

"Clara," he said in a weak but steady voice, "why don't you look at me? I know it is you, but, you see, it may be my imagination that has created an image like that one." He pointed in the direction of the stereoscope. "Prove to me that it is you. Turn round to me, look at me, Clara!"

330

CLARA MILICH

Clara's hand rose slowly—and dropped again.

"Clara, Clara, turn to me!"

And Clara's head turned slowly, her drooping eye-lids opened,—and the dark pupils of her eyes stared steadily at Aratov.

He recoiled a little and uttered one long-drawn-out, trembling "Ah!"

Clara looked intently at him, but her eyes, her features, retained their former wistfully stern, almost discontented expression. It was with that expression on her face that she had come onto the platform on the day of the literary matinee—before she caught sight of Aratov. And just as then she suddenly blushed: her face became animated, and her eyes flashed, and her lips parted in a joyful, triumphant smile.

"I am forgiven!" cried Aratov. "You have conquered. Take me! For I am yours and you are mine!"

He rushed towards her. He tried to kiss those smiling, those triumphant lips—and he did kiss them. He felt their burning touch. He even felt the moist chill of her teeth—and a triumphant scream filled the half-dark room.

Platosha, who had run into his room, found him in a dead faint. He was on his knees; his head was lying on the armchair; his outstretched arms drooped powerlessly; his pale face was filled with the ecstasy of great happiness.

Platosha sank on to the floor beside him; she put her arms round his waist, murmuring, "Yakov, dearest! Darling Yakov! My poor little darling!" She tried to raise him in her bony arms—he did not stir. Then Platosha began screaming wildly. The servant ran in. Together they somehow lifted him, made him sit down in a chair, and began sprinkling water over him—holy water from the icon.

He came to. But in reply to his aunt's questions he only smiled, and with so beatific an expression on his face that he made her more worried than ever, and she kept making the sign of the cross over him and over herself.

Aratov at last pushed her hands away gently and, still with the same beatific expression on his face, said, "What is the matter with you, Platosha?"

"What's the matter with you, Yakov, dear?"

"With me? I'm happy—happy, Platosha. That's what's the matter with me. And now I'd like to go back to bed and sleep."

He tried to get up, but felt such a weakness in his legs and in his whole body that he was not able to undress and get into bed without the help of his aunt and the maid. But he fell asleep very quickly, still with the same beatific, ecstatic expression on his face. Only his face was very pale.

18

When Platosha entered his room the next morning she found him still in the same position, but the weakness had not passed off, and he even preferred to stay in bed. Platosha did not like the pallor of his face, in particular. "What can it be, O Lord?" she thought. "Not a drop of blood in his face, won't touch bouillon—lies there and smiles, and keeps telling me he's perfectly all right!" He refused lunch too. "Why, my dear," she asked him, "you don't intend to lie like that all day, do you?" "And why not?" Aratov answered gently. This gentleness worried Platosha even more. Aratov looked like a man who has discovered a great secret, a secret that pleases him very much, and is jealously guarding it and keeping it to himself. He was waiting for the night, not so much with impatience as with curiosity.

"What next?" he was asking himself. He was no longer amazed or bewildered; he did not doubt for a moment that he had entered into communication with Clara; that they loved each other, he did not doubt, either. Only—what could be the outcome of such love? He recalled that kiss and a rapturous shiver ran swiftly and sweetly through all his limbs. "Such a kiss," he thought, "not even Romeo and Juliet exchanged! But next time I shall not give way so quickly. I shall possess her. . . . She will come with a wreath of small roses on her black curls.

"But what next? We can't live together, can we? I shall have to die in order to be with her, shan't I? Was it for that she came? And is it like *that* that she means to take me?

"Well, what does it matter? If I have to die, then let me die. Death no longer frightens me now. It cannot destroy me, can it? On the contrary, it is only like *that* and *there* that I shall be happy—as I have never been happy in life, as indeed she has never been; for we are both of us—untouched! Oh, that kiss!"

Platosha kept coming into Aratov's room; she did not worry him with questions; she only peered at him, whispered, sighed, and went out again. But he would not touch his dinner, either. That really was a bad sign. The old woman went to fetch the local doctor, an acquaintance of hers, in whom she believed only because he was not a drinking man and had a German wife. Aratov was surprised when she brought the doctor to see him, but Platosha began imploring her darling Yakov so persistently to allow Paramon Paramonich (that was the doctor's name) to examine him, "just to please me," that he agreed. The doctor felt his pulse, looked at his tongue, asked a few questions, and declared at last that it was absolutely necessary to auscultate the patient. Aratov was in such an agreeable frame of mind that he consented to that too. The doctor bared his chest tactfully, tapped, listened, hummed and hawed, prescribed some drops and a mixture, and advised the patient, above all, to keep calm and to avoid any strong emotions. "I see," thought Aratov. "Well, my dear sir, you're a bit late!"

"What's wrong with Yakov?" asked Platosha as she handed the doctor a three-rouble note at the front door.

The local doctor, who, like all modern physicians—especially those who wear a uniform—liked to show off with scientific terms, told her that her nephew suffered from dioptric symptoms of nervous cardialgy and also from febrility.

"You'd better speak more plainly, my dear sir," Platosha cut him short. "Don't try to frighten me with your Latin. You're not in a chemist's shop."

"His heart isn't in very good order," explained the doctor, "and—well, there's also a little fever." And he repeated his advice about keeping calm and observing moderation.

"There's no danger, is there?" Platosha asked sternly. ("Don't you come to me with your Latin again!")

"Not for the time being."

The doctor went away, and Platosha looked very sad and worried. She did, however, send to the chemist's for the medicine, which Aratov refused to take, in spite of her entreaties. He also refused to take the herb tea for his chest.

"What are you so worried about, Auntie, dear!" he said to her. "I tell you I am now the healthiest and the happiest man in the whole world!" Platosha merely shook her head. Towards evening he had a slight temperature, but he insisted all the same that she should not stay in his room but go to sleep in her own. Platosha obeyed, but she did not undress and did not lie down; she sat down in an armchair and kept listening and whispering her prayers.

But she was beginning to doze off when suddenly a terrible, piercing scream awakened her. She jumped up and rushed into Aratov's study and, as on the night before, found him lying on the floor.

But he did not regain consciousness, as on the previous night, in spite of all their efforts. The same night he became delirious, and his high fever was complicated by inflammation of the heart.

A few days later he died.

A strange circumstance accompanied his second fainting fit. When he was raised from the floor and put to bed they found in his clenched right fist a small strand of a woman's black hair. Where did it come from? Clara's sister Anna had had such a lock of hair, which she had taken from Clara; but why should she have given Aratov something she had treasured so much? Unless, of course, she had put it in Clara's diary and not noticed it when she gave it to Aratov.

In his delirium, before he died, Aratov referred to himself as Romeo—after the poison; he spoke of his consummated marriage, about how he knew now what real felicity meant. Particularly terrifying for Platosha was the moment when Aratov, after recovering his senses a little, and seeing her beside his bed, said to her, "What are you crying for, Auntie? Because I have to die? But don't you know that love is stronger than death? Death! Death, where is thy sting? You should not weep, but rejoice, the same as I rejoice."

And again on the face of the dying young man there shone the beatific smile which made the poor old woman feel so terrified.

Bougival, 1882

335